Angela Huth has written three collections of short stories and several novels, including *Nowhere Girl*, *Virginia Fly is Drowning*, *South of the Lights*, *Invitation to the Married Life* and *Land Girls*. She also writes plays for radio, television and stage, and is a well-known freelance journalist, critic and broadcaster. She is married to a don, lives in Oxford and has two daughters.

Also by Angela Huth

Wives of the Fishermen

ANGELA HUTH

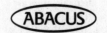

An *Abacus* Book

First published in Great Britain by Little, Brown and Company 1998
This edition published by Abacus 1999

A CIP catalogue record for this book is
available from the British Library.

ISBN 0 349 10851 X

Typeset in Berkeley by M Rules
Printed and bound in Great Britain by
Clays Ltd, St Ives plc

Abacus
A Division of
Little, Brown and Company (UK)
Brettenham House
Lancaster Place
London WC2E 7EN

For Prue Penn

What is a woman that you forsake her,
And the hearth fire and the home-acre,
To go with the old grey widow-maker?

Rudyard Kipling

Wives of the Fishermen

Part I

It is the habit of fishermen's wives to glance at the horizon many times a day, but only one of their own kind will recognise the furtive looks, the tightening of anxiety behind eyes that have grown prematurely old from checking distant sea.

A moment too late Myrtle Duns flicks her eyes back from the window. Annie, looking up from her cards, has seen.

'Ach, stop worrying,' she says.

She watches Myrtle lift the black kettle from the range, pour boiling water into a brown pot. Unbroken cloud, divided into squares by the panes of a small window, is powered by enough brightness to light the sides of the old teapot with colours of petrol flung upon water: threads of gold and incandescent mauve. Annie knows that Myrtle will now take two mugs from hooks, two tin spoons from a drawer, pour milk into a souvenir jug from Dundee. She will lift the pot with both hands, testing its weight, judging the amount of water to be correct before transporting it to the table with a listing movement that bends and splays the pleats of her long woollen skirts. The rhythm of tea-making is familiar from hundreds of such afternoons spent together.

All the time Annie watches her friend the cards flicker in her hands. Sometimes they rise in fans. Then, disapproving of such petty skill, quick fingers snap them back into a neat pack. The silky sound of their activity is the single noise in the room, for now the kettle has stopped its spluttering. Myrtle stands motionless by the range, waiting for the tea to brew.

She is a large woman, hands rough as salt cod, tall. The kitchen ceiling clears her head by only a few inches. She moves with practised skill among the narrow spaces, managing her wide hips with dignity. Archie says she sometimes put him in mind of an opera singer, the way she glides. It's as if there are wheels under her skirts, he says. For Lord's sake stop scoffing at your wife, Archie, she answers, pleased by his observation, for she recognises the admiration beneath the teasing.

3

But in response she would clench her hands and punch him gently behind his ear till he caught her big wrist and forced it to a halt, the muscles in his arms rising like waves of bone.

'Archie,' says Annie, slapping down the cards, 'is the best skipper any boat could have. You know that.'

'Aye.' Myrtle sits. She arranges the tea things protectively in front of her. The apparent passivity of her face hardens. Blank eyes. Neither mouth nor nose twitch. She no longer has consciously to remind herself that any remark Annie makes about Archie should be greeted with an impassive expression.

'How's Janice?' Myrtle asks after a while.

'She's bonnie. High marks at school again.'

'That's grand.'

Annie finds it hard to resist informing Myrtle of her daughter's high marks several times a week.

'I think they're beginning to see her worth,' she says.

'That's good, too.'

Annie shuffles the cards.

'Mrs Singer said to me not two days ago: "Mrs Mcleoud," she says, "your Janice is on her way to being a great beauty as well as a scholar."' She pauses, looks down. Modesty, or the nearest she can get to it, webs her eyes. 'I couldn't say that to anyone but you, Myrtle. But I believe there's some truth in it.'

'Oh there is, that's for sure,' says Myrtle warmly. She accepts a pile of cards slimy with age. It's not yet time to pour the tea. Her look slides from Annie's small, busy hands to her face: the tiny nose with its nostrils the shape of horizontal petals, the opal eyes, the mouth whose dividing line in repose is the subtlest of shallow curves – a mouth that can jump from solemnity to laughter with astounding speed. In the rubble of dark curls, Myrtle observes that Annie has a few grey hairs. But her friend has changed very little over the years. She was the prettiest child in the school, the village, for miles along the coast. Her looks had tempted admirers from Fife to Dundee. It is no wonder her only child, Janice, is set to follow her mother's reputation. Myrtle sometimes wonders if Janice will cause as much chaos, as much agony of spirit, in her friends. She wonders if she has inherited the same powers of persuasion of her innocence, so that she will always be forgiven. Everyone had always forgiven Annie, Myrtle most of all.

As children, Myrtle and Annie walked to school together holding hands. On cold mornings, Myrtle wore mittens of scratchy wool. Annie wore gloves. The bare ends of Myrtle's cold fingers would burrow into the warmth of Annie's angora hand. She longed for gloves herself. But in her mother's cautious mind they were an extravagance not even to be considered. Very quickly Myrtle gave up hoping her mother would relent. Dot Stewart was not a woman accustomed to changing her mind for the benefit of others. Locked into the narrow disciplines of a hard life, her beliefs in everything – from the rewards of the afterlife to the number of blankets a healthy person should be allowed on the bed – were unchangeable. The firmness of her convictions was a matter of pride. To be caught changing them, no matter how persuasive an argument, would be despicable weakness. Myrtle and her father, understanding these things, learnt it was easier to agree with Dot, do her bidding. Any opposition caused scenes so fraught, so emotionally exhausting, that they suffered the cold of dreaded winter nights rather than try to persuade Dot of their need for more blankets.

In the classroom Myrtle and Annie shared a desk. Myrtle's half was sparsely furnished: pen, text book, exercise books. Annie's was chaotic: school books a despised territory over which things of more interest were strewn. There were skeins of wool, electric colours, that Annie liked to weave into a long tube that grew into a hideous worm from nails punched into a cotton reel. There were plastic hairslides, boiled sweets whose horrible colours were scarcely dimmed by their twists of transparent paper, and cuttings from magazines – shampoo advertisements, lion cubs, travel brochure sunsets. For several months, at the age of ten, Annie was a compulsive cutter-outer. The pictures she chose gave no clue to her interests. She snipped randomly, attracted by bright colours that hurt Myrtle's eyes.

Often the clutter on Annie's side of the desk would drift over its boundaries. Myrtle would gently push the stuff back. She was patient, unreprimanding when it came to Annie's untidiness. And when Mrs Williams began pacing the aisles between the desks, weak eyes straining to detect any hint of something Not in the Rules, in loyalty to her friend Myrtle would hide things under her own books. Sometimes she was rewarded. There was a day when Mrs Williams was particularly disinclined to believe Annie's excuses for the mess on her desk, and Myrtle found herself declaring with extraordinary conviction that most of the offending objects were hers. Punishment was just avoided though there were warnings, as always, that Mrs Williams' patience was running out.

On that occasion, when the bell went for the end of the lesson, Annie turned to Myrtle and hugged her.

'You're my friend, Myrtle,' she whispered. 'I can always count on you.'

In the heat of gratitude and pride Myrtle did not ponder the truth of this statement. When Annie was at her best, and her best was irresistibly endearing, it was easy to forget the other times. Myrtle stood by the desk rubbing her still icy hands. The bell rang out the joy of her secret feelings. Her loyalty to Annie was often rewarded by a suggestion of doing something together in the playground: she hoped this would happen today. Myrtle held on to the back of the chair, its wood still smeared with a shadowy warmth from her own back. She waited, hoping. Watched Annie's eyes flick round the others. When Ross Wyatt passed them he handed Annie an emerald rubber.

'Yours,' he said.

'Thanks,' said Annie. She gave him one of her half-smiles that, despite the braces on her teeth, boys found irresistible.

'Coming outside?' Ross sniffed and wiped his nose on the back of his hand.

'Right.' She turned to the boy standing behind Ross. 'You coming too, Archie Duns?'

The boy nodded, not looking at her. She moved into position behind Ross, in front of Archie. Thus flanked by the two best-looking boys in the school, Annie moved with the queue to the door. In a moment she was across the room, and had forgotten to invite Myrtle.

When all the children had left the classroom Myrtle sat down again. She looked up at the beams that spanned the vaulted ceiling, a roofscape where she often found ideas. The cobwebs that dulled the skylight, she noticed, seemed to have thickened in the past year. But as Mrs Williams often joked, on the occasions her glance rose from the blackboard, how long is a broom? Never long enough to reach the skylight . . . It was during that lunch break, in early winter, alone in the classroom, voices outside rising and falling like small garments hung out to dry in a wind, that an uneasy thought struck the ten-year-old Myrtle: Annie, her best friend, sometimes preferred to be with boys than to be with her.

Several more games of rummy have been played, several more cups of tea have been drunk. Myrtle wants Annie to go. She wants to get on with the evening – peel the carrots, take the folded clothes from the airing cupboard and put them in their place in Archie's drawers. But Annie shows no keenness to leave. For all that her own kitchen is a smarter place than Myrtle's – white tiles, the occasional one stamped with a sea horse, and formica tops, speckled and shiny as eggshells – she seems to prefer the shabbier kitchen in the Duns' house. Sometimes she does suggest that Myrtle should come over to her place. But then, just as Myrtle is setting out, by chance Annie is passing by. She has come to 'fetch' Myrtle, she says. But as Myrtle has not yet put on her shawl, and Annie is already taking off her coat, it seems pointless to walk up the hill, wind swiping their faces, to the council estate. So they stay. Friendship, as Myrtle points out when guilt spurs Annie to bring the occasional gift of a bannock or oat biscuits, is not about whose house is the meeting place.

'Won't Janice be back?' asks Myrtle. 'Are we forgetting the time, all this card-playing?'

Annie smiles, reassuring. Perhaps she is unaware of Myrtle's impatience. It is more likely she is not.

'She's going over to Joey Brick for her tea. I'll pick her up later.'

'The red-haired one? Does a paper round?'

'That's the lad, aye. She likes a boy with freckles, Janice does.'

7

Myrtle waits a moment, weighing caution. She has learnt it's all too easy for Annie to detect some note of criticism in anything she might say about Janice.

'Starting young,' she says at last.

'They're grown up at twelve these days. Know just what they want long before that. There's no stopping them.'

Myrtle thinks that if she had a daughter, there would certainly be some stopping her.

'Pity,' is what she says.

They hear footsteps outside, Archie's lopsided tread on the steps. The door opens. A smell of sea comes in on the wind. Archie's dark jersey twinkles with raindrops. Some are perfect sequins. Others are smeared like the trail of an off-course snail across the coarse wool. His face is haggard, exhausted. He smells of cod, rope, pipe smoke. His eyes go straight to Myrtle. Annie stands up.

'Ken's home,' he says to her. The sharpness in his voice has its effect on both women. The defiance in Annie's eyes, that had automatically flared when Archie came in, quavers.

'His supper'll not take a moment in the microwave,' she says. She and Ken bought the microwave, special offer, a couple of months ago. Myrtle and Archie are familiar with the accounts of the magical way in which it changed their lives. 'But I'll be going.'

When Archie has shut the door behind her he moves to the range, leans his hands against the chipped enamel of its side. Then he raises his warmed hands to hold his wife's face. He looks at her silently, re-assessing the rock firmness of the floor, with the eyes of one who has been tossed by a fairground swing, or a stormy sea. He will kiss her later. For the moment he lets the sensation of being home flow through him. The warmth of his own kitchen is what he remembers, if there's a moment to think, at sea. When the boat rocks crazily in giant waves and rain hard as sheet glass crashes into his eyes, there's a lightning flash in his mind: the old stove, his wife beside it, alert to his need of no questions, ready to pour the tea.

*

The kitchen was always the warmest room in the house. Until 1953, just before Myrtle was born, it was the place where Dot Stewart baited the lines. She used to throw a length of tarpaulin over the flagstones and Sandy, who delivered the lines in his cart, would drag in a load so huge that sometimes, Dot said, just the sight of it brought tears of despair to her eyes. The lines, with their lethal hooks, were alive with pernicious intent – snagging, pricking, drawing blood. Dot's hands had bled so many times that the scar tissue criss-crossed the ruddy skin in abstract, knitters' patterns. When her hands were in repose, slumped together on her lap, from Myrtle's side of the table they looked like bundles of silvery twigs. She remembered thinking that from a very young age. She felt very sorry for them, wanting to kiss them. But she did not dare approach her mother's lap. Dot Stewart was not one who took kindly to physical gestures of comfort or sympathy.

Once the lines were stacked on the floor, Sandy would haul in the sacks of mussels. They made a crunching, screeching noise as they scraped the flagstones on landing – a noise, Dot said, that hurt her ears: a noise that she could no more forget than her own cries when Myrtle was born. Often she was left to face the task alone, though on occasions, with no warning, old Cecily, Dot's mother, would drop in to help. Even in her eighties Cecily could work faster on a length of line than women half her age – scoffing all the while at the slowness of the modern young girls. Dot preferred it when Veronica gave a hand – one-eyed Veronica who had lost an eye in a fish-hook accident as a young child. Veronica baited with a recklessness that unnerved every woman in the village, lacerating herself without complaint, bloodying the mussels as she attached them to the hooks, and leaving red smears round her mouth when she licked a flowing thread of blood from a finger. Veronica, in her brief pauses, made Dot laugh with her lively surmises about the fishermen. With no evidence to back up her stories, she recounted such scurrilous tales that to Dot invention became more powerful than reality, and she found it hard to look many of the staid men in the eye. Veronica's slanderous tongue lightened the long mornings.

The women sat on low wooden chairs to do their baiting, thick-stockinged legs slung wide apart to make a copious lap for a clump of line which, once mussel-loaded, would slip on to the floor. They were skilful with their knives. Years of experience had driven them to finding the weakness in the shell before it was visible. A flick of the wrist (no indication that there was any restraint in the shell) and it was jarred open. Two liquid wings lay for a moment in the palm of a hand. Then pitilessly the silvery glistening meat would be gouged out with another flick of the knife, slipped over the next hook. The empty shell was cast to the floor by a movement of the knee, to be swept up later. The women's fingers worked automatically, swift as machinery, their rhythm only broken by the drawing of blood, the quick suck of a damaged finger. They rarely spoke: Veronica's outbursts came only at occasional moments. The small thuds of shell on tarpaulin, and the scrape of line as it was tugged along to the next hook were the only interruptions in the fish-stinking silence. The smell was always there: in the women's hair, clothes, skin. Even on Fridays, baking day, bread in the oven, the black smell of sea depths from which the raw shell-fish had come out-reached the warm brown smell of baking bread. They did not think of listening to the wireless while they worked. Music did not occur to them. Besides, the wireless, with its elaborate Bakelite façade sculpted like a miniature Odeon, was in place of honour on the dresser in the front room. The wireless was for weather forecasts and news: an evening thing. But when the window was open and there was a strong breeze, they could hear the water break against the harbour wall. That was music enough.

Myrtle had listened to her mother's descriptions of all this many times – Dot enjoyed recounting to her daughter all the small details, conjuring the smells and sensations vividly in Myrtle's mind. Dot never read her stories, was never much of a reader. But she was an observer with a beady eye whose visual accounts were her legacy to her daughter. And now that she was grown up, alone in her kitchen, Archie away at sea, Myrtle often felt that time had intertwined itself and she had actually been with Dot and Veronica, baiting the lines. She knew what it was like to watch chapped fingers making the same movement a hundred times an hour; she could feel the same pain those women had felt in their shoulders as they crouched hour after hour over their work. Sometimes, sweeping the floor, she would come across a minute glint of mussel shell, a speck of diamond ground into the cement between the flagstones, and she felt awed at the ease of knowing how it had been in those hard days. Compared with then, present life was much less physically exhausting, though never without worry. There was the same fear through the years – no fish, no money. Many was the time – weather too bad to go out – Myrtle and Archie had been down to their last few pounds. And the shadow that could never be erased was the anxiety. Inherited from generation to generation of women whose men make a living at sea, anxiety was a moth trapped in their insides that flutters, batters, can never escape, is rarely still. When one spell at sea is over, and the fisherman home for a few days, these wings of fear are stilled for so short a time that the places they have damaged cannot hope to heal. As clean clothes are stuffed into a bag ready for another week at sea, the whole inner turmoil began again, the effort to conceal it tightening the skin of pale faces so that the very scalps of the fishermen's wives seemed to be pulled back, exposing the worry in their eyes.

Archie, at the table, is asleep. His head is couched in his arms. A mug of tea cools beside him. Myrtle touches his hair. It's divided by the wind into stiff points, salt-crusted. She strokes his cheek. He hasn't much time for shaving on the boat, though does his best on the day of homecoming. The stubble is thick on his jaws. His top lip, clean-shaven, reveals cracked lips: small shavings of dry white skin that will scratch Myrtle when he kisses her. Archie has been away for five days and four nights.

When he wakes, what shall she tell him? Myrtle wonders. There has been no news, here, apart from the day the washing machine went mad. It was clogged up with a million fish scales from a load of sea-soaked clothes. Water had gushed out on to the floor of the cold little room where the machine is housed. But it was not plain soapy water. Myrtle, in her panic, had seen it as a surreal cascade, full of living eyes horribly twinkling at her among the bubbles. As it soaked her feet, her ankles, thousands of the tiny scales stuck to the hem of her skirt. The dead fish smell was sickening as the water sloshed ruthlessly about, proud of its glitter. Myrtle had run from the house, wet wool skirts hampering her legs, to find Alan, one-eyed Veronica's son and the nearest thing to a plumber in the village. He had swiftly and kindly dealt with the crisis, and helped her mop up the mess. Once she had re-washed the jerseys, and dried them, it had taken her many hours to pick the scales from the wool. Now the garments lay folded in the airing cupboard, neatly as always, as if the drama had never occurred. There was no reason to trouble Archie with a disaster that was over, no point in telling him. Myrtle liked to protect her husband from such trivialities: with so little time together, it was the important things that should consume the hours – plans for the summer holiday, re-acknowledgement of love and wellbeing.

Again Myrtle touches Archie's hair with her big, gentle hand. Grains of salt scratch her fingers. She loves these moments – Archie here and yet not here; exhausted, yet soon to wake, to eat the supper she has made him, to re-settle. Many of the fishermen go straight from the boat to the pub, arrive home drunk and useless with no apologies. Not Archie, thank God. His priority is his wife. Soon as he's ashore, he hurries home. He's best pleased when he finds Myrtle alone. Annie's constant presence annoys him. About this evening, Myrtle will apologise, explain why she was unable to get rid of Annie in time, today – the cards, the chatter. With a silent nod of his head Archie will signal he understands: he, of all people, knows how difficult it is to dislodge Annie. He dislikes her, but does his best to contain that dislike. He understands Myrtle needs a friend when he's away, and Annie is a good friend in many ways, so he lets the matter be. All he asks is that Annie should not hang around when he is home. Myrtle is thus left to the delicate job of keeping her husband and her friend apart. Neither of them can know how difficult this is, what tact and skill it involves. But she has grown used to it and mistimings, like today, when Archie made no effort to conceal his annoyance, are rare.

Every time Archie returns Myrtle thanks God: she imagines the wives of pilots and soldiers and war correspondents – men in dangerous jobs – must all do the same. But the thought is never far off that one day there will be reason to curse God, just as her mother did when Jock Stewart died. The day that Archie does not come back has festered in her mind for so long that the picture is sharp and polished. She described it once – a week of foul weather – to Annie, who said such thoughts were morbid and wicked. Since then she has kept them to herself, tried to extinguish them, but has not succeeded.

Her father died at sea, though not on the fishing boat. He was only half a mile from the shore, a Saturday afternoon, in his rowing boat. Smoking his pipe, most likely, which Dot would not allow in the house. Dot and Myrtle were used to his disappearances when he came home. He did not like many hours to pass not on or near the sea. And when he was 'playing about', as Dot thought of it, in the rowing boat, she was not afraid. A man who had spent his life at sea, respected it, knew its ways, he would not be likely to take it out if he had reason to suspect bad weather was brewing. The afternoon he died there was a strong April sun, sea flat as tin, scarcely a breeze.

When he didn't appear for tea, and darkness gathered, Dot reluctantly put out the alert, worried such foolishness would annoy him. His boat was found quickly, empty. Oars askew. A black-head gull was pecking at a packet of half-eaten sandwiches. It was Archie's father, Ben, who towed the small boat of chipped green paint, *The Happy Wanderer*, back to the harbour where Dot stood waiting, scarf fiercely tied under her aching jaw. He came without a body. Every boat in the harbour had been searching miles of empty water. No body, no drifting clothes – nothing.

Two weeks later Jock Stewart's body was washed up on a beach a mile along the coast. Ben Duns told Archie (who years later, at Myrtle's insistence, passed on the description word for word) that it was a swollen mass of blubber, horrible. The eyes were still open. They seemed to have spilt over their rims, cloudy as jellyfish: though in the quick glance, before he had to turn away to vomit, he could not be quite sure that was really so, he said. But it was the sight of Jock's feet that made him cry: toes the colour of shale, skin blown up so taut – as if the wind itself had been playing balloons – that you could see the passage of every vein. The indignity of seeing a good fisherman, his skipper, stripped of his boots was the thing, Archie confessed, that broke his father, and he had seen many a drowned man.

A post-mortem showed Jock had died of a heart attack. But how had he fallen overboard? Dot liked to think that, knowing he was dying, Jock had decided to speed the process by heaving himself into the waters he loved. She looked at her husband, lying in the morgue, too full of disbelief to shed any tears. The black bruise colour of his skin glowered through the pinkish matt make-up that the mortician had employed to disguise the actuality, and had only succeeded in making it worse. Myrtle, eleven at the time, remembered clearly the bitterness of the rain at the funeral. Cheeks were confused with rain and tears: Dot's brave face was blurred by so much water. Best of all Myrtle remembered Annie, who had pushed her way close to the open grave. Annie took a peppermint from a soggy paper bag of sweets, held it up to Myrtle and said, 'Shall I drop it in?' That was the moment that Myrtle herself felt the warmth of tears collide with rain on her own cheeks. Later, Annie tried to apologise, said she only did it to make Myrtle smile.

Archie is awake, eating. He crams wodges of butter into a huge baked potato, splits his sausages and fills them with English mustard. Between mouthfuls he leans his forearms heavily on the wooden table. Myrtle can tell by the hunch of his shoulders that he is pleased to be home, beginning to relax. Half a day before returning to sea he grows more upright, tenser. He frowns. First evening home, the short nap over, the sea-going frown unclenches.

'How was it?' Myrtle can expect only the barest information.

'Not too bad. We had to go a long way for a fair catch. Mighty small fish again. Always the small fish, now. I don't know . . .'

Archie is so weary of the politics of fishing these days he is reluctant to discuss them. There are old fishermen in the village who talk about the time when fishing was one of our proudest industries, when a man went out knowing there were limitless fish to catch and no one to fight. It was always a hard life, but you could make a decent living. They say the cod war, in the early eighties, was the beginning of the end of the good times. And now it is the fight with the Spaniards with their too-fine nets; the scientists advising about quotas; the rows about TACs; pontificating politicians who don't know a haddock from a herring . . . and all the time over-fishing causing such a disastrous lack of fish that early into the next century there could well be no industry left. What then? Archie does not like to think about it. There is an unspoken rule among the men on his boat that no one should speculate. In the past, speculating on the future had caused too much gloom. Archie did not want to skipper a bunch of downhearted men – they needed to function with all the fire they could muster, these days, to go further, fish longer and, despite the pathetic size of the fish, bring home a decent catch. Archie smiles at his wife.

'Have you been hearing much news of the microwave, then?'

'Aye.' Myrtle smiles in return. 'You can have no idea of the brilliance of that machine. It's brought a whole new dimension to their lives.'

Archie studies his wife's face.

'You can always have one if you're wanting one: you know that, don't you? If it would make a difference to you.'

'Not on your life.'

'We can still afford a microwave.'

'I don't want one, Archie. What would I be doing with it? I don't mind waiting for things to unfreeze slowly, do I? I don't feel the urge to cook things in a moment. Besides, it's not the same. You'd not have a crispy baked potato like that out of a microwave . . .' She laughs.

'Just wanted to make sure I'm not depriving you.'

'Never.' Myrtle rises to take a bread pudding from the oven, and two warmed bowls. 'I'm sorry about Annie. God, how she stays.' Guilt at Archie's homecoming is still within her.

'She's not strong, Annie, on knowing when she's not wanted.'

'No: but she's a good heart.'

'I was never interested, you remember, in her heart, or any of the rest of her.' They both laugh. 'Poor Ken. Does he have any idea what goes on in the wifey's mind? Any idea what she gets up to? Does she say anything to you?'

'No: but it's not hard to guess,' says Myrtle after a while.

Annie has learned, very slowly, that when the men are home she and Myrtle should see less of each other. She keeps up the pretence that this arrangement does not exist, but at the same time she is careful not to drop in on Myrtle if there's a chance Archie might be in the house. What she has not yet done – and pride might never let her go that far – is to caution her daughter, Janice. The child, she feels, should remain ignorant of past events that have led to the present situation, and if this means Myrtle must suffer awkward moments – well, that's something that, as Annie's oldest friend, she must put up with.

It's the morning after Archie's return. He's in the small bathroom, shaving. The first shave, after days at sea, always takes a long time – half an hour, perhaps, among carbolic soap and sweet clean towels. Archie also takes a shower. The water – in the shower he installed himself a couple of years ago – never quite achieves the strong gush he hopes for, but it is very hot, and soon the small room is packed with dense steam. Archie shampoos his hair, washing out the stiff salt, and brushes his teeth more vigorously than he does at sea, with the toothbrush he always keeps at home. All this is a ritual of the first morning back, before breakfast of porridge and bacon and the thick grainy bread that Myrtle has left to rise overnight, and has put in the oven to bake at dawn.

Myrtle stands by the stove stirring the porridge. She listens for Archie's step. She waits, aware of an internal warmth that is never there on mornings when he is away. Through the window there is a bright, colourless sky. On days like this the sea, too, will have cast off its plumage of blues and greens and purples and chosen austerity to match the sky. Later, Myrtle will go with Archie down to the harbour.

The door, rarely locked, opens. Tentatively. Myrtle shifts her position, at once alert, protective of her husband's time. Who has come to disturb him?

Janice stands there. Janice Mcleoud. She has her mother's enquiring eyes, slanting under heavy brows. She holds the bottom half of a biscuit tin filled with hay, or dried grass.

'Mrs Duns? My mother said . . .'

She moves towards the table. Puts down the tin. Lifts from it a brown hamster which she keeps in her hands.

'There's something the matter with him. He's not eaten for two days. My mum said –'

'I don't know what makes your mother think I'm any better than she is with animals. I know nothing of hamsters.' Myrtle moves quickly from stove to table. 'Here, let me have a look.'

Myrtle raises Janice's hands so that the animal is almost on a level with her own eyes. It does not move, its nostrils twitch very slowly. Its eyes are dull.

'The poor wee thing,' says Myrtle. 'He looks quite poorly.' She sees Janice is close to tears. 'I'm afraid I can't say what's the matter. What's he been eating?'

'Just the usual,' says Janice. 'What can I do?'

'Go to the vet, would be my advice.'

'Mum says she's not spending money on the vet just for a hamster.'

'Then do your best for him. Keep him warm. Try a little tepid milk.' Myrtle is sorry for the child, but she wants her to go. Archie will be here in a moment. Janice returns the animal to the tin.

'Can't *you* do anything, Mrs Duns?'

'I'm sorry, but I really can't, Janice. Now if you don't mind, I must be –' She returns to the stove, picks up her wooden spoon, begins to stir, aware the earlier calm has gone. Bother the child. Her own father home, why isn't she calling on *him* for help if Annie is no use?

'Surely you can do *something*?' Thwarted, Janice is cross now, as well as upset.

'No. Nothing. I'm not an expert on hamsters. Now please, Janice –'

'But Mum said that once she remembered when you were children that you found a gull with a broken leg and you made a kind of splint and looked after it till it was mended. If you could do that for a gull, Mrs Duns –'

'That wasn't hard.' He is on his way now. Archie's tread in the passage is heavy with anticipation. Myrtle's voice rises. 'Now Archie's here wanting his breakfast. Go back to your house, Janice. Your mother'll be wondering –'

'She won't! She knows where I am.' Janice turns to see Archie standing in the doorway. His look unnerves her. She picks up the tin, smiles her best smile straight at him. The extraordinary prettiness of her devious little face, so like her mother's at the same age, makes Myrtle's own expression harden. 'I'm sorry, Mr Duns, if it was too early to call, but my hamster is very ill and I thought Mrs Duns –'

'Bugger your hamster when I'm just home,' says Archie, very quietly, and the child, pressing the tin to her chest, runs from the room.

Myrtle spins round.

'What d'you want to go and say that for? She's upset enough.'

'Little minx. Thick-skinned as her mother.'

'There's nothing wrong with Janice except that she doesn't know when she's not wanted.' Archie sits at the table. Myrtle brings him his bowl of porridge.

'I'm sorry about that,' she says more gently, 'but I couldn't be too hard on the child. The creature will be dead before the day's out, and if I know Annie there'll not be too much sympathy. It's not the sort of thing she minds about.'

'Right as usual,' says Archie.

In all the years of Myrtle and Annie's friendship there have been many rows, but only a few they can remember. The first one, that became so violent that Dot had to pull them apart, was when they were five or six years old. That occasion, never forgotten, they laugh about now, but neither speaks of the crystallising of the differences between them that became apparent that day, though at the time both girls were too young to understand why they were struck by uncomfortable feelings which later they realised were jealousy, resentment, partial longing for each other's way of life.

Dot had taken the girls for a picnic on the beach – the very beach where her husband's body was to be washed up some years later. Annie's mother Mag had agreed to come too. But, as Dot had expected, at the last moment she had changed her mind. She sent a message with Annie saying she wasn't well. Of a nervous disposition, Mag was rarely well enough to do anything that did not suit her. Reading romantic fiction occupied most of her day. The fantasies played out in her head had given her over the years a vague, distracted look. It was hard ever to feel you had her full attention: Annie gave up trying from a very young age and her father, an Irishman who had come to Scotland looking for work, returned to his native country weeks after Annie's birth. (He still sent what money he could every month.) In Dot's private opinion Mag suffered from agoraphobia, though in those days the condition was less well recognised and no one knew how to help her. She lived on tranquillisers – the doctor's only solution – and the practical help of kind neighbours. It was always Dot who dropped Annie home from school: she and others 'picked up a few things' for Mag whenever they went shopping. Life at home for Annie – mother's greasy head forever in a book, scant food, no interest in the outside world – was both bleak and boring. It was no wonder that much of her childhood was spent in the Stewart household.

For some reason, that particular day, Annie had believed her mother really would come on the picnic, and was excited by the prospect. So when, once again, at the last minute Mag changed her mind, Annie felt the familiar pebble of disappointment shift round her insides, a physical pain that made her cry, though she could not explain her tears to Myrtle and Dot. But it was a fine day on the beach, which they had to themselves, for the breeze was as stinging cold as the edges of the sea they paddled in – and once Annie had hungrily eaten Dot's banana sandwiches and drunk a bottle of home-made lemonade, she found herself more cheerful. She and Myrtle wandered down the beach to look for shells. Dot perched herself against a small rock, took her knitting from a cavernous bag of ancient patchwork. Lulled by the movements of her own fingers that needed no eyes to guide them, her glance went back and forth between the empty grey sea and the two small girls, bending and shouting, some twenty yards away. She had no idea how much time had passed before she heard the screams – thin scraps of sound muted by the breeze and the brush of breaking waves. But their urgency made Dot leap up from her reflections with no further thought. She flung her knitting down on the sand. The children were hitting each other – kicking, scratching, pulling each other's hair. Dot ran.

The shell Annie had found Myrtle did not particularly want: it was not a special shell, for all its size. But Annie had been nasty, annoying, all day: and now Myrtle wanted her *not* to have the shell more than anything in the whole world.

'I want this one! You've got more than me.'

'*No!* Can't have it! It's mine –'

Myrtle snatched at the shell in Annie's hand. Annie flung a small claw at Myrtle's cheek. Her nails, sharper than shells, tore down the skin. Myrtle grabbed a clump of Annie's curly hair, chaotic in the breeze, and pushed her to the ground. Annie scratched, kicked – any part of Myrtle she could. She bit her arm, tasted salt. Seared by the pain, Myrtle pushed a thumb into a wet red eye. Annie screamed louder. Myrtle felt the slippery flesh of the eyeball, wondered if she pushed hard enough it would fall right back into Annie's head. Annie spat. The glob of slime, cracked by the breeze, splattered across Myrtle's bleeding cheek. Then two large firm hands were pulling the bodies apart, Dot's angry voice telling them to stop at once: disgraceful little fools, they were.

The girls sat one on either side of a panting Dot. She wiped faces, eyes, hands with a hopelessly inadequate paper handkerchief: screwed up the mess of blood and sand and tears and stuffed it in her pocket. Then she lifted the hem of her long skirt and applied it more vigorously to the sniffling children.

'It was her fault,' Annie was the first to say.

'*Her* fault,' said Myrtle.

'I'm not interested in whose fault it was: just remember you've both spoilt a good day.'

'She's bigger than me: it's not fair,' said Annie.

'She's prettier than me,' said Myrtle. 'Her curls.'

'Life isn't fair and I'll not be listening to any more of this stupid talk,' said Dot.

Fight over, they were cold. But they stayed where they were, huddled next to Dot, who did not put her arms around them: physical gestures of comfort or affection she deemed to be unnecessary. They might have remained where they were for some time while Dot gathered the energy to take two unhappy and exhausted children home. But then a divine intervention, as she later described it to Jock, came to the rescue. The knitting! All three of them saw it at once – powered by the wind, the long scarf of intricate colour and design, into which Dot had knitted many hours of her life, was racing towards the sea. The needles, still attached, made funny stiff-legged walking movements that made them all laugh. When the needles fell over, they laughed harder. Then with one accord they all leapt up and began to run towards the water. The children reached the edge first. By now the scarf was curling about on the white spume several yards out. Ignoring Dot's cries, they both high-stepped towards it, lifting their skirts over their bottoms. They each grabbed an end, and tugged it back to the shore with an air of triumphant partnership. Dot, in her wet shoes, was still laughing, praising. The girls, shivering, helped her wring the water from the sodden wool. One needle was missing, but Dot said that was not important. On the walk back to the bus stop the wind dried their clothes. Once on the bus itself they chose to sit together, bare legs splayed wearily across the bristly seat, touching. The warm and smelly air – petrol, sea, discarded food – sent them to sleep in moments. Dot, on a seat beside them, felt the heaviness of her own eyes.

The days that the fishermen spend at home are always edged with the knowledge that time is short – too short to be wasted with disagreements about how they should be spent: and yet, because these breaks are so regular, a part of normal life, they cannot be thought of as holidays, times for treats or unnecessary extravagance.

Myrtle tries to assume an exterior that gives no hint of her feelings. It would be no help to Archie to know the depth of her anguish every time he was away, and she had no wish to risk hindering him with desire of his constant presence when he is home. The luxurious times are when he is working on something in the house. As she goes about her own household jobs, the tap of his hammer or the sawing of wood, signifying his presence in the next room, is the kind of joy that gives lightness to her step and speed to her fingers.

Between chores, Archie takes trouble with his wife. They would go for long walks, often along the beach beneath the church of St Monan's, where they were married. They would have a drink in a pub out of their own village: Archie has no wish, he says, to have to talk shop with his crew – he hears enough of their opinions at sea. Myrtle's private view is that he has even less wish to run into Ken and Annie, who spend much of every shore leave in pubs. Sometimes, on a fine day, Archie would spontaneously suggest a real excursion: the bus to Edinburgh for a day, where Myrtle would filter slowly round the large bookshops, Archie at her side encouraging her to buy. It was high time he made some more bookshelves, he said: he is proud to think she's read every book that was on the shelves he had already made. Sometimes, summer, they would get out the old bikes, pedal in uniform solemnity out to fields of long grass starry with buttercups. Archie would beat down the grass to make a sheltered hollow where they ate their sandwiches, drank their cider.

There was a particular place they loved, where the flat lands behind the village gave way to a gentle rise, scarcely high enough to be called a hill. But at the summit of this rise was a church from which life – apart from a rare service attended by a scant congregation – had fallen away. It was surrounded by graves long since attended to, housing dead too long forgotten to be saluted with flowers. Archie and Myrtle loved this place best in May, when the cow parsley was breast high and the dense shade of the dark trees was scattered by a warm breeze. From the grave-yard where, they decided, to eat their lunch was not a profane act, they could look down on to fields of wheat silvered by the spring sun. In the distance these rippling fields merged into the darker flank of the sea. Bass Rock, from here, was no larger than a human tooth sticking up from the water – for all its distance, a menacing shape. On a clear day, the Lammemuirs beyond the sea were a switchback line against a huge sky. This place, Archie often said, reminded him of north Norfolk, where his parents once took him on holiday as a child after they had been fishing at Lowestoft. The gentle incline of land behind Brancaster, the expanses of sky and sea were very similar to the East Neuk of Fife: this part of the coast was untypical of much of Scotland.

Once, pushing their bikes back down to the main road, Myrtle and Archie passed the open gate of an old stone house, the former manse. It was simple in its architecture as a child's drawing: four large windows and a handsome front door dividing its friendly façade. While Archie admired the thickness of the hawthorn hedges that divided the garden from the lane, Myrtle was excited by the glimpses of lustrous curtains at the windows: even their linings, she reckoned, were made of quality stuff. She imagined herself looking out of one of these windows, waking to see the small herd of enormous white cows that grazed in the field beyond the garden. She could see herself growing familiar with their habits, their movements about the field at various times of day. How easy it would be to grow fond of them, to watch with a drugged, lazy pleasure their heavy stride as they lolled about in their small patch of earth, tails heavy as bell ropes sloshing from side to side to reveal pink-skinned glimpses of fatly upholstered thigh . . . How easy it would be to let time pass standing at an upstairs window, arched by curtains of frosted damask, and to stare down upon these dignified creatures, and the world denied to them beyond, where wind-bent trees became smaller and smaller in their progress towards the sea. Myrtle wondered who were the people – the person – whose good fortune it was to live in such a place: and did they love it as much as she would, given the chance?

'Imagine living here,' was all she said to Archie.

'I canna,' he said, mounting his bike with a suddenness that disturbed Myrtle's reverie.

'Well, I can live with my dreams.'

'You can, too.'

Myrtle, heaving on to her own bike, gave a small, deprecating smile that Archie did not see. He was already some way ahead of her, pedalling fast, as he used to as a child. His mind was on other things. He whistled. Myrtle could just hear the sound of the plangent tune which was carried up to her on the breeze.

*

She stands outside the front door, pot of paint in hand. Archie has gone again. Five more days.

The paint is the Christmas green of holly leaves. There was nothing close to the colour Myrtle had in mind in the chandler's store. She had gone by bus to St Andrews and found exactly the right thing there – a whole afternoon, the expedition had taken her. She liked it when whole mornings or afternoons were taken up by a single project: such demolitions of time hurried the days to Archie's return. Myrtle's sense of perfectionism sometimes unnerved Archie, though it also made him proud. It was a wonder, the way she paid such acute attention to detail that others would regard of no importance. But then, with no bairns to keep her busy, time had to be skilfully marshalled. He could not criticise her way. It was best for her and, for all his gentle teasing, affected him in some funny, pleasurable way, too.

The days with Archie here, as always, have gone so fast. When time is precious, pottering about, getting on with normal chores, does nothing to slow the hours. Archie spent the best part of one day preparing the front door for the new paint: sanding, filling in, smoothing. From her place in the kitchen, Myrtle was lulled by the scrape of sandpaper, the occasional bang and thud of implement on thick wood, indications of sweet proximity. Archie had brought home several pounds of red fish (even in the depths of her subconscious Myrtle, superstitious as all fishing people, never thought of it by its real name: to say the word *salmon* is to dice with fate. They must avoid it as actors avoid *Macbeth*). They had the fish for three meals – grilled, kedgeree and fishcakes. Myrtle, huge in her kitchen, floury hands swiping down her apron only to be re-floured again, listened to the scraping and the sanding which became confused with the distant rasp of the sea, and felt the familiar churn of security which alighted when Archie was home, all the more vital for its transience.

One afternoon she went with him down to the boat – a thing she did not much like doing, for it was all too easy to imagine such a small vessel at the mercy of tumultuous waves. Archie always assured her it would take a storm the like of which he had never seen to capsize *Skyline II*, but Myrtle could not be convinced. Not long ago

Archie had confessed that his father's boat, the old *Skyline* (which Ben Duns had bought from Dot after Jock's death), had once rolled right over, but righted herself. If it came to it, he said, *Skyline II*, an even finer boat, bought in the days when fishing was profitable, would do the same.

Myrtle, standing on the harbour wall, had tried to push such thoughts from her mind. She did not share Archie's affection for the boat, or his faith in her. *Skyline II* was far from the youngest, or most handsome, boat in the harbour: snub-nosed, wide-girthed, her black paint worn away and scratched like an old table. Her decks were an incomprehensible clutter of wires and winches and nets: Myrtle watched in awe as Archie scrabbled among the mess looking for something. He was better acquainted with *Skyline's* decks than he was with his own sock drawer, she often thought. Somehow, before returning to sea, he and the crew always managed to have her ship-shape. To Myrtle she was a boat that looked tired, spent: foolishly, she had once said this to Archie, and angered him. She was an ignorant woman when it came to boats, he said, and should keep such opinions to herself. *Skyline II* had years of buoyant life in her yet. So Myrtle contained such thoughts, but could not rid herself of them. When Archie disappeared into the cabin, she could feel her eyes lock with concern. The boat scarcely moved as the brown harbour water flopped against her sides, a languid low tide. She had the look of an old carcass, awaiting the vulture gulls, shrieking low overhead, to rip her to pieces. Archie, all smiles as he ran up the ladder carrying a cardboard box, caught her stricken face. He put an arm about her. They walked with huge fast strides back along the harbour wall, Archie deflecting her thoughts with some story about Ken's eagerness always to be first to help with the worst jobs. He was the one who most frequently volunteered to clean up the galley or unblock the sink. In a moment Archie had recharged his wife's spirits, and they both silently anticipated the long, quiet evening ahead. And on the last night of this shore leave he put his hand round the back of Myrtle's neck even before they had gone upstairs. He gathered her to him with all the constant love that he found difficult to declare, but

Myrtle had come to recognise in the complicated maze of his natural diffidence.

By noon, the undercoat is finished. Myrtle stands back, contemplates her work. With any luck the paint will have dried hard enough for her to begin the top coat this afternoon. Archie advised her to leave it for twenty-four hours, but an impatience for its completion spurs her to ignore such advice. Archie will never find out – and if he does it would not be the kind of infidelity that would concern him. Then, if the topcoat is really hard by tomorrow morning, Myrtle goes on to think, she can spend a good many hours polishing up the black crust of the old brass knocker. That should take care of most of Tuesday.

Until two years ago, when Dot died, the days when Archie was away were charged with duties that did much to speed their length. Dot, who eventually required more expert nursing care than Myrtle could give, went without protest to the Evergreen Home just outside the village. Myrtle and Archie felt all the ubiquitous guilt at organising this move, but as far as they could judge it caused Dot no traumas.

'I shall no longer be a bother to you,' she said with one of her toothless smiles. 'I'll be able to sit and sit and sit, no trouble to anyone.'

At the home, within a very short time, Dot had established that her sedentary life should not be in the company of others. On their first visit, Myrtle and Archie arrived to find she had persuaded the nurses to move her armchair to the bay window overlooking the sea, as far as possible from the rigid circle of other fishermen's wives who dozed round a television set from morning to night. Dot's small body, dwarfed by the rose-blown cushions of the armchair, seemed to have closed in on itself in this new place – its edges reaching hopelessly towards each other like a shell prised half open. Her tiny head, lowered on to her chest, strained upwards so that her eyes could meet the horizon. She was watching, she said, for *The Skyline* to return for her: that was occupation enough till she died. She convinced the nurses this was truthfully all she desired to do, and they soon gave up trying to persuade her to join the others' undignified activities. The 'exercise' class, she told Myrtle – old arms struggling to rise in time to 'Pack up your Troubles' – was worse than any sight she had come across in eighty years on land or sea. It was *indecent*, she declared, and she wanted no part of it. But then Dot had never been one inclined to join a crowd, and in the last two years of her life in the home she rallied gestures of independence with the energy she had left. From her solitary position at the window, she scorned the woollen garments of pale pinks and blues that drizzled from the shoulders of her peers. Dot insisted, despite the stuffy central heating, in wrapping herself in her mother's old Shetland shawl, a woollen garment dyed in natural dyes – 'hedgerow juices', she called them – that she declared must be her shroud. Gloomy, the nurses called it. Why do you want to wear this old thing, dear? Your daughter could bring you a nice bright cardigan. But Dot wanted neither nice bright cardigan nor carpet slippers. She insisted on wearing the lace-up boots, their brown leather polished to a silvery bronze, that she had preserved for thirty years. These were the clothes she had worn when she waved Jock off from the harbour, or went to greet him: and these were the clothes she wished to be in when he came for her again.

'She's what we call our wee Bohemian, your mother,' a nurse once said to Myrtle. They could never understand.

In the two years that Dot was in the home, Myrtle visited her every day. Archie came with her any Sunday he was not at sea. The visits imposed a pattern which Myrtle found soothing, though each one brought evidence of further decline, and each one was heightened by the knowledge that time was running out. Myrtle would sit on the floor beside her mother's chair – thus, their eyes were on a level, though rarely met. Dot's patient gaze was on the sea. Her hands lay side by side on her lap, unmoving, like two small dead fish about to be cast back into the water. Sometimes the fingers would make involuntary movements, as if trying to pluck at an invisible line, or fix bait to a hook. At such moments Myrtle believed her mother to be remembering, but she was often wrong.

'What are you thinking, Mother?' Silence. 'Are you remembering baiting the lines?'

'No,' Dot said, after a long while, and still not moving her eyes. 'Why should I be?'

They would not talk much, mother and daughter. Myrtle found little to say. She knew the only news to interest Dot – before she ceased to take in anything at all – was of tides and winds, so that she could calculate the progress of her dead husband. She had no interest in the present politics of fishing, or how scant were the catches. News of Annie, whose shocking behaviour had once caused her a certain glee, held no interest either. Only the death of one of the old widows stirred her into brief liveliness.

'She fell forward in her chair, Clarrie McFair she was, her Andrew on Jock's crew for a year or two, spit coming out of her mouth in great bubbles like our goldfish Sammy used to blow. You remember Sammy? She upsets her tea all over the place, face a nasty colour. Blow me if she isn't gone, the nurse says. And she'd walked back from the dining room, no help, not an hour before.'

'How did you see all this, Mother, your back always turned on the circle, your eyes out to sea?'

'If you hear a commotion, you turn round, don't you? It was a sight. Some of the old ones, they just kept their eyes shut. One or two of them cried, a horrible noise, and tried to get up to help. But the nurses pushed them back in their chairs. There was nothing they could do – nothing anyone can do when a heart pegs out like that. I turned back to the sea. Poor old Clarrie, I thought, though I'd not seen her for years. I'll be the next one to go, I thought. I'll be the next one to go, though not before your father's come for me.'

When Dot died, Archie had been at sea for two days and was not due to return for another three. Myrtle, who arrived at her usual time at the home in the morning, was told her mother had had a restless night but now appeared more settled. Dot was in her usual position, staring out over the white-chipped sea to the horizon. Her hands were clasped restlessly together as if holding some secret excitement. When Myrtle lowered herself on to the floor beside her, Dot raised one of her hands – the silvery scars so faded they were almost invisible – but did not move her eyes.

'He's here at last,' she said. 'Look: there's *The Skyline*! On the horizon.'

Myrtle looked out to sea. There was indeed a ship on the horizon, though it looked a hundred times the size of her father's fishing boat. More like a tanker.

'That's good,' she said.

'He'll no' be long now.' Dot's hands unwrapped themselves, fell back on to her lap. She did not speak again. When Myrtle left her, an hour later, it was clear Dot had more important things to concentrate on than the farewell. Myrtle made her way past Clarrie's empty chair – still not filled, though it was three months since she had died – thinking that although her mother's reason had now completely gone, at least she seemed happy. She did not fret, or complain, or shift about in her chair. Consumed by her long, irrational watch for her husband, her extraordinary firmness of purpose gave her calm, resolve, a kind of peace.

Myrtle had not been back home an hour when the telephone rang. Dot had died moments after she left. Kind timing – to spare me the commotion, Myrtle thought. She sat at the kitchen table, busied herself making a list of things that must be done. She wished that Archie was home, and that she could weep away the diffuse sensations that gather when a much-loved mother dies. But for the moment no tears came, and eventually she telephoned the minister of the kirk to arrange the funeral for the day after Archie's return. Dot's wish was to be buried beside her husband, in a corner of the graveyard that overlooked the sea.

By mid afternoon the front door was finished. Myrtle stood back to consider her work. It would be hard for Archie to find fault, she thought, even if he did not appreciate the subtlety of the green. It was well painted, handsome, lustrous. It distinguished the small stone house, whose roof was now in perfect order, and Archie had done a grand job on the window sills and frames only a year ago. Myrtle was pleased. Impatient for Archie's approval. Four, maybe five days . . .

*

Number five Arbroath Street had been the McGregor family house for many generations. It was a traditional East Neuk village house of thick stone walls, crow-stepped gables, slate roof and well-spaced windows of more aristocratic proportions than are usually found in small village houses. Two flights of stone steps, joined at the top by a stone landing place, led to the first-floor front door. Two hundred years ago the ground floor, a single large room the length of the building, was rented out to a firm of sailmakers. When steam drifters came into general use at the beginning of this century, and sailmakers were made redundant, Myrtle's grandfather had plans to turn the space into part of the house, linking the two floors with an inside staircase. These plans never materialised: Hamish McGregor spent most of his life at sea, and when he was home the last thing he felt inclined to do was building. As there was no possibility of paying anyone else to do the work, the room fell into disrepair. It became a general store for neighbours, and was soon full of ancient nets, rusting machinery and all manner of useless objects.

When Dot and Jock were married they lived, at first, with Dot's parents upstairs. The lack of space meant this was an uneasy arrangement of which they soon tired. Apart from the kitchen, where all daytime life was conducted, there were only two small bedrooms. The first one, hastily converted from the original parlour, was occupied by the elder couple. Dot and Jock were left, albeit gratefully, with a slip of a room into which only a single bed would fit. After a year of discomfort, Jock took a couple of weeks' holiday and put the old storeroom downstairs to rights. It was cold, sunless, damp, in no way luxurious: but it was private. When Jock was home he and Dot kept to themselves in their quarters, the heavy thud of parental feet overhead spurring them to restrict family visits as much as possible. Myrtle was born in that room, five minutes before the midwife arrived. Jock was at sea. It was a stormy day, but according to a much-repeated story of Dot's, no sooner than the baby was born the clouds disappeared and a bar of sunlight made its way into the room, lighting the darkness.

Myrtle was two years old when her grandparents moved to a small modern flat. For the last decade of their life they enjoyed an electric stove, central heating, a bath and inside lavatory (for years they had had to climb down the outside steps, torch in hand on dark nights, to a shed in the scrap of earth they called the garden). Dot and Jock and their young daughter moved upstairs: it was warmer, cosier, lighter, and they could see the sea from the kitchen window. Once again the downstairs room was neglected. Mould grappled the walls, evil-looking fungi sprouted up through the floorboards. By the time Archie and Myrtle married it was in a state of such sad neglect they did not even contemplate making it their first home, poor though they were. They started married life in a council flat of the meanest possible proportions, and hated all that their grandparents had so enjoyed: air stiff with central heating, cheap windows, lack of shelves or space, a bleak and tacky kitchen whose geometrically patterned formica, orange and brown, caused Myrtle daily anguish. So when Dot became ill and needed constant help, to convert the downstairs room in Arbroath Street, and make it into a small flat, was a quick and happy decision.

In the last two years, since Dot had died, Myrtle and Archie had gradually been putting the house further to rights. They moved upstairs to sleep in order to wake up to the view: the two small bedrooms were knocked into one, the old fireplace was unblocked. Sometimes, on cold winter nights, they lit a wood fire in the bedroom. Pale ash in the grate, the occasional red eye of a still-living ember, was their first sight on waking. For them it was a shared pleasure to rise from the warmth of the bed into the bitter air, their breath spectral bulbs of air floating in the semi-dark of dawn. But it was always warm in the kitchen: the ancient range, a temperamental old object that suffered various crises and needed constant pampering, gave out a good heat. In the tradition of Myrtle's forebears, she and Archie spent most of their time there: Archie's old armchair was by the stove, Myrtle's books were thrust between china and jars on Archie's fine shelves. It was the place they felt most at ease, the room where greetings and farewells took place: its window was the vantage point from which Myrtle would daily read the sea. Neither of them could ever imagine spending more time elsewhere.

In the landing between the kitchen and bedroom they had put a spiral staircase to the downstairs room – thereby achieving at last Grandfather McGregor's plan. Their old room was now changed once more: a door led on to the 'garden', now a paved courtyard where Myrtle grew herbs and geraniums in discarded baker's trays. The small bathroom they had put in when they came to live there was furnished with a more amiable bath, and a corner of the room was partitioned off to house the washing machine. They painted the walls white, bought a huge old sofa, and a desk for Archie's accounts. Thus it became the living room, referred to by the jealous Annie as a 'bloody great ballroom'. But rarely did they use it. Sometimes, summer evenings, they would sit by the open door looking out at Myrtle's flowering pots, but they felt oppressed by the high walls of the courtyard. All they could see, from down there, was a few yards of sky: no sea.

Arbroath Street, once only known for the poverty within its thick-stoned houses, was by now a generally smarter place. Neighbours had preceded the Duns with their improvements: roofs were patched, window frames gloss-painted, the wood of old front doors turned yellow and red and blue. Strangers with cameras, in clothes to match the front doors, were often to be found wandering down the street these days – their eyes more dulled than amazed by the sight of what one of them explained to Myrtle was surely 'living history'. And tourists were not the only problem: men with profit in mind had also discovered the east coast of Scotland.

One day Myrtle opened the door to a man who wore a tartan tie and the sort of expression that indicated he was confident of a welcome. He said he hoped it would not be untoward if he were to compliment her on her house.

'A very desirable residence, if I may say so,' he ventured more cautiously, in response to Myrtle's face. 'Now would you ever have it in mind, I wonder, to rent out your quite exceptional – if I may be so bold – home?'

Myrtle stepped back into the kitchen. So preposterous a thought deprived her of an immediate answer. The estate agent, as Myrtle imagined him to be, took the liberty of moving inside as well, where his expert eye took in the decorative order of the place in a moment. As Myrtle was still locked into her speechless state, the man was able to grant her the benefit of his advice.

'You could pick up a nice little rent, place like this, summers,' he said. 'Of course, a modicum of investment, dare I suggest, might be required – nothing to alarm the coffers.' He gave a narrow smile of encouragement, exposing teeth the colour of young bark. Myrtle, lulled by his Morningside accent, sinuous as the cooing of a distant wood pigeon, folded her arms and stared down at his head of man-nered hair. 'There are others in this very street in the process of *considering*, aye. Indeed, there are some that have more or less made up their minds: I'd put my money on that, Mrs – eh?'

'Never,' said Myrtle.

'I think you would be wise to reflect on how much you could gain from so little trouble –'

'I said never –'

'The mere changing from the, eh, delightfully *historic*' – here a dark smile was flashed towards the stove – 'in some cases, to the more contemporary aids of modern life that weekenders, bless their hearts, seem more greatly to favour . . .' At this point a small sniff was quickly extinguished by the genteel dab of a tartan handkerchief. He somehow managed to convey that while he himself was not one to approve the vulgarity of modern convenience, he was naturally obliged to consider the taste of his clients. 'What I'm saying is, with a nice little modern stove in here you could command a very fair rent indeed.'

'You're wasting your time,' said Myrtle. She wished desperately that Archie could have been there. He would so have enjoyed Mr Morningside.

'I can assure you that our agency is a very old establishment of highest reputation,' he persisted. 'Your interests are our business. We let all manner of properties on the east coast of Scotland, and, indeed, even further afield . . .' He trailed off. Glanced at the chipped paint of the window frame, the only one still awaiting Archie's attention.

Braced himself for one last attempt. 'You cannot imagine, Mrs eh? just how many satisfied customers we have on our books . . .'

'I'm sorry I can't help you by joining them, but no amount of money in the world would ever tempt my husband and I to let out our house to strangers. Now if you wouldn't mind, I have things to be getting on with . . .'

Myrtle sets about polishing the brass lion's head door knocker. She is impatient to finish the job, has no wish to be interrupted.

'Myrtle? I say, your door looks grand.' Myrtle, when she sees Annie, smiles. Annie, whose presence has the power so often to dissipate Myrtle's agitation or annoyance, has reached the top of the steps by now. She stands beside Myrtle on the stone landing, peering at the door. Eventually she reaches out a finger, touches the hard gloss paint. 'I want to talk to you.'

Myrtle sighs. She feels the sudden chill of evening on her shoulders. The sky is feathered with purple and grey clouds.

'We'll go in,' she says.

In the kitchen Myrtle automatically puts on the kettle, reaches for the tea caddy. Annie doesn't sit in her usual chair. She remains standing. Myrtle sees a tightness in her face that spells trouble. She knows at once when there is something up with Annie. She wonders if she can deflect whatever it is her friend has come to expound: she's in no mood for a confrontation.

'Did you and Ken get to Edinburgh?' she asks.

'We didn't. Ken had to be away a lot with the van. Business.'

'I don't want to talk about that.' Archie has been aware of Ken's 'business' for some time: as skipper of the boat he cannot approve, for it means that days ashore are far from a rest for Ken, who returns to the boat exhausted, unable to pull his weight, though his helpfulness – perhaps fired by guilt – continues. Archie has warned Ken several times he cannot put up with Ken's double life much longer. There have been arguments, rows. At some point, both wives know, there will have to be a showdown. Archie is increasingly suspicious as to the nature of Ken's 'deliveries'. He does not think they are all furniture removals. He has reason to believe that crates of black fish – fish surplus to the legal quota that should be returned to the sea – are stowed among the furniture and delivered to someone in a chain of traders flouting the law. Archie has confessed his suspicion only to Myrtle. When he is angry, he threatens to 'catch Ken out'. Myrtle keeps hoping that he will never do this.

'You asked,' says Annie. 'But I want to know what you meant by Saturday morning. What you did.'

'Saturday morning?' Myrtle's mind spins back, confused.

'You upset Janice, you upset the bairn. She came back in tears.'

A muffled snorting noise comes from Myrtle's nose. Annie takes this to be derision. She pulls back a chair – not her usual chair – with an angry scrape. Sits down.

'There was nothing I could suggest to cure the hamster,' Myrtle says.

'It wasn't that, so much. It was the general feeling you gave Janice of not being wanted. Not welcome.'

'Well she was right, there. She wasn't welcome.' Myrtle slams down two mugs. 'What do you imagine? Archie just home, wanting a bit of peace and quiet for his breakfast, and your daughter comes running round with an ailing hamster. That's not what I'd call good timing.' She pours tea. Annie, silent, has deep pink cheeks, the same marks stretching from eye to jaw that used to appear when she was an angry child.

'The hamster died,' she says at last.

'I'm sorry.'

'I thought you loved Janice as if she was your own daughter.'

'I've never quite said that.' Myrtle sits down heavily, the far end of the table from Annie. 'But it's true I'm very fond of Janice.'

'Sometimes, you wouldn't know it. You're often sharp with her – too sharp, to my mind.'

'There are moments when a child must know the truth. She's too cocky, young Janice. Too pleased with herself. It's not up to me to tell her how to behave in general. But as she seems to be in this house almost as much as she is at home, I've every right to tell her how to behave here. She should learn when she's not wanted. When Archie has just come home – that's one of the times she's not wanted. Doesn't seem unreasonable to me. But I don't blame the child entirely. *You* should tell her, Annie, not to come round here when Archie's –'

'So that's it.' Annie pushes away her empty mug. 'You know what your problem is, don't you? You're just jealous: jealous of Ken and me and Janice. Jealous of any couple with a child.' She takes in the scorn that travels across Myrtle's face. 'That's always been the case. That accounts for your behaviour – everyone says so. Of course, it's not that you don't have our sympathy. You know that. There can't be anything much worse than wanting a bairn and not being able to have one. But who was always at your side, tea and sympathy, when you were going through all those dreadful tests? Me, you remember. And how do you think I felt, having a bonnie wee daughter when you were unable –'

'Stop this, Annie –'

'How do you think I felt? How do you think I still feel? I remember saying to you soon after Janice was born: Myrtle, I said, you can have as much share in her as you want.'

'Stop it! There's no point in all this.' Myrtle is very pale. Her big hands grasp her mug of hot tea. After a while she says: 'I've told you before: if we're not going to quarrel then we should avoid this subject. Besides, you've no idea how I feel about not having –'

'You can't tell me you're not jealous of Janice's existence. You don't like the fact that I have a daughter and you don't.'

'I don't like it, no – not the fact that you have something I don't – I'm pleased about that, you know perfectly well. But the fact that *I* can't, ever, for Archie. I can't have Archie's child. Don't you see? That doesn't make for jealousy of you or anyone else who has children. It makes for something far more deadly: the persistent sense of failure. Of course, there are many advantages in having no children, no ties. We can do all sorts of things that you and Ken can't – just go off for the day on a whim. For all I know, you and Ken are jealous of our freedom. And then we're better off than some, with no children's things to pay for. But nothing can compensate . . . Failing to have a child smoulders away . . . You accuse yourself, all your life. There, I've said my bit. That's it, please. End of subject.'

Annie folds her arms, looks up at Myrtle.

'I'm sorry,' she says. 'I don't often fly off the handle like that, do I? We've been having a time, Ken and me. Up and down, all over the place – him out so much with the bloody van we never have time to settle. What do I do once he's gone again? Take it all out on you.'

Myrtle, webbed with thoughts which for the most part she manages to keep at bay, gives her a distracted smile.

'That's no matter,' she says. There's a long silence between the women. While both want to regain the old equilibrium between them, both are still too encumbered with their own preoccupations to come up with a declaration of good intent. 'If I was jealous of you, Annie, there'd be all sorts of good reasons, nothing to do with a bairn. You were always the pretty one, the lively one, the one the boys fought for. But I didn't mind any of that when we were children, when we were young, because you were always such a loyal friend, sticking up for me, insisting I share everything except for the boys – well, they didn't want me, so that wasn't your fault.' She gives a small laugh. 'You did everything to make sure I couldn't feel jealous and I was very proud that you, the most popular girl in the school, were my friend.'

The anger in Annie's cheeks, long since vanished pink, now returns, diffused, in the guise of a blush.

'Well I couldn't have done without you,' she says. 'You were my rock. Still are. Besides, you're remembering all wrong. I'd make you cross as anything. Still do.' Both women laugh. Annie moves towards the door. 'Will I come for cards usual time tomorrow?'

'Aye.'

'I must be gone. Janice'll wonder where I am.' Myrtle takes a bar of chocolate from a shelf.

'Give her that from me,' she says.

When Annie has left Myrtle remains quiescent in the semi-darkness. She feels such desolation that to remain sitting is all she can do. Her hands lie unmoving on the table. She wonders if one of them will shift of its own accord, and break the spell. She senses that rocks have been moved within her, and shale is pouring down between newly made crevices. Her devices for keeping untroubled the friendship with Annie usually work. They can go for months at a time with no arguments, no increase of tension. The sort of flare-up that took place this evening is both rare and, to Myrtle, disturbing. Annie, more volatile than Myrtle, has probably not given another thought to the disagreeable scene, and is heating up Janice's supper in the microwave as if nothing out of the ordinary had happened. Lucky her, thinks Myrtle: Annie's ability to take things lightly – *that* is the area where some fragment of envy lodges. Myrtle watches as her hands – no feeling within them, disconnected things – quiver up to grasp her temples. The emptiness of the room is so acute she knows she must leave it for a while. She picks up her shawl, shuts the window. For some weeks she has not visited her mother's grave. She will go there now for the certainty of quiet and the hope of peace.

Annie's acts of kindness to Myrtle, as a child, sometimes caused her trouble. There was the day when Ross Wyatt, who had been pestering Annie for months, made a final stand for her, and was rejected in favour of Myrtle.

'Come on out in the playground with me, Annie. I've something to show you.'

'I'd rather not, thanks, Ross Wyatt.'

The boy, Myrtle remembers, was desperate. He could not decide how best to appeal to the snooty girl who stood before him. His hands were in the pockets of his shorts. Myrtle could see the fingers whirling round. There were smears of high colour on his cheeks.

'I didn't mean the playground. I meant . . . let's go down to the harbour. Get us some chips.' His voice was breathless, odd. He suddenly turned away from them, flung his head back. Myrtle was alarmed. Was he ill? Should she get someone? But Annie didn't seem to think anything was amiss. She was used to boys having to turn from her, weak with love.

'No thank you,' Annie shouted. 'I don't want to go anywhere with you, ever. So don't bother to keep asking. Do I, Myrtle?'

There was sudden confusion in Myrtle's mind. Not three weeks ago Annie had told her just how much she fancied Ross Wyatt. She couldn't think why he was taking so long to do anything about it, she said. It was clear as anything he fancied her, too. So this peculiar change of mind, now Ross was actually making some move, took Myrtle by surprise. What should she do? Annie nudged Myrtle.

'No she doesn't,' said Myrtle, quietly. 'Annie doesn't want anything to do with you, Ross.'

'There! What did I tell you, Ross?' Annie was thrilled by her friend's quick thinking, her loyalty. 'Myrtle knows. Myrtle's my friend. Come on, Myrtle. We're going.'

Ross spun round to face them, deeply flushed. He looked healthier, despite his high colour, Myrtle thought. The fit, or spasm, or whatever it had been that struck him, had definitely passed. He fixed Myrtle with a look of total scorn.

'You! Friend? You're nothing more than an ugly great parcel, guarding Annie for dear life for you know *you'll* no' ever get a man wanting to get into your pants –'

'You foul-mouthed bugger! Don't you dare speak to my friend like that,' screamed Annie, and threw herself towards him. Myrtle tried to pull her back, but it was too late. Annie kicked Ross very hard in the balls. He went white, moaned, bent double. Myrtle dragged Annie back.

'Leave him, Annie,' she shouted above Ross's moaning, 'the scumbag –'

'I'll kill him!'

'You'll pay for this, bitch.' Ross unfurled himself painfully. Upright, one hand still clutched his groin. 'You stick around with your friend Myrtle, and I'll tell my friend Hamish if he wants you then he'll have to have your ugly friend too!' He laughed.

'Don't you dare!' There was a quiver in Annie's voice. Myrtle knew at once that Ross's threat meant something to Annie. Hamish? Perhaps there had been no chance for Annie to tell her whatever it was about Hamish.

'I'll say to Hamish not to bother with you – you're more concerned with this great parcel, Myrtle Stewart, who no boy would touch if she was the last girl on earth –'

'Get out,' Annie screamed again, 'before I fetch Mrs Williams.'

Ross turned and left the classroom with the air of one who had no intention of wasting any further insults on such despicable girls. His back view conveyed tedium with the whole scene. He slammed the door behind him.

Annie turned to Myrtle with tears in her eyes. Myrtle put an arm round her.

'You shouldn't have stuck up for me so hard like that,' she said.

'Course I should. I won't have anyone saying such beastly untrue things about you. It's wicked.' She sniffed. 'I'll kill him if he goes and messes up everything with Hamish.'

'I don't know what's up, you and Hamish, do I?' asked Myrtle, passing Annie her handkerchief. 'You go so quickly from one to another.' Annie suddenly giggled.

'I liked Ross for a bit before he looked at me. Then when he started up with all his pestering and soppy notes I thought he was revolting. Then just this morning in assembly Hamish winked at me – well, sort of winked at me – and I thought he was nice. I mean, I like curly hair.' She giggled again. Myrtle smiled, conspiratorial. She always enjoyed the turbulent progress of Annie's love life. 'Sorry, I didn't have a moment to tell you.'

'But how,' asked Myrtle, 'if Hamish winked at you only this morning could Ross know already that you –?'

'Och, he just guessed.' She gave a wry smile. 'Suppose you could say that sod Ross Wyatt is a good guesser. And next time he insults you I'll kick him so hard he'll never get up again.' She was punching the air with a clenched fist, pretty eyes flashing. 'No one's rude to my friend.'

It was one of Myrtle's proud moments. Annie's fierce declarations of loyalty filled her with more happiness than anything, surely, that any stupid boy could provide. She knew she had no chance with boys, anyhow. They either ignored her or were rude to her. But none of that mattered so long as Annie loved her and stuck up for her. And she couldn't imagine, even when she was grown up, that she could love any man half as much as she had always loved Annie. The two girls hugged each other, aware of the faint honey smell of each other's tears; then were parted by the clanging of the bell for games. They were twelve years old at the time.

Myrtle stands beside her mother's grave. It is dark by now: the flaked clouds of early evening have given way to a smooth darkness that becomes faded rags round the moon. Its light makes a highway across the sea. There are no ships, no waves. The meeting of sky and sea is lost in velutinous black. How, Myrtle wonders, do people think of the dead?

She herself finds it hard to picture her mother as a whole figure. The images in her mind are scattered miniatures. There are the scarred hands, the deep-lidded eyes, the wary smile, some small questioning gesture of head, the shoulders bent in old age. It's hard to remember her upright. Sometimes, frighteningly, it's hard to remember her face at all, and Myrtle has quickly to turn to a photograph to remind. The scent of her comes back more frequently: fish – the powerful whippy smell of brine – and the milder scent of lavender water. Dot, on Sundays, would dab homemade lavender water on her neck to disguise the fish. Myrtle, as a child, was allowed to give her mother the briefest goodnight kiss: it was enough to catch the familiar combination of fish and lavender on her skin. The smell was there even in the home: the fish marinated into skin over the years, the lavender now daily applied. A terrible extravagance, this, Dot once told Myrtle. But she feared the fish smell still clung, and she had no wish to give offence.

The voice was the part that lived most clearly. Dot's was a sweet, melodious voice, the Scots accent brittle as glass, the intonations choppy as small waves on a windblown sea.

'Myrtle: will ye come here?'

'Myrtle: you've grown into such a fine big lass – your faither's bones.'

'Myrtle, look: there's *The Skyline* on the horizon. He'll no' be long now.'

Dot's voice chimes ceaselessly through Myrtle, all times of night and day. Its persistence is what makes her think the dividing line between life and death is narrower than we might suppose. Perhaps the voices of those we love will never die, she thinks, and that is of some comfort.

'Myrtle, is that you?'

This is not a voice from the grave, but a man's voice. Canadian. Myrtle turns.

Martin Ford stands nearby, one hand at rest on a granite cross almost his own height. His hair is blonded by the moon, his face is in deep shadow.

'Och, Martin.'

'Hope I've not given you a fright.'

'Never.'

'I was caught up on a job, back late. Just wanted to see where I have to start digging in the morning. Rusty Burns. Ninety-three, I believe.'

'I heard. Poor Nancy's in a terrible way.'

'Last of the great bakers, these parts, I'd say.'

Martin is a stonemason. He came over from Canada with his parents when he was seventeen, and served his apprenticeship in the south. But he returned to Scotland to be near his parents – they share with him a divided house just beyond the village. Lack of work has always been his problem. He has established a reputation for being the most skilled stonemason on the east coast, besides the most reasonable – many is the time he has charged merely for the price of the stone. He is kept fairly busy with headstones, the odd monument, or memorial tablet for a church, but each job is long and painstaking and his profits do not reflect the value of his craftsmanship. To supplement his paltry income he digs graves. Martin is a strong and fast digger, and reliable. Indeed his reliability is renowned – always ready to help others, he has never been known to let anyone down. He is generally liked in the village, thought a good man considering he's from overseas. But no one, so far as Myrtle knows, is close to him or is privy to much of his life.

Martin shifts his position.

'Your mother – how long is it, now?'

'Two years almost exactly.'

'She was a rare woman.'

'Aye, she was.'

'And you?'

'I'm doing fine.'

'Archie away so much. Must be hard for you wives.'

'You get used to it.' The lie reverberates down Myrtle's spine. She pulls at her shawl.

'I must be on my way. Would you like me to walk you home?'

Myrtle shakes her head.

'Thanks all the same,' she says. She lets the fingers of one hand alight on the headstone of her mother's grave, then quickly fly away. Dot's name and dates, along with those of her husband, were beautifully carved by Martin. There is no epitaph. Myrtle has still not been able to think of one that she considers perfect.

'You've not come up with something for me to add?' Martin asks.

'Not yet. But I'm thinking.'

'Poor old Rusty. Nancy says RIP is all she can afford. I said don't be silly, I'll do him a line for nothing.'

'That was good of you,' says Myrtle.

'He deserves an epitaph, a baker like that.'

Somehow they are walking side by side down the narrow path between the graves, their feet making a shushing noise in the stone chippings. Martin shuts the cemetery gate behind them. Myrtle stops while he does this. It is the smallest indication that she does not mind his company. She has said she does not want him to walk her home, but when he continues by her side down the road she does not think of objecting.

No one is about in the village. The houses, so friendly-looking by day, have shuttered themselves behind a haughty, defensive look, which is their custom by night. Curtains are drawn. Lights, suffused through unlined fabrics, trick the eye with their three-dimensional quality: the windows appear to be luminous bricks suspended in the dark.

Myrtle and Martin walk in silence. Number five Arbroath Street is soon reached. Myrtle, who has been wondering whether to spend the rest of the evening with a concert on the radio or her book, stumbles on the bottom step.

'Careful.' Martin whips a torch from his coat pocket. A bright beam carves the stone staircase into wodges of light and shadow. The wool embroidery on the hem of Myrtle's skirt becomes ruby-red flowers.

'Whatever am I doing?' she asks. She can feel Martin's hand under her elbow as she remounts the bottom step, easily this time. She pauses there, one hand on the iron rail. Turns to him.

'Cup of tea? Something to eat?'

Martin thinks for a moment. Releases her elbow from his hand.

'Better be getting back,' he says at last. 'Thanks all the same. But I'll have to be up at four if I want to finish Rusty's grave before I go off to see about some marble.'

Myrtle pictures him alone in the churchyard, spade plunging into trim dewy grass, dawn sky lighting the dark earth as he digs fast and deep. She wonders about his life these days. It's not something she has thought about for a long time.

'Very well,' she says. 'It was good of you to walk me home.'

She flies up the steps now, keen to be inside. Martin keeps his torch shining for her. He waits till she has turned the key in the newly painted door before he puts it out. Then he waves: but it's too late. Myrtle has shut the door. Martin is as alone outside as she is within.

It is almost midnight. Myrtle shifts about, unable to sleep. As always, she envisages Archie far out to sea – an image she hates, but one which recurs every night. Then, the endless black water in her mind turns to sea dancing with sunlight, a calm day in the harbour. Martin, newly arrived in the village, strolling along the harbour wall, hands in pockets. He had a modest air as if he wished to be invisible. That was hardly possible, for he is well over six foot tall and wore his blond hair in a wild mess. Already he had become the object of desire of all the local girls: rare sightings increase speculation as to his availability and character in general. Annie, who at the time was going out with one Roddy Fairburn, found that her affection for a good but dull Scots boy did nothing to impede exciting possibilities provided by the Canadian.

'He's a smasher,' she whispered to Myrtle. 'I could do with a bit of him.' Myrtle could not deny the desirability of Martin, but kept this to herself. The idea of his even noticing *her* was laughable.

From a distance they watched him move slowly along the harbour wall, stopping to contemplate each anchored fishing boat.

'Here's our chance,' said Annie. 'Why don't we just go over and be friendly?'

'Not me,' said Myrtle, who learnt long ago the disadvantages of acting as chaperone to Annie. 'You can go alone. But he's too old for you, seventeen.'

'I'm nigh on sixteen,' said Annie, whose fifteenth birthday was not a week past, 'and anyhow everybody takes me for seventeen.' She fluttered her eyelashes, stiff with purple mascara. 'You're just a rotten sport, Myrtle. Never one for taking a chance.'

'There's Roddy,' said Myrtle. 'I thought you were going out with him.'

Annie laughs with a scorn too sophisticated for her years.

'Roddy? What good's he?'

Myrtle guessed Roddy's days were numbered. She had heard that laugh before. Martin had moved to the far end of the harbour wall, back to them. His concentration was now on the horizon.

'Thoughtful type, Martin, if you ask me,' Annie said. She shrugged, then laughed more agreeably. 'Course, the one he'd be really good for is you.' She smiled at the thought of any such impossibility. 'The height, I mean. He's about the only boy around taller than you, isn't he?'

'Don't be daft, Annie.' Now that Annie seemed to have forgotten about approaching Martin, none of her silly suggestions could alarm Myrtle.

'I'm not so daft, you'll see. Just a matter of waiting.' Annie took Myrtle's arm. 'All I ask is a chance to have first go. I don't half fancy him.'

'You do what you like,' said Myrtle. 'I don't *want* Martin.' But they were running fast now, late for school. Annie didn't hear.

The unexpected meeting with Martin has brought back this long-past scene very clearly to the sleepless Myrtle. She goes on to remember Annie's next move, and smiles to herself. Then at last she sleeps.

Annie, shuffling cards at Myrtle's kitchen table, is unusually quiet. She has brought a small pot of crocus bulbs which, she says, will be out for Christmas. This, too, is unusual. Annie is not by way of making such gestures very often. She does not describe the bulbs as a peace offering: but this is what they are, Myrtle well knows, and makes much of her pleasure and thanks.

Although the women play in silence for a while Myrtle is aware that something is on Annie's mind. She knows her friend so thoroughly. She knows exactly the cheeky tilt of head that precedes some overture to a man. She knows the look of hopeless caution that means she is doing her best to keep a secret. She knows the fingers that jump faster through the cards when she is harbouring some thought or knowledge she finds hard to contain. Myrtle watches her patiently, amused. Sometimes she feels most fond of Annie when Annie is struggling. Her inability to conceal, her candour, are among the things Myrtle loves her for. Annie knows she is being watched. She enjoys keeping Myrtle waiting. She pretends to concentrate very hard on her hand of cards. But eventually she says:

'So you caused a scandal last night.'

Myrtle meets Annie's mischievous eyes, gives a deprecating smile. 'I don't know what you mean.'

Annie flings out a look that says of course you know what I mean.

'Arm in arm with Martin, all through the village.' Myrtle is already laughing. 'Under cover of darkness. He sees you in, right in. Door apparently *bangs*! What happens then, Myrtle?' In Annie's playfulness there is an edge of suspicion. Myrtle's laughter increases, the warm, bubbling, cooing noise that Archie calls audible hot chocolate.

'There was no one about,' she says. 'Who were the spies?'

'There are always spies behind the curtains.'

Myrtle lays down her cards, folds her big hands. She cuts off the laughter, takes a deep breath.

'This village! I've never heard anything so ridiculous in all my life. The day Myrtle Duns causes a scandal ... .' The laughter breaks again.

'The truth, then. Tell me the truth.'

'It's not in the least interesting. After you left I went down to the churchyard for a while. Martin was there, looking at some plot where he had to dig a grave this morning. Aye, we walked home together – not arm in arm, as you can imagine. He shone the torch for me to get up the steps. I asked him in for a cup of tea – we haven't seen him for some weeks. He said no. I shut the door. Big scandal, that, I suppose.'

'Big scandal. I believe you.'

Myrtle, too, aims for playfulness.

'I should hope so.'

'He's a mystery, that Martin. There's not one of us knows about his life.'

'You got the closest.' It's Myrtle's turn to tease though she thinks, too late, that the subject of Martin and Annie is still, probably, no joking matter.

'Didn't get very close, as far as I can remember. He was always on about this other woman he loved.'

'I do believe you were really taken by Martin, all that time ago.'

'I was. You know that. Well, you know me. Not being able to *get* spurs the attraction. But it was more than that, what I felt for Martin. He represented something good, honest, strong: things I aspired to beneath all the flirting, whatever you may have thought. Last time I saw him he'd put on a fair bit of weight. He looked quite sad, I thought. I'd have liked to have ruffled his hair and said: come on, Martin, I'm still your friend. But I didn't dare. I'm not sure he'll ever like me again.'

'Nonsense.'

'If my carefree days were still here, I could still fancy him. There! Now I've said it. It's brought on your disapproving look.'

Myrtle laughs.

'You'll be fancying people – and they'll be fancying you – till the day you die,' she says. 'I can just see it, when the time comes you have to go into the home: the old boys'll no' stand a chance against you. You'll be chasing them down the passages on your Zimmer. You'll be pulling your armchair across the telly room to make sure you get beside whoever –'

'Now you're being daft. Besides, Ken'll be in there with me. There's no way we're going to be parted in our dotage. At least, that was a plan we once made.'

'How is Ken?' asks Myrtle. They don't normally enquire much about each other's husbands. Myrtle asks in a thoughtful way, perhaps to fill an uneasy silence. Annie shuffles her cards, eyes down, the extraordinarily long lashes making jagged shadows on her cheeks.

'It's not a good time,' is all she says.

Ken, at school, was for some years proud to be the joker in the class. He was always the one to come up with the cheeky answer, to make the others laugh at the teacher's expense; the one to be punished most often. The standard punishment was to be made to stay in after school and learn a hundred lines by heart, either from the Bible or Robert Burns. Thanks to this form of reprimand Ken discovered he had an astonishing memory. It took him moments to learn what would take others an hour or so. Not ten minutes after he had been shut into the empty classroom with a passage of St Paul's letters to the Corinthians, he would hail the teacher with the news that he had 'got it'. To the teacher's amazement, this was true. He would gabble the whole thing off, heedless of punctuation or intonation, but word perfect. Then, just to keep up the sharp edge of his renowned cheekiness, he would offer to learn a couple more passages if that was what was wanted. But no: he was always let off, accused of having a photographic memory, and warned this was nothing to be proud of. With great glee he would recount all this to his class mates who, already admiring of his cheekiness, doubled their respect. In order to be given more passages to learn by heart, Ken had to continue in his irreverent ways to gain punishment. Soon he began to ask if he could branch out from both Burns and the Bible. He was given the *Oxford Book of Verse* and told to learn whatever he liked so long as it added up to a hundred lines. Thus he was introduced to the poets, and came to love them. For two happy years he kept to the busy routine of punishment and learning, punishment and learning. He was kept so busy that he had no time, unlike the majority of the other boys, for thoughts of girls. They did not come into his scheme of things. He spent any free moment dreaming of becoming an actor. This he confessed one day to Myrtle and begged her to keep the secret to herself. If he mentioned the idea to his family, he said, who had been in the fishing business for generations, they would assume he was suffering from some weakness in the head and send him to the doctor.

In those days Ken held no interest for Annie. She was so dizzied by the compliments and desires of almost every other boy in the class that to make a play for one of the few boys who showed no interest in her was pointless. Had Ken been a generally acknowledged good-looker, like Archie, she might have made some effort. But as his sparse charm was more cerebral than physical, she saw no point in wasting her time. She merely joined in the laughter when Ken asked one of his funny but impossible questions, and equally joined the general respect for so singular a boy. Ken, for his part, could not help noticing that Annie was the prettiest girl in the class by about a million leagues, and that his peers – with the exception of his shy friend Archie Duns – made daily fools of themselves trying to please her.

The summer term that Ken turned sixteen there was a post-exam expedition to St Andrews organised by the school. There was to be a picnic by the beach, swimming, games. Not at all the sort of thing that appealed to Ken, but he knew there was no getting out of it. He arrived at the meeting place late to find there were just two seats left, at the front of the bus. He sat by himself, took out his copy of *Hamlet*, which he had disguised in the cover of a thriller for fear of ridicule. The engines started up, the coach was about to go, when there was a cry from Myrtle: Annie! Where was Annie?

Five minutes later, delayed not wholly by chance, Annie made her entrance up the steps. It was clear she had made a stupendous effort, was taking this outing more seriously than most. She wore tight black jeans and a scarlet elastic top, so thin and tight it might have been skin. The nipples of her small breasts played hide-and-seek between the chunks of stone, beads and leather thongs of her ethnic necklaces. It must have taken her at least an hour, Myrtle thought, to perfect her face: eyelids a translucent violet sheen, lips a creamy gloss, cheeks burnished a coppery pink, and long earrings of silver filigree jittered among her dark curls. The sight of her caused a general intake of breath, followed by a whooping and caterwauling which spurred Annie to smile benevolently up and down the bus at her less colourful friends. There was not a girl or boy there who did not recognise that she was in a different class, somehow . . .

Who was it that day Annie had set her heart on sitting next to? Myrtle could not remember. But whoever it was already had someone beside them. The only free seat, Annie saw from a racing glance up and down the bus, was next to Ken. She frowned. Then, not wanting to be unfriendly, she smiled. Both expressions were lost upon Ken, who moved as close as he could to the window, and opened his book.

He need not have feared that he would be interrupted. Annie swivelled round, back to him, and started chattering to those in the seats behind her. The journey, luckily short, passed in a cacophony of voices that Ken, concentrating on his book, tried to shut out. The thing he could not ignore was the smell of Annie: he tried to work out what it was – some kind of warm, honeyed flowers, perhaps. It was the only thing about her that did not intimidate. Rather, it gave him a strange new feeling. Confidence, was it? Whatever – it drew him from his book. He looked up to see the bus was entering the town. At that moment Annie gave one of her flashing turns – this time, towards him. For an infinitesimal moment she dropped a hand on his knee. The second was also an eternity, for in it Ken had time to observe in the minutest detail the shape, weight and contours of that small hand, nails the size of ladybirds blazing with scarlet polish, luminous skin of the fingers scarcely rippled at the knuckles . . . It was a hand that carried some strange venom which punctured his own skin with a thrilling sensation that sped up his thigh and reverberated through his body. The hand had flown, disinterested. But its touch continued to quicksilver through Ken, confusing.

'Ken!' He heard her voice from a long way off. 'You old bookworm, you. You should get together with Myrtle.' There was laughter from somewhere, and Annie had turned her back to him again and carried on her entertaining. As he climbed down the steps of the bus a few moments later, Ken felt curiously weak and tired, as if he had just accomplished some mammoth physical feat.

That day, Myrtle remembered thinking, was not perfect for a picnic. There was an unbroken grey sky and a cool wind which whipped the sea into petulant waves. But free from their exams at last, the pupils made the most of it. They set up a ball game to keep themselves warm, they played silly childish games of hopscotch and leapfrog. They patterned the clean beach with graffiti – the teachers decided to turn a blind eye – and ran random races, pulling each other on to the ground for a skirmish in the sand before they would right themselves and be off after another friend. After a short game of rounders Myrtle detached herself from the crowd and went to sit next to the solitary spectator, Ken. His melancholy air enclosed him like a shadow, but Myrtle was the only one to observe it. He sat hugging his bare, goosepimpled knees, pale of face as if struck down by a sudden illness. A book was stuffed into his back pocket. His eyes were on Annie. As she raced about, followed by some dozen boys, his look never left her. There was a moment when Sandy Strachan, who had caught her in one of the races, flung her to the ground. There were cheers as he rolled quickly over her, mashing her breast with his hand and plunging his mouth into her hair. Ken winced.

'You all right?' Myrtle asked.

'Fine, thanks.'

He was concentrating on Annie's escape. She fled down the beach, soon no more than a small red dot, classmates stringing out behind her. Suddenly she swerved towards the sea. From where they sat Myrtle and Ken could see the splashing and chasing of the faraway crowd. Spume, tossed into the air, made brief arcs that freckled the sky, and the squeals of laughter came to them tiny as the sounds of distant sea birds. Myrtle waited for Ken to make some joke, but he kept his agonised silence. Oh Lord, Myrtle thought: another one.

Later, when the others returned for the picnic lunch, Ken continued to keep his distance. Annie invited Myrtle to come and sit next to her, thus dashing the hopes of at least four boys who had been hoping to be granted this privilege. Pupils and teachers sat on the rounded grey stones that jutted through the sand, gritty hands clamped to thick sandwiches, hair blasted across their eyes by the breeze, the taste of salt on their lips. Overhead, puppet seagulls dipped and rose on invisible strings. Ken, with the air of one to whom noise and collective conviviality are unbearable, got up and wandered down the beach.

'What's the matter with him?' asked Annie, uninterested. Hamish was playing with her shoelaces in what she took to be an erotic manner. Myrtle shook her head, didn't answer.

On the way home, Annie contrived to sit next to Hamish while Myrtle took the place next to Ken. He looked terrible, she thought. Grey, shaken. As soon as the engines started up she enquired at once if anything was the matter. After a long silence he answered so quietly Myrtle could hardly hear him.

'I feel as if I've been in an *accident*,' he said.

'Anything to do with Annie, could it be?'

Ken nodded miserably.

'Your friend,' he said. 'Is she a witch, or what?'

'She's a beguiler,' said Myrtle. 'But she's good, too. She wouldn't want to hurt anyone intentionally. It's just that no boy can resist her – well, you can see why. But then if she doesn't fancy a boy back – there's the suffering.'

'I never gave her a second thought. Never really looked at her, even. Until today. Then she has to go and sit next to me and next thing I know . . .' Ken sighed. Myrtle suspected his discovered tragedy was not altogether disagreeable. 'There's a Keats ode,' he said, 'one of my punishments. "When a melancholy fit shall fall, sudden from heaven like a shower of rain, then glut thy sorrow on a morning rose . . ." Bloody stupid suggestion. Unlike Keats.'

'Quite,' said Myrtle. 'You need more than a morning rose.' She looked at his miserable face. 'I'll tell you something about Annie: for all that she's flattered, she gets a bit overwhelmed by all the adulation. The thing that really intrigues her is a boy who doesn't seem to notice her. So maybe if you go on lying low for a while, give no indication she's made you feel so . . . sick, when she's older and wiser it might come into her head that Ken Mcleoud is the one to interest her.'

Ken gave a pessimistic shrug, but half a smile.

'Thanks for the tip,' he said. And then, a while later he asked: 'Do you know that melancholy ode?'

'Lord, yes: aye, I do. It was after I first read it I thought to myself I'd like to be a teacher.' Ken seemed to be listening intently. His interest encouraged Myrtle to confide further. 'I was in the library one day and I pulled down this book of Keats' poems – I'd never heard of the man. I began reading – I couldn't stop. I took the book home – I couldn't learn so much by heart, like you, but I know it all, it goes all through me. And I thought, why don't we do this stuff at school? Why do they think it's too difficult, we wouldn't like it? And then I thought, if I can get so much out of it there must be others who can too, if only they had the chance . . . That's why it came to me maybe I should be a teacher, explain poetry to children, help them to love books.' By now Myrtle's cheeks were crimson. She knew she had gone too far and would regret this silly outburst to a boy she had scarcely exchanged a word with before today. But he was listening sympathetically as he dug rims of sand from under his nails with the point of a pencil.

'You'n me've got quite a lot in common,' he said.

Myrtle felt the heat of relief. He wasn't scoffing, as Annie would have done had Myrtle confessed such things to her. He seemed to understand. But then she silently laughed herself to scorn – quite a lot in common was of very little worth if you were big and clumsy and generally known to be the plainest girl in the class. Quite a lot in common with Ken would get her nowhere, and the pity of it would remain one more secret in her heart, for she warmed to his sympathy and liked the good nature in his brown eyes.

After this exchange on the bus Ken did not mention Annie again.

But the day at the sea marked some profound turning point in his life. The cheekiness, the spirit went out of him. He no longer entertained the class, he no longer committed deeds fit for punishment. He became one of those whom Annie described as 'no one in particular'. Myrtle watched his confusion and pain with concern. But his aloofness was not easy to broach. As he did not seem to require friends, she felt diffident about the offering of comfort. She liked to think, though, that he trusted her, and one day they would talk to each other again. Myrtle waited patiently, but Ken did not approach her. It was as if their talk on the bus had never taken place. That caused Myrtle herself a certain chafing of regret. But she never allowed herself the indulgence of much hope where boys were concerned, and the feeling faded within a few months. She was able to continue waiting for him to confide in her again with a steady heart.

For once, Myrtle is in Annie's house. Here, they don't play cards. They stand edgily in the box of a kitchen. The microwave has been placed in a position that catches the eye as soon as you're through the door. It has displaced familiar objects, Myrtle notices. A wooden salad bowl filled with wax fruits, and a china jug from Portugal, both things that once were Annie's pride, have now been relegated to distant shelves. A clear space has been left round the microwave, the better to appreciate the symbol of high technology and even easier living.

A bright sun polishes the lime green of the formica tops and the plastic cupboards, and reflects on to Annie's face and bare arms. She boils the kettle with the air of one who is reluctantly using an inferior machine. Had Myrtle wanted a cup of coffee, Annie would have boiled the milk in the microwave, just to prove how brilliant it was at boiling milk. Myrtle smiles to herself. She finds Annie's delight in a machine, undimmed in the six months since she has bought it, touching. Their various simple pleasures are, and have always been, so different, she thinks. Annie regards nature, landscape, walks, as utterly boring. For her the pleasure of an afternoon alone is to lie on her leatherette sofa studying a high-class mail-order catalogue, microwaved pie to hand, feet warmed by the heat of a gas fire that she likes to think looks like the real thing. Gregarious by nature, she avoids aloneness as much as possible. She has never been able to understand Myrtle's odd way of striding off for an afternoon by herself: for her, the vicarious experience is enough. 'You've been five miles in this weather?' she would say. 'Wonderful! I can imagine just how you feel.'

This morning the lime-tinged Annie has something on her mind that cannot wait until they are settled.

'I'm the one to be causing a scandal now,' she says.

Myrtle assumes a look of particular interest. Nothing puts Annie out so much as a blank face in response to an important fact or opinion.

'Martin,' she says, and hands Myrtle pale tea that sways in a cup stamped with an orange flower of no known variety. 'Ran into him not an hour ago. We walked a good hundred yards down the street together, seen by everybody. He was on his way to Creele to buy some crabs for his tea, he said. He said he'd seen you up at the cemetery, and that was nice.' She smiles.

'Big scandal,' says Myrtle, smiling back. In joining in the joke she knows that Annie will be further assured that their recent squabble is forgotten.

Annie gives a beguiling toss of her pretty head so that the green light scatters into a translucent mosaic over her skin.

'To think how I fancied that man, once.' She sighs. 'So, anyway, to make conversation I tell him the news.'

'The news?'

'I would've told you first, but he happened to be *there*.' Annie is amusing herself tantalising Myrtle by drawing out the suspense. Myrtle can tell by the set of her mouth there is still some way to go before the eventual climax of the story is revealed. 'Let's go next door and sit down,' says Annie.

She leads the way. Each of them has one hand beneath their saucer, the other controlling the cup that is in danger of skittering on its bone-china base. Myrtle finds all this cup-and-saucer business tiresome. It's one of Annie's small snobberies. Some years ago, when fishermen were better off, Annie spent a fortune on useless knick-knacks, expensive china and cutlery and crystal glass, all destined for an unused life behind the glass doors of a reproduction cupboard. For *showing off*, Myrtle had once teasingly observed, and Annie had agreed. While clothes held no interest for Annie, status symbols of a household kind she found irresistible. It was her persistent desire to spend that drove Ken to his nefarious ways.

In the living room, as Annie now calls it (upgraded from the front room) the carpet is a frozen sea of blue and green whirls. A sofa and matching armchair are covered in expensive imitation leather the colour of cement. They are at an angle to the complicated fireplace, a patchwork of overdefined brick and filigree wrought iron that both surrounds and overwhelms the small gas fire. The wall above all this frantic brick and iron work is hung with a collection of horse brasses, though as far as Myrtle knows neither Annie nor Ken has ever had any interest in horses. The only indication of Ken's life is the single ornament on the mantelpiece – a miniscule sailing ship made from matchsticks, sailing on a fragment of blue cloth, the whole tiny seascape preserved in a bottle.

Myrtle sits down. The armchair squeaks. Annie, cup and saucer now held high, lowers herself on to the sofa. It greets her light weight with a different set of groans from the chair. Sitting down at Annie and Ken's, Archie once said, put him in mind of an orchestra tuning up. Myrtle smiles at the thought. It must be some years, now, since he made the observation. These days, the men rarely visit each other's houses.

Annie is twitching her spiky little ankle. Northern sky full of slow, drugged clouds, is bright through the panoramic window, illuminating her uncontainable smile. She can hold out no longer.

'I'll tell you what then,' she says, 'I've taken a job.' She shifts excitedly. A pale wave of tea flips over the aristocratic cup into the saucer. The sofa quietly moans.

'Oh Lord, Annie girl,' Myrtle replies at last, trying to suppress a sigh. 'Whatever is it this time?'

Annie, in her time, has tried so many jobs. Up and down the coast she has worked, for grocers, hairdressers, butchers, bakers and newsagents. She had a short spell – some three days – in the baked potato shop, a brief attraction designed for the tourists one summer. But the locals scoffed at the idea of paying someone else ridiculous money to bake a potato, and the enterprise did not survive its first winter. From there, after one of her longer pauses for reflection on the desirability of working at all, Annie graduated to the Breeks a' Serks shop, but soon left on account of its musty air that caused her hay fever. The last job that she 'held down' (as she referred to it if she had remained in place for more than a week) was in Ladies' Fashions, an elderly establishment in a staunch old building inappropriately close to the harbour. When the wind came off the sea, customers were in danger of their purchases being snatched from their hands as they left the shop. On occasions, floral skirts and cobweb scarves had been whisked away and furled irretrievably into the waters of the harbour. Annie, from her place behind the counter in Ladies' Fashions, enjoyed her view of the boats, the feeling that she was at the centre of some small but important part of life. Selling clothes, in her estimation, was a superior business to selling bread or meat. But she could not reconcile herself to the fashions themselves. Her boss, a Mrs Helen Grundy, had a distinct vision of what high fashion on the east coast of Scotland should constitute: that her opinions were not a little out of keeping with current fashion in the wider world, no one but Annie dared suggest. Annie took the liberty of pointing out, one customerless morning, that here was evidence of her opinion: if things were a little more up to date, customers might more eagerly come running. Mrs Grundy was so affronted by such criticism that all she could do for several silent, raging moments was to stroke the stoat-paw brooch (mounted on a swirl of silver) on her lapel. She would, Annie later told Myrtle, have sacked her on the spot – but there was the matter of two dozen boxes of easy-iron blouses to be unpacked, and Mrs Grundy's elevated position in the fashion world precluded her from unpacking anything. Tension between boss and employee remained high, and furnished Annie with many a lively tale to entertain Myrtle. The end came in early summer, when Mrs Grundy asked Annie to cover the windows with thick sheets of transparent yellow paper that would, she said, prevent the merchandise from fading. Annie pointed out that, displayed behind the yellow glare of protective paper, the slumped dresses and lifeless cardigans would look even less alluring. Mrs Grundy could take no more of such impudence and asked Annie to leave within the hour.

It was always the employers' fault that caused Annie to leave her various jobs: they could never come to terms with the irregular hours she was able to work. Although compromises were sometimes aimed for, they were seldom reached. In the end, for all her charm and winning ways with customers, employers became impatient with Annie's singular attitude to work – she was doing them a favour, not the other way round – and dismissed her with mixed feelings. By now Annie was impervious to dismissal. It meant nothing to her, was certainly not a sign of failure, but the evidence of how unreasonable employers are. She could always get another job, she said, if and when she felt like it. And despite the lack of work locally, and her reputation for unreliability, she always did. Myrtle was familiar with the whole recurring pattern of Annie's working life. First, the enthusiasm.

'Come on,' says Myrtle. 'I've waited long enough.'

Almost imperceptibly, Annie shivers.

'The new café up at the museum,' she says. 'I'm to be a part-time waitress.'

'Waitress?' Myrtle is surprised. Annie serving others is a role hard to imagine. 'Making pots of tea, carrying plates of sandwiches . . . surely that's not the sort of thing you enjoy?'

Annie, choosing to ignore her friend's observation, puts down her cup and saucer with an exaggerated gesture of care, clumsiness banished at will.

'It's so nice up there,' she says, 'what they've done. Fresh tablecloths, homemade scones and cakes. The place always full. You feel life is *going on* up there.' She gives Myrtle a look. 'You're not being too hasty with your congratulations.'

'Congratulations,' says Myrtle. 'I'm pleased for you. I really am. Though I don't understand. You don't need the money.'

'That we certainly do. Ken is going to have to lay off his . . . business or he and Archie will come to blows –'

'I can imagine,' says Myrtle quickly.

'Besides, I want to see the wider world. It would be a way of meeting new people.'

Myrtle laughs.

'The wider world? It's just tourists you'll get up there. Not much time to chat between orders, I don't suppose. You could be disappointed by the bit of the wider world that makes its way to the museum.'

'Think what you like, I'm looking forward to it.' Annie's faint huffiness shows in her risen shoulders, the ankle that suddenly stops swinging. 'It's not often we get the chance to see new faces. The claustrophobia of this place could drive you mad sometimes.' She gazes longingly out of the panoramic window at some convivial imagined scene that Myrtle cannot envisage. Suddenly, she gets up. 'Come on, let's go out. I start Monday. No more free afternoons after that.'

'Where?' asks Myrtle, who has but an hour before she must return to her part-time job at the home.

Annie shrugs.

'The harbour, why not? Who knows: we might run into Martin.'

Sometimes, unplanned, Myrtle and Annie find themselves behaving like girls again. In the harbour lies the brown silk water of a low tide, exactly matching the mud beneath. They can see the bones of the harbour wall, steel girders fixed into the stone. On the wet stone steps they can see the sparkle of barnacles and the slimy curl of seaweed. There are no boats. The emptiness lends a misleading grandeur to the place. When the boats are in it becomes small, crowded, protective.

They walk closely side by side, the large woman and the small one, alert to the possibility of something to laugh at: the scene is too familiar for serious comment. A man in a municipal plastic overall of livid orange, a few yards ahead of them, switches on his machine. He begins to power-hose the empty fish boxes. The jet of water makes a savage hiss, air-renting as a dentist's high-powered drill. Steam rises, chasing low-flying gulls. They scream in protest. Annie clutches Myrtle's arm.

'Do you see who I see?' she asks.

Myrtle, following Annie's glance, sees Mrs Grundy slink out of Ladies' Fashions. Mrs Grundy looks about to make sure no one will notice her nefarious mid-morning break. She does not look seawards or notice Myrtle and Annie, but hurries off towards the newsagent, hand in hand with the stoat paw on her lapel.

'Stupid bitch,' says Annie. 'You go and hide yourself round the corner, make sure she doesn't see you on the way back. I'm going to fix her.'

It's one of those moments when there's no time to question Annie's demand: Myrtle simply obeys. She finds herself running, skirts heavily flapping. What has Annie in mind? Myrtle takes her position, panting, in a doorway. She will not be seen by Mrs Grundy on her return to the shop, but she has a clear view of Annie's territory.

Annie is whispering something to the man with the hose. Myrtle can tell from the way her friend tilts her head, and smiles, she's using her coquettish act to persuade him of something against his better judgement. Then she sees them both laugh. Annie briefly touches the orange plastic arm, then darts away to a hiding place of her own. As soon as she is out of reach, the man points his hose to the sky and draws an arc of water over the gulls, who leap higher in screaming indignation, and a million curved sparks of water are silvered by the pale sun before they fall. Myrtle knows that Annie will take the hoser's gesture, the making of such a beautiful aquatic archway, as a compliment.

Mrs Grundy comes out of the newsagent. A magazine is under one arm of her emerald jacket. Her free hand still clutches the stoat paw. She totters uncomfortably across the uneven ground, eyes down. Daft shoes for such a place, Myrtle thinks. Serve the snooty woman right if she comes a cropper.

The hosing man has his back to Mrs Grundy, apparently concentrating his water jet on stacked boxes that face the sea. How he hears her unsure step Myrtle will never know. But without turning his body, his hosing arm swerves to the left – an involuntary movement, it seems – then speeds back to its old position. An arc of sparkling water catches Mrs Grundy's high-fashion jacket with its full force, at once darkening the terrible emerald stuff and disarranging the neat package of her hair. Her plum mouth opens, but her scream is killed by the noise of the jet. The damp magazine falls open-winged to the ground. She hobbles, bent double with unheard curses, to the safety of her shop.

Annie and Myrtle run from their hiding places, meet in a laughing embrace. Tears are falling from Annie's eyes, mascara zig-zags down her cheeks. She gives a little skip, just as she did as a child when she was pleased, so that for a moment her eyes are almost on a level with Myrtle's. Myrtle sways in her mirth, joy at the silly prank scattering inside her, making her weak, keeping her closely locked to the small Annie in her arms. It all comes back, the fun of their childhood. For several hours the aching, the anxiety, the longing for Archie, have been curtained off, unable to disturb.

'It's good to know we can still be so daft, sometimes,' says Myrtle, the words all cracked up in the laughter.

'Magic,' says Annie.

A moment later they are on their separate ways. Myrtle reaches the corner where she must branch off up the hill. Still buoyant from the happy encounter, she turns to give Annie a final wave. But Annie, back to her, is waving to someone else, and does not see. Myrtle screws up her eyes, inexplicably put out. She focuses on the distant figure of a man carrying a heavy box. It is Martin. Myrtle thinks he nods his head in Annie's direction, but from this distance she cannot be sure.

When Archie is away Myrtle wakes every morning at four thirty. This is the time, she knows, that his first shift begins and she likes to feel he is in her thoughts as he wakes. For a while she lies imagining him brutally disentangling himself from his duvet – that does little to disguise the discomfort of the bunk – and taking a single step to the vile little sink whose tap provides a thread of water to splash on his face. She thinks of him pulling on his trousers and salt-stiffened jersey before pushing an egg round the frying pan that none of them ever considers cleaning. She sees him eating fast, efficiently, mopping up a yolk with a piece of sliced bread favoured by the mates, stomach lurching in time with the rise and fall of the boat. Myrtle imagines it all so hard that sometimes she feels she has become bodyless, weightless. She is transported out to sea, she's an invisible passenger. It's only when she slides a foot to Archie's side of the bed and finds the sheet, smooth and chill, that she knows she is not there, miles out at sea with Archie, but here, alone The powerful feeling has tricked her again. It is these tricks of the mind, so mysteriously strong and comforting while the illusion lasts, that Myrtle considers her kind of magic. (She can hear the way Annie says *ma-gic*: it chinks in her head like small beads. Annie's kind of magic, though, is quite different from her own.)

A small breeze through the open window makes the curtains pucker: their gathers are puffed up with air. Soon she must pull them back, begin the day, try to shuffle small tasks into the kind of order that will best speed the hours. Her hand moves from her own lonely pillow to the plumped-up hillock of Archie's. Denied his presence, her body is morose. There is no vigour in her blood. Without him, she moves less keenly by day, lies more heavily by night.

It's five o clock. Myrtle shuts her eyes but knows that she will not sleep again. Archie is at the galley sink now, rinsing his greasy plate. Or perhaps he is already on deck, zipped into oilskins, assessing sea, sky, fish . . . She never likes to question the exact order of his day for fear he should guess her reasons. With a great effort of will Myrtle puts Archie from her mind, and thinks of Annie.

Magic: the word resounds again – the magic of Annie. There are few days when her extraordinary powers are not reflected upon by Myrtle. For years she has tried to analyse them, for years she has failed. But then perhaps the gift of enchantment, which is bestowed upon very few, is not meant to be analysed, but accepted as a gift that should exist without question. All the same, Myrtle is permanently intrigued. She watches constantly for clues, but the clues give no real answer. What is it about Annie that draws people of both sexes and all ages to her, wanting to please her, wanting to be in her presence? The extraordinarily pretty face is obviously the first signal, but it is far from the whole solution. The solution – and by now, after so many years of trying, Myrtle suspects she is beginning to understand – is to do with the feeling Annie unconsciously conveys that she is the centre of an important part of the universe, and whoever is with her shares that place. Myrtle remembers so well that (then amorphous, inexplicable) feeling as a child: with Annie at her side, she was certain she was at the centre of life, in some kind of mainstream place, even though reality, a small Scottish fishing village, said this logically was not so. In Annie's company, she felt important, courageous. Without her, time was flatter, duller. Annie brought a gladness to bear wherever she was, and it brushed off on others like gold dust. The fact that she was petulant, spoilt, sometimes ill-mannered, frequently thoughtless and constantly selfish made no difference. Annie's mysterious quality of life-enhancement was so strong that her faults were forgiven. Boys, snubbed by her, ridiculed and generally spurned, never gave up hope that at some future time they would be forgiven. To this day there were married fishermen in the village who would confide that Annie, in their youth, was the love of their life: Ken was regarded as the luckiest man on earth. While teachers and other grown-ups – in particular Dot Stewart, who feared Annie's influence over Myrtle – declared they could 'see right through her', they were no less enchanted than Annie's contemporaries when Annie chose to concentrate upon them. Nowadays, no matter how Myrtle disapproved of her friend's behaviour, or was irritated by her self-centredness, she still felt a sense of infinite loss without her. So whatever rows or disagreements they had, Myrtle found she could never go for more than a few days before returning to Annie – who bore no grudges when Myrtle berated her, and was always pleased to see her back. They would resume their old pattern as if there had never been a disruption: games of cards, cups of tea, occasional spontaneous events such as the hosing of Mrs Grundy. Annie would forever scoff at Myrtle's superior intellect, provoking her admonition with too much talk of material matters – the marvel of the microwave or the price of Janice's new boots. But even when Annie's trivial chatter most annoyed Myrtle she felt the warmth of her presence which had been essential to her since early childhood, and she could not imagine life without such nourishment. Myrtle liked to think – though she could not know for certain – that Annie would feel equally deprived were she to lose her own devotion, which she could count on at all times.

Myrtle's own experience with boys had been almost entirely vicarious. In the last couple of years at school, still too lacking in attraction for any girl to think of her as competition, she found herself in the role of confidante, adviser. (This last role amused her. On what experience could she base her advice?) But her peers were grateful for her careful listening, her considered opinion. For such services rendered she won a measure of popularity, and in her turn was grateful for that.

Of all the vicissitudes of young love that Myrtle so attentively listened to, there was none half so interesting, so amazing, as Annie's. There was not a boy in the class who had not at some time been beguiled by her, tried his luck, been rejected but still lived in hope. Since the age of seven Annie had been receiving notes from boys throughout the school. She used to gather them together, a day's takings, small, crumpled bits of paper torn from exercise books inscribed with passionate and ill-spelt declarations. After school she and Myrtle would go to their hiding place behind a bush in the Stewarts' garden, and read through them. *You are the cristal in my heart*; *I shall love you till the world stops and you and me are left alone on a sea of eternitty*; *Please come to the moon and back with me, I will buy you roller skates when I am a rich man*; *When I look at you in maths or some lesson my heart begins to pound and my legs go weak and I feel ill as if I had a fever, I love you so.* At first, Annie enjoyed the notes: they made her squeal with laughter. But over the years, as there was no decrease in their delivery, she grew blasé. They began to bore her. Often she would screw up a whole collection without reading them. 'Same old thing,' she told Myrtle. 'Nothing very original. There's no real romance to be found in this place.'

It was real romance, she confessed to Myrtle a thousand times, that she was after. Her disappointment was to find that her suitors were not of like mind. All they wanted, as quickly as possible, was sex – no hanging about. Annie, who had made flirting into her highest art, let them have a little of their way. (By the time she was sixteen, she once confessed to Myrtle, she had kissed twenty-three boys in the school. But only kissed.) Their impatience was their undoing. No sooner had they made their carefully plotted pass, clutched her with sweaty hands, clashed brace-bound teeth with hers, ground their restless hips against her and whimpered oh, so soppily, Annie's interest died. She would push them away, regard their silly look of frustrated desire with undisguised scorn. Several boys, realising their impetuousness had lost her for good, were reduced to tears. Annie had no pity. Rather, her contempt was increased. She would run away, laughing, to tell Myrtle details of the latest pathetic attempt at seduction.

There were two boys in the class who never attempted to kiss Annie: Archie Duns and Ken Mcleod. Archie, alone of all the boys in the school, did not fancy Annie. When asked why – a question he was often asked – he declared her too small, too spoilt and too flirtatious. He admitted her looks were exceptional, but looks were not what interested him as much as kindness and calm. For such sentiments he was considered by his friends to be a fool. Annie, aged twelve, lured by Archie's resistance, did once offer her mouth behind the coal shed. But it was her turn to be rejected. Archie, who had no intention of becoming another number on her list of snubbed suitors, told her very firmly to go away. It was three days before Annie, more amused than humiliated, was able to bring herself to pass on this information to Myrtle. She'd never really *fancied* Archie, she said – too dour. She was just annoyed he ignored her so blatantly. All she was after was a quick snog to prove to herself she could get anyone she wanted.

As for Ken, since the day out at St Andrews, he had been so tortured by love for Annie it was impossible for him to speak to her. If by chance he found himself close to her, he would move quickly away. Surrounded as always by her admirers, it took Annie some time to notice Ken's avoiding tactics. When she did, she found herself, at last, faintly intrigued. Why was he so unforthcoming? His lack of response to her most coquettish appeals became something of a challenge – only a *wee* challenge, she told Myrtle. Ken was nothing particular, she said. But for the fun of it she made a few overtures. They were always met with silent blushes. Eventually she gave up, left him alone, puzzled. Myrtle advised her there was no point in fretting over one shy boy when she could have her choice among so many who were eager. Even as she produced that small homily, which Annie accepted with a winning smile, Myrtle suspected her own motives. She was aware that, deeply embedded beneath her altruistic good sense, some small hope had risen from the brief closeness of confession on the bus. She also knew that for self-preservation she must do everything she could to ensure this hope did not flower.

By now it is seven o'clock. Myrtle is in the kitchen alone at the table. Archie will have been at work for three hours. He may be in the galley for a ten-minute cup of tea. He may well be sitting next to Ken. How do they get on, at sea? Myrtle often wonders. It's funny to think that the only two men in her life end up on the same boat. Not that Ken was ever exactly *in* her life. Indeed, to this day she cannot be sure that he was aware of the turmoil he caused. Her love for him was a secret she kept from Annie, from everyone. She knew the humiliation that could come from confessing hopeless love: those who confided in her had described it so vividly, pathetic in their despair. She was sometimes amazed that Annie did not guess what was going on in her heart, but then Annie, so consumed by her own preoccupations, was not a keen observer of other people's plights. Besides, it would never occur to Annie that Myrtle, so plainly unappreciated by boys, might fancy anyone. 'You'll find yourself a good solid husband one day,' Annie once told her. 'Older men aren't so worried about looks. What they want is a faithful wife who'll cook their dinners and mend their shirts and be happy with a quiet life.' Myrtle knew this was Annie's idea of consolation – she could not remember what event, or inadvertent hint of weakness in her own armour, brought it about. Naturally, she kept to herself what pain this 'comfort', this patronage caused.

Myrtle goes to the window, waits for the kettle to boil, waits for the familiar sound of its chugging steam to break the silence in the room.

Outside the sky is that naive grey peculiar to early mornings in October. Very high overhead (Dot always said it was worth checking the top of the sky if you wanted to judge the day), there is a lemony thinning of cloud, suggesting that later the sun might break through. Myrtle can smell the sea, but not hear it. The calm, usually some comfort, is disturbed by her thoughts of Ken. For the truth is that of late she has come to despise him. She despises his treachery, his betrayal of Archie. When Ken first became a mate on *Skyline II*, his loyalty was total. Now, since he has taken up his second job of 'removals and deliveries', that loyalty has become divided. He returns to the boat a weak link in a strong and devoted crew. Myrtle knows all this is taking its toll on Archie, though he never speaks about it in detail. Myrtle also senses the rows between the two men are increasing – though never at home – and dreads the moment control is lost, and in temper some violent act is committed. She also finds it hard to accept that the once quiet and morose boy Ken has turned into a weak and dishonest man. The nature of the 'deliveries' has never been specified, but Myrtle has her suspicions, though she cannot guess which law-breaking friend Ken might be helping. He is taking risks merely in order to pay for the silly status symbols his wife demands. He is a fool. He should condemn Annie for her greed, not pander to it. He should know by now that Annie responds well when she is thwarted in her desires for material things, if only for a time. Then Myrtle remembers that before Ken fell for Annie, in his early teens, he was daring in his lack of respect for authority. He was bold and imaginative in his nefarious acts. He enjoyed his punishments, he enjoyed his era as a hero among his peers. Now, there were no punishments – yet. And Annie was the only one to benefit from the profits of his foolishness. When Myrtle had loved him it had been during his quiet phase. Withdrawn, melancholic, his sad dark eyes had wrenched her heart, though shortly after the day at St Andrews she had given up all hope he would ever confide in her again, and her small, foolish spurt of hope had subsided into calm compassion, unspoken sympathy.

But she had always remained on the alert, lest one day there should be a hint of things changing. For a long time she had felt guilt about her advice to Annie to give up trying with Ken, although Annie's interest in him was so half-hearted it petered out very quickly. Even his embarrassed refusals to respond to her overtures could not spur her to keep trying. *Had* Annie, just for the fun of the challenge, won him over – well, that was a situation, in those days when Ken was Myrtle's only hope, she could never let herself contemplate. And when Annie finally declared herself not interested in pursuing Ken further, a warm rush of safety filled Myrtle's being. She herself could never hope for Ken to pay her the attention she craved, but at least there was consolation in knowing that Annie (who still had no notion of his tortured feelings, Myrtle having kept this secret) would leave him alone. This comfortable, if unfulfilling, state of affairs lasted three years. Then came the day of the gala.

Even as she remembers it, Myrtle pulls her shawl tighter and her large body tips forward a little. One hand spreads, and lingers over her ribs. There is still the echo of the pain at that time, a spectre of hurt that she buried long ago, for the sake of her friendship with Annie. But from time to time it rises again to haunt, to mystify – to make Myrtle think there is reason never quite to trust even the closest of friends.

That time: that summer's day. And later, the darkness of the days that followed Annie's innocent, gleeful confession: the past can be so cruel in its clarity, its tangibility. Myrtle, knowing her own foolishness, puts out a hand. She can feel the warmth of Ken's sinewy young arm beneath his rolled-up sleeve, where her finger dared to go. She can see – she will see for ever – the mixture of horror and guilt in his eyes as he bent towards her. For her, that was the end of the night. For him, it was the beginning.

There were galas, then, every year. As children Myrtle and Annie would go down to the harbour, watch as the boats, dressed up for the day in flags and bunting and flowers, sailed out of the harbour in their fancy dress. They made such a pretty flotilla, their normally chipped and battered hulls hidden under skirts of looped flowers, greenery and ribbons that fluttered with every bounce of the waves. Each boat had its chosen Fisher Lass, a beautiful young girl in some extravagant dress that was the result of weeks of indecision and excitement in its creation (and happily paid for by the skipper and crew). The Fisher Lass would sit at the head of the boat, refulgent face tipped up towards the horizon, unmoving as a masthead, self-importance fighting with queasiness if the sea was rocking. Behind her, family and friends would drink and sing. Soon entangled in the ribbons and flags, they would lean merrily over the ship's sides and let the spray cool their faces. All this Myrtle and Annie learned from Dot, who had herself once been a Fisher Lass, and went out every year on *The Skyline* until her husband died. When the children were older, she assured them, someone would invite them on to their boat. The young Myrtle and Annie, eyes never leaving the small, fluttering trail of boats until it vanished into the distance, longed for that time.

It came the summer that they were both seventeen – Annie only days after Myrtle. Archie Duns' father, Ben, had been an old friend of Jock Stewart. Ben's wife, who had broken her leg that year, suggested Dot took her place on the boat, and help with the food. She was invited to bring the two girls, whose intense excitement – they had been waiting for this occasion for so long – was increased to breaking point when they learned that Annie had been chosen to be the Fisher Lass. There followed several weeks of flurried plans concerning her dress, hair, make-up, shoes . . . She would make no decision without Myrtle. The supreme importance of these plans, which seemed to occupy every moment of Annie's thoughts, Myrtle found a little tiring. The excessive talk about scarlet or green or blue, about silk or satin or muslin, began to pall. But she managed to maintain at least a semblance of interest, and was as helpful as she could be. Her greatest contribution to Annie's happiness was in persuading Dot, a natural seamstress, to make the dress. Annie had long since despaired of finding the perfect thing, so clear in her mind, in a shop: Myrtle's suggestion that Dot should make something saved her from a nervous crisis. But when it came to describing the imagined dress to Dot, Annie was surprisingly inarticulate. The picture was clear but hazy, she said – by which time Myrtle, suffering from plan-fatigue, was too exhausted to point out the incongruity of this statement. Annie explained she would recognise the stuff she was looking for when she saw it, which meant dozens of visits to drapers up and down the coast, Myrtle her weary companion. Eventually she lighted on a bale of pale mint lace, and declared all the trouble had been worth it to find the right thing – did not Myrtle agree?

Dot, by now in a panic that there was so little time left, moved the furniture to the edges of the room, cut out the lace on the floor. As the dress progressed, an incredulous Annie came more and more often to try it on, querying every seam, every tuck, requesting that the neck should be a pinch higher, an inch lower, taxing Dot's patience to the limit. While Myrtle slouched in a chair looking, looking at Annie in new wonder, Annie jiggled in front of the small speckled mirror, frustrated at being able to see only her face and neck reflected through its tarnished surface. Impatiently, one day, she snatched it off the wall, then held it facing different bits of her body. As she could never, *never* see the whole, she wailed, it was bound to be a disaster. Myrtle looked on in sympathy, unreasonably cross with her mother because there was no long looking-glass in the house. Dot, tried to the limit by Annie's ungracious striving for perfection, let fly. 'Och, stop your complaining, girl, or I'll no' put in another stitch. And I'll have you put back that mirror on my wall this very minute or I'll –'

Annie's quick smile of contrition, her apology for her nervous state, quelled Dot's fury. She put back the mirror, not looking at her face. She stopped jiggling her hips. The skirts – pink imitation silk beneath the mint lace – froze round her knees, stilled. The room was strangely quiet without their rustling. But it was sour with the scent of Annie's sweat. Myrtle thought how lucky she was, being Annie's friend, to be part of all this excitement. She wondered if Annie had any idea of the extent of her beauty – in the dull evening light, at that final fitting, Myrtle realised with awe that Annie's prettiness, which she had become so used to she scarcely noticed any more – had given way to looks of wondrous and extraordinary beauty which would procure privilege for life. She looked down at her own hands – wistful, but she felt no envy. Then she looked at her mother crouched on the floor fussing with the hem of Annie's dress. She watched as Dot tried to put on her silver thimble. But her fingers had swollen in the many years since she had last used it. It kept falling off. Dot's own moment of shadowy regret was ended by Annie suddenly sliding impatiently out of the dress, standing in childish vest and pants, thin parted legs, bare feet hidden in a rock pool of green lace through which the pink silk petticoat sparkled like sunlight.

On the morning of the gala, Annie and her mother came round to the Stewarts' house soon after seven. While Dot cut sandwiches and Annie's mother inefficiently made a pot of tea, Annie herself jittered about unable to sit down for more than a moment at a time. Myrtle had never seen her in such a state of excitement. She refused to eat anything, saying food would make her sick. She kept touching the dress, which hung on the door: she'd never seen anything so beautiful in her life, she said. Every few moments she hugged Dot, which interfered with the speed of Dot's sandwich-making, and thanked her a dozen times. By eight o'clock she could wait no longer. She slithered into the dress and spun about, making its skirts flash and dance. Everybody laughed at her happiness. Suddenly, facing Myrtle, she stopped: held out her arms.

'What about you, Myrtle? What are you going to wear?'

In all the flurry of organising the Fisher Lass's clothes, Myrtle had given no thought to her own appearance. In answer to Annie's unexpected question, her immediate thought was what does it matter what I wear? I'm only to be part of your audience.

'I'll think of something,' she said. 'It's early yet.'

'You'll wear your jacket,' snapped Dot. 'There's a stiff breeze.'

'In that case, Annie'll be frozen.'

'The Fisher Lass,' said Dot, with some authority, 'will no' feel the cold. There'll be too much on her mind.'

There was already too much on Annie's mind further to concentrate on anyone else: silver shoes to be taken from their tissue paper, earrings to be secured, hair brushed to a shine that would defy the wind – so much trouble all for so few hours of glory, Myrtle thought, as she ate her own large breakfast. But perhaps that was the whole point of glory – the anticipation, the preparation. When the event was actually taking place there might be a sense of anticlimax. She would be watching Annie very carefully.

For all her early start, in the end Annie had no time to put on the carefully planned and purchased make-up. Besides, her hands were shaking too much to apply unsmudged shadow and knife-edged lipstick. The small plastic bag, a cornucopia spilling out its hoard of coloured pots and wands of mascara, was left on the table. But Annie was in no need of artificial aids to her beauty, thought Myrtle, as the two mothers and two daughters walked to the harbour. With silent awe she looked as if for the first time at every inch of her friend's face. She marvelled at the incandescence of Annie's skin, and the black-lashed eyes whose every restless movement sparked a chip of diamond in the blue irises. She wondered at the simplicity of beauty – the undulations of a mouth that by a fraction of a millimetre made it unique, the smile that pushed dimples into cheeks. This was the first day, Myrtle thought, that her friend was really grown up: excited but confident, cool, but generous in her appreciation of others' approbation, she exuded more potently than ever her mysterious sense of centre-life which warmed those in her wake. From today, Myrtle realised, things might happen to Annie that had never happened before. And she, Myrtle, would be left far behind. Perhaps she would no longer even be granted the vicarious experiences. Perhaps, now they were grown up, a new shyness would mean some privacy, and their close ways would diverge. When they reached the harbour wall, they stood looking down at the waiting boat. Annie was laughing at its fancy dress – the crew had done a grand job with flags and bunting. At the point of the bows a chair had been transformed into a magnificent throne of greenery dotted with flowers. Annie's place. Myrtle saw the goosepimples on her friend's upper arms, and was glad of her own clumsy jacket, and was suddenly afraid though she could not define the fear. She moved closer to Annie, in attendance, before the Fisher Lass was urged towards her seat.

Myrtle's own forebodings were further strengthened by the sight of so many passengers on board: a crowd of Archie's friends – Ross Wyatt, Sandy, Roddy, Ken, Hamish. Annie was waving to them, calling their names, acknowledging their catcalls of praise with a series of small bows. A gust of wind flattened her lace skirts against her legs and scrambled her hair into a thousand curls. The boys, looking up, hollered more loudly. Then Archie's father, Ben, made his way through the small noisy crowd, leapt over the side of the boat and ran up the steps of the harbour wall. In a quick, swooping movement, like a predatory bird pouncing on its prey, he lifted Annie up in both arms and carried her down into the boat. There was more laugher and cheering. Myrtle's own mouth felt rigid. She had to make an effort to prise it into a smile.

While Annie was seated on her throne, with much elated help from the boys, Myrtle and the two mothers, clutching boxes and baskets, made their way unaided down the slippery steps. Archie, the only boy who seemed to have no interest in Annie's enthronement, received them: first helping the two women with their loads, then putting a firm elbow under Myrtle's arm as she stepped on to the cluttered deck. Events were now beginning to spin in her head, but beneath them a heavy thought persisted. She knew that Annie, despite all the clamour around her, would not be too preoccupied to notice that Archie was paying her no attention. Only recently Annie had observed that the god Archie had *never* paid her any attention since the 'silly incident' when they were children, and she found this insulting. At some point his stand-offish behaviour would have to be challenged.

Myrtle also realised that there was no point in trying to sit near Annie in the bows. Annie was surrounded by admirers who had no intention of moving. There was no place for Myrtle there. She made her way to the back of the boat where Dot, legs slung wide to make a table of her lap, was already sorting food. Beside her sat Ken, pale face well back into the hood of his plastic windcheater. He nodded to Myrtle. She sat next to him – the only empty seat. This undreamt-of proximity to Ken stirred Myrtle in some vaguely pleasurable way. She would enjoy sitting beside him, would not mind his silence.

The boats set off at last, a line of seven of them, their loops of flags all twittering in the breeze, their Fisher Lasses upright in the bows, heads high, stiffly smiling. They wore dresses of bright primary colours that flashed in the clear light, though none of them had managed the subtlety, the style, of Annie, Myrtle thought with pride. Once the boats had left the harbour they veered off, a rougher line, though all in the same direction.

Distance quickly grew between them. Details of the other boats became indistinct, though the Fisher Lasses remained bright specks. Small clouds of gulls hovered above each mast, puzzled by the flags. Their screeching, above Ben Duns' boat, added to the cacophony of noise from Annie's admirers.

Myrtle had never liked the sea. As a young child, the first time Jock and Dot took her for a treat on *The Skyline*, she had been secretly terrified. She had stared down at the moving surface of water, trembling at the thought of what might lie beneath it, convinced that any moment a demon wave would rise, snatch her up in its curled fist of giant foam and drag her to black depths too horrible to imagine. But later, older, watching with Annie as the gala boats sailed away, she had longed to join them. That would be different, she thought. That would be safe.

That gala day, with the revellers at last, Myrtle's fear of the water had faded to a thin, untroublesome vein that caused nothing more than a feeling of tension which was confused with the excitement. There was a swell, and small coxcomb waves broke randomly over bigger ones, but they were playful rather than threatening. The boat rose and dipped with a rhythm that sometimes broke, and surprised. Then the boat would tip at an unexpected angle, jostling the passengers. On several occasions Myrtle found herself pushed into Ken's side. She apologised each time. He did not seem to mind.

But he kept his silence, so Myrtle concentrated on the distant Lammemuirs, and the way Bass Rock was becoming gigantic as they approached it. By mid morning there was a high sun, though the breeze was still cold. The sea, so far out, was a dense navy – so different from the dead brown water in the harbour. (Why, Myrtle wondered, did such blue not feed into the brown?) The light on the water had a strange thinness, as if it had been dragged over by a feather to enliven the blue, but not to change it. This light made a wide path across the waves which the boats seemed to be following.

Myrtle had not thought of sharing her observations, but suddenly she was aware of herself murmuring to Ken:

'Don't suppose the fishermen, out all the time, are surprised by all this sort of thing.' She nodded in the direction of the path of light. 'Probably don't even notice.'

Ken gave a reluctant movement of his closely packed lips, which Myrtle took as a comprehending smile. Before he could muster a reply, Dot pointed out that they were turning for home now. And indeed Myrtle saw that all seven boats were curving round, their backs now to the Rock and the mist of hills, and were facing the home coast.

Although her fear on the outward journey had been only slight, Myrtle felt a sense of relief now that they were going home. She helped Dot unpack sandwiches and pour out plastic cups of lemonade.

'Take something up to Annie,' said Dot. 'She'll be famished, behaving all this time like a regular masthead.'

Myrtle made her way along the deck, the wind keener now she was upright. The boys, still crowded round Annie on her throne of greenery, its leaves now splashed and sparkling, made way for her.

'She's gone all silent, silent as a bloody statue,' said Hamish.

'We canna get a word out of her,' said Ross.

'She's the dumbest Fisher Lass, that's for sure,' said Hamish, 'and it's very boring.'

Myrtle reached Annie's chair. She saw at once what Hamish meant about a statue. Annie sat upright, rigid, her head thrown back, staring at the horizon, apparently unconscious of her surroundings, impervious to the boys' provocative jibes which by now had replaced the compliments. For a moment Myrtle was alarmed by the look in her friend's eyes. They seemed to be fixed on some invisible place, another world. Her cheeks shimmered with a thousand tears of spray and the front of her green lace dress was darkened with water. Myrtle put out a hand, touched Annie's arm. It was icy cold, rough with goosepimples.

'Here, Annie, I've brought you something to eat,' she said. Annie did not respond. Myrtle touched her again. 'You're so cold. Shall I get you a jacket?' Still no word. 'Come on, Annie. What's the matter? Would you like an egg sandwich?' After a long moment Annie very slightly shook her head. The boys behind them cheered. Still with her eyes locked into some distant place, Annie murmured that she would like Myrtle to go away, leave her. The boys did not hear this request and Myrtle, defeated, moved away. One of the boys snatched the sandwiches and drink from her hands. They jeered at her for having no effect on the sleeping beauty. Fed up, now, with Annie's very long silence, they began to move back towards the boat's stern and help themselves to Dot's food and drink. Myrtle did not join them but stood by the cabin watching Ben at the wheel. Archie stood behind his father, smoking. Archie's eyes sometimes passed over Annie's upright little back view, but without curiosity or interest. Archie was some two inches taller than his father: broad and strong and stern, his blond hair jagged about his forehead. He smiled briefly at Myrtle, shrugged: a message, through the glass of the window, that Annie was a hopeless case, the least entertaining Fisher Lass he had ever seen. The thought flashed through Myrtle's mind that Archie was the most desirable boy along the coast, and had she been a different sort of girl then she might have allowed herself to fancy him. As it was, there was not the slightest possibility that one as exceptional as Archie Duns would ever have reason to be interested in her. He was beyond the scope of her own aspirations, though she did not doubt that Annie's eventual seduction would be successful. Ken, on the other hand – Ken with his nice eyes but sullen ways, his lack of friends . . . if she waited patiently, made no move that would alarm, then perhaps one day Ken would turn to her.

Myrtle saw the hump of a large wave, which had sneaked up on them from nowhere, now only yards away. As it tipped the boat in its hurried way, she could not help a small scream as she was flung to one side and fell on to a pile of coiled rope. In the next instant she saw one of Annie's thin white arms, pearled with water, shoot into the sky as the boat righted itself. Then she felt a strong hand under her own arm, and the nasty blue of Ken's waterproof filled her vision as clumsily he dragged her to her feet. She turned to thank him, but he was gone. And Annie's arm had returned to her side. Still rigid as before, her head was tipped further back. Myrtle had the impression that Annie could feel the clouds on her skin; she had become part of the blue of the sky.

Months later, on one of the many occasions they talked about the gala day, Annie explained she had wanted the journey on the boat just for herself, holding the brief hours to her so that they would be imprinted in her mind for ever, and she could call them up again whenever she needed them: sun, sea spray, cloud; the movement of the boat, the noise of gulls and boys. She went into a kind of trance, she said, which she could not allow anyone to break. The boys might have thought of her as stand-offish, silly, but that was the truth of the matter. Those hours of being locked into herself were the beginning of one of the best days of her life, and not for anything would she have spoiled them by larking about with the boys. That was to come later.

Early afternoon the boats reached a harbour some miles up the coast, the home of a few small craft that went out for lobsters and crabs. Behind the harbour white-painted houses clustered on a small hill. Some had scarlet geraniums at their windows, and front doors of yellow and green. It was a prettier place than Dot and Myrtle's village, and discovered by tourists who came to buy the fresh crabs, sold from a small hut, for bargain prices.

A makeshift dais had been put up a few yards from where the passengers alighted from the boats. It stood in a tangle of torn nets, lobster pots and coils of tarred rope: a precarious-looking little structure to which a skirt of salmon-pink crêpe paper had been inadequately pinned. Quite a crowd had gathered to watch the proceedings – tourists and locals. Dot, an old hand at every moment of the Fisher Lasses' progress, secured herself a place on a lobster pot near the dais. Myrtle stood beside her.

She could see that Annie, tripping up the wobbly steps with the other six Lasses, was showing some sign of nerves. She clutched at the damp skirts of her dress – the pink silk now shone through the lace more dully – and looked vaguely about with an unnatural smile. In bright sun, close at hand, the choices of the other girls' dresses were painfully clear – bundles of spangled netting, glossy red satin cobbled together with clumsy seams, wilted muslin fit for a milkmaid. Diamanté necklaces glinted above deep cleavages: one girl also wore a tiara. Annie was the only one with no jewellery and no make-up. All the girls' cheeks were buffed to a deep red-brown by the journey through the wind, and their carefully organised hair blew free from its various combs and ribbons. They were happy, bonny faces, as Dot observed: but only one was beautiful.

They stood for what seemed an age, shifting from uncomfortable foot to foot – stilettoes of pearly leather seemed to be the ubiquitous order of the day – casting expectant smiles at whoever they knew in the crowd, and giving shudders of exaggerated fear. Briefly Annie's eyes met Myrtle's. Her statue pose a thing of the past, she now allowed herself the odd anticipatory jiggle of the hips further to encourage the compliments of her admirers, proud of her now, which flew up from the crowd.

'This part always takes far too long,' said Dot. 'It's terrible up there, the waiting.'

'Do you reckon Annie's going to win?' Myrtle's own heart was beating very fast. She could imagine just how it was for Annie, up there on the stage, so many calculating eyes upon her.

'You can never account for the judges' taste. They might think Annie too wee for a good Lass. I've seen certain winners disappointed.'

There was a movement in the crowd. The harbour master, another man and two women who, with undisguised looks of self-importance had been conferring near the crab stall, now moved with self-conscious steps, as if they felt they were famous, towards the dais. The harbour master alone mounted the steps – the added weight of his fellow judges would have meant disaster. Revelling in the attention, he slowly shuffled a few scraps of paper on which, it was plain, nothing was written. He took his time, the harbour master: milking his brief moment of eminence, enjoying the sudden hush, palpitating with the importance of his imminent announcement. Get on with it, you old sod, Myrtle thought, and others began to express the same sentiment. But the master of ceremonies – and as there were few ceremonies in his small harbour to be performed he was naturally keen to make the most of it – started with some hesitant little speech about tradition, the necessity of maintaining old-world customs in this lacklustre age, and so forth. Myrtle, her ears pounding with impatience for the climax of his declaration, missed the sonorous words that led up to the announcement of the winner. But she saw the harbour master bend to take the banner from someone in the crowd, and approach Annie with a lascivious smile on his face. There was a roar of approbation that drowned the squealing of the gulls. Dot jumped up from the lobster pot, jumping higher than she had for years, shouting Annie's name like a wild thing. Myrtle, silent but clapping her hands, saw the harbour master fumbling to put the banner over Annie's head, and Annie impatiently pull it into position herself. Fisher Lass 197– was now loud across her bosom. The harbour master then handed her a shield which would later have her name engraved on its silver face. For a second Annie held this away from her, smiling at her own reflection. Then she moved quickly to the very edge of the dais, shut her eyes and stretched both thin arms above her in a gesture of ecstasy.

She opened her mouth to scream with joy, but the scream went unheard in the general noise and excitement. Then she leapt, impossibly high, into the sky, eyes still shut. A dozen arms shot up to catch her. But somehow, mid air, her body twisted, avoiding them all. Annie fell on to a bare patch of cobbles at the side of the dais. Instantly a chaos of admirers were there to retrieve her. Myrtle caught sight of her shocked face and a badly grazed arm. Her own help was unnecessary for the moment. She moved her eyes from the writhings of the crowd and saw that Archie was walking beside his father towards the harbour's edge. And that Ken, still in the safety of his plastic hood, was talking to a fisherman by the crab stall, plainly not interested in Annie's triumph or her fall.

That evening there was the traditional gala dance at The Seafarers' Hotel. The place was crowded with the friends and relations of the Fisher Lasses who had been on the boats, and many others besides. It was evident that most of the Lasses had spent the afternoon celebrating. One of them, who had to be supported to the supper room, dissolved on to a chair and fell asleep at once. Unconscious of the merriments of the evening, her presence served as a reminder of what could happen to an overexcited Fisher Lass. One look at the slumped figure in the corner, in her slippery pink dress – which by cruel coincidence exactly matched the spikes of gladioli that rose in a giant halo behind her drooping head – and they sipped more slowly at their beer or wine.

Annie herself had had nothing but tea all afternoon, and a rest on the Stewart's sofa (her own mother by now was bored with the whole event and had gone home to read her new magazine) where she relived every detail to an attentive Myrtle. So by the evening her energies were restored. Absolutely sober, she was fired by an internal adrenalin. Her object tonight, she told Myrtle, was to win over the elusive Archie. And when she entered the supper room – entrance nicely timed, everyone else was seated – and made her way to the place of honour at the top table, there was a general gasp of admiration. Applause. Before she sat Annie cast her eyes up and down the tables, assessing her audience, it seemed. Myrtle knew better. She knew who Annie was looking for. Her eyes paused at last on Archie's back view – he had deliberately turned away from her, it seemed to Myrtle. But she had no doubt of Annie's power tonight. She would end the evening with Archie. Myrtle would have staked her life on that.

After supper the reels began. By now Annie's stand-offish demeanour had disappeared. She was revelling in the race among her admirers to be her partner. With good humour she tried to distribute her favours fairly. As she twirled up and down the lines, she bestowed smiles on Ross, or Harry, or whoever was the current partner, making each one feel he was in with a serious chance again, no matter how many times he had been spurned in the past. But Myrtle saw that Annie's eyes were also conducting secret hunts that were invisible to anyone else. At safe moments they darted quicker than a lizard's tongue towards Archie. Whenever a reel came to an end, Annie led her partner towards the place Archie stood or sat. Her proximity signalled many times her desire to dance with him, but Archie refused to recognise her invitations.

Myrtle herself watched the progression of Annie's evening from a chair at the side of the room. She knew that her place on such occasions was to be a spectator and she accepted this role with no bitterness. Rather, she was deeply curious. How would the evening end? Above all, she did not want Annie to be hurt by Archie's very obvious rejection. She had complete faith in her friend's powers, but by eleven thirty it was plain she was far from achieving her goal.

Dot came to sit next to Myrtle. She had reached the time in her life when a party is a place for keen observation from the sidelines, rather than an occasion to participate in the dancing. All the same, she found it hard to stifle memories.

'You should take to your feet, dear,' she said. 'When I was your age you couldn't keep me off the floor.'

'I don't like dancing,' said Myrtle, sullen.

'Nonsense! All young girls like a reel. Why don't you go over to the bar? There's a crowd of your friends. One of them's sure to ask you for a dance.'

Myrtle blushed, furious. She resented both her mother's concern at her lack of partners, and her well-meaning help. She had a headache from the bagpipes that sawed through her. She felt large and uncomfortable and longed to go home. But she knew she could not leave until Annie's predicament was resolved.

Ben, Archie's father, came up.

'I can't get Myrtle here on to the floor,' Dot said. In her chair she swayed from side to side, feet tapping on the floor, longing to get there herself.

'Perhaps she doesn't care for reeling any more than Archie,' Ben said. He turned to Myrtle, smiling. Sympathetic. 'Is that it?' Myrtle nodded, aware of the hot red of her face. 'How about you and me have a go at this eightsome? They're looking for a couple, over there . . .'

He was a kind man. Myrtle could not refuse him. Besides, she wanted to get away as far as possible from Dot. She stood, realising she was taller than Ben. He made her feel like an awkward giant, dingy in her beige skirt and white blouse. She wished she had made more effort, but had reckoned that not to be desired when you have made no effort is less humiliating than not to be desired when you have done your best to look alluring.

Myrtle and Ben joined six couples. One of them was Annie and Sandy. Annie raised her eyebrows at Myrtle. But before the flash of a friendly smile could disguise it, Myrtle saw her friend's look of pity. Myrtle, forced to dance with Archie's father . . . such a crying shame. The words were written all over Annie's face.

Never had Myrtle hated an experience so much in her seventeen years. While Annie's delicate little feet twittered skilfully through the steps, and Annie's lean back and arms bent like saplings as the boys twirled her keenly round, Myrtle's huge clay feet struggled to keep in time and place. The boys, who whooped when it was their turn to hold Annie, were silent when it came to Myrtle. She felt them struggle to get their arms round her waist. She felt them pushing her as if she was some piece of large and awkward furniture. Only Ben, old man Ben, gave her an encouraging smile when once again she turned in the wrong direction. Myrtle felt tears burn her eyes. She thought the misery would never end.

When it did, when the bagpipes stopped their dreadful wailing at last and the group broke up, Myrtle thanked Ben and left his side as soon as it was politely possible. She made her way to the crowd by the bar. If she helped herself to a glass of wine, she thought, and just stood, not moving, perhaps no one would notice her. And the wine would blur the pain. She drank fast, took up a position. A moment later Archie passed by.

'Saw you give my old man an enjoyable time,' he said. As far as Myrtle could tell he was neither scoffing nor laughing at her. 'That was kind of you.'

'It was kind of him,' said Myrtle. They both laughed.

'I've had enough of all this,' Archie said then, finishing his drink. 'Not my scene. I'm off. Like me to walk you home?'

For an immeasurable time Myrtle was unable to answer this question. It was the kind of surprise that was too great to be digested instantaneously. Archie, the most elusive and desirable boy in the school, the village, for miles along the coast, asking her, Myrtle . . . While disbelief within her almost snapped, and her cheeks burned outrageously, Myrtle thought very fast. Two very obvious things came to her at once: Archie was only asking her out of kindness. Escorting her home – he had to pass her house on the way to his – would be no trouble. And were she to accept his extraordinary invitation, Annie would never speak to her again. Even as all this was balancing in her mind – shuffling into position for a firm refusal, to be precise – she felt the heat of distant eyes upon her. Perhaps Archie felt them too, for he and Myrtle turned at the same moment and caught the full blast of Annie's look.

Annie was at the other side of the room, furious, puzzled eyes perched on the rim of a glass of lemonade. The knowledge of her misery was a physical blow to Myrtle. To have walked home with Archie would have been the kind of small shaft of excitement she could never have hoped for. She would have read nothing into it, known it was nothing but kindness on his part. But Myrtle would sacrifice anything to avoid Annie's unhappiness. She looked straight at Archie. A terse voice disguised her real feelings.

'I think I'll stay on a while, thanks.' She forced a smile. 'My first Fisher Lass dance – better make the best of it.'

Archie shrugged. He did not care one way or another whether Myrtle came with him. He just wanted to leave as soon as possible.

'Very well, then. I'll be off.'

Myrtle saw Annie's eyes follow his exit. She saw the tears. But in her own misery she had not the heart to go over to her friend and try to comfort, to explain. Suddenly she was exhausted by the whole day – pleasure or unhappiness, experienced vicariously, are more tiring than the real thing. She, like Archie, wanted nothing more than to be home.

As soon as she knew Archie would be well on his way, she slipped unnoticed from the room – there was another reel in progress. Annie, dancing with Sandy, again an uneasy smile on her face, did not notice Myrtle's departure.

Myrtle hurried through the arched passages, their patterned carpet moving like shoals of red and blue fish beneath her feet. Although she had drunk nothing but a single glass of wine all evening, she felt unsteady. Sharp lines trembled; wall lamps had the hazy, perilous look of jellies. In the reception area yet more gladioli were menacing as daggers. She ran towards the revolving door. Captured within two spread glass wings, she found herself going round so dizzily that she missed the moment of escape. Forced to go round again, streamers of light and dark fluttered through the glass, entwining her like maypole ribbons. And suddenly, trapped in two opposite wings of glass, was a figure, the face cut into jagged reflections. In irrational panic, this time Myrtle managed to slip out on to the pavement as the doors spun by. She was aware of a full moon, her own beating heart, the smell of sea in a black wind. Then, the other figure escaped too.

It was Ken. He was smiling.

'More fun than the reels, going round and round,' he said. 'Not my sort of evening.'

Myrtle smiled back. Gradually, the spinning of her head was slowing down.

'I've had enough, myself,' she said.

They began to walk. In silence, at first. The amorphous warmth Myrtle had felt in Ken's presence on the boat was still there, but it seemed to have slid to a deeper place. Above it, like a foolish frill, were more ruffled feelings concerning Archie.

'It was certainly Annie's day,' said Ken at last. Shyly, he took Myrtle's arm, but she could tell from his loose touch it was not her he was thinking about.

'It was.' Myrtle sighed. She slid Ken a sideways look. He was biting his lip. 'Do you still love her?' The unplanned question came out with a harshness that Myrtle instantly regretted. 'I'm sorry: I shouldn't have asked. It's none of my business.' But Ken was not perturbed.

'You don't stop loving someone just because there's no visible hope, do you? You keep thinking something might be possible, one day. The thought keeps you going.'

By now they had reached the house in Arbroath Street. They

stopped at the foot of the steps. In the light from the bright moon Myrtle could clearly see the fatigue of long, hopeless love in Ken's eyes.

'As I told you, that day . . . Annie's intrigued by what she can't easily capture. If you're patient enough . . .'

'But she's so many after her. The whole world's in love with Annie. Do you think she's ever actually . . .?'

Loyalty to Annie rose at once in Myrtle's throat: she could not discuss such private matters with Ken. On the other hand, he had suffered too long. He deserved some crumb of comfort. The devious serpent that thrives on the convolutions of all friendship stirred uncomfortably within Myrtle. If she could be the one to put his mind at rest, then his gratitude to her might even flower into some . . . closer friendship.

'If you're asking what I think you're asking,' she said, 'the answer is no. No.'

Ken's relief was visible. He straightened himself, grew taller. His face was now on a level with Myrtle's.

'Thanks,' he said. 'You've a good heart, Myrtle. Annie's lucky to have such a friend.' He put a hand over Myrtle's. She could feel it was strong with resolve, and felt pleased with herself. This was some compensation for the yearnings of the day. Then, so suddenly she was forced to totter backwards, Ken moved his head towards her and kissed both cheeks. She believed the edges of their mouths just touched. Emboldened, Myrtle ran a cautious finger up his bare arm, under the rolled-back sleeve: warm muscle under hard skin. Dear God, how thrilling it was. Ken pulled swiftly back. Her prying hand was left at a loss.

This was the first time Myrtle had been kissed since she was eleven years old, when Ross Wyatt's lips had brushed her forehead to win a bet with Jake Mackingtosh. The speed and unexpectedness of Ken's kiss left Myrtle with a feeling of ecstatic disbelief. Even as she began to climb the steps to the front door, Ken's departing footsteps merry chinks on the road, she wondered if it had actually happened . . . Only an hour ago Archie's invitation had stirred some hopeless new possibility. Now, that was dead. Ken's kiss may have been merely out of kindness, but the secret warmth for him, contained so long, rushed back. More than warmth, even. Some strange, effervescent feeling that made her catch her breath.

Wholly preoccupied with the sensations of her body, and panting audibly as she turned the key in the door, Myrtle did not look at Ken again. It occurred to her, for some silly, superstitious reason that she was in no condition to analyse, that it was important not to look on him again tonight. So she did not see in which direction he had gone.

Sometimes fragments of that day and night return: today, one of the three days a week Myrtle helps out at the Evergreen Home, it is with Myrtle in its entirety. The pictures push into her vision as she stuffs vein-laced old arms into cardigan sleeves of clotted wool, or spoons melted ice cream into flabby mouths. All day at work she suffers double vision. The kaleidoscope of the gala is superimposed on the reality of her duties. The white scars on a fragile leg are flecks of sunlight on the gala sea. The pink of a shawl is the pink of the gladioli that accosted her before Ken appeared in the revolving door. With her vision playing such tricks, Myrtle thinks perhaps she is sickening for something. She goes to the small room where tea and coffee are made – beverages, the matron insists on calling them. She sits on the only chair waiting for the kettle to boil. There is a strong smell of disinfectant. Someone has hung six blue cloths on a line of string to dry. Boat flags. Myrtle's hand is trembling. One of the helpers, a nervous young girl with a sheen of sweat on her top lip, rushes in. Mrs Bruce has been taken poorly, she says. Collapsed. Would Myrtle come quickly?

Clarrie Bruce is the last of Dot's old friends. As Myrtle feels for her pulse she remembers the toffee apples for which she was famous. She would bring them round to the house, one for Dot, one for her. Sometimes, even better, she would bring homemade doughnuts, warm and bursting with jam. She had bright green eyes, Clarrie: she and Dot were always laughing. As Myrtle pulls her up more comfortably on the pillows, she feels the regret of another imminent death. Mixed with it is the sickness of horror that ended the gala day. But that must be resisted for the moment, for the ambulance has arrived and Clarrie Bruce must be hurried away.

At the end of the long, lost day, Myrtle decides not to go home at once. Despite the low metallic sky she takes the road out of the village to the fields that slope upwards to the hidden church and the old manse. The gorse, so glaringly bright in June, is reduced to random specks of dying yellow on a few bushes. In the distance there is a slash of rapeseed cutting through the duller greens of the earth.

Myrtle walks fast. Speed might submerge the pictures, she thinks. But it's too late. They have gripped the day. Their blight will not cease until the story has rerun to its end. She walks with lowered head, the unclear grass running past her eyes.

What she did not see, or guess at, was the ending of that gala day. She observed that Annie was unwilling to talk about it, which was puzzling. Myrtle had expected her to relive each important moment a thousand times. All she said about Archie's premature exit from the dance was that she was briefly put out. Really, it hadn't mattered to her, she assured Myrtle. There would be plenty more chances. She had enjoyed the dance, she said. She was flattered by all the squabbling between her partners – who wouldn't be? But that was all. Perhaps Myrtle had misjudged the significance of the event in her friend's mind, she thought, and questioned her no more.

Three months went by in which nothing more about the gala was said. Myrtle was working hard, the penultimate year at school, for her exams. She spent less time with Annie, whose attitude to work was frivolous. When they did meet, Myrtle found Annie to be curiously withdrawn, edgy. At school she almost gave up her brazen flirting. All at once she was grown up, Myrtle reflected. Calmer, less thoughtless of people's feelings – though sometimes, when she caught a sly look between Annie and one of the boys, she wondered if something was going on that Annie had decided, in a new phase of life, to keep to herself.

But Annie's habit of telling all to Myrtle, demanding her opinion, was strong. At the beginning of the summer holidays they took a picnic lunch up into the fields – the gorse, then, flamed across the landscape – and Annie (whether by design or by mistake, Myrtle never knew) confessed.

'I've done it,' she said.

'Done what?'

'Don't be silly. You know.' She was plaiting three pieces of grass. Concentrating hard.

'Who with? Sandy? Ross? Harry?' Certainly she'd been much in conversation with Harry, of late, come to think of it –

'Ken.'

'*Ken?*' Myrtle held a sandwich half way to her mouth. She dropped it. Her fingers stung. She was made of glass, ready to break any moment. Annie shrugged, careless.

'It seemed like a good idea at the time.'

'When was that?'

'After the gala dance.'

'*After* –?' Myrtle could not repeat the words. Needles of sun pierced her eyes. Annie sat in so bright a halo that her edges were all shirred.

'I was getting fed up, towards the end of the evening, Archie behaving so rottenly and everything. I saw Ken leave – just after you, I think it was. But then he came back.'

'He came back.' It wasn't a question, but a dumbfounded echo. Annie had no idea what she was saying . . . what she was doing to her friend.

'All the others were arguing about who'd take me home, so I put an end to it all by saying I was going home with Ken as he was the only one who hadn't asked. He looked pretty surprised, I have to say. Blushed deeply.' Annie laughed. 'Well, the others ribbed him a lot, as you can imagine. But they eventually got fed up and left us alone. We started to walk towards home. It was quite awkward, actually, Ken being so silent. I began to think I would have done better to have taken up one of the other offers, though of course the only one I really wanted to be with was Archie. And he'd buggered off, the bastard. Anyhow, Ken was rather sweet. He put his jacket round me. Talked about some seagull he'd found in his garden with a broken leg. He'd been trying to mend it with a splint made from a pencil.' Annie laughed again. 'Not at all the usual sort of conversation you get with boys. Anyway, on and on about this seagull he went, once he'd got going, and somehow we were still walking – towards St Monan's. Ken said: let's go down on to the beach, such a fine night. From him, it didn't sound at all like a filthy suggestion. I really believed he just wanted to walk on the sand. So we climbed down. My feet were hurting like hell by now – all day in silver shoes, imagine. So I kicked them off and we walked by the water's edge. It was lovely, the cold sand under my squished toes. I couldn't be bothered carrying the shoes. I threw them into the waves. Don't know why I did that, I really don't. It was a spontaneous thing, just came to me. Throwing away such expensive shoes. Anyhow, it made Ken laugh. He laughed and laughed. Quite bent double, he was.'

While Annie smiled at the remembrance, Myrtle pulled up her knees in an effort to blanket the audible beating of her heart. She said a small prayer for strength. Please God, don't let me break down until I'm alone. Don't let Annie see what this means to me.

'We went back up to the stones – you know, those big flat stones – and sat down. The moon was so bright it was almost like daylight. If it'd been with someone I'd really fancied, it would have been pretty good. Ken was still laughing about my shoes. Or maybe he was pretending it was that and really it was something else. Hard to tell what's going on in Ken's mind. So there am I, end of the best day of my life, thinking here's the moon and the sea and all that stuff – what a waste. Can't end it just sitting . . . Next thing I know I'm asking Ken to kiss me. And he does.'

Annie paused, scrutinised Myrtle's face. Myrtle prayed she would think the watering of her eyes was caused by the hurting sun.

'And we do it.'

Myrtle could think of no response. She could not speak.

'It wasn't up to much, really. Bit of a disappointment. Ken hadn't a clue . . . Not at all what I'd imagined.' She paused again. High above them a skylark's sudden song cascaded down into the silence. Myrtle moved her eyes but could not see the bird.

'Then, well, it was over. No big deal. But at least I knew I could trust Ken not to slag me off to the others. I knew he wouldn't say a word. We got up, brushed ourselves down. Then an awful thing happened.' Annie bit her lip. 'He began to cry. Really sob. I said come on, Ken – what's the matter? It was horrible, the noise he made. I was glad no one was near. Just us and the sea. Took him ages to calm down. Then he said something about not wanting me to think it was just any old occasion – it meant more to him than he would ever be able to tell me. Well, I reckon he was overcome – his first time, too. And boys are sometimes more sentimental than girls. I said brace up, Ken, you don't have to say anything. I'm glad the first time was with you, I said, lying through my teeth. But don't let it give you any ideas, I said. It was just the end of my Fisher Lass day. We're not going out, or anything. He said that was fine by him, sorry about the crying, and we walked home. Sun coming up.'

Annie lay back on the grass, shut her eyes and covered them with one arm. Myrtle, convinced God had answered her prayer and given her strength, gathered herself. Caution tightened her words.

'Why didn't you tell me before?'

'I couldn't. I tried, but I just couldn't bring myself. I had to work out how you'd take it. You always used to warn me, so sternly, when we were younger. Remember?'

'We're seventeen, now.' Myrtle's lightness of tone was edged with laughter.

'Exactly. So you're not shocked?'

'Of course not.'

Annie sat up again, brushing dry grass from her hair. Their eyes met.

'And since then?' Myrtle could not resist. The agony of not knowing would be unbearable. 'You and Ken?'

Annie shrugged.

'Next day I asked him about his seagull. He said it had died in the night. End of story, really. I wouldn't go with Ken again. He was just the end of the Fisher Lass thing, like I said. He doesn't pester me, I'll say that for him. Seems to have gone back into his shell. Poor old Ken.'

'He's someone you can trust,' Myrtle said.

'More than you can say for the others. Most of them can't keep their bloody mouths shut, can they?'

'What about?'

Annie lowered her eyes to concentrate on plaiting more blades of grass again. Her demeanour suggested a closeness to shame Myrtle had never seen before. Annie answered quietly.

'After Ken . . . I found myself saying I don't mind. Ross – poor old Ross, he'd waited so long; Harry, Sandy . . . Don't know why really. They were all so impatient.'

The skylark had moved away. Myrtle's shock beat like wings in the silence.

'Archie?' she asked, at last.

'Not Archie. Yet. I've been too occupied to have a go at him. One day.'

'They must have been rather surprised, the other boys. You turned them all down so often.' If she kept talking about anything except Ken, Myrtle thought, she would manage to sound quite normal.

'I think they were, rather. Maybe they just thought the right time had come. Sandy said I was showing a green light. News to me.'

'Well,' said Myrtle.

'You're not shocked?'

'Perhaps a bit concerned. I wouldn't want you getting . . . I wouldn't want you to be thought of as some sort of –'

'Easy lay,' interrupted Annie, who knew Myrtle was uneasy with such jargon. 'That's a risk you have to take if you want a bit of fun. Just hope they're not laughing too much behind my back, comparing notes. As for the other – don't worry. I make sure they all take precautions.'

'Good. Though it's not *that* that really worried me.' A feeling of great weariness had begun to overwhelm Myrtle. She was eager to go, now. Be by herself. Reflect on all the things Annie had so innocently confessed. She wanted to be free to cry without restraint, as Ken had, to Annie's scorn, that night on the beach just an hour or so after he had kissed *her* . . . A kiss that had left an indelible imprint. Whereas to Annie his lovemaking had meant nothing more than the proper end of an extraordinary day. The unfairness –

'Sandy's top of my list at the moment,' Annie broke in. 'He's a sweet lad, funny. And a quick learner.' She giggled. 'We came up here one evening –'

Myrtle did not want to know. Quickly she stood up. Unable to bear any more, she hurried off, leaving Annie to the unaccustomed job of packing up the picnic bag. When she had gone some way, running, she heard a shout.

'Have I said something?' Annie cried.

Myrtle did not answer or look back, but ran faster into the lacerating sun.

The impact of Annie's confession and the thought of Ken's innocent betrayal consumed Myrtle for the first few weeks of that summer holiday. She and Annie continued their normal life together when Annie wasn't off with one of the boys. Myrtle managed to conceal her own disturbed feelings. The last thing she wanted Annie to know was that she had ever entertained the most fragile hope of serious friendship with Ken, the boy Annie had used merely for her own gratification to round off a memorable day, and then cast aside careless of his response. It was the first time in their lives Myrtle had ever kept anything concerning her own most private feelings from her friend. Until now there had never been any crossing of interest. Myrtle had kept her docile place as Annie's friend and confidante, never supposing that one day some boy might come between them. Ever since Ken had revealed his secret to Myrtle on the bus, she had kept it securely – securely as her own inclination towards him. As he had never spoken to her about Annie again, she had come to assume that his obsession – love, could it be called? – for her had waned. The friendliness he had shown Myrtle after the dance, followed by the kiss, had briefly fanned these hopes. It had not occurred to her a boy would kiss (albeit chastely) one girl and make love to another within a matter of hours. (Ah, such innocence, she thinks.) Then Annie's news, that Ken plainly still loved her, added to the shock. She felt deeply for Ken, she felt for herself. So much suffering, and it had to be kept secret. She could only sob at night when Dot was asleep. For a while, she was exhausted.

Then, perhaps because she was determined to be rid of the discomfort, her own feelings for Ken slid invisibly away. She awoke one morning to find they had evaporated. Her affection for him, and her sympathy, were still there. But the idea of having some deeper relationship with him made her laugh. She laughed out loud at breakfast, surprising Dot. Ken, with his lack of romantic impulse and his underdeveloped biceps, would never be enough of a man, for her, any more than he would be for Annie. There were visible fissures of weakness in his character she would have come to despise. Ken! However could she have contemplated . . .? How could she have maintained the slightly excited feeling ever since she was fourteen? She supposed the answer was that youthful fantasy has to have flesh and blood to feed on and Ken, being there, flattering with his confessions, had understandably become her object of possibility. She laughed again. Dot observed she hadn't seen her so happy for weeks.

In the void left by thoughts of Ken, Myrtle tried to sort out the sensations Annie's promiscuous life caused: alarm, worry, some diffuse thing that could be jealousy. Not that Myrtle would want or approve such behaviour herself, but she would like occasionally to experience the luxury of being desired. She would like the chance to say no. The boys who were now Annie's lovers were her own friends: they had given up their banter years ago, and treated her kindly – still seeking her advice, though not about Annie. But it never occurred to any of them to think of Myrtle as a girl: not one of them had ever given the smallest indication he fancied her, and this was a denial Myrtle had to endure. As for her friendship with Annie – it was a difficult time. In her daily exuberance, charged with hormones, part of the excitement was to relate every detail to Myrtle. But Myrtle had no wish to hear the sexual skills or failings of the boys she had known most of her life. She begged Annie to keep them to herself.

'Very well,' Annie eventually agreed. 'I won't tell you a thing except the really dreadful bits, or the really funny bits . . .'

They laughed over this arrangement. They still laughed, often. But it was the beginning of the parting of their old ways. There was now careful choice in the exchange of secrets, conscious restraint. At that time, too, Myrtle began to wonder whether there was an element of treachery somewhere in her friend. She despised herself for such misgivings but, unlike the unhappiness caused by Ken, she could not quite extinguish them.

Even today she cannot quite extinguish them, though often they taunt more wildly when Annie is not there than when they are together.

Myrtle walks back through the village weakened and ashamed by her day in the past. She sees Annie come out of the museum door, pause for a moment to glance at the harbour empty of boats. Myrtle curses herself. Had she been less preoccupied with her own pointless thoughts she would have remembered it was Annie's first day at her new job, and dropped in to see how she was getting on. She shouts. Annie turns. They run towards each other.

'It was marvellous!' Annie is all smiles.

'You didn't drop a thing, gave the right change?'

'It was all fine, fine. Wonderful. I'm going to be happy there.' She looks at her watch. 'Like I told you, the whole world is drawn to the museum café . . .'

'Really?' Myrtle knows well enough that Annie's whole world most probably has a single name.

'There was this chappie, Bruce, from the north. Gave me a huge tip, all for one cup of unspilt tea.' She laughs again, so happily. 'Well, we get talking. He asks me would I like a drink this evening. He has to be on his way tomorrow.'

'What about Janice?'

'She'll think something's held me up, first day.' Annie looks at her watch again.

'I'll go round, tell her. Tell her you're held up a while, I mean. Stay with her till you get home.'

'That would be kind.' Annie's mouth puckers. So often Myrtle has seen her like this, torn between right and wrong. To urge in the right

94

direction is always counter productive. 'Only a drink,' Annie repeats, suddenly impatient. 'There's no need for that face.'

In Annie's house Myrtle finds Janice in the kitchen. She sits on a stool at the table, exercise books unopened before her, watching television. Her school shirt has one button too many undone. The sleeves have been rolled up to show the tiny wrists and forearms. Conscious or unconscious, such loosening of clothes? Myrtle can't be sure. But she recognises the signs. Janice's eyes flick from the television screen to Myrtle and back without interest. Since the death of the hamster her usual warmth to Myrtle has been noticeably absent.

'Mum's late,' she says.

'I caught sight of her. She said to tell you she'll not be long.' She paused, contemplating the untruth she was about to tell on Annie's behalf. 'First day in a new job – you know how it is. Sorting things out.'

'Aye.'

'Will I get you something to eat?'

Janice shakes her head.

'Not hungry,' she says.

'Or to drink?'

'I been home ages,' she says, 'but I'll wait till Mum gets back.'

The promise of considerable beauty in Janice, so apparent in babyhood, has receded. Now, at eleven, Janice is nothing like as pretty as Annie was at the same age, but she has the same wide-apart eyes fuzzy with thick lashes, and a languid smile, rarely given, that could lead to success when she is older. What she lacks is Annie's spirit, animation. She suffers from lethargy, or boredom. A dull acceptance of her lot Myrtle finds alarming. No childish ambition seems to goad her: her hamsters and her cat are the central interest in her life. She tolerates the attentions of boys but her natural disinterest means they keep their distance.

Myrtle recognises much of Ken's character in Janice. But, of late, there have been signs of her mother, too. Janice automatically strikes provocative poses. Even alone in the kitchen, expecting no one but her mother, there is an elegance in the slouch across the table. This, too, fills Myrtle with misgiving.

'Very well, then. I'll go next door. Don't want to disturb your home-work.'

Her lack of admonition is greeted with a cheeky grin.

'OK. I'll start soon as this is over.' Janice hitches herself up – a childlike gesture that dispels the disagreeably grown-up pose.

In the front room Myrtle lowers herself on to the sofa. The imitation leather gives its usual squeak. She contemplates the pile of women's magazines on the table but does not pick one up. She wonders how long Janice will be, and who is this Bruce it's so important to have a drink with – and what are they doing? She wonders what it would be like to have a child of her own doing homework at the kitchen table. She wonders if she would have been a good mother – better than Annie, most probably, though at moments, at times convenient to herself, Annie takes great trouble with Janice, and even encourages the child's slow, low-key laugh. Through the panoramic window she can see the sky is darkening – the sullen dark of a gathering storm rather than the darkness of nightfall.

The distant scrape of voices stops. Janice must have kept her word, turned off the television. Myrtle wonders what fragment of history or literature or biology now taxes the child's mind. She is inclined to go and find out. It would be good to discuss Janice's school work with her. But she does not want to disturb. Myrtle continues to sit, unmoving, on the hostile sofa in the ever huskier brown light of the room. Then there is a tap at the glass of the panoramic window. Myrtle turns her head. She does not see a bird, but imagines it must be one who has not understood the glass. But no: it's a small clutch of raindrops, the pebble-hard, vicious kind. They begin to tadpole down the long stretch of glass. Their long, smeary tails, reflecting some grain of light outside, glint like strands of tinsel. They are jolted into sudden speed by a loud crack of thunder. The terrifying noise is sharp, clean as gunshot. It is followed by a second of absolute silence. This is broken by a livid crashing and growling (clouds head-butting and breaking, Myrtle imagines) and rain squalls across the sheet glass so hard Myrtle fears it will break. She jumps up to run to the kitchen: Janice is clearly alarmed. At that moment lightning flares through the room, flooding the dreary colours with its silver-milk liquid. In her dash from sofa to kitchen Myrtle feels she is drowning in this surf of strange light. Then there is darkness again, leaving her confused and afraid as she stumbles along the passage. More thunder overhead. There has been no warning of this storm – is it raging at sea? Janice's cries chime like small disjointed bells in the greater clamour of more thunder. Myrtle takes the child in her arms.

By now she is almost hysterical. She clings to Myrtle, hot-limbed. Her tears darken the wool of Myrtle's jersey. With each new bark of thunder Janice tightens her grip. When the lightening comes she shouts that it is blinding her.

Myrtle concentrates on soothing Janice: stroking her head, murmuring that it will be over soon. Janice is curled into a babyish position, legs askew, cheeks blotched with tears. A child who so often appears mature, now seems younger than her years. Myrtle thanks God she decided to come. What if Janice, so afraid of storms, had been alone here while Annie was out with this new Bruce? And what was Annie, at this very moment, thinking?

Half an hour goes by. As Myrtle and Janice cling to each other, it seems much longer. Anger with Annie, and pity for her child, clash within Myrtle. She rocks back and forth, willing Annie to return. Gradually outrage drains from the thunder. Its fury almost spent, the growling after each clap gives way to quieter murmurings. The lightning ceases its erratic flashing, leaving unlit rain to run down the window.

'I hate thunder,' says Janice, for the third or fourth time. 'I think it's coming to get me.'

'It was a nasty old storm but it's on its way out now. Listen, no more thunder.' They listen to the rain. Myrtle dabs the child's face with a handkerchief.

'Do you think they'll be all right in the boat?' Janice repositions her head on the comfortable expanse of Myrtle's breast.

'They'll be fine. They've been out in weather much worse than this.' Myrtle tries to sound convincing.

'I hope so.' Janice sniffs. 'I'm hungry now.'

'I'll get you something.'

'You're very kind, Myrtle.'

'Nonsense.'

'Were you sad to hear my hamster died?'

'I was. Of course I was.'

'I cried a lot. Mum said stop blubbing, Janice, it's only a hamster, we'll get another one. She couldn't understand it wouldn't be the same.' For a moment Janice puts her arms round Myrtle's neck. Myrtle is touched. Janice is a child who, like her father, makes little show of her affection. To disguise her feelings, to stop thinking of the child she and Archie will never have, Myrtle knows she must be brusque.

'Now run upstairs and wash your face. I'll butter you a scone.'

Janice obediently slithers off Myrtle's knee.

'We've no butter,' she says, dully. 'We're always out of butter.'

'We'll manage with jam, then.'

'Don't suppose there's any jam either. Mum's not so good at remembering things like that when Dad's away.'

Ten minutes later Janice is eating hot butterless toast, and Myrtle is drinking a cup of tea, when Annie returns. She is dark with rain, clothes dripping, sodden curls flat against her cheeks, exposing the fine bones. Her eyes skitter with guilt – well they might, thinks Myrtle. Were Janice not there she might have risked telling Annie what she thought of her as a mother, the anger is so fierce. But she says nothing.

'I'm sorry,' Annie shakes her head. Water patters on to the floor.

'Where were you?' Janice gets down from the table.

'First day in a new job – I was kept, didn't like to hurry away –'

Janice is out of the room. They hear her running upstairs. A door bangs. Annie picks up a dishclóth and begins to rub her hair.

'She wasn't alone. You were with her,' she says.

'I might not have been.'

'You said you would be. I would have come straight away, otherwise. Always ready to jump down my throat about Janice, you are, Myrtle Duns. Always accusing. What do you know about children?'

'I know that if you're lucky enough to have them, then they should be your priority. How was he, this important Bruce?'

Annie picks up a bunch of spoons and forks from the draining board, throws them into the sink to make an infuriating clatter.

'That's no business of yours, is it? But if you must know, he didn't turn up. Stupid bastard. Men. I waited. Gave him half an hour then ran back here fast as I could.'

Myrtle stands up.

'If I hadn't been here,' she says, 'God knows what Janice would have gone through on her own. She's terrified of storms, or perhaps you didn't know that –'

'Fuck it, Myrtle,' Annie shouts. 'I've had enough of your preaching! Your *goodness*, your *thought* for others, your *priorities* – they make me sick. You may be more saintly than me, I grant you that. But there's one thing you know nothing about: that's *motherhood*.' She is scarlet-cheeked, furious, panting. The damp cotton of her shirt is stuck to her lively breast.

Response flares up within Myrtle, but she fights against it. She hates such quarrels. They are rare, but unsettling. Telling Annie what she thinks of her as a mother will do no good. References to Janice, except in the most superficial way, are rightly taboo. She curses herself for her lack of restraint. This row will mean several days of unhappy tension, each waiting for the other to apologise, forgive.

'I'll go now, leave you to Janice,' Myrtle says.

Home, the telephone is ringing. Archie, on his ship-to-shore telephone, says the storm has hardly touched them: all is well. Myrtle sits heavily on an upright chair. The good news is clouded by the scene with Annie. Fury with those you love best, she thinks, is unlike any other fury in its destruction. She has not felt more weary, more drained, for months. She sits listening to the rain, gentler now, longing for the day to end. The telephone rings again, startling. It will be Annie – Annie to apologise. Charged with unexpected relief, she hurries to answer it. For a moment she does not understand, or recognise the voice, a man's. Martin? Yes, Martin, he says. Happens he's been given a fine lobster. Would she like it if he brought it round to share?

'That would be grand,' says Myrtle, not giving herself time to think. She is still confused, heavy. Stupid to have supposed Annie would make amends so soon. She fills a huge pan with water, puts it on the stove. It will be good not to have to spend the evening alone, but she doesn't much relish the thought of having to make polite conversation with Martin. As she waits for the water to boil, and for him to arrive, she becomes aware of a lack of sound rather than clean silence. The rain has stopped. Through the window Myrtle can see a scattering of stars in a sky suddenly cleared of cloud. Moments later there is a knock on the door.

Martin comes in carrying the lobster wrapped in newspaper. He is embarrassed to find Archie not at home. Had he been down to the harbour, seen no boats, he would not have come, he says. Myrtle tells him they'll be back tomorrow night. She smiles to see him clutching at his parcel, not sure, as Archie is not here, that sharing his supper with a married woman is in order.

'Perhaps I'd better go,' he says. 'I'll come another time, when Archie's back.'

'Put your lobster down,' says Myrtle. 'Archie'd never forgive me if I turned you both away. Besides, I'm in need of company tonight. I've had a day. Shall I beat up some batter for pancakes while the lobster's boiling? I seem to think you like a pancake with treacle.' How did she remember that? He must have mentioned it, the Lord only knows how long ago.

'Can't think of anything better, if it's not too much trouble.' Martin sits at the table, avoiding what he knows to be Archie's chair. As Myrtle prepares the food they talk about matters they both under-stand: the shortage of fish, problems with the delivery of marble. When they have finished eating, Martin congratulates Myrtle on her cooking.

'I could do with a wife like you,' he says, laughing. 'You should see the stuff I eat. Takeaway, takeaway, the occasional grilled herring. I dream sometimes of coming home and finding a supper like this on the table, a good wife to spend the evening with.'

Myrtle likes the Canadian drawl of his voice, less distinct now than when he first arrived, but far from lost. He has adopted a few Scots words which sound so peculiar in his Canadian accent that people smile when he uses them. She grins, trying to imagine him as a husband. Signs were he'd be a good one: faithful, gentle, sensitive to his wife's desires. Had Archie not existed, Martin was the sort of man Myrtle would have aspired to, though not with much hope. He was a rare figure in this small community: a target for many in search of a husband.

'You could do with a wife, aye,' she says. 'But you've not got one for the lack of offers, have you? Every girl along the coast was after you. Two dozen girls, you could have married, if you'd wanted . . .'

Martin looks down, reddens. Myrtle sees him as he was: blond hair, bronze skin – some had thought he must have Norwegian blood – diffident, shy, awkward among all the sea-going young men of his age. She remembers the excitement, as an unexpected stranger suddenly in their midst, he caused among the girls. She remembers Annie's unusual reticence. 'He's all right,' she said to Myrtle at the time, 'but not really my type. If he knelt at my feet and begged me to marry him, I'd not be interested. You'd not catch me emigrating to Canada.' She was utterly convincing. Myrtle remembers this declaration very clearly as she pours cream over the treacle on Martin's pancakes. She herself has eaten an unusual amount, and feels happier. The day has fallen away.

'None of them was right,' says Martin. 'I had a picture in my mind of just what a wife should be. None of them came anywhere near it. I could never bring myself to go for second best. And now it's something I don't think about very often. Happy in my work. Preoccupied. I've given up looking, I suppose. Given up trying.'

'That's ridiculous,' says Myrtle, sounding fiercer than she means to. 'There are good women about. One of them'll cross your path one day when you're least expecting it.'

'Perhaps,' says Martin, not meeting her look.

Later, when the dishes are cleared and the lamps are lit, they move to the wooden chairs (Myrtle takes her mother's old rocking chair) either side of the stove. Martin declines Myrtle's offer of a dram of

Archie's whisky, but accepts a bottle of lager. Myrtle herself makes do with a mug of tea. The conversation turns to Annie.

'I see your friend, Annie, darting about,' Martin says. 'A real will o' the wisp, she seems to be. Marriage hasn't much changed her, I'd say. How is she?'

'She's fine.'

There's a long, easy silence between them. Myrtle is in half a mind to tell Martin about today's row, but loyalty wins. She says nothing. Martin, the dark skin of his cheeks deepening again, nods his head. It occurs to Myrtle that he looks more weathered than many of the fishermen, which is strange considering most of his working life is spent in a shed. Martin wipes his mouth with the back of his hand.

'I suppose I could have married her,' he says.

'Married Annie?'

'Well, don't think me boasting if I say this, but there was a time when – if I read the signals right – she seemed keen.'

'I didn't know that,' says Myrtle, after a while. Her heart begins to beat as wildly as it did some hours ago, when Annie shouted at her. Irrational feelings of possessiveness consume her. Martin has always been *her* friend – hers and Archie's. She has never understood Annie's lack of enthusiasm – hostility, almost – towards him, though has never questioned it very far.

'Don't suppose she wanted to say too much . . . it was all very awkward at the time. I was younger, inexperienced.' He smiles briefly. 'Couldn't think how to begin to cope. Didn't have any friends, in those days, whose advice I could ask.'

'Annie is very . . . well, there's no one else quite like her.' Questions roar through Myrtle's head that she is determined not to ask. Somehow, she must keep her astonishment to herself.

'That's for sure.' Martin meets her eye now. 'I imagine you did know . . . about Archie. I mean, it was when she was all out for Archie, trying to add him to her list.'

'I knew about that – Lord, I did. Was she a pest, forever telling me about her pursuit of the elusive Archie?' Myrtle laughs so Martin will see all that – events so long ago – means nothing to her, now.

'The way she put it to me was that Archie was a kind of challenge. She didn't really fancy him, didn't love him – nothing like that. No pretence of any great feeling there: she said he was too solemn for her, she couldn't have stood his lack of smiling for long. But, Jesus, did she want to . . . just for the prestige, just to prove to herself she could get any man she wanted, I suppose. Then, I don't know why, she seemed to give up on Archie. Turned her attention to me, instead. Heaven knows why. I didn't do a thing to encourage her. Rather, I kept my distance.'

'That's always been the great encouragement, in Annie's case,' says Myrtle. She has to make a great effort to keep her response low and calm. She can see that Martin has no idea the impact his news is causing.

'Funnily enough, the impression I got was that she was a little . . . afraid of me. Nervous. There was no flirting. None of that come-hither stuff I'd see her exercising on others. Then the letters began to come. Strange, wild, beautiful letters. It seemed she thought she'd fallen in, eh, love with me. Deeply, hopelessly, she said. For all the boys she had accommodated – I remember thinking what an unlikely word for her to use – she'd felt nothing. Nothing. But for me – for some goddamn reason she couldn't explain, and I certainly couldn't – she was eating her wretched little heart out for me. She said nothing of this to you?'

Myrtle shakes her head. Her mind spins back to that time: Annie daft and laughing as ever, looking vaguely for a new job, having been sacked from the post office for unpunctuality. Annie drinking with all her short-time lovers in the pub. Drinking a bit too much sometimes, perhaps. But not unhappy. Certainly never mentioning Martin. As for writing good letters – the idea is beyond comprehension. Myrtle scours her memory for any clue, any incident of no significance at the time but which would in retrospect indicate the truth. But she can remember nothing. Only that Annie had always said that she, Myrtle, was the one privy to her secrets: her secrets then concerned the hope-lessness of inexperienced boys at sex, and if she couldn't win over Archie then she'd have to be off to find an older man. It had all been lightly said. Not a hint of hidden love. Not a clue that for the first time in her life her own feelings were unrequited.

'So what did you do?' Myrtle, desperately curious to hear the rest of Martin's story, feels this question is permissible.

'I have to say I was touched by those letters. Anyone would have been. Beautiful writing, poetic sort of stuff straight from the heart.'

Annie writing beautiful letters? It's hard to believe! Annie who never put pen to paper if she could help it: Annie consistently bottom in English, scoffing at Myrtle's love of Keats . . . Myrtle feels all understanding has been wrenched from her. She shifts abruptly in her chair.

'Does that surprise you?' Martin asks.

'It does, a little.' Myrtle's incredulity is so overwhelming she wonders that Martin cannot see it.

'She became what I can only call obsessive. Following me, jumping out at me at unexpected moments to declare this great love. Needless to say I never laid a finger on her – it wasn't that she seemed to want – or gave her one iota of encouragement. Quite the opposite. I tried to explain she was caught up in some fantasy. Wanting affection, I said, she'd fixed upon me as a figure to provide it, though she didn't know me at all. She wouldn't listen to a word of that.' Martin pauses, smiles. 'I'm no analyst, but I think I had a point. Father gone long ago, little love or attention from her mother – certainly no guidance. Then this great flurry of boys – quick fancies, disillusioning sex. What she was after was something more solid, real, though perhaps that was something she hadn't worked out for herself. So happened she picked on me, almost the only one she hadn't been to school with, hadn't known all her life. I got the impression she was fed up with boys just fancying her, just wanting her for sex. She's a romantic at heart, Annie. What she wanted was love. But I couldn't give it to her.'

'You didn't feel anything for her at all?'

'Only pity. Sorrow that I couldn't help. Of course I saw she was an exceptionally attractive girl, beautiful. She's still an attractive woman. But not for me.' He pauses for so long that Myrtle fears he is not going to continue. She fetches him another bottle of lager from the fridge. Presses him a little.

'So how did you . . . resolve it?'

Martin sighs. He opens the bottle, fills the glass then puts it on the floor without drinking.

'It had to stop. I was worried about her state of mind. Inevitably the end was untidy. She taxed my patience once too often . . . She came round to my place in the middle of the night, woke me up throwing stones at the window. She was sobbing, desolate. I had to let her in – didn't want my parents to be woken. She'd come to tell me of her new resolution, which was to wait for me, no matter how long. God forbid, I said, it's not a matter of waiting, Annie. Don't you understand? I don't love you, I never will love you, and all this nonsense must stop. I'm fed up with it, bored. I rather lost my cool I guess. I wasn't as gentle as I might have been. All I wanted was to get rid of her, stop her preying on me. As usual, my words had no effect. So I decided I'd have one last try at jolting her irrationality. I told her I loved quite a different sort of woman – a quiet, gentle soul who'd never flirted in her life. You mean *dull*? she said. Not dull at all, I said. Unattainable, sadly, but so entrenched in my heart I've no hope of ridding myself . . .' He petered out, embarrassed to have gone so far.

'I didn't know that,' says Myrtle.

Martin reaches down for his glass, drinks.

'No: well, I keep things to myself.'

'And how did she take the news?'

'She said I was making it up to try to put her off. She said it wouldn't make a jot of difference to what she felt – ever. Poor Annie. She was so white. I remember she was leaning against the wall, fists clenched, her head tilted up at me awkwardly. Then – well, this bit is rather shaming. Shall I go on?' Myrtle nods. 'I regret it – but I regret the whole thing. She said I'll strike a bargain with you, Martin Ford. Give me one kindly kiss on the cheek, and I'll leave you alone. I'll not bother you any more, she said. I can see it's useless, now. But one day you'll see how foolish you were to let me go – and I'll still be there. She sounded so . . . pathetic. I said I was sorry I had shouted at her, but I didn't know how to get the truth through to her. Then I did what she wanted. I kissed her gently on the cheek. But as soon as my mouth touched her skin, she fell away from me as if I'd struck her. She was suddenly a heap on the floor – fainted just like a character in a romantic novel. I gave her some whisky, brought her round. She apologised for being a nuisance. I couldn't help seeing how real her fantasy had become – girls don't faint away when they're kissed on the cheek, these days, and I felt for her profoundly. After all, I knew all about unrequited love myself, though I didn't tell her that. Anyway, true to her word, she stopped her pursuing after that. Left me alone, thank God. Avoided me for a while, then just acted normally as if nothing had ever happened. Though she did once ask me to burn her letters.'

'And did you?' Martin has stopped again.

'I did. With some reluctance, I have to say. They were so strange – not about her and me, so much, as about the tricks love plays on daily life . . . I doubt I'll ever have such letters again.' For the third time in the evening he reddens deeply. The magenta skin of his high forehead shines brightly against the blond hair. 'But that was all a long time ago,' he goes on. 'I can't say we're close friends, but she's not unfriendly. Her irrational behaviour, for those few months, was no more than an illness in the form of an illusion. Kind of thing that often strikes confused, unhappy people, I daresay. But it seemed to pass as quickly as it came. I doubt Annie ever gives me a thought, these days. Or if she does, it would only be to laugh at her youthful folly. She seems to be happily married to Ken, doesn't she?'

'Aye. Ken's a good husband to her.'

Martin looks at his watch, stands up.

'My, how I've been going on,' he says, 'tongue running away with me. I'm sorry. It's late.'

Myrtle goes with him to the door.

'And your own . . . unrequited?' she says, not meaning to say anything and not wanting to mention Annie again. 'I'm sorry about –'

'Yes, well, you get used to the insurmountable. You learn how to readjust. Even if the shade – is that the right word? – never quite goes. Anyway . . . thank you for . . . listening, whatever. I've never told that story before. Thought you knew it all, being Annie's friend.' He puts a hand on Myrtle's arm for a moment. His touch ignites a flare of sympathy – is it sympathy, exactly? – through her body. The sensation is faintly unnerving.

'Thank you for coming round,' says Myrtle. 'I like your visits. Thanks for the lobster.'

'My pleasure.' Martin inclines his head.

Myrtle smiles at his old-fashioned courtesy. She sees that once more his face is blazing. Funny how she has never noticed his easy blushing before. But then in all the years they have known one another they have never had anything like tonight's conversation. It is past midnight when Myrtle closes the door.

And sleep is not possible. Myrtle returns to her chair. In her confusion the words *betrayal, disillusion, disaster* swarm through her head. It's not the first time Myrtle has reflected on the treachery of friendship: that happened when Annie confessed about her night on the beach with Ken, and the news was devastating. But even in her youth Myrtle had forced herself to understand, and to forgive. Since then – foolishly, naively, she now sees – it has never occurred to her that Annie, the person she has loved so much for so long, has carried on keeping important parts of her life to herself: vital parts which Myrtle could never have guessed at. The fact that Annie, obviously so unhappy at the time, did not require Myrtle's help, or advice, or sympathetic ear, is a blow of such magnitude that she is consumed by a physical wrenching that leaves her no strength to work out reasons. She shuts her eyes and listens to questions that whimper across her mind. How many other events, loves, losses, has Annie not told her about? How was it that she failed Annie so badly? How could she have been so unobservant, seeing Annie daily, and yet not even suspecting that there were secret traumas in her life? They had sworn, at a very young age, to be best friends and tell each other everything, always. A childish pact, perhaps. But one they had believed in. For so long Myrtle had reason to trust that Annie was keeping her part of the arrangement. Annie confided so many thoughts (mostly about the nature of boys, though some about her wayward mother) that it had never occurred to Myrtle there could possibly be much besides which she was keeping to herself. For Myrtle's own part, she kept scrupulously to the agreement, though inevitably she had fewer secrets to contribute than Annie. Myrtle's life was duller. But – with the single exception of her feelings for Ken – she tried to supply Annie with private information. Sometimes, with a feeling of disloyalty, she would confess that her mother's eccentricities – the stringency over blankets, for instance – depressed her. Or that she was disappointed she had not a higher mark for an essay. Most private of all her secrets was to do with the shame of her large hands and feet. But she had felt bound to confess something of even this most delicate subject to Annie, confident she would receive sympathy. She had told Annie that while she knew she would never be the kind of woman who would attract men, and she had come to accept that, she wondered if physically she might improve? Annie had said yes, of course; everyone gets better once they've lost their puppy fat. Carelessly she said it. Annie was never much of a comforter with words – small, unexpected gestures was more her way. And in truth, Myrtle was aware from a very young age, Annie was not much interested in Myrtle's confessions. They were neither surprising nor exciting. So the pact soon became mostly a one-way thing. The whirligigs of Annie's existence, delivered in exhausting detail, far outweighed Myrtle's own diligent contributions. But she had no intention of ever breaking her youthful promise to her friend, so continued to supply some secrets, no matter how dull Annie found them.

Myrtle remains in her shocked, unmoving state for a long while in the chair. She hears that it has begun to rain again, a gentler rain than earlier, shimmying down the window panes. And she remembers – the memory gathers unfocused as smoke – but there it is, a day of light rain. She and Annie were standing looking in the newsagent's window. Annie had red, puffy eyes. She said she had some infection: already they had been to the chemist for ointment. Outside the newsagent Annie was acting strangely. She was whispering out loud all the names of the magazines. Her face was very pale. Myrtle asked what was the matter? Nothing, said Annie. Nothing now. *Now* is the word that in these nocturnal reflections hurtles weightily as a cannon ball. *Now* meant nothing, then: or not more than some reference to the future healing of her eyes now that the ointment had been acquired. *Now*, in the middle of Myrtle's night of agonising, is so obvious in its significance that Myrtle wants to roar her regret out loud. *Now* meant *now that something has happened. Now that something important is over. Now that I've given up all hope of Martin's love.* How could . . . how *could* Myrtle have been standing so close to Annie and had not the smallest inkling of what her friend was going through?

Shocked by her own insensitivity that day, that time, Myrtle curses herself years too late. And one further memory returns. It is in the street, possibly later that day. Definitely outside, for Annie's swollen cheeks and eyes glistened wetly – tears, rain? Myrtle did not know which. Annie tugged at her sleeve. She told Myrtle, with a pathetic attempt at light-heartedness, that her plan is to have one more attempt at seducing the elusive Archie. Myrtle thought nothing of this declaration at the time: a mere passing guess that Annie's determination would achieve her desire in the end. Certainly there was no reason to think that was a courageous or defiant remark. But now, almost two decades after the moment has passed, Myrtle sees the bravado of it, and the fury against Annie, that has been uncoiling itself since Martin's story, begins to ebb. She remembers instead all Annie has been to her since they were children: the exuberant leader, the encourager, the one so generous in her small acts of unpremeditated kindness – the joker. Their friendship has often astonished others – no one can understand its fine balance. But the point is they understand it – Myrtle the rock, Annie the spark. The pattern is rarely upset, it suits them both. And perhaps, Myrtle thinks, deceit of a certain kind among friends is a form of self-preservation. Small betrayals must be forgiven. She is calmed by the thought. She knows that an act that would break them for ever is unimaginable, and that in the end her love for Annie will overcome everything.

When Archie returns the following evening Myrtle can tell at once that he is in good spirits. The signs are in his movements rather than in his expression. A slow, ponderous tread is his normal gait – it becomes even slower if he is anxious. But happiness, or relief, spur him a little faster. The indications, this evening, are clear: he slaps down two hunks of fish on the table rather than bothering to find the usual tin plate that raw fish is kept upon. He throws his damp jersey at Myrtle rather than hanging it over the back of his chair.

'What's all this, Archie?'

Archie smiles. The taut solemnity of his face is broken up into unaccustomed lines and dips and puckerings round eyes and mouth.

'Here, wifey,' he says. She goes to him.

'I thought of you through your storm yesterday afternoon. Wish to God I'd been here.' Archie laughs and Myrtle privately rejoices: she never likes to ask Archie whether he thinks of her at sea. She can taste salt on his lips. His rough jowls scratch her cheeks. His hands are on her breasts, covering them. Myrtle feels strong. The traumatic journeys of the night may have acted like depth charges upon her soul, but her body is impatient. Eager.

'Let's not eat for a while,' Archie says.

They go to the bedroom, lie on the bed in their clothes. Archie, as always on returning, smells powerfully of sweat and fish and cold salt water. Myrtle smiles to herself: storms have always been an aphrodisiac to Archie. She can remember a jumble of nights with thunder crashing overhead while the two of them have risen and fallen like wind-lashed waves in this bed. Archie puts out her smile by clamping his mouth to hers. Sometimes he is not gentle, and on those occasions Myrtle is glad of her size. She takes one of his hands, guides it to her neck. His salt-stiff fingers pull at the small buttons. Clumsy in his impatience, it takes a long time to undo them. Myrtle, engaged in other overtures, does not help him. She likes his urgency, the way that the heavy solidity of his body seems to lighten in its quivering. She likes the way he begins tunelessly to hum, or moan. The noise reminds her of wind in sails, the calls of dolphins and the depths of the sea.

But it is not in bed that Archie will tell Myrtle what has caused him gladness beneath the storm-induced desire. Myrtle knows she must not ask. He will tell her in his own good time. Or will he? For a moment, pulling on her skirt again, pushing back her enlivened hair,

Myrtle wonders whether Archie, too, keeps things from her . . . She knows she must dismiss such absurd thoughts, but since last night it will not be easy.

After supper Archie says he is going down to the boat to fetch his large torch. He wants to inspect the roof of the house, fearing the storm may have dislodged some weak slates. Myrtle says she will go with him.

She takes his arm. His smell, now, is of carbolic soap and the clean cotton of his shirt. Myrtle feels that curious combination of melting weakness and newly lighted strength that comes from perfect love-making. This, perhaps, she thinks, is the meaning of being at one with someone: a transitory feeling, but so long as it keeps recurring, then there is little to worry about. They make their way, in step, down to the harbour. There are lights in some windows, but it's still not quite dark.

'How's Annie?' Archie asks out of habitual politeness every time he comes home.

'She's fine.' Myrtle's response is automatic. She knows Archie's feelings about Annie, has no intention of boring him with her news. This is a calculated reason for keeping the matter of Annie private, she quickly thinks in her newly alert-to-secrets way. It is simply to protect him from things that he would find of no interest.

'She's not going to be so pleased with Ken, this evening. He made me a promise. We thrashed it all out – went over it all for hours one night. Finished up shaking hands on it. No more of his bloody stupid "deliveries". He's going to sell his van. Live on his fishing wages like the rest of us.'

'That's all good,' says Myrtle.

'I've told him. If he's off again, driving himself to the useless mate he's become – that's it. He's out of the boat. None of that'll please Annie, I reckon. It'll mean less microwaves, less expensive rubbish.'

'She's got a new job,' says Myrtle. 'Waitress up at the museum café. That should make up a little –'

'That won't last long if the others are anything to go by.' Archie cannot resist a trace of scorn in his laugh.

'Who knows? Maybe she's found the right thing this time. She thinks she's going to meet a lot of dynamic folk up there.'

'Another of her illusions.'

A feeble moon struggles for recognition among passing clouds. The clouds are reflected smearily in the dark, high water of the harbour, crowded with sea-battered boats of coarse and thickset build. Myrtle and Archie stand looking down at the scarcely visible deck of *Skyline II*. The particular set of its funnel and bulge of its bows are so familiar that even Myrtle feels she could instantly recognise it in a crowd of a hundred similar boats. She feels the kind of affection for it that is inspired by inanimate objects whose function is to provide and to protect.

Archie lowers himself down the iron ladder cut into the harbour wall, jumps on to the deck. Myrtle can hardly see him. She can hear thuds as he tramps about (sated, his movements have slowed down again) pushing coils of rope, and boxes, out of his way. Then suddenly there is a whiplash of light scouring the boat. For infinitesimal moments Myrtle catches sight of a dozen objects that are part of Archie's life – line, nets, empty crates – and seeing him among them, trapped in the picture made by the torchlight, she feels as close to him as she did just an hour ago in bed.

It is cold by now. Myrtle folds her arms under her breasts and draws her mother's old shawl more tightly round her. Patiently she waits. At last the skipper's face appears over the wall, and she cries out with wordless delight, as if he had been away for a long time. She takes his arm again. With his free hand Archie drags the light of the torch across the harbour water. The tricks of shadows, finely edged in the foreground, fade in the distance. There is no dividing line between the boats' sides and the water they rest on: solid black sea-shadow indicates depths that always make Myrtle shiver, and thank God she is on dry land. She has always been apprehensive of empty boats – *that* was something she once confessed to Annie, who had not been interested. There is a ghostliness about them that perturbs her. Tonight, their stillness on the flat water, their creaks in the silence, their cargoes of machinery and nets etiolated by moonlight and torchlight, make them a spectral fleet which Myrtle would not have had the courage to stand close to on her own. But with Archie beside her she feels courageous, safe. She can smile at her own foolishness.

'How about going for a drink?' Archie asks. 'Would you like that?'

The invitation is so unusual that Myrtle has to pause before answering that she would love a small whisky. She is cold by now. The thought of the warmth and noise of the pub is appealing, though normally she has no desire ever to join a crowd in a public place.

'Very well, then. A wee drink it shall be. Tomorrow we must up to the cemetery, you remember.'

'The cemetery?'

'Dad.'

'Och, aye. Ben . . .' She hopes she does not sound as if she has forgotten the anniversary of Ben's death. How many years is it? Myrtle cannot remember and does not like to ask. A long time. But a long time gone so fast.

Ben Duns died of cancer in a hospital in St Andrews. It was the same hospital in which his wife had died of the same illness ten years before. Her fortune was that the end had been swift – a matter of weeks after the tumours were found. Ben's own death had been a slow and appalling process observed by Archie, in his early twenties, with increasing horror and desolation. For as long as possible Ben stayed at home, looked after by Archie and the district nurse. His bed was dragged to the window so that he could see the harbour, watch the boats come and go. His loyal crew, who had all been together many years, visited his bedside each time they came ashore and reported on catches, weather, problems. Their fading skipper gave his orders as if he was still on board. 'Clear up that bundle of nets, Billy,' he would say, and his look defied any of them to observe they were sitting in his bedroom. They assured him that all on board was shipshape.

Ben was transferred to hospital for the last month of his life. Archie, who scarcely left his side, watched the encrustations gather over his father's face, chest, arms – the rest were hidden by the sheet – and tried to answer the constant question: 'Why can't this dying business be hurried along?' Then one October morning, sun bright on the hospital sheet and hideous skin, Ben pulled himself up on the pillows with a rare show of strength and declared it would be a good day at sea. He'd be down at the harbour in a moment, he said. He patted Archie's hand, told him to be a good skipper, then closed his eyes and died.

To outward appearances the only sign of Archie's devastation was a harder setting of the solemn expression, a feeling of greater distance, detachment. Only to a very few did he reveal the profound sense of loss and despair he was determined to conceal. At first, he occupied himself with reorganising the boat, replacing old members of the crew who wished to retire, now Ben was gone, with younger ones. He arranged longer trips than usual to sea – the new young crew, all unmarried and keen to make money – did not seem to mind. On his return home he would find bunches of flowers and kindly notes from girls he had briefly fancied at school. Whereas their teenage offers had been flirtatious, they were now of a more practical nature. How can I help? Let me do your washing. I'll send you over a pie, just needs warming up.

Archie was touched by such kindness, and accepted food pressed upon him, but never requested help. And after some months, instead of passing most of his shore leave in his house – where Ben's things lay untouched – he began to pass the days in the Stewarts' house. Dot and Ben, after the deaths of their respective spouses, had become great friends. Ben had been almost a father replacement to Myrtle, just as Dot had mothered Archie after Sarah Duns had died. So it was in Dot's kitchen he felt most comfortable, eating her copious meals, listening to her familiar stories of disasters at sea. He was used to Myrtle's silent ways, her diffident smile, her care not to intrude. Archie had been one of the few boys at school who had not joined in the teasing. Armed with gratitude for this long after they left school, Myrtle regarded him with the affection of a sister. She often wondered where he would find a girl fit to be his wife. Safe in the knowledge there was no possibility of Archie ever regarding her as anything other than a loyal friend, she was able to act towards him with an openness, a lack of awkwardness, that eluded her in the company of other young men. In the period after Ben's death when Archie frequently began to come round, while her mother did the chattering, Myrtle's assuaging of Archie's grief came in the unconscious form of a warm and sensitive presence, always ready to fall in with his wish for a game of cards or a walk in the fields behind the village.

One day, some three months after Ben's death, Dot gave the command that Archie should go through his father's things – throw out the rubbish, take the clothes to a charity shop, generally reorganise a new life in the small house. Archie indicated his reluctance to such a job, but there was no disobeying Dot. 'Go on with you,' she said, 'it's got to be done sometime. Myrtle here will help you.'

The house, untouched by a woman's hand for the last decade, was a sad shambles. In the stuffy air there was a smell of dust and salt, and damp clothes that had dried to an alien crispness over a string line in the kitchen. Archie's efforts at domesticity were not impressive. Myrtle found a surge of unwashed cutlery and pans; opened tins, half full of mildewed beans and soup, crowded the table. It was no wonder he spent so much time under the Stewart roof, was her sympathetic thought.

'It's not usually this bad,' he apologised. 'Just lately it's all got rather out of hand, being at sea so much . . . Let's get the worst over first.'

He led her up the short flight of steep, narrow stairs – carpet worn to its strings – to Ben's bedroom. This had plainly not been visited since the day Ben was taken by ambulance to hospital: sweat-stained sheets pulled back into a violent twist of coarse cotton; thick dressing gown abandoned like a shot-down body on the floor; a hairbrush in which a bramble of grey hairs was woven through the greasy, greenish bristles. And over everything a mildewed look of dust.

'Oh, God,' said Archie, hand to his nose.

A smell of impending death had been trapped and horribly preserved in the airless room.

'Open the window,' said Myrtle.

Archie struggled with the small casement. Fresh sea air gushed in, cutting through the stale-death stench within, but not extinguishing it. Myrtle made her way to the small cupboard, pulled open the thin little door. The short rail was by no means fully occupied by Archie's parents' clothes. There was Ben's Sunday suit, a brown pinstripe. The stripes were worn and smudged round the back of the collar, where two grey hairs clung and moved like ghostly tendrils. Two pairs of stiff, sea-stained heavy jeans, and a light jacket, also badly marked. Pushed to one side, its sense of isolation almost alive, was a dress of drooping crushed velvet, the blue-pink of old gums. Circles a deeper pink of long-dead sweat were dotted like beading under the arms. A moth wavered out from its skirt and flew towards the window. Archie turned, saw the clothes.

'Oh God,' he said again, 'Mother's wedding dress. Da would never throw it away.'

He took a step backwards, sat heavily on the bed. He held out his hands, one on top of the other, fingers pressed together as if he was about to receive a communion wafer. Then slowly his head descended into the shaking receptacle of his own hands, and he began to sob. At first it was quite silent as his body swayed back and forth. Tears thick as blood fanned out from his closed eyes and fell over his fingers on to his knees. Then he began to moan, a deep, pitiful noise that reminded Myrtle of a sea cave she had once dared enter as a child, where strange echoes lobbed between the rocky walls.

She had never seen a man cry before, and was alarmed. It occurred to her she should run and fetch Dot, who would know what to do. Then she saw that she should not leave Archie in his wretchedness. Bereft of comforting words, at least she should just be there.

She sat on the bed beside him. After a while she put a hand on Archie's heaving shoulder. The strong, acrid smell of his sweat added to the other pungent smells in the room. Sometimes a puff of wind through the open wind would shift them a little, then they would congregate again, claustrophobic.

Myrtle had no idea for how long the two of them sat there. A couple of hours, perhaps. Eventually, the sobbing lost its strength.

Finally drained of tears, Archie took up a clump of the dirty sheet and wiped his face, fiercely scrubbing at his eyes. Myrtle removed her hand. He threw back the bit of mangled sheet, stood up.

'Sorry,' he said. 'That hasn't happened before. Won't happen again. Thanks for being here.' He picked up a plastic rubbish bag, shook it open. 'I'll hold it. You shove in the clothes.'

'No,' said Myrtle, rising too and taking the bag from him, 'we'll not do that. It's a job best done by Ma and me. We'll do the whole house for you next week when you're at sea. We've plenty of time. We're good at that sort of thing.'

Archie shrugged, attempted a smile with his bloodshot eyes. He had no energy to protest. Myrtle smiled strongly back.

'You'll come back to find everything sparkling,' she said. 'Ma and I will enjoy that. Let's go now. There's a stew for dinner. You must be hungry.'

Archie followed her downstairs. A pink envelope lay on the doormat. Myrtle picked it up: Annie's ill-formed writing. Whatever? She handed it to Archie.

Archie evidently did not recognise the writing. Exhausted, he opened it without interest. He read the single page quickly to himself, then handed it to Myrtle.

Dear Archie, she read, *I'm sorry I'm such a long time in writing but I thought you must have so many letters all at once. Just to say how sorry I am about your dad. He was a good man with not an enemy in the world, wasn't he? I will never forget when he chose me to be Fisher Lass on his boat and told me that as skipper it was his duty to pay for my dress. I asked him how much that should be, and he said you go ahead lass and spend whatever is necessary. I thought that was very nice of him, very generous. Do hope by now you are not still too much down in the dumps. Love for now, Annie.*

'Good of your friend,' said Archie.

What was Annie up to? wondered Myrtle. What was her idea? She had threatened one last assault on Archie some time ago, but the plan had to be postponed because of Ben's death. Myrtle chided herself for such uncharitable thoughts: Annie was merely showing her sympathy, like everyone else in the village. It was a friendly letter, unlikely to be part of some grand scheme. It meant nothing to Archie. Myrtle imagined his horror and amazement should he have any idea that Annie still had intentions towards him. As teenagers he had rejected her overtures so many times, distanced himself. Only in the last few years had he become a little more unbending, talking to her occasionally, innocently thinking that her youthful fancy was over. These brief encounters, Annie reported to Myrtle, had given her hope. Myrtle had tried to tell her it would be better to forget any such hope, but Annie was stubborn in her anticipation and could not believe otherwise.

Archie threw away the letter. He and Myrtle returned to the Stewart house for Dot's long-simmered stew. Myrtle was aware of a disturbing unease. She knew it was nothing to do with having been witness to Archie's exploding grief: that was an occasion she would keep to herself for ever. As they sat at the table, Dot busying about with hot bread from the oven and homemade barley water, she was also aware of the warmth of the thought of rescuing Archie's house from its present depressing state. She was not, like her mother, a natural lover of cleaning and polishing. But to have Archie's house all ready for him when he next got back from fishing . . . to surprise him with fresh air and tidiness and order, Ben's old clothes magically all gone – now there was a secret, strangely exciting thought. She was aware of the calmness of her surface: *Come along, Myrtle lass, eat up. I will, Ma, I will. I'm just not very hungry.* Beneath the non-reflecting glass of her normal appearance, a curious excitement simmered, a new feeling she could not put a name to at the time.

She and Dot worked hard on Archie's house. He returned from the next fishing trip to find it transformed into a welcoming place, clean and shining and full of fresh air. Myrtle had put a jug of cornflowers on the kitchen table and bought a new linen dishcloth (which he did not notice) illustrated with pictures of fishing boats, some similar to Archie's *Skyline II*, the boat with which Archie had replaced *The Skyline* some years after Jock's death. Archie's delight, though apparent, did not inspire him to unusual rhetoric. He merely said the place hadn't looked or smelt so good since his mother was alive, and he thanked them. His pleasure was evident in his absence, after that, from the Stewart house. He still paid visits, was asked to meals, did small jobs for Dot round the house, but he spent far more time at home now that the place was no longer alien. Alone, Myrtle imagined.

She found herself more carefully observing Annie than usual. Annie's moods fluctuated, as they always had: she seemed restless, more prone to melancholy which she could not explain. She was irritated by Myrtle's part-time job (coaching children to read for several hours a week, payment a tin of shortbread or sometimes a pound) while she herself was unemployed. Seeing her friend's plight, Myrtle suggested they should take a short holiday together – neither of them had ever been far from home. They spent a few days in the Shetland Isles, one fine spring. Myrtle persuaded Annie to walk with her over the treeless hills for the best part of most days. Once they took a boat to one of the smaller islands and spent the day listening to the clatter of a million birds which soared in huge arches over their heads, darkened the sky for a moment, then broke up like a million pieces of tumbling masonry. Annie, despite herself, seemed to be enjoying the enforced dose of nature. She visibly cheered. They talked idly of mutual friends, though Archie was not mentioned except when Annie, with unusual generosity, praised Myrtle and Dot for all their good work on his house. She did mention, on the only afternoon heavy rain blighted their walk through the heather, that she thought her best plan would be to marry soon. *Though God knows where I'll find a good man in our neighbourhood, Myrtle.* Myrtle replied with feeling that there were plenty of good men: Annie would do better to put her mind to some form of employment. She said this so sharply that it had effect: on the long train journey Annie made no further reference to her matrimonial hopes, but did say she would apply for the job in the post office as soon as they got back.

Annie took the job, and bided her time. For a while she went out with a fisherman from Aberdeen. But his erratic visits and the closeness of his eyes did not suit her. He was given his marching orders after six weeks, an event which Annie recounted with much glee.

Once this luckless character had been made to understand he was no longer required in her life (a bucket of water over his head had been Annie's final desperate gesture to underline the seriousness of her meaning) she was manless and restless again. Her past boyfriends – Ross, Sandy, Hamish – were marrying girls from their old class. Archie, on the few occasions she saw him, in the street or in the post office, looked more cheerful. Time, Annie told Myrtle, to have one last lighthearted attempt. Nothing serious, she assured her. *You know I'd never think of marrying a serious man like Archie, don't you? Archie will end up marrying some serious woman just like him, and they'll be happy ever after*. She laughed her scoffing laugh, and Myrtle felt so sick she put her hand to her mouth and turned away. It was just four months after Ben died, and a winter of particularly vicious cold.

A week or so after Annie's announcement Myrtle went to the post office early one morning for stamps. Annie was behind the counter. She wore angora mittens. The sight of them brought vividly to Myrtle's mind those cold mornings of their childhood walking to school, the soft furriness of Annie's small hand in Myrtle's large one. The thought made her smile. But she received a freezing look in return.

'Didn't work, did it?' she said. 'Silly bugger. Doesn't know what he's missed. We could have had some fun, but he's too bloody serious.'

'It was a bit soon after Ben's dying,' ventured Myrtle. There was such a leaping of relief, such a gladness of heart within her that she had to control her words very carefully.

'You can't mourn for ever. Life's got to go on. I'll tell you all about it one day. It was quite funny, quite amusing, I'll say that.'

Later that day Archie came round for tea before returning to the boat for a long trip. He was his usual quiet self: hung a picture for Dot, asked Myrtle if she would keep an eye on the flowers on his parents' grave. He liked it always to have fresh flowers. No mention of Annie. From his behaviour, it would have been impossible to guess anything untoward had taken place. The only unusual thing was that he asked Myrtle if she would like to walk down to the boat with him: she could carry the tin with Dot's cake while he managed other supplies.

It was an icy, black night, frost already fuzzing the edges of stone walls. Archie was to sleep on board: departure was at dawn next morning. A punctilious skipper, he always arrived first at the boat and took the stuff on board. Then he climbed back on to the harbour wall to tell Myrtle to hurry home. He didn't want her to catch cold, he said, and patted her arm with a distracted little frown. Myrtle obeyed him, much though she wanted to linger for a few moments. On her fast walk back through the streets she wondered if her imagination was playing cruel tricks, but did not allow herself to think too far in that direction.

For some time after Annie delivered her letter to Archie, Myrtle could not help wondering if she then took any further steps to carry out her plan of seduction. There was no evidence of any progress, and Myrtle asked no questions. She did not want to risk anything to do with Archie coming between them, and after a while she put the whole matter from her mind.

It was not till some years after she and Archie were married that she learnt the full story. Archie had been up in the woods collecting kindling for the fire. The place reminded him, he said, of the whole silly incident with Annie which had completely gone from his mind until his return, by chance, to a particular bit of the wood. Myrtle believed him. By now Myrtle felt secure enough to hear whatever had taken place. As Archie recounted the tale her overwhelming feeling was one of puzzlement, sadness, that Annie had chosen not to tell Myrtle the story herself.

Archie had had a feeling, he said, that for some time after she had written the pink letter, Annie had been following him, spying on him in a mild way. Several times she turned up at the same place as him, too often to believe it was coincidence. On the first occasion, at the baker, he had thanked her for her letter and they exchanged a few words. On subsequent occasions they didn't speak, merely nodded agreeably. Then came the winter evening Archie had gone for a walk in the fields with his gun, thinking he might pot a rabbit for supper. Or to give it to Dot to deal with, he said. In fact the fading light made shooting impossible. But Archie, needing to stretch his legs after a week at sea, wandered on, further than he meant, into the woods. He liked to listen to the roosting pigeons.

He had not gone far along the path when he heard a crackling of twigs and someone calling his name – Annie, it was. Her voice friendly. Archie turned. Annie stood some yards behind him, an innocent-looking Red Riding Hood figure if ever there was one, he told Myrtle, in some sort of knitted cape with a hood. Black with flecks of white in it so it looked as if she had been walking in snow. In fact the only thought in Archie's mind at that moment – nothing had alerted his suspicions, although in Annie's presence he was always on his guard – was that perhaps it had started to snow, but they were protected here in the woods. It was cold enough.

Annie carried a bundle of hastily gathered twigs under one arm. Having observed that it was funny to run into Archie here, of all places, she explained that she was gathering firewood for their neighbour, an old man with arthritis unable to get out. The explanation was rather too long and elaborate. There were details about the neighbour's recent fall and general misfortune. (Archie felt a warning buzz down his spine. There was something odd here, he thought: the firewood story was very unlikely. Annie was not a known walker. From harbour to pub to home was as far as she ever went. Had anyone in the village heard she was off on a winter's evening to gather kindling in a wood half a mile away, they would have been very surprised.

Annie chattered on, impervious to his silence: the sudden cold, the pity he hadn't got a rabbit, her slight fear of woods, her relief when she had seen a familiar figure ahead of her. When her bright little remarks ran out, she suddenly pushed past Archie on the path, and made her way ahead of him, calling out that she was going back to the road through the other side of the wood, and it had been nice seeing him. In a moment she was out of sight round a bend of the path. The light was very poor by now.

Archie remained where he was, wondering what to do. He could not help feeling that the enjoyment of the evening had been spoiled by Annie's unexpected presence. There was also the uneasy thought that the meeting had been arranged by devious means. The idea of Annie spying on him, tracking him down, was disagreeable. On the other hand – Archie's foremost thought – it was not safe for a young girl to be alone in these woods on a dark evening. He had better make sure she was all right.

Gun hitched over his shoulder, eyes on the murky distance, Archie carried on down the path. He walked quickly, expecting to see Annie after a hundred yards or so. But no sign. He stopped, listened. From behind a tangle of bushes on his right, he heard laughter. His name was called again. Annie urged him to join her in a little clearing she had found. Had he got a match? she shouted. She rather fancied putting a light to her bundle of sticks. Having a bonfire.

Annoyed, Archie made his way round the clump of brambles into the clearing. It was divided by the trunk of a fallen tree, long dead, its roots a giant scraggy fist raised in the air at one end. Annie was sitting on her cape which she had laid across the trunk. She was swinging her legs against it, banging the sodden bark with her heels, childlike. Her wood was scattered on the ground: it had never been a very serious bundle. Annie grinned up at Archie, laughed at what she called his solemn face.

At this moment in his story Archie paused to try to impress upon Myrtle the sudden strangeness of light – or, rather, the dusk – which confused him. On the path it had been a normal winter gloaming, brownish among the bushes and trees. But there in the small clearing, the density was a surprising blue-white, like sea mist. The close trunks of the trees had turned the dull navy of gaberdine. It was these dreamlike, dull-grained blues, he tried hard to explain to Myrtle, that unnerved him, made him unsure what to do. Most disorienting of all was the fact that Annie had thrown off her cape. Beneath it she wore a cardigan the exact blue of her eyes. It was made of soft, fuzzy wool, done up to the neck with a line of small pearl buttons.

They stood looking at each other through all the dark blue. The wood pigeons had begun to purr. The occasional flutter in high branches was the only sound. Eventually, as if to make some gesture to free himself, Archie put down his gun. He asked Annie if she wasn't cold. She replied she never felt the cold. The only thing she felt was romantic.

Even as she said this, head tilted, eyes fluttering as they had a thousand times at a dozen boys, one hand ran up the line of buttons, pulling them apart. The two sides of the garment were thrown open – the efficiency of the gesture added shock to the confusion of other feelings rampaging through Archie – and was flung to the ground. Archie's eyes followed the progress of its silent wings till it landed. He then looked slowly, reluctantly, up to Annie's feet. She was still banging her heels against the tree. Finally, inexorably, his reluctant eyes climbed further, rested on the bare breasts. *There*, said Annie.

At twenty-three, this was Archie's first view of naked breasts. He had not had much experience, physically, with girls. To date his knowledge of their bodies had been confined to their curious, soft rises and slopes explored under cover of darkness. He had never encountered a girl so bold as to sit before him, naked. Trust Annie to have no such inhibitions . . . In the indigo gloom the outlines of her breasts were hazy, but clear enough to make Archie feel a shortness of breath. There was a noise like loud water in his ears. He sensed his hands stirring – desperate, for an appalling second, to cover the skin which must surely be icy cold. In the nightmare of the moment, he told Myrtle (anxious to furnish her with the most trivial details of the story), the phrase *marble breasts* came to him from some dimly remembered text at school. He had never known what it meant. Now, he did: these were marble breasts, all right: not a vein in sight, the nipples no more than the faintest smudge on skin the blue-white of skimmed milk. He clenched his fists and kept them firmly at his sides, smiling at the thoughts. Foolish, that. Annie took his smile for encouragement. She wriggled her shoulders. The milky, ethereal shape of her, which every second was becoming harder to focus upon, moved gently in invitation. *I'm here for you, Archie*, she cooed – yes, *cooed*, he snarled, at this bit of the story. Took it into her stupid head to imitate the wood pigeons – as if that would make any difference.

It was her voice, the pathetic little phrase attached to her offering, that broke the spell. Archie's previous turmoil of feelings, which he was too ashamed to name, was replaced with embarrassment, anger. He shouted at her to put on her clothes, come to her senses. He didn't want her – he never had wanted her and never would want her. Surely she had understood that when they were teenagers? And now, he ranted on, if she didn't make herself scarce for ever, she'd be sorry. She was nothing more than the village slag – used by everybody, loved by no one, and serve her right for her years of revolting behaviour. Yes, she was beautiful, but she was an unfeeling bitch not worthy of a good man, so if she had any plans for future happiness she had better change her ways. Yes, he went too far. He put things more fiercely than he meant to – spurred by guilt, perhaps, for having briefly contemplated an ignoble act.

By now it was completely dark. Annie was no more than a pale smear, her vague shape suggesting she had moved into a hunched position, head on raised knees. Archie could hear her sobbing and was unmoved. He knew that the smallest word or gesture of compassion would be misconstrued. He left her to her misery in the cold night, stumbled clumsily back through the thicket to regain the path. When he reached the edge of the wood, still far from calm, he fired his gun into the air. He had no care for the alarm this would cause the wretched Annie. He wanted only that she should know that the gunshot was the end of the matter, an evening for both of them that should be forgotten with all speed. After that, Annie avoided Archie cunningly as she had previously stalked him. They did not speak again for many months.

It's the last afternoon of this shore leave. Though neither has found it necessary to mention the fact, both Archie and Myrtle have had a particularly good time. Some shore leaves are too cluttered with jobs in the house or meetings with the bank manager or the FMA – general administration – for any real peace or pleasure. This time, unexpectedly, there has been little to do but enjoy themselves. The four days have flown.

Archie is down at the boat. Myrtle is not expecting him back for a couple of hours. She is aware that the pleasure of the last few days has softened her edges. She feels sleepy, although she is not tired. She drifts about the kitchen, moves pieces of china on the shelves that don't need moving but there is nothing of real importance to do while she waits for the bread in the oven she has baked for Archie's tea. Once he has gone she will return to her normal, faster pace. Resume her usual efficiency. But for the moment she is enjoying her dreamlike state, the infusion of pleasure that makes the solid things of every day to dance.

There is a knock on the door. A visitor will break the spell Myrtle wants to last, a warm, protective covering, till Archie leaves. Her shout to come in is reluctant. She guesses it's Annie – they haven't spoken since the storm – and composes her face.

Ken comes into the room. He is agitated, she can see at once. He keeps rubbing a hand over his mouth and jaws as if with an invisible towel. Myrtle tells him to sit. Unknowingly, he sits in Archie's chair at the table. Automatically Myrtle puts the kettle on to boil.

'Annie wants a car,' he says.

'What?'

'A *car* – can you believe? She's off her head. How can we afford a car?'

'She's not mentioned it to me.'

'It just came to her last night, late. We were arguing about something quite different. Then all of a sudden, this ranting about a car. Says she's stuck here, a prisoner. Can't get out. She's at the mercy of public transport, she says. Buses out of the village are hopeless. What she wants is to get in a car and drive about when she feels like it. Drive about where? I took the liberty of asking. Besides, I said, you only drove for a few months after your test. You're not an experienced driver, Annie, I said. I'd not like to think of you alone on the roads.'

Ken sighs, pushes his thin, highly strung fingers through his hair.

'Perhaps the novelty's worn off the microwave and she has to have something new to aim for. You know our Annie.' Myrtle hands him a mug of tea.

'I do,' says Ken. He sounds rueful. 'I expect Archie's told you,' he goes on, 'of our agreement. We shook hands on it Friday night. It's a relief, I can tell you. I mean, I'm not a man to enter willingly into the black economy. Apart from anything else the lack of sleep, working nights when I come home, is taking its toll. But Annie . . . I only did it for Annie. She wanted so many things I couldn't afford to buy otherwise – things for the bairn and herself. I like to please her. I like to keep her happy. I mean, it's a rough life for you wives, us away so much, the worry, the small bits of time together that are never enough.'

'But Annie must be pleased you and Archie have sorted things out, put it behind you. She can't have been happy in her bones, knowing her husband was heading for a breakdown, putting in all those hours. She must have seen you couldn't keep it up much longer, something bad would happen.'

Ken shrugs.

'To be honest, I'm not sure she was all that bothered.'

'Oh, I'm sure she was.'

'You're a good friend to Annie, Myrtle. Don't know what she'd do without you. She relies on you for so many reasons. But I sometimes wonder what the hell you get from her in return. I used to wonder that even when we were at school. You'd follow her around – very quiet, you were – supporting her at every turn, helping her with her homework, giving her good advice about how to handle all the boys – and what did you get out of it? Bugger me if I could see.'

'I got a lot,' says Myrtle, a defensive look hardening her eyes. 'I loved Annie when I was a very small child, and I've loved her ever since, no matter what. Beneath all the nonsense there's a good heart, and a special way with her that's hard to describe. She's impatient with people, dismissive. She sometimes judges too quickly. But, my good-ness, when she's concentrating on you she makes you feel on top of the world. She gives you a kind of hope . . . I'm not putting this well, but there's nothing I'd not do for Annie.'

'I know what you mean,' says Ken. 'It's that mostly unseen bit I fell in love with when she was a girl.' He pauses. 'You remember the very day . . . Well, you were there. I told you. I had to tell someone. Couldn't keep it to myself. You were very understanding, far as I remember.'

While he speaks Myrtle remembers his face on the beach at St Andrews: soft with youth but contorted by his sudden confusion, the dark eyes almost black with yearning. The image melts into one a few years later, the night of the Fisher Lass ball, when some dull old hope had settled into his longer, harder, thinner face. She looks at him with the complete dispassion of one whose feelings have once been engaged, but are now totally severed. She is filled with the kind of wonder that comes in such situations. How *could* she ever have been so drawn, even for a short time, to the difficult, clever but bloodless Ken? How could she ever have thought that it was some form of love? She remembers the agony of humiliation, the feeling of having been betrayed by Ken when Annie had told her, on that sunny picnic, how the night of the Fisher Lass had ended. She smiles to herself at the thoughts of youthful innocence, and senses the gush of strength that comes from feeling *nothing*, now, for the man opposite her who had once caused her so much anguish.

There is a silence. Myrtle assumes Ken is remembering the day itself: his triumph and rejection, the one following cruelly after the other on the cold beach. Did he ever know, Myrtle wonders, the despair similar to his own that he caused her that night?

'How can I help you?' she asks at last.

'I thought you might persuade her, if she says anything to you, that it's a bloody silly thing to want, a car. Make her see sense. She knows we can't afford it. She knows I don't want any more hire purchase payments hanging over me . . . It's one of her madder ideas.' He finishes his tea, stands up: a thin, hunched figure with arm muscles lean as leather straps. Archie says he's stronger than you'd expect. And not clumsy, like some of the mates. He can untangle nets faster than any man on board and works fast and well at whatever job is at hand. It's only since he's been doing his deliveries that he's become inefficient, made mistakes in his tiredness. Not two weeks ago Archie reported Ken had misread the radar system and taken them miles out of their way. Archie had blasted him: such miscalculations cost precious time and money. Ken had apologised, admitted he'd not been concentrating. Myrtle sensed such tensions between Ken and Archie were increasing. All the same, she knew Archie would hate ever to lose Ken from his crew.

'I'll do what I can if she mentions any car nonsense to me,' says Myrtle. 'Try to avert her mind to something cheaper.'

They both smile: recognition of their mutual love for Annie, and understanding of her singular ways. Then Ken makes his way to the door.

'Have you seen anything of Janice, of late?' he asks. His back is to her, so Myrtle cannot see his face.

'I was with her during the storm. She doesn't like storms. But she was fine. She's a bonnie lass, growing up fast –'

'Where was Annie?'

'Her first day at the museum. She was held up.'

Ken nods.

'Well, thanks. Nice talking to you. Keep an eye on both mother and daughter, if you would.'

Myrtle, standing by him at the open door, sees a quick, grateful smile, but the anxiety still there.

'Of course. I'll do what I can. Maybe now all this . . . business is over we can all four of us get together again. We haven't done that for a long time.'

'Maybe,' says Ken.

When he has gone Myrtle takes the bread out of the oven. It is a little burnt on top. She curses herself for leaving it too long, holds it like a brick between her hands, feeling its heat through the oven gloves. The smell of new bread Ken would never find in his own kitchen, she reflects, but that is not something he would mind about. She continues to think of him. His anxiety has rubbed off on her. It's evident all is not well between him and Annie, as Annie recently hinted. For Ken himself to come to Myrtle signifies a possible seriousness Myrtle has not previously guessed at. She catches her breath, saddened. Fearing to imagine what might happen, her mind takes refuge in the past. She remembers a cold afternoon, here in the kitchen, a week or so after Annie had announced – but given no details – that her assault on Archie had gone wrong. They were eating a plate of Dot's scones, Myrtle remembers. Annie piled hers high with home-made raspberry jam.

'You'll never guess what I'm doing tonight, Myrt,' she said.

'No,' agreed Myrtle. Her friend could scarcely keep still in her chair. She was wriggling about, good-humoured, licking up jam from the plate with her finger. Her pleasure seemed to be more childlike than the grown-up anticipation of some romantic assignation.

'I'm going for a drink with Ken.'

'*Ken?*'

'Well, he asked me, didn't he? Why not? I thought. There's not that many that ask me out these days. Ken's an old friend, isn't he? He's kept his word, not bothered me since . . .' She looked down but did not blush. 'How long ago was it, the Fisher Lass dance? So anyway, I said all right, Ken. But no funny business, mind. Well, no one could *fancy* Ken, could they? He didn't seem to mind. Understood. Can I have the last scone?'

'Go ahead,' Myrtle said. The warmth of her own feelings for Archie guarded her against any retrospective jealousy. But having become used to the fact that Annie had no interest whatsoever in Ken, she was not unshaken by an irrational irritation: here was Annie *messing* with a kind and innocent man who remained Myrtle's friend.

'Don't you go causing him any harm,' said Myrtle, lightly.

'Course not.'

'Not that you would on purpose. It's just that Ken's held a candle for you for so long. Suddenly taking his hospitality might make him think there's some hope. Besides, it's hard for a man never to be allowed to lay a finger, especially as there was one occasion in the past.'

Annie sighed, impatient.

'Trust you to take it all so seriously. One drink is all that's on the cards. We may never go out again, according to how he behaves. So you don't need to worry.'

Myrtle remembers their conversation went something like that. The next day Annie reported Ken had borrowed his father's old car and they'd driven to a pub several miles inland. Had a good time, Ken the perfect gentleman, no suggestion of anything else. Hadn't even held hands, hadn't even brushed hands lighting their cigarettes. Top marks, he got, first evening, Annie said. As a reward, she accepted another invitation. From then on, although she still went out with one or two others, who she swore were nothing more than platonic friends, her chaste relationship with Ken continued. There was no hope of that ever changing, she said. But Myrtle, observing Ken, remembers she could not agree.

The men have returned to sea. They went at five this morning. It's late afternoon, almost dark. Myrtle is back from a hard day at the home, too tired to iron Archie's shirts. She plans to sit down with a cup of tea and ring Annie. It's been six days, now, since the storm. Six days since they last spoke. Too long. Out of touch with Annie, albeit due to some silly squabble, makes Myrtle uneasy.

The door opens. Myrtle spins round from the stove, kettle in hand. Annie, who never knocks, stands there smiling.

'Janice is over with a friend for the night,' she says. 'Thought I'd come round. It's a long time since we had a game.'

She takes a box from a paper bag she is holding, puts it down on the table. A new pack of cards. Their backs are decorated with a thistle head set against tartan.

'That's great,' says Myrtle. 'We needed some new ones.'

'I got them from the museum. The gift shop. Staff discount. If there was more I wanted in the gift shop I could save a lot of money.'

'You're enjoying it, then, still?'

'Oh, aye. It's not a bad job. Better than some. I'll stay a while.'

They sit at their usual places at the table, pot of tea between them. Annie pushes the cards over to Myrtle. Their hard new edges warn they could cut her fingers. Their stiffness will take some getting used to – to be honest, Myrtle prefers the soft slappiness of the old cards. But she shifts them about, shuffles them, her big hands cold from the walk home, inaccurate.

'Do you know what happened?' asks Annie. 'I asked Ken for a car.'

'Why ever do you need a car?'

'Freedom. Just to be able to go off at will, when I want to. Not to have to be forever at the mercy of the bloody awful buses.'

'Like a lot of us.' Myrtle pushes the cards towards Annie, watches her delicate fingers deal with them more skilfully.

'I daresay. That doesn't stop me wanting . . .' She pauses. 'Did Archie tell you he and Ken have come to an agreement?'

'He did.'

'They shook hands on it.'

'I'm glad.'

'Me too. Though, mind, all Ken was doing was *deliveries*. Removals and that.' She gives Myrtle a look. 'Seems reasonable to me. The mates are having such a thin time –'

'The skippers have no' done much better –'

'– that it's hard to blame them. The price of children's shoes – not that you'd know about that.'

Myrtle quickly decides to let this pass, despite the anger in her throat.

'Archie knows your reasons, Annie. But the whole business is over, now. Let's not talk about it again.'

'Aye, you're right.' Annie begins to shuffle the cards. Myrtle refills Annie's cup. There is nothing to lose, she decides, in just one attempt to make Annie see reason.

'Do you really want a car?' she asks. 'It's not just the buying price, it's the upkeep that's so expensive. I mean, isn't that pushing Ken a bit far? He gives up the source of income that's paid for the microwave and all your gadgets, and you immediately ask for something way beyond his means. Is that fair?'

Annie sighs.

'Perhaps not. He went away worried, I'll say.' She gives a small laugh. 'I said Ken, we can sell the van now, get a car with the money. He says we'll not get more than a hundred pounds for it if we're lucky. Perhaps I'll shut up about the car for the moment. Suggest a better telly. He could run to that, I daresay . . .'

They begin their game, play in silence for a while. Both rub their fingers round the edges of the cards, unconsciously to speed familiarity with their strange feel.

'Janice is very fond of you,' Annie says after a while. 'You were very good to her the other night.'

'That's all right. You know I love the child.'

'I don't think I said thank you for that. I felt badly when you'd gone.'

'I would have rung you tonight to say –'

'We always get over these silly skirmishes, though, don't we? We can't always agree. You can't expect even the oldest friends not to drive each other potty now and then. It was my fault the other night, Myrt. I know that. You're very patient, very forgiving. I never forget that. Me, I've not been myself lately and you still put up with me.'

'I wouldn't say you've been that much different.' They smile at one another, lay down their cards in fans on the table. 'Shall we have a glass of whisky?'

Annie nods. Myrtle fetches bottle and glasses.

'Nerves about the new job – I mean, nobody could call me a *quali-fied* waitress, Myrt, could they? And Ken being so on edge . . .' They chink their glasses together. 'Archie'd never believe this, would he? The wifey drinking behind his back?' She laughs again, more easily. Her cheeks are pink after the first sip of her drink. 'I've a favour to ask you . . . concerning Janice. She's not doing too brilliantly at school. Well, you know how it is: they don't have the sort of teachers we had. No one to inspire. She's bored out of her mind, doesn't try, gets rotten marks. I was wondering, might you have time to fit her in with a little coaching? I'd pay you . . .'

'Don't be silly. I'd love to help Janice.' The idea instantly appeals. 'But only on condition there's no further stupid talk of money. I'd not take a penny to help young Janice.'

'What would I do without you? You're a brick.' Annie giggles. 'You've been a brick, the best brick ever, all my life, though I could only say that after three sips of this. Come on, your turn to deal. God, we haven't played for too long.'

Warm and flushed on their small but unaccustomed amount of whisky, the two women return to their silent game. For once, thoughts of their men at sea are put aside. They concentrate wholly on the cards, by now more familiar in their hands. The hours, secure, pass magically fast as always. Annie does not stir, and pull on her thick coat, till past midnight. Myrtle, too, puts on her shawl so that she can see Annie down the stone steps.

It's a dark night, moonless. No lights in other houses in the street. Myrtle takes Annie's arm. Annie's hand jerks down the iron rail. They feel their way cautiously down the steps, hunched figures, dark against dark. At the bottom, they hug.

'Fool I am! I forgot, I've brought my torch.' Annie pulls it from her pocket. She swoops its narrow blade of light over sleeping façades.

'Will you be all right, walking back alone?'

'What do you think I am? A helpless woman?' They both laugh, happy. 'You know what? Ken says there'll be snow before Christmas.'

Annie moves away. In a moment she is consumed by darkness. The slanting light of her torch appears to be a ghostly walking stick travelling on its own. With a small shiver Myrtle returns up the steps. There's a hard, dark scent in the black air that often comes before snow – could be Ken is right. Its purity warns that the gravid sky is ready to burst: a smell Myrtle will associate with a particular Christmas for the rest of her life.

That Christmas, almost twenty years ago, the traditions of the Stewart household were the same as always. But there was a reason for the sharpened edges of familiarity: Archie was coming for lunch. The kitchen was fugged up with steam, the smells of warm bread and fresh pastry were almost tangible. At the table Dot was preparing mince pies and chopping up chestnuts – enough food for half a dozen hungry eaters, though Archie was to be the only guest. Myrtle opened the window to clear the air, clear her head. It was then she sniffed the bright crispness of impending snow, and Dot said the clouds would break tomorrow, Christmas Day.

She was right. Archie turned up at one thirty, flakes on his shoulders. It was so dark outside that they lit candles as well as the lamps, and afternoon felt like evening. After they had eaten they exchanged small presents – Archie had bought Myrtle an ivory comb which to this day sits unused on the bedroom chest of drawers – and drank his bottle of red wine, and watched the thickening snow slam silently against the window and pile high on the ledge. Intrigued by the snow, no one wanted to draw the curtains. The tree, with its tiny coloured lights, stood on the window ledge speckling the high ridge of white with dots of red and blue and green. In the warm clutter of the room Dot and Myrtle and Archie played three-handed whist until it was time for the Christmas cake bound in scarlet ribbon, and Myrtle wanted the day never to end. It had been ages since Archie had spent so long a spell in the house, and she dreaded his going.

But he would not stay for supper, left soon after seven. Myrtle stood watching him hunch his way up the street in the densely falling flakes, white figure soon invisible in the greater white that swirled through the darkness. His footsteps were covered in seconds. No traces, Myrtle thought, with a heaviness of heart. He had not said when he would be round again. She wondered how long it would be before they next saw him. That Christmas evening she could not quite hide her sudden melancholy, and was aware of Dot's enquiring looks. After a light supper of vegetable soup, she apologised to Dot and went early to her room. There, she looked at her reflection in the mirror, but from some distance. She combed her hair with the ivory comb for a long time, deep in thought, before she drew the curtains over the window against which a bank of snow now almost reached the top.

She woke next day feeling the hollow rattle of Boxing Day – the emptiness of a day that follows celebrations. She wondered how she would pass the time, and how she would keep from Dot the agitated feelings that made her so restless she could not concentrate on any task for more than a few moments. After a small breakfast she looked out of the window.

'What are you after, I wonder?' Dot could never contain pressing questions.

'I was wondering, the weather . . .'

'Snow's melting.'

It was, too. Melting fast under a bright sun. Shrinking from the edges of the street, edging away from window panes. Myrtle longed to go out, walk. Walk anywhere, very fast. Be far away from Dot, whose silent perception made her uneasy. But she could not leave for fear of questions, surmises. Dot gave her some chore at the table – carrots: scraping, chopping. The morning loomed up like the side of a vast mountain Myrtle had no energy to climb. She picked up a knife, listless. Then there was a bang on the door.

Archie. Such a fine morning, he said. Pity to waste it. Would Myrtle like to stretch her legs? He planned to walk a few miles.

'I'll do the carrots,' said Dot, with the voice of one who had had every intention of doing them all along. 'Don't you bother, child. Put on your warm boots, won't you?'

Myrtle, exasperated by her mother's keenly approving eyes, could not stop herself blushing. She dragged on boots, thick coat, was at once too hot. She and Archie hurried down the steps. The village was deserted, silent except for the wail of a lone gull. They made their way up the wynd that led to the main road. The thaw had destroyed the untrammelled whiteness of yesterday. Roofs were slatted with thinning snow: gutters ran with melting water.

'How many days do you have off?' Myrtle asked. She hoped Archie would not observe the new unease within her.

'We've given ourselves a week or more, depending on the weather.' He took her arm to cross the road, something he had never done before.

They walked along a path beaten hard as rock beside a ploughed field. Dark earth showed through its chipped icing of snow. Sometimes one was ahead of the other, sometimes they were abreast. A thorn hedge protected them from a south-easterly wind and the sky, flax blue, was stripped of cloud.

'The postcards never get it right,' said Myrtle.

'What?'

'The blue.' Myrtle lifted her head, eyes scanning the heavens. She instantly regretted so foolish a remark, but was relieved when Archie laughed.

'You do say the oddest things. Who but you would go on about the precise blue of the sky? You're a very precise woman.'

Myrtle smiled. She still thought of herself as a girl. It would take a moment to become accustomed to *woman*.

'I would have thought fishermen were acutely aware of every shift in the sky, the slightest change in colour,' she said.

'No. It's just fair weather or foul. We're not poets.' Archie had stopped just ahead of her. Turned to look at her. 'What are we doing, talking about the sky?'

Myrtle felt the chill of her own foolishness. Beneath the hugeness of the heavens she would not mention again, she regretted her silly observations. There was an iridescent sliver of sea behind Archie that merged into the distant outline of the Lammemuirs, indeterminate as horizontal smoke. (Another fanciful notion Myrtle would keep to herself.) This was the view that was part of her vision most days of her life, but now its familiarity was blighted by the foreground figure of Archie with his accusing eyes. Backlit as he was, she could not see the humour, and so failed to find comfort.

'Wouldn't it be better if we talked about getting married?' he said.

Myrtle stumbled backwards off the path. She could feel thorns snarling into her coat, tearing at her hands (in her hasty confusion she had forgotten gloves) as she stretched them to support herself.

'Am I to drag you out of the hedge before I get an answer?'

Archie took both her hands, impatiently pulled her back on to the path. Myrtle's immediate thoughts were for the snagged wool at the back of her coat. Whatever would Dot think? Archie was dragging her towards him, smudging the stupid thoughts as he put his arms round her shoulders. Their heads were on a level. He kissed her on both cheeks with an ironic formality that seemed to please him, for there was a smile on his lips. The stubble on his jowls scraped Myrtle's cold skin. So this is a proposal, she thought, looking at herself from a long way off.

'So is it to be aye?'

'Of course, Archie. Aye a thousand times. Yes, yes, yes.'

'I've not proposed before, as you may have guessed. It's not worked out too delicately.'

'Oh, I don't know. I'm not experienced in proposals, either. But I'd say you've managed it beautifully.' Both laughed, newly shy.

'I'd been working up to it. Christmas Day, I'd planned. But somehow there was never a chance.'

'No.' She dared very gently to put a hand on his arm.

'So it's late, but at least spontaneous. It suddenly came to me. Ploughed field, I thought: good as anywhere.'

A long silence then quivered between them.

'Why do you want to marry me?' Myrtle asked at last.

'Always known you'd be the best wife in East Neuk, in the world I daresay. Always loved you.'

'*Always loved me?*'

'Well, years and years. Since school.'

'Since *school*? You never gave the slightest clue.'

'Course not. Had to be sure. Takes a long time to be sure, when a man is choosing a wife.'

'But . . . all those other girls after you. I always knew you were quite out of my range – just a distant hero. Then you became a friend, and I couldn't believe my luck.'

'And then?'

'And then, quite lately, friendship turned into something else. I didn't dare admit it, even to myself. I thought I should go to my grave loving Archie Duns, and no one would ever know.'

Archie turned suddenly away from her with the stiff, dignified movement of a man who turns away from a lowered coffin, wishing to hide his powerful feeling.

'Thank God it's turned out like this,' he said.

'I love you,' said Myrtle.

'That's all I wanted to hear. Hoped it might be the case. I'm a lucky man, but I'll have to warn you: I'm not a man of many fine words. Well, you must have gathered that by now.' He patted Myrtle's hand, still on his arm. 'This could be the only time we say all these sort of things to each other. But you'll know it's there, my love for you, for ever, God willing. I'll be a faithful, loving husband, though I can't promise many frills.'

'We're grown up,' said Myrtle. 'I don't need roses. Just assurance.'

'That's fine, then.' Archie was a little brusque, looking at his watch.

'I'd planned a good long walk but we've been a while, all this standing about. Maybe we should be getting back to Dot, have a cup of tea, tell her.'

'She won't be surprised,' said Myrtle.

'That she won't,' said Archie. 'There's nothing she misses, your mother.'

They walked back the way they came, pushed together by the narrowness of the path. The pale sun defrosted their faces and soon, walking briskly, even their bare hands began to feel warm.

They spent a chaste week making their plans. Dot, in her total delight, offered them the ground floor of her house so that they could sell Archie's house and have money to invest. Archie was pleased by the plan. He had never liked his parents' house, and since his father's death it was too full of unhappy associations, despite Dot and Myrtle's efforts to clean and cheer the place. Now, he wanted to distance himself from the memories, start somewhere new with his wife. Archie put the house on the market and returned to sea early in the New Year. He said that he would break the news to Ken when they were some miles from the shore, and ask him to be best man.

Not until he had been gone for some days did Myrtle tell Annie: harbouring the secret had provided a peculiar pleasure. Until now she had had so little excitement to share with Annie. Now the time had come she wanted to keep it to herself, unbroken, for a while. She feared that once Annie knew the whole precious matter would be splintered and swept up like broken glass – Annie with her opinions and enthusiasm and overwhelming surprise. When she did break the news at last, Annie went so pale that Myrtle thought she was close to fainting. But in her state of shock, and annoyance at not having been told sooner, Annie did manage suitable congratulations. Her show of pleasure, though, was less – immediately – than Myrtle had anticipated. Then Annie took a hold of herself and behaved in character. Even her friend's important news could not deflect Annie's natural references to herself.

'Oh Myrtle, it's wonderful! I never thought you'd make it up the aisle before me.'

'You probably never thought I'd make it up the aisle at all.'

Annie laughed, ignoring, or not noticing, the slight waspishness of Myrtle's tone. Then they hugged, glittery-eyed.

'Nonsense. You'll be the best wife. I'll never make as good a wife as you.'

'Course you will.'

'Never. I know it in my bones.'

'To be honest, I never imagined I could end up so lucky. I still can't believe it. Archie Duns! . . . *Me.*'

Annie moved away, not much concentrating on her friend's incredulity.

'I hope you won't think too badly of all that silly business when we were at school,' she said. 'Me threatening to go after Archie. Dreadful mistake. We'd never have been right for each other. But you know me: always spurred on by a challenge. I always knew I'd never get any-where. It was nothing at all serious. I'm sorry.'

'I'll never give it a thought. It's forgotten for ever.'

'Do you think Archie forgives me?'

'I doubt it ever enters his mind. Besides, he knows you're my friend and nothing will ever alter that.'

'Marriage will, a bit.' For a moment Annie was downcast.

'Not really.'

'I'll have to find myself a husband too. God forbid: where to start? So what will the wedding dress be? Big and white?'

Myrtle laughed.

'Big and white'll have to be for your turn. My size, I'd look like a fridge.'

'You'll look beautiful – honest.'

They laughed and hugged again. At twenty years old they were on the brink of the new era in their friendship that Myrtle's marital status would cause. Anticipating the reality was not easy. Best to smother the anticipation by envisaging less serious matters.

'So what do you have in mind? Oh Myrt, I'm so excited for you! So jealous.'

'Ma's got out the yards of velvet she's had stored away for years. She bought it for curtains in a sale when she was just married, then never had time to make them.'

'Old curtains won't make you a very fashionable bride.' Annie looked appalled.

'I'm not after being a fashionable bride, am I? That would scare Archie to death, wouldn't it?'

'I wouldn't have thought so, but then I don't know Archie, do I?' Annie sighed at the hopelessness of her friend's lack of romantic vision. 'But I expect you'll get away with it. Long as you expect me over first thing, morning of the wedding day, Carmens to the ready. Promise? By the time I've finished with you, you won't know yourself.'

'I wouldn't want to surprise Archie too much,' said Myrtle. 'He seems to love me as I am, amazing though that is.'

Annie put out a hand and held up a clump of Myrtle's heavy, straight hair.

'Trust me,' she said.

Dot spent a week cutting out and sewing yards of musty-smelling velvet the colour of loganberries. The fittings, in contrast to those of Annie for her Fisher Lass dress, were silent, serious occasions: Dot pinning and tweaking with slow and loving care, Myrtle impatient and uninterested, urging her to hurry. She was agitated by Archie's absence – the beginning of feelings that were to grow and torment for many years to come, the first taste of the chronic anxiety that becomes the norm for fishermen's wives. There had been storms. There was scarcely a moment of the day she did not imagine the man she loved exposed to a wild sea. One afternoon, her impatience for his return almost unbearable, a wearying fitting was interrupted by a knock on the door.

Martin came in. He carried a small box.

Myrtle turned so swiftly – for a foolish moment thinking it might be Archie home early – that Dot, on the ground, hands working on the hem, was swung round on her knees in a slipstream of velvet. Martin was silenced by the sight of the bride swathed in the gloomy stuff, its shadows melancholy in the thin violet light that came through the window. They stared at each other: Myrtle in friendliness, Martin still too surprised to speak. He had not imagined he would be intruding on such a scene.

'I'm sorry,' he said at last. 'It seems to be an inconvenient time. My goodness, Myrtle: you're looking grand.'

'No it's not,' said Dot, through the pins in her mouth which kept their balance on her lips. 'Come and sit down and tell us what's going on.'

'You're the ones with the news,' Martin said.

Myrtle felt a tug on her tacked skirt. Her mother was lumbering up from the floor. She moved automatically to the kettle.

'I heard,' said Martin, turning to Myrtle. 'You and Archie. That's good.' He held out the box. 'Small wedding present.'

'Martin! There was no need. Thank you. Our first wedding present.' (So strange, so thrilling to say *our*.)

'I was wondering if I might appoint myself . . . official photographer?' Martin gave a hesitant smile. He was not a man experienced in the art of selling himself. 'I've just bought myself a new . . .' He took a small instamatic from his pocket. 'I thought – just outside the church. I wouldn't be any bother.'

'I'm sure Archie wouldn't mind,' said Myrtle. (Oh, the luxury of having to consider and imagine the opinion of the man she loved.) 'Though we hadn't planned any photographs. There'll be nothing much to – I mean, it'll be a very small affair.'

'All the same, it should be recorded.' Though his voice was light, Myrtle found herself touched by his clouded look – a mixture of joy and regret.

'Course it should,' said Dot, glancing at a faded record of her own wedding to Jock, the sepia print diminished by a brass frame polished till it blazed with light.

'Very well, then; of course.' Myrtle found it hard to concentrate on Martin's plan, and Dot was chivvying the folds of the skirt again. She did not open the box until Martin had left. It was a lump of rock crystal, its tiny milky peaks glittering with a faint voltage on so dark an afternoon. But Myrtle could imagine how it would be on a bright day, and bent to show it to Dot, who complained that never had she known so fidgety a bride.

The very small affair took place on a bitter February afternoon in St Monan's church. It was so cold Myrtle was forced to wear her grandmother's old cape, thick as a horse rug, over the velvet dress. But unassailed by vanity, even on her wedding day, it did not occur to her to be put out by such an ungainly addition to her wedding clothes. Her concern was not to be distracted by the cold.

She and Dot and Annie were driven to the church by a taxi that heaved over the lumpen roads like an old boat. An onlooker might have thought that Annie was the bride, her dress being more appropriate wedding material than Myrtle's. Also, she carried a small bunch of snowdrops. She remembered to give these to Myrtle just as they were alighting from the taxi into the heavy rain. They found Archie and Ken waiting in the porch, shifting uneasily in their unaccustomed suits. Archie wore a tie covered with small anchors. His shirt, to Dot's dismay, was missing a button.

The small group went into the church where the priest was lighting the altar candles. This job done, the gloom was only slightly dispelled by two murky halos of light. The place smelt of the ineradicable damp that comes from centuries of sea spray bashing against stone. As Myrtle's eyes travelled round the whitewashed walls she saw that patches where the wet had seeped through were the colour of old men's sweat.

Bride and wedding guests stood beneath the fine model of a sailing ship that hung from the ceiling. Each one looked about, eyes not meeting. They were unsure how to proceed. The priest eventually turned from finding a page in the Bible and invited them, being so few, to walk down the aisle together. The red carpet – a touch of modernity incongruous in so ancient a place – was only wide enough to accommodate three. Ken and Archie flanked the bride. Dot and Annie followed them. There was no music, the organist being indisposed with flu, but rain was hard on the windows.

As they progressed up the aisle Myrtle found herself remembering the stories her father told her, as a child, about this church. Built in the time of King David I of Scotland it was, at the end of the eleventh century – a time too far past for Myrtle to imagine. Had other brides, nine hundred years ago, walked down this very aisle feeling the same mixture of strength and peace and nervous anticipation that assailed her now? Had brides through the centuries felt their minds escaping like a cloud of butterflies, settling on irrelevant thoughts, even as they neared the moment they were to take their vows? The cold little stems of the snowdrops had become warm, she realised, in her hot fingers: was that a timeless thing, a common experience through the years? Her father had always dealt so easily with past and present, finding events hundreds of years before his birth no harder to envisage than events of last week at which he had been present. He often spoke of Scottish kings as if they were friends, contemporaries.

'He was a good man, the first King David,' he would say. 'The legend goes that he suffered a terrible arrow wound, and the monks of St Monan's saved him. As thanks, the King had this church built for them.' Myrtle remembered her father lifting up her hand to run it over the rough carving of one of the twelve consecration crosses carved into the walls. She hated the feel of the chill, bristly stone, but had said nothing for fear of offending him.

So slowly, they walked up the aisle, passing the carvings. Her fingers, grinding the snowdrops, remembered the feel of the stone noses just as fingers remember scales on a piano taught long ago. David II, her father told her so many times, was the next king to take more than an interest in the church. He, poor man, was caught in a fierce storm when sailing from Leith to Ardross, just a mile from St Monan's. He swore that if he landed safely he would rebuild the church. This promise was carried out between 1362 and 1369 at a cost of £750. Why should she remember that on her wedding day? And the carpenter was paid just £1 13s 4d for his labours. Whenever Myrtle's father told her that – and he was inclined to repeat his favourite stories – he whistled through his teeth at the paucity, even in those days, of the sum. Myrtle could hear that off-key whistle, full of spittle, against the pebbling of the rain against the windows. She wished he was here, escorting her up the aisle in conventional fashion. She wished he could see her, know of the happiness he had always wanted for her but had doubted she might achieve. 'You're such a big girl,' he used to say, sadly, as if that was an impediment to happiness. And indeed, for many years it had been, although Myrtle's way of coping with it was to take her father's advice: *don't hope for anything, lass, and then you might find yourself surprised.* Surprised! Surprised scarcely described it, here at the altar at last, struggling through the flock of butterfly thoughts to the present, trying to persuade herself this was not a ridiculous dream, but the elusive present which would only become solid in her mind once it was over. Here he was, Archie the unobtainable, smelling of mothballs and toothpaste, about to become her husband, 'with no frills', in the eyes of God.

When the simple ceremony was over, bride and groom, priest and congregation, stood at the church door looking out at the rain that bulleted down on the sea. The sky was so low and heavy it was hard to know where light came from to illuminate Bass Rock, a distant spectral monument in this weather. They were all standing there, the small crowd, wondering when to make a dash for the taxis, when a sodden figure suddenly appeared from behind a gravestone – Martin. He approached them, camera in hand. First he photographed them huddled in the porch, then he persuaded them out on to the squelchy slopes of the graveyard, backs to the sea, for more pictures. One of these, blown up and framed, has stood on the chest of drawers in the bedroom for the Duns' entire married life. The enlargement enfeebled the original colours, but the spirit of the moment was caught: black rock covered with the slime of weed; thrashing waves, lifesize granite crosses above gravestones and the startled, disbelieving faces of the wedding group – Annie the only one bearing a proper wedding smile. Curiously, the light that shone so mysteriously on Bass Rock does not show in the photograph. Sometimes Myrtle wonders whether it had been a figment of her heightened state.

Later, after food and drink in a pub, Myrtle and Archie made their way on buses and trains to Mull. There they spent a week in a small guesthouse overlooking the island of Iona. Myrtle was fascinated by the provision of flannels in the pristine bathroom – a whole pile of them, of unimaginable fluffiness, in different colours. Archie was more intrigued by the size and quality of the breakfasts.

The honeymoon was a time of relentless bad weather, landscape all but obscured by dense mists. They ventured out only briefly each day. Mostly they kept to their room. Archie confessed that, desirable though he may have been to local girls (a modest blush accompanied this admission), he had never slept with anyone. Myrtle laughed at the solemnity of this announcement, deeply relieved. She liked to think of their starting out to discover this unknown territory of physical passion together. It gave her confidence. On the first night she walked naked across the room to the bed, where Archie awaited her, huge shoulders looming above the sheet. He murmured about the wonder of her.

It was in Mull that he fell in love with his wife, and she with him. The exhilaration of those early days of lovemaking, perhaps fuelled by Archie's absences at sea, never seemed to flag. Myrtle had observed in Dot the destructive effect of chronic anxiety when the men were at sea. Married to Archie, a stern and wise skipper who would never contemplate any risk to his men's lives, it was her turn to live the regular days of unease. But she understood that it was this threat to life itself that heightened the value of the times she and Archie had together. Each homecoming was a celebration, a reason to be thankful. At each departure they both secretly prayed for *Skyline II* to be spared. Even after years of surviving storms, they resisted any measure of complacency. For their entire married life Myrtle and Archie remained alert to the shadow of mortality, which endows all love and pleasure with its cutting edge.

In the eighteenth, and even the nineteenth century, Myrtle explains to Janice, fishing boats were still remarkably similar in design to their Viking forebears. She shows her a picture of a *sixern*, or six-oar boat, found rotting in the Shetland Isles quite recently. She does not mention the feeling of distaste the picture holds for her. Myrtle's dislike of rotting boats is even greater than her dislike of empty working boats:

wrecks, rust and softened wood, old boats that are leaking but just afloat, fill her with peculiar fear. She has always kept her distance from ship skeletons, disturbed by their lack of life, though that same lack of life in deserted buildings holds no menace. Once, as a child, she came across a rotting rowing boat, its bows split and gaping, its paint raised in dozens of blistering sores, tipped up on a stretch of shingle. Unaccountably, she burst into tears, would not go near it. Annie had wanted to creep into its shade to play houses, but Myrtle refused. Loony, Annie had thought her. 'Loony loon,' she had shouted over the crack of pebbles as Myrtle ran away. Well, yes, she was: a fisherman's wife, and still a bit odd about boats.

But now, indicating nothing of her own feelings, she points a firm finger at the picture: the faded sepia of the dead *sixern* at Vemmenty in Shetland. Janice, close to her, is intrigued.

'I'd like to see it,' she says.

'Doubt it'd still be there. It would have broken up long ago.'

'I'd like to go to the Shetland Isles.'

'Your mother and I went, once. Long before you were born.'

'I'd like to go.'

'The birds! Millions of them. The noise!'

'Maybe one day you'll take me.'

They are at the kitchen table. Janice sits in the place Annie usually occupies when she comes to play cards. Several books are spread open between them. Janice is at work on a project on the local fishing industry. Myrtle has agreed to coach her in several subjects. This project, it turns out, is Janice's favourite. Originally, she had hated the whole idea of such a boring old project. Who wanted to know about boats? she asked. The harbour was stuffed with them. Her father talked of nothing but fish. She'd had it up to here with everything to do with stinking fish. She wasn't going to try. Nothing could make her interested.

But somehow, with Myrtle, fishing did become interesting – fascinating. Myrtle put things quite differently from her boring old teacher Miss Simmons, who droned on in a voice that sounded as if she was talking through a mouthful of scones. Myrtle tells stories, asks Janice the sort of questions it's actually good fun to answer. Then, Myrtle *listens*: she listens to Janice as if she is really interested, which makes Janice want to go on and on with her ideas to please her. Myrtle has persuaded Janice what fun it is to go to the library at the museum and look through old documents and records, find photographs which can be copied for her book. Janice has done this and triumphantly produced the fruits of her excavations. She received high praise and homemade cinnamon biscuits from Myrtle. She is beginning to feel she is not as stupid as they say she is at school. Her marks are rapidly improving. The lessons with Myrtle go too fast. She looks forward to them, she loves them. In just a few weeks, as Annie observed to Myrtle, the child has *blossomed*. She loves the poetry Myrtle is now introducing her to – comes home talking about people called Sorab and Rustum. Only yesterday Janice refused to go home until they had finished reading *The Ancient Mariner*.

'You ought to be an all-the-time teacher,' Janice says, 'so that lots of children can have all this fun, not just me.'

'Maybe: one day. I've often thought of it. But I've no training.'

'Surely that doesn't matter. You'd be brilliant.'

Myrtle is gathering up photocopies of pictures of ancient fishing boats. In preparation for these lessons she herself has spent hours in the museum. Mornings, thus engaged, have flown by. Sometimes she has broken off to go down to the café to see Annie, by now the accomplished waitress. Annie brings coffee with all speed, 'on the house'. 'You the tutor, me the waitress,' she says, laughing. There is both admiration and jealousy in her comment. She would like to inspire her daughter herself, ignite her enthusiasm for learning in a way that Myrtle has so quickly managed. But she knows that is beyond her. And she is pleased that at least her childless friend is able to play an important part in Janice's life. To Myrtle, Annie likes to think, Janice is surely second-best to a daughter of her own.

'On to the herring industry, tomorrow,' says Myrtle. 'I've found pictures for you of clinker-built ships knee deep in herrings. I'll be telling you all about the disaster in 1848 when a hundred boats and a hundred fishermen died.'

'Good.'

'But it's time to go, now.'

Janice does not move. She concentrates on writing HERRINGS in elaborate capital letters. Eyes down, her lashes, thick and curly as Annie's, make spiked shadows on her cheeks. Her hair, of late, has become curlier, more abundant. There are red lights in the brown. It falls over her eyes. She makes no attempt to push it back. Annie was just the same, at that age: stubborn about her rebellious hair. 'Tie it back, Annie, or you'll earn yourself a black mark,' the teachers used to threaten. Annie earned herself dozens of black marks and didn't care. Past and present interweave confusingly. For a moment Janice is the child Annie. She looks up, smiles the same smile. Dimples press into her cheeks, plumper than Annie's ever were, and she's herself again. Eleven years old and full of spirit. Her father's heavy jaw means her own looks will never quite equal her mother's. But there is an unruly appeal, a wicked eye, that will be both invaluable and dangerous when it comes to grown-up life.

'I'd better be off, then,' says Janice. 'Though I don't want to go.' She stands, gathers up her things. She looks round the kitchen, memorising its geography to take home with her. Myrtle notices her nails are bitten to the quick. 'There's a boy at school called Arthur Dilk. He writes me such silly notes.' Myrtle smiles. Again, history repeating. 'I haven't told Mum – don't say anything.'

'Of course not.' There were dozens of boys writing silly notes to Annie, too, when she was eleven, Myrtle remembers.

Janice moves round to Myrtle and kisses her quickly on the cheek. This is something she has not done since she was a very small child.

'I'm looking forward to hearing about the disaster,' she says. 'I wish my dad and Archie and all of them didn't have to keep going to sea. I'm never going to marry a fisherman. I hate men being fishermen.'

'Not much choice for a man, here,' says Myrtle.

'Then I'll move. I quite fancy the thought of the south. Stratford-on-Avon, or Weston super Mare – I've read about that. Perhaps you'd tell me about lots of nice places in the south next geography lesson?'

'Perhaps.' Myrtle goes with Janice to the door, big hand lightly on small shoulder. 'See you tomorrow at five.'

'Twenty-three hours till then.'

'Aye.'

'Hope they go quickly.'

Myrtle watches Janice's slow progress down the steps, one side of her slight body weighed down by her satchel. She fears for the child. She loves her.

The time when Archie and Myrtle were trying for a child of their own is a time that both of them have closed away. They never reflect on the weariness and disappointments of those days: there is too much else to be glad of in their lives. But regret can be perennial and to deny that it did not assail them – Myrtle in particular – from time to time would be an untruth. News of friends giving birth, the constant sight of babies in prams, the well-meaning invitations to be a godparent – such things could not but remind of their own 'failure', as Myrtle saw it. Long ago both she and Archie had come to accept this 'failure'. But accepting is different from growing accustomed. It was growing used to the idea of impossibility, short of a miracle, that savagely eluded them. Sometimes, they wondered if this anguish would be with them for the rest of their lives.

Myrtle's attempts to conceive went on for almost five years. First, came the natural hopes. Myrtle pictured herself running down to meet the boat with news of her confirmed pregnancy, too excited to await Archie's return home. But as there was no reason for any such event to take place, Myrtle began to suspect something was wrong. She was the first to be subjected to tests, questions of a loathsomely intimate nature, examinations. While Archie was at sea she would spend many hours waiting in hospital corridors, hope writhing like some wretched, dying bird within her. Sometimes the pregnant Annie would come with her.

'Well, if nothing happens, you can share this bairn – Jesus, how it kicks! Feel it kicking, Myrtle.' Innocent of Myrtle's reaction to this offer, she would tap her stomach with long silver fingernails. To

Myrtle they represented an alarming sign of Annie's less than instinctive maternal feelings. 'How'll I ever manage looking after one myself? Oh, it's not fair. Though you mustn't give up for a long while yet. Then just when you're least expecting . . .' Annie did her best, in those sleazy hospital waiting rooms, to raise her friend's hopes and spirits, always innocent of her own blundering.

When months of ignominious examinations finally came to an end, the answer was that nothing seemed amiss. And so it was Archie's turn to be confronted. Perhaps he was the 'culprit', as the gynaecologist put it. Archie's misgivings at subjecting himself to tests, that made him feel sick to think about, he kept to himself. But for the sake of a child, for the love of his wife, he would go through anything. And so, refusing Myrtle's company, one shore leave he braced himself for the bus journey to the hospital. He faced the appalling indignity, at nine in the morning, of being shown into a sterile cubicle armed with a plastic jar and a couple of very old magazines. How many other hopeless, desperate hands had trembled unwilling through the crumpled pages of obscene buttocks and breasts? 'Just do your stuff,' commanded a stiff little nurse, her own breasts buttoned tightly into a lust-defying uniform. Superior, pitying, mocking she managed to be, in the few dreadful moments of their acquaintance. Archie hated her. She shut the door behind her with a smug, all-knowing look. Imprisoned in the silent white cube, it was only the thought of Myrtle's last hope that gave him the strength to carry out the disagreeable command.

But there were no problems concerning Archie's sperm count, it turned out: nothing amiss with him, either. All a great mystery, as the consultant put it in their last interview. How about trying the fertility drug? With one accord Myrtle and Archie dismissed the idea. Then it was in God's hands, the man went on, attempting to be helpful but too busy to spend a long time trying to persuade so adamant a couple. Obviously there were sometimes pyschological barriers to pregnancy that could be excavated through long sessions with a therapist . . . This parting shot met with equal distaste. No thank you, said Myrtle and Archie again. In that case it's up to God, the consultant repeated wearily, closing the Duns' file before him. He glanced at his watch, indicated that in his opinion even a barren couple should not be allowed to overrun their time too long. Yes, God was probably the best – the only – hope, he went on, standing up. Indeed his own father was a minister of the kirk and had taught him the power of faith. He looked down on his patients with an encouraging little turn of his mouth that was a poor substitute for a smile. Archie and Myrtle stood. Now they could look down on him, the man they could not help despising because he could do nothing further for them. The consultant's final advice was not to give up hope – and, who knows, the good Lord might provide them with a surprise in his own time. Remember, His ways were mysterious, He could not be hurried . . . With that, the consultant's own rising hurry could no longer be contained, and he showed the Duns to the door.

Not greatly encouraged by his little homily, to await God's surprise was all Myrtle and Archie could do. But His mysterious ways did not include, for them, the provision of a baby. Meantime Annie gave birth to Janice, a healthy girl. Myrtle, for the first two years of the child's life, helped greatly with her upbringing. She grew to love the child – not like her own, no use pretending that – but without reserve. Archie observed his wife. He understood how she felt, and was grateful that there was at least a baby upon whom Myrtle could bestow her naturally maternal feelings. But he himself harboured an amorphous kind of antipathy that he could not bring himself to fathom. Something to do with resentment? Why should the undeserving Annie be blessed with a child while his own, far superior wife, was denied this gift? Janice was a beguiling and pretty child: no denying that, though by three years old she was already showing the dangerous precocity and petulant ways of her mother. On the occasions that Archie was accosted by the child (often he would return home to find her on Myrtle's knee) he behaved as well as might be expected – dandled, swung, told stories of mermaids and fishes, made her laugh. But in truth he could never feel much affection for the child. By the time she was eleven his indifference had turned to keen animosity. He requested that she should visit the house as little as possible while he was home. His intention to avoid her did not go unheeded by Annie. Myrtle was saddened by the confusion of Archie's strong feelings, though she could not fault his behaviour.

'I'll never understand why you've got it in for her so, Archie.'

'Something about her.'

'She's an innocent wee thing, for heaven's sake.'

'Not so innocent.'

'What do you mean? What rubbish you talk! She's not twelve years old.'

'She's manipulative as her mother.'

'That's unfair. Pure prejudice.'

'Let's not discuss her. You'll see I'm right, one day.'

'Nonsense.'

Janice was the only source of disagreement between them, though the discomfort she caused them for the most part lay fallow. When arguments did erupt, they were quickly extinguished, but left both parties resentful, angry, unreasonable. The air was clouded for a day – 'wasting precious, happy time', Myrtle said. But Archie, back from an hour's work on the boat, would return with his normal, equable mood reinstated and rest his head on his wife's shoulder, like a contrite child, seeking forgiveness for his outburst. In comforting him, Myrtle herself was eased. The strength of love for her husband ran eagerly through her as she stroked his coarse and sea-bleached hair, and they stood locked together in their kitchen chiding themselves for their stupidity. How could they be so foolish as ever to let Annie's daughter come between them?

The day after Myrtle and Archie came back from their honeymoon Archie went to sea. Within moments of his departure, Annie dashed round to the house. Her state of excitement was unconnected with Myrtle's return. She hurried through some perfunctory questions about whether Myrtle had had a good time, then her own uncontainable news burst forth.

'I'm engaged!' she shrieked, and held up her left hand. A minute speck of red stone perched like a firefly on her fourth finger.

'*Engaged?* Who to?'

Annie tossed her head, dismissing the importance of that part of the question. She twisted the almost invisible ring, assuring herself of its significance.

'Ruby,' she said. 'Or maybe garnet. I don't remember which. I just wanted something red. Great, isn't it?' She waved the finger under Myrtle's nose.

'But Annie – you're engaged who *to*?'

Annie fluttered her eyelashes, blushed, put on her most mischievous look. She liked to surprise.

'Ken,' she said at last.

'Ken?' Myrtle sat down, heavy with astonishment.

'Ken himself.' She looked down, rubbed the firefly again. Myrtle's incredulity was embarrassing.

'How on earth did that come about?'

'Well, he's loved me for ages, hasn't he? I made up my mind following you down the aisle. I thought to myself – why not marry Ken? He's a good man. I'm fond enough of him. Not everyone has to be passionately in love, you know, to have a happy marriage.' There was a sneer in her voice so faint that Myrtle might have imagined it. She looked away. She could not face her friend's eye.

'Are you so surprised?' Now, she mocked.

'Yes, in truth.'

'I thought you'd be *pleased*.' Myrtle's less than enthusiastic response to her news was not at all what Annie had envisaged. She pouted, petulant. 'It may not be the love match of the century like you and Archie Duns, but he loves me all right, you know that perfectly well. You're the person he confessed to. He'll be good to me, and I'll try to be a good wife.' She gave a wisp of a smile. 'We'll get on, see if we don't.'

Myrtle sighed. She made a quick decision to ask just one question, and then to brace herself for loyal support.

'But you've avoided Ken for so long,' she said. 'Scoffed at him, even. The idea of *marrying him* . . . you would have laughed at the very suggestion a few weeks ago. You've never loved him. You don't love him. As far as I know you don't even fancy him. Is it fair to marry him?'

Myrtle's tone was less harsh than her words. Annie shrugged.

'You have to be a bit practical when it comes to marriage, in my reckoning,' she said. 'There's not much choice left, locally, is there? I don't want to move away. I want to stay here. I've never had anything positive against Ken, except embarrassment that I flung myself on him in that silly way. But he's been a regular gentleman about all that – never mentioned it again. I think I could grow to love him. If he wasn't a good man he'd no' be Archie's friend, or yours. I respect him, and that's important in marriage, respect. So if one half loves, and the other respects – well, that's more than can be said for a lot of marriages. I think we'll be fine.'

'I hope so.'

'We both want a lot of bairns. We both want lots of the same things – we made a list the other night. Really. Don't look so worried. There's lots going on for us, I promise.' She giggled. 'Having waited for me for so long . . . I'll tell you something: he's a grand lover, Ken. I can hardly walk.' Annie moved round in a small circle, legs bowed, limping like a wounded bird. She laughed at herself, encouraging Myrtle to laugh too.

But Myrtle looked away, a confusion of feelings contorting her face. She controlled them, rose and went to her friend, kissed her on the forehead. Briefly they clutched each other's hands.

'That's all good, then, Annie,' she said. 'I'm pleased for you. I hope you'll be very happy.'

'We will be.' Annie laughed again. 'It gave him quite a shock, I can tell you, when I proposed. You should have seen his face!'

'When *you* proposed?' The calm Myrtle had fought for so hard now erupted again into shock.

'Not an hour after you and Archie had left on the train for Mull. Ken was walking me home. I mean, there weren't many wedding guests to choose from to walk home with, were there? I said how about you and me getting married, too, Ken? He said I'd had too much to drink. I said no, I'm serious. He said if you're serious, and I doubt it, I'm on. Of course I'll marry you, he said. I've loved you for years. Never in my wildest dreams, he said. Then he grabbed me. God almighty, how he grabbed me. We raced down to the beach, didn't stop till next morning . . . Came back wet through from the rain, and icy cold, but *engaged* . . .'

Myrtle's determination to disguise her horror failed her at this point. Annie was quick to try to quell her friend's misgivings.

'The wise thing Ken said was – and he's a wise man, believe me – he said all marriages involve risks, and we've got a lot more going for us than some. Provided, he said, I make it my business to be a faithful wife, there shouldn't be any problems.' She fluttered her eyelashes, suddenly red-cheeked.

'And when will you be getting married?' Myrtle asked primly, for there was no point in speculating on the likelihood of Annie's future fidelity.

'Oh, that. Sometime soon, I expect. Haven't had time to discuss it all really, have we? The important thing is, we're *engaged*, Ken and me.' She went back to rubbing the firefly stone on her finger. Like real fireflies, in daylight its glow was scarcely visible. Myrtle's disapprobation, she felt, was so plain she must distance herself from Annie's gaze. She moved to the stove, put on the kettle.

'Then there's cause for celebration,' she said. 'I'll make us a cup of tea.'

It's an hour or so after Janice has gone home. Myrtle notices a darkening in the room. She goes over to the window. Outside, a haar, thick as custard, obliterates everything in its greyness. There are no gulls' cries to splinter the silence. Myrtle wonders whether the haar has spread twenty miles north over the sea, where Archie should be casting his nets. It is time for supper. She contemplates taking the baked potato from the oven, but does not feel like eating it. A sense of isolation has wrapped itself round her like a caul. 'Archie,' she says out loud.

Then the dense quietness that has drifted over the village is split by a shriek – the shriek everyone most dreads: the rockets. The alarm scorches through the walls of the house, attacking the silence like a wild animal, pounding against Myrtle's entrails, making them hot and fluid. She trembles. It can't be Archie, she thinks – she hopes, she prays. He would have rung her on the ship-to-shore had anything been wrong. But some boat is in trouble.

Myrtle grabs the big torch, runs without her cloak from the house. It is dark, now, as well as foggy. There's confused shouting in the street. The rockets continue to savage the air, terrifying invisible gulls who have set up their own alarm system of petrified screams.

Myrtle follows other blobs of light. Down at the harbour, the lights are gathered at different heights, like the lanterns held by a group of carol singers. Their beams are useless little swords in the impenetrable air. Lustreless. Myrtle, looking down, cannot see her own feet, let alone the water in the harbour.

There's a boat in trouble on the rocks, someone says. *The Swallow*, says another. Myrtle's heart contracts with relief. The fear still grips, but when a disaster does not include your own loved ones, the fear is different. Relief breeds acute sympathy. Other faces nearby reflect the same feelings. Thank the Lord there's no' a rough sea, says one: that's one blessing. The lifeboat went off ten minutes ago. Someone's gone for brandy. Mary Tunnit, shouts a voice, is coming over queer. Mary Tunnit, wife of *The Swallow*'s skipper, is calling to the wives of her husband's mates to be calm. Her face is thick with creamy sweat, her hair wet and black. There's a catch in her voice. Myrtle remembers that catch. At school, always uncertain, called upon for an answer Mary could only produce one in a broken voice. She was never a leader. Now, in an emergency, she has to be the good influence, the calm and sensible one, or her skipper husband Duncan Tunnit would want to know about it.

'They're going to be all right,' she shouts, 'so stop panicking, for God's sake.' Firm of voice, now: shyness forgotten. She wipes the sweat from her face. In a flash from a lamp Myrtle sees Mary's skin is pale as oatmeal, unshining. Faceless voices chime, swinging this way and that. Myrtle feels a cold hand in hers: Annie.

'I was looking for you,' she says.

'I was looking for you.'

'Bloody rockets break up your heart.' Annie is trembling too. There's not a woman in the crowd unshaken. In the darkness the general quivering can be seen in the stirring of the lamps. Then the screech of the rockets stops.

The silence is dense as a cushion. The wives fall back on it, faces still alert but no longer clenched. Footsteps crump on the invisible ground. A man's voice shouts the good news: boat located, crew all safely on their way back in the lifeboat. Not much damage done: a line will get it off the rocks soon as the haar has risen. In the morning, most probably. Not much anyone can do in this murk. Footsteps retreat.

In the collective sigh of relief the lamps bob about faster, almost gaily. Mary Tunnit lets forth a wail of joy. The wives of *The Swallow*'s mates lumber about to hug each other, clasping at others on their way. Annie, still close to Myrtle, takes her arm. She must go home, she says: Janice is on her own.

The two women push their way out of the crowd. Relief, almost tangible, runs like a lighted fuse through the figures who are bloated by mist and thick clothing.

'Thank God,' says Annie, crossing herself – although not a believer, she likes the fancy gestures of the Roman Catholic Church. 'It could have been . . .'

'This has happened so often, hasn't it?' says Myrtle. 'There's good weather, you're conscious that the general worry has faded a bit, then something like this comes to shock you . . . You know you should never trust the bloody sea for a single day, but sometimes you're ground down, worn out by not trusting. I suppose we can only ever have limited moments of peace, when our men come ashore.'

'And I wouldn't say *they* were all peace and light and happiness,' Annie says sourly. 'Hell: who'd be married to a fisherman?'

Arms still tightly linked, they follow the guiding beams from their torches – inadequate little sticks of light in the dark and swirling gloom.

*

Once, when they were children – eleven or twelve – Myrtle and Annie were lost in a mist. Dot was walking them home from school. She stopped to go into the baker, urged them to wait for her outside without moving. But some devil, as Annie later told Myrtle, snuck up and twisted her guts. She was overcome with the desire to see what it was like running into dense mist. She imagined it would feel like running through clouds, she said. Or perhaps it would feel like being blind. She spun round and ran, without a word.

In the moment Myrtle realised she had gone, her instinct was to follow. She did not think to tell Dot, but plunged into the mist calling Annie's name. No response; no answering call. Myrtle panicked. She had lost all sense of direction. She had no idea where she was going, but kept running. The comforting smear of shop lights had disappeared. She sensed she was no longer in a narrow street, but had reached some sort of clearing. She stopped, listening. The density of the mist bound her like a dank shroud. But suddenly there were voices: boys' voices, calling Annie's name. There was laughter, too. How could they laugh? This was no ordinary game of hide-and-seek. This was frightening. This was horrible. Myrtle recognised Ross's voice, Ken's, Sandy's stupid giggle. She could not see them and the voices moved about, sometimes far away, sometimes a little closer.

Then her own name was called, and it was Annie calling. Annie ignoring all the boys: Annie calling her. Myrtle felt a great sob of strange happiness jerk through her. She called back. Somehow their voices led them blindly to each other. Their cold hands stretched out. Smudgily they touched. Annie was crying, too, more loudly than Myrtle – saying what a fool she was, how frightened she'd been. What would Dot say? What would her mother do when she heard? Myrtle mumbled words of reassurance. They held hands, stumbled along guessing the way. The boys' ragged laughter grew fainter. Some immeasurable time later they found an anxious Dot in the baker's shop. In her relief at their return, she handed them doughnuts instead of a scolding. Their fright had been punishment enough, she reckoned.

The incident had not lasted more than ten minutes, endless though it had seemed to the girls. On their way home, one firmly each side of Dot, Myrtle looked at Annie, saw the mixture of sugar and tears round her mouth, and felt an odd satisfaction. Although too young to work it out at the time, she was aware that, in a crisis, it was she, Myrtle, who Annie needed. She was consumed by thoughts of boys in ordinary life, but when something horrible happened it was Myrtle Annie could rely on. Myrtle would be the one to come and rescue her from the mist. It was Myrtle she called for, Myrtle she counted on.

That small event of many years ago – probably long forgotten by Annie – Myrtle regarded as a significant confirmation of her friend's dependency. In moments of carelessness, waywardness or unkindness on Annie's part, Myrtle often looked back on that frightening afternoon, and the memory reassured her. On the night of *The Swallow*'s grounding, she is reminded. The memory is so powerful she licks her lips, half expecting to taste sugar among the salt of tears. Always, when the haar comes down, the sharp and the sweet come back to her. She is glad to be with Annie.

It is with particular grateful joy that fishermen's wives welcome their husbands home after there has been a drama at sea. When Archie returns, two days after *The Swallow* has been dragged off the rocks, Myrtle leaps from her chair when she hears his footsteps outside, and runs out to greet him.

He looks surprised. He takes her in his arms, kisses her briefly on the cheek, but without attention. His mind is elsewhere. Even as Myrtle follows him up the steps she is aware of his distraction.

'They got *The Swallow* off,' she says. 'She's not too badly damaged.'

'So I hear.' He conveys no interest. Normally, if one of the harbour boats has been in trouble, Archie is the first to go down and offer help, consolation. Myrtle is puzzled. Anxiety, which usually fades when he comes through the door, spirals through her. What has happened? She waits.

Archie takes his place at the table, eats hungrily, preoccupied. Myrtle keeps her silence. She knows he will not welcome questions. It's the belief of fishermen that wives should be spared from incidents at sea. Myrtle's father waited ten years to confess to Dot that once *The Skyline* had rolled right over, and it was a miracle they had not drowned. Archie had taken even longer to pass on this information to Myrtle. The world of the men at sea is a shut-off place, its realities unimaginable to anyone who has not spent several days imprisoned in a fish-stinking bark bashing lonely over the waves; a place where off-duty hours must be spent in cramped and foul quarters never free from the smell of old frying, never free from the close proximity of unwashed fellow members of the crew. When they come home, the men want to forget all that. They want to put out of their minds the savagery of storms that try to kill the boat, tossing it without mercy from one cliff of wave to another, drenching decks and men over and over again, leaving them frozen, exhausted, numb, but still hanging on. They have no wish to recollect the rows, the flaring of tempers miles from home under an alien sky, the sickening disappointment of a poor catch. Fishermen want their lives to be divided, even from their wives.

So Myrtle allows this unusual silence to lumber on. It is so heavy she thinks a crack of explanation must come soon. Whatever the rules, Archie cannot leave her in this sort of suspense. She polishes the stove, going over and over bits that have no further need of polishing. Her back is to Archie.

At last she hears him put down his empty glass, push back his chair.

'It's Ken,' he says. 'He'll no' be much longer on the boat if he carries on.'

Myrtle turns. At some point when her back was to him Archie must have run his hands roughly through his hair. It stands up in stiff, clownish points. He looks a little crazed. Saddened.

'What do you mean? I thought it was all agreed. What's Ken done now?'

Archie shrugs. Myrtle can see he is still undecided whether to tell her. At last he says:

'Same old thing again. For a week or so he was back to his old self. But this trip he wasn't pulling his weight, hell he wasn't. Driving the lot of us mad with his moaning. Complaints of chronic tiredness. Of course you're tired, I say. Shore leave's for a mite of rest, not working yourself to the bone delivering stuff in that old van all over Scotland – of course you're knackered, I say. Besides, we agreed he'd give it up. We shook on it, didn't we? But he's not been keeping his word. And I'm afraid a lot of it is Annie's fault – nag nag nag as usual. He says she's given up asking for a car, but she despises him for not getting one. And now it's a lot of other stuff she's demanding – new shoes for the bairn, a tumble dryer, whatever. Daresay he's being driven beyond the bounds of rational behaviour . . . but he's going to have to make up his mind finally. Is he a fisherman or a removal man? And what exactly is he fitting in with his removals? So far I haven't asked him, straight out. But he knows I've a pretty good idea. If he's delivering black fish for Charlie Roberts . . . I tell you, his days are numbered. My patience is running out.'

Archie gets up from his chair, moves over to the window. He is flushed. He stands, looking out, back to Myrtle. His big shoulders block the light. The room is evening-dark and it's still early afternoon. Unnerved by the strange atmosphere, Myrtle keeps her place by the stove, leaning against it.

'Annie's dropped small hints,' she says carefully, 'but I'd no idea of so much . . . bad feeling still between you and Ken. She told me not long ago Ken was planning to sell the van and they'd spend the money on a holiday.'

'Well he's obviously made some effort, but has changed his mind. I warned him before we came off the boat this morning. I said Ken, this is your last chance. You sell that bloody van or get off the boat. God, how I hate all this. Until Ken went to pieces we were as good a crew as you could find along the coast. I say that myself. And now there's an atmosphere. I want it cleared. I want to trust Ken'll come to his senses, not be so bloody daft. But I don't want to bother you with all this. I only mentioned it because a crisis is looming. I'm surprised Annie hasn't been on at you about it all. She must know something's still up, be aware of the tensions. She's no fool, your friend Annie. Just ruthless when she's after something.'

'Sometimes,' says Myrtle, allowing a moment to register all Archie has said, 'even after all these years, I get the impression I don't know anything that's going on in Annie's head. She likes to make me think she's telling me everything, but I doubt that's the truth.' In her loyalty, she chose the word *doubt* rather than the phrase *know that's not*.

'If Annie betrayed you one day, I wouldn't be surprised.'

'She'd never do anything calculated to hurt. She's a good heart.'

'I'm not so sure.'

'Of course she has! You've never liked her, long before the stupid business in the woods.' Myrtle hears her voice rising. 'You've never tried hard enough to understand her.'

'Oh, I have. But seeing her through different eyes from you, it didn't seem worth the effort.'

Myrtle shifts her position. She wishes Archie would turn to face her. But he remains mesmerised by the view he knows so well beyond their small window.

'Well, anyway,' she says, attempting a lighter voice, 'whatever you say or think about Annie will make no difference to my feelings for her. You know that. I'm familiar with all her faults, all her cunning ways, and it doesn't make any difference. I love her. She's my friend.'

Archie gives an almost inaudible laugh. Myrtle can just hear the note of scorn within it.

'Aye: she is, too,' he says. 'More's the pity, sometimes.'

Silence flops between them again. Myrtle is conscious of the alarmed beating of her heart. She wants this uneasy exchange to come to a quick end, things to return to normal. However did they drift into talking about Annie? She was the one subject that they had both learnt to avoid with such skill . . . A single gull flies past the window with a long and dreary moan. Myrtle watches Archie's head move a little, following its flight.

Then the quiet is blasted by a battering of footsteps outside. There's angry banging on the door. Before Myrtle can urge the caller to come in, it's flung open. Annie runs in, scarlet-faced, ugly smears of red running down her neck and on to her chest. She does not look at Myrtle, but pummels the table – the place where she usually fans out her cards – and screams.

'Archie Duns! You've a lot to answer for! What is all this? What the hell have you been saying to Ken?'

Archie turns round very slowly. He looks down on the furious woman battering his kitchen table. Myrtle steps quickly forward, puts a hand on Annie's leaping shoulder.

'Get off, Myrtle! Leave me alone. I'm here to speak to your husband.'

'What seems to be the matter?' The languid voice of Archie's question infuriates Annie further.

'What's the matter? What d'you think's the matter? You've no idea why I'm here, I suppose?' A small pellet of spit flies out of her mouth and lands on her own flailing fist. 'I'm here because Ken, my husband Ken, comes home a broken man. You've been getting at him again, not a month since your agreement, and he can't take it any more. And nor can I. I don't want a broken husband. Beneath your – your *boring* exterior, Archie Duns, you're nothing but a sodding great bully, and I hate you for it. What has Ken ever done to deserve such a bashing from you?'

'Calm down, Annie –'

'Shut up, Myrtle. This is between Archie and me.' Annie moves quickly to the window. With small fists still whitely clenched, she reaches up and punches Archie on the chest. 'I want an explanation!' she shrieks.

'Stop it, Annie!' Myrtle cries. In a lightning shift of time Annie's angry hands become her childhood hands, the nails tearing at Myrtle's own face, the screams of fury ripping through the wind on the beach. 'Stop it, please. For heaven's sake . . .'

She sees Archie looking down on Annie with a disparaging smile, an expression she has never seen on his kindly face in all the years she has known him. He touches the place Annie has just punched on his chest. Her small fists have made no more impression on his bone-hard muscles than two alighting butterflies. Her pathetic gesture seems to amuse him.

'You shouldn't go hitting people,' he says, 'especially those a lot larger than yourself.'

'I'd willingly kill you for what you've done to Ken.' Annie no longer shouts. Her rabid fury is abating.

'What have you done, Archie?' Myrtle asks. 'I'm at a loss here.'

Archie's eyes pass thinly over his wife, and return to Annie.

'If you want an explanation, a proper explanation, you shall have one. Ken's been a dead loss on the boat for months, now. All his old energy gone, his enthusiasm. You of all people know very well the reason for this. Ken can't be relied on any more. What I said to him this morning was that he could have one last chance – sell the van and give up his deliveries, as we agreed a month ago, and get back to being his old self. The old Ken. As it is, we can't afford to carry a man like him on the crew. He's useless.'

'That's your story,' says Annie. 'You've always had it in for Ken. Always been looking for a chance to get at him. He was fine till you started to put the boot in.' She moves backwards, away from Archie, so that now she is equidistant between husband and wife.

'I've been warning him for months,' says Archie. 'He keeps promising things will be different. But they aren't. We made what I took to be a final agreement. He broke it.'

'Ken's done nothing wrong.' Annie is sullen now.

'I'm sorry to say, Annie, he has. I don't like reporting tales from sea, but the time's come for you to face the fact that Ken's going off the rails. Last week he couldn't even cope with the job he's best at, the nets. When Ross came to help him, he got nothing but abuse. Then a punch on the chin. Ross flung him on a bunk where he slept for three hours. Woke up saying he wasn't used to brandy and he'd had a slug or two to give himself energy. Meantime, two hands short, we were up against it. This can't go on. You must see. He's taken too many liberties, affected the general well-being of the boat.' Archie is quiet, forlorn. Annie shrugs.

'Well, I don't know. You must sort it out for yourselves.'

'Can't have a man on board who not only doesn't pull his weight, but could be a risk –'

Annie cuts him off with a laugh.

'Don't be pathetic, Archie! So dramatic. It doesn't suit you. How could Ken be a risk? If you'd stop nagging him, he'd be all right. You're the one who gets his wick. I'm telling you, if you ever put Ken off the boat, there's no accounting for how the score will be repaid.'

'Please, both of you . . .' says Myrtle. She feels an outcast, kneads her skirt.

'I'll not put Ken off the boat if I can help it,' says Archie. 'Last thing I want. But you better warn him. You better stop pestering him for things he can't afford. *You're* a lot to blame for all this, as you must know.' His eyes are hard on her.

'*Me?* I do nothing but support him.'

'You goad him. You want this that and the other, a lot of material rubbish you can't afford. You do your best to make him feel a wimp, not being able to afford the things you want that you have some daft idea will bring you happiness. So what does Ken do? Because he loves you, stupid bastard, he spends his shore leave running round in the van trying to earn a few quid to buy the junk you want. The more you get, the more you want. The last straw was your idea of a car. How the hell can Ken afford a car? You know perfectly well what the fish have been like lately. We're all having to cut back –'

'I don't want to hear any more such rubbish!' Annie cups her hands over her ears. She used to do that as a child: block her ears should a teacher scold her. Anger flares in her eyes again. She shakes her head – so pretty in her fury – and folds her hands firmly under her breasts, as if to support herself. 'I ask Ken for a few mod cons, yes, all right. What wife doesn't, husband away most of the bloody time? And yes, money's tight. Some of us haven't had the luck of a father's house to sell – money in the bank.' Her eyes lash from Myrtle to Archie. 'But to say I goad him . . . That's just the vicious side of you, Archie Duns. That's the side Ken and I know about.' She looks at Myrtle.

'Vicious?' says Myrtle, appalled. 'There's not a kinder man in the world. Archie says nothing without good reason.'

Annie gives a small laugh.

'The supportive wife! The perfect couple, so brave about no children –'

'Shut up.' Archie goes white. Annie tosses her head at him, defiant.

'Well, I will say you were right about the car. But you're out of date, so happens – we don't pass *all* our latest disagreements on to you two, so happens. I did want one, I don't deny that. But I've changed my mind. I've come round to thinking a better telly would be more within Ken's means.' She gives a contemptuous laugh. 'But here's one thing you know-alls don't know – Ken *likes* his moonlighting, earning a bit to get me things . . . That's why he broke the agreement, hasn't sold the van yet. And anyway, unlike some people, we're not the sort of couple who want to spend four days' shore leave sitting by the fire holding hands. We've got better things to do with our time – and what we do is bloody well nothing to do with *you*, skipper Duns –'

'It is if it affects Ken's job as one of my crew.'

'You're nothing more than a bully. Everyone says so. Ken would be better off without you. There's plenty who'd like him.'

'Then he can go.'

A trace of alarm flickers over Annie.

'I'm not saying he wants to go.' She moves to stand beside Myrtle, back momentarily to the door.

'What's that?' Ken's voice startles them all. He stands in the doorway. None of them has heard him coming up the steps. Myrtle, close to Annie, feels her shock.

'I told you not to come here, Annie.' says Ken. He is pale, unshaven – same look as all men when they come back from a stint at sea. But there is no immediate evidence of the broken man Annie declared had returned to her.

'I couldn't take any more,' Annie says. 'If you won't stick up for yourself, Archie's bullying, then I'll have to do it for you.'

'I can stick up for myself, thanks. Sorry about this, Myrtle. Archie and I can work it out between us. It's a private matter. It's nothing to do with the wives.' He turns to Archie. 'Shouldn't have blurted it out to her: sorry.'

Archie nods briefly: apology accepted for that. But he looks no less grim. Myrtle puts on the kettle. Ken's young face, blanched by moonlight, fills her mind: his quick, tantalising kiss, while all the time he was thinking only of getting back to Annie the Fisher Lass. The betrayal between friends is as punishing as loss, as death, she thinks. Myrtle sighs, misery coming at her from all directions. She wonders how this horrible scene is going to end.

'Tea, everyone?' she asks, and registers a general nodding.

Annie slumps, all energy spent, into the chair that is always hers for the card games. Now Ken has arrived, interrupting her confrontation, the fight is leaving her. Ken dithers beside her. She tells him to sit, too. But Ken remains standing, eyes warily on Archie. Myrtle pours tea.

Then Archie moves towards Ken, hand outstretched.

'Look here, Ken,' he says, 'this has all gone too far. Things shouldn't have got to this.' Ken looks at the hand with suspicion. 'Besides: what are we doing to our wives, involving them in all this? Can't we call it a day? You know what I'm asking. I don't want to lose you from the boat. I'll give you one more chance.'

'Go on, Ken,' says Annie, subdued.

The men shake hands. Ken turns his head aside so that he does not meet Archie's eye. Myrtle, in a warm rush of pride at her husband's magnanimity, puts mugs on the table. Ken gives a wan smile, sits beside Annie, who sniffs. She is scornful of a second deal sealed with a handshake.

'Do my best by both of you,' Ken says. 'But I'm a torn man.' This, Myrtle realises, is supposed to be a small joke. Ken is the only one to smile. Archie takes the huge pot from Myrtle and sits beside Ken. Myrtle sees how tired Archie looks. She also sees, beneath the charitable front he has fought for, that he remains determined to carry out his threat should Ken fail him again. That this really is Ken's last chance is in no doubt. Myrtle prays that Ken will not be so foolish as to break his word a second time. Though if what Annie said is true about his *liking* the moonlighting, the firmness of his purpose could easily be shaken again. And then . . . but Myrtle will not let herself think of the consequences.

It's a long time since the two couples have sat down together round a table, and this unplanned gathering is not the easiest of occasions. But united in their disturbed feelings – each one different from the other – they make an effort to cover the awkwardness. The easiest way, having all known each other so long, is to resort to talk of the shared past. Archie tells the story of some childish escapade on his uncle's boat, and they manage to laugh. But a void remains beneath the paper-thin politeness. Not one of them is free of concern that the smallest mistake could cause a further explosion. They drink their tea swiftly.

Then Archie gets up and says he is taking Ken to the pub: they deserve a drink. The gesture is so out of character that Myrtle is unable to suppress a look of astonishment. Unlike most of his peers, Archie is not a man who frequents pubs often, and when he does it is for the sake of others.

It is for the sake of Ken, now, Myrtle realises: the last piece of his extraordinarily charitable behaviour in the past hour. Alone with Ken, he obviously thinks, the final agreement about Ken's future can be decided. And then, please God, may the matter be put away for ever.

As the four of them scrape back chairs in the dimly feathered light of the kitchen, in Myrtle's eyes Archie shines with benevolence. Although she is still innocent of much detail, she knows that Ken has caused Archie serious trouble for the last few months, and forgiveness can't be easy. But Archie has put aside his own anger about Annie's insults and accusations. For his wife's sake he has offered forgiveness, peace, a last chance. Never has Myrtle been so moved by his goodness. Tears approach her eyes. Through a blurring of vision she sees that Ken, following Archie out of the door, wears a feeble, guilty smile.

The two women are left alone. Myrtle turns away from Annie to dab her eyes with a dishcloth. Now is her chance to berate Annie for all the loathsome and untrue things she said about Archie. Now is her chance to ask what exactly has been going on, all these months, that everyone has known about but her.

She takes a deep breath, for control. Then, as she knew they would, sympathy and forgiveness surge over her. Annie, in a rage, had surely been saying things she did not mean. There had been deep trouble between her and Ken that Myrtle could only guess at – and the slight hurt of Annie's keeping these matters from her, Myrtle feels, is not worth dwelling upon. In a word, she deems it wise to carry on as if the storm had never happened. Annie would be expecting her support.

Myrtle turns round. Annie is sitting down again, pushing away things on the table in front of her, clearing a space as if for a game of cards.

'Glad that's over,' she says, airily, as if the whole incident had been nothing to do with her.

'Aye. No one can have enjoyed it.' Myrtle sits, too.

'Archie was the pourer of oil, I'll say that. Ken should never have come round.' She sniffs, searches for something in her pocket.

'Perhaps it was best it's all come to the boil. God willing, every-thing'll be back to normal now.'

Annie gives Myrtle a look in which a hint of defiance is still just visible.

'Maybe. Hope so. Bad things were said.' This, Myrtle realises, is the nearest Annie will ever come to an apology. Annie pulls an old packet of cards from her pocket. 'Shall we?' she says.

Myrtle nods. The cards are slapped down, the friends bow their heads in concentration. They are safely back in a place they know. This kitchen and the familiar game fortress them against the discom-forts of the world outside. For a while, as calm returns, they play in silence. Then Myrtle looks at the clock.

'Gone two hours,' she says. 'They must have a lot to talk about.'

'Ken's got to be off at nine. A delivery first thing in the morning. He'll have to drive through the night.'

Myrtle puts down her cards. 'But I thought . . .?'

'Just one final job, worth a bomb,' Annie says quickly. 'Maybe Archie'll persuade him against it, but I doubt it. Maybe they'll agree it's the *very* last job he does.'

'For God's sake, Annie! After all this. I can't believe it. We have all this discussion here not an hour ago, and Ken fails to mention he's another job lined up for tonight. Archie'll . . . I don't like to think what Archie'll do.'

Annie looks impatient.

'What none of you understands, as I said to Archie, is that Ken *likes* the extra work. It gives him a real buzz, coming home from some delivery – an easy drive up to Aberdeen and back. It gives him a real buzz to hand me over a wodge of notes and tell me to go and spend them.'

'Well I don't know, but it sounds to me pretty daft, and anyhow the arrangement is . . .' Myrtle fights hard to sound uncondemning. She is determined to say nothing that will resurrect the row. But fear for a troubled future returns. If Ken, encouraged by Annie, is unable to honour his promise to Archie, then God knows what will happen. Annie shrugs.

'Don't worry, Myrt,' she says. 'It'll all work out all right.'

Myrtle has little faith in this declaration. Unsettled, she concentrates hard on the cards again. They play in silence until they hear the sound of footsteps. The women's eyes meet in mutual relief. But the man who enters is neither Archie nor Ken, but Martin.

He carries, as he often does when he drops in on the Duns, a newspaper parcel. It's usually either a lobster or a crab, given to him by his parents. In return, he gets an hour or so sitting with Myrtle and Archie, who realise that beneath the cheerful exterior lodges a lonely man.

Tonight, Martin has miscalculated. He thought he would find the Duns on their own, enjoying one of their quiet evenings together. He has never run into Annie in their house. Knowing her visits are in the afternoon, to play cards with Myrtle when the men are at sea, he is careful to avoid those times. Seeing her at the table, he is confused, put out.

His feelings are transparently clear to Myrtle, who makes a quiet but firm show of welcoming him. While she fetches beer from the fridge, he hesitates over which chair to take at the table. Eventually he seats himself beside Annie.

His choice delights her. In a trice her various black moods of the past hours are gone, and a rosy blush spreads over her face and neck. She taps Martin's forearm with mock severity. His horror at the sight of her long silver nails comes upon him too fast to conceal.

'So! You bringing a lobster to my friend! You've been caught out, Martin. You never bring a lobster to me.' Annie pouts, childlike. Martin smiles, shrugs, lifts his arm to take a bottle from Myrtle, so that Annie has to remove her hand.

'I wanted Archie's advice,' he says to Myrtle. 'I've been offered a job part-time filleting. I've got the time. I could do with the money.'

'*There!*' Annie bangs her hand on the table, triumphant. She swerves round to Myrtle. 'How about that? Another one who isn't afraid of two jobs! I'd say it was fairly normal practice, these days, wouldn't you, Martin? If you're offered the work, you'd be a bloody fool not to take it.'

Martin and Myrtle exchange a look. On an evening not long ago they had touched upon Ken and Annie's problems, and the trouble they were causing Archie, though Myrtle could only tell Martin the little she herself knew. Martin plainly has no wish to be involved in an argument whose traces still linger in the air.

'Part-time grave digger, part-time filleter, part-time stonemason – and I'd still be far from a wholly employed man,' he says.

'Well,' says Annie, deflated by his unhelpful response, 'I daresay . . .' She tries another tack. 'So what have you been *up* to? Why haven't I seen you for so long?' The questions are accompanied by her most flirtatious look, a beguiling widening of the eyes. The expression is deeply familiar to Myrtle, who turns away. But not before she notices Annie's bottom lip quiver like a child's about to cry. Perhaps she still loves Martin, or imagines she still loves him, Myrtle thinks. Perhaps, in the blindness of this love, Annie will fail to see how pathetic are her small efforts still to attract him and – there being few other excitements in her life – she will go on making a fool of herself for years to come. Even as such harsh thoughts run through Myrtle's mind, sympathy overtakes them. For all her extraordinary appeal, Annie has had nothing but empty disasters with boys, with men. Ken is a compromise husband, not the man she loves, or even pretends to love, with the kind of energy that seals a marriage. Perhaps her real love – or the love most potent in the crowd of her fantasies – is Martin. But Martin has little respect for Annie – no interest. However she behaves, it's unlikely his feelings for her will change. So even if, in some future calamity, Ken and Annie part, Martin would not be the man to come to her rescue.

Myrtle is so entangled in her own thoughts that she has not been concentrating on Annie and Martin's last few exchanges. Now she notices that again Annie's approach has changed. She is talking in a more ordinary way, and Martin is paying more attention. She is talking about Janice, and how she is enjoying her private lessons. Martin is definitely interested. Myrtle busies herself unwrapping the lobster. As she moves back from the fridge she sees that Annie has pulled up her skirt over her crossed knees. The top leg swings gently while she spins her tiny ankle. It moves like a well-oiled mechanism whose works never fail. Martin's eyes trail the turning foot for a moment: then, conscious of a look flashed from Myrtle, he quickly shifts his look. Myrtle has no intention of joining their conversation even though much of what Annie is telling Martin is wrong: it's plain Janice has not bothered to tell her mother precisely what Myrtle is teaching her. Martin's interest appears to be increasing. He smiles at Annie, something he has not done for a long time. She blushes, and the ankle twirls faster.

Myrtle feels the necessity of occupying her hands. The events of the evening have made them shake. She takes a place at the far end of the table from the other two and begins to fold the sheets of newspaper in which the lobster had been wrapped. They are damp and limp at the edges, and smell of salt water. Myrtle folds them into small squares very carefully, as if they were to be preserved. Martin's eyes are still on Annie – more polite than interested, now, Myrtle thinks. She wonders how the encounter will end. She longs to know, though realises that is perverse. A new kind of unease, to which she cannot put a name, begins to possess her. She fears something worse than the previous row is going to take place. But then she tells herself that it's merely the trauma of the whole evening that fills her with such irrational thoughts. With hot, swollen, clumsy fingers she finishes her pointless task of folding the newspaper, and Martin, with surprising suddenness, rises and leaves with a perfunctory excuse about not wanting to be late.

'Well, that was a nice surprise,' says Annie, when he has gone. Her ankle no longer twirls. 'You're lucky in your visitors, I'll say that.' Myrtle is saved from answering by Archie and Ken's return. Archie, it's plain to see, is upright and sober as when he left, while Ken sags by his side, a benign but stupid grin on his face. Archie turns to Annie.

'As you can see, Ken here has to postpone his job. He's in no condition to drive the van tonight. But he'll be off in the morning, and that'll be his last job.' He says this with good humour, but casts a forbidding look at Annie. 'That's our final arrangement and I have every reason to suppose Ken will keep to it.'

Various reactions shift across Annie's face. There is an annoyed frown for Archie, a scornful glance for Ken. But what Myrtle sees rising most powerfully in her friend is the hopelessness of a woman married to a weak husband. Annie opens her mouth to say something, but thinks better of it. Ken moves his grinning face very slowly, like a mechanical toy whose battery is running down.

'That's our arrangement,' he says, slurrily, and puts out a hand roughly in Annie's direction. 'Home.'

He needs support. But Annie, dizzy with so many charged feelings, chooses not to indulge him. She sweeps past both Archie and Ken and out through the door without a word. By the time Ken has yanked round his eyes to follow her progress, she is gone. Archie takes pity on his helplessness, puts a hand on his arm and guides him to the door.

Archie and Myrtle, with the place to themselves at last, silently acknowledge the need to extinguish the traumas of the evening.

'Let's hope that's final,' Archie says. Then he laughs. 'What did you think of my way of stopping Ken's delivery until the morning? He just downed the whiskies, happy enough. No thought!'

'Grand,' says Myrtle.

They move to the window. Myrtle opens it. Frosty air gushes past them eager to devour the warm pad of the room. It's a clear night, full of stars. Archie's eyes rise automatically across the skyscape with the kind of humility that is natural to fishermen who put their trust in the sky – a look of his familiar to Myrtle. She never ceases to wonder at his knowledge of the stars, how he can use them to chart his path on the sea, or warn him of the weather. To her they are a confusion of twinkling specks, to Archie they are a well-worn map.

'See if you can find me the Bear,' he says.

This is an old tease. For years Archie has been trying to teach his wife the way round the night sky, but she remains at a loss. He never scoffs at her – just explains it's a knack, like the knack she has of observing curious things about people that he would never see for himself.

'I can't.' Myrtle's eyes are frantic among the millions of sparkling tracks, searching. She wants to please him. She wants to surprise him, as she sometimes can, and wave triumphantly to the Bear. But tonight the sky is smeared too densely with scintillating lights, and the air is very cold on her bare arms.

'The Plough, then. The Plough's so clear.'

'Really, Archie. I'm trying, but I can't. It's cold.'

Archie puts an arm round his wife's shoulder, and laughs.

'One day you will,' he says. 'One night you'll suddenly see it clear as anything, your way round the stars, and you'll wonder however you couldn't see it before.'

Myrtle feels the weight of Archie's arm on her shoulders, and bends her head against him. She wonders how it's possible to be so close, and yet so far apart in different kinds of knowledge. Archie is a man who knows about winds and currents, preying storms almost as soon as they have left their distant lair. He can read signs in the waves and remember where hidden rocks lie, across hundreds of miles at sea, without having to consult his radar screen. Better than any skipper along the coast he knows where the fish are gathered: some instinct draws him to them like a magnet, though each time he finds them he confesses surprise – Ken told Myrtle this years ago. Archie's knowledge has always been a mystery to her, a mystery that fills her with excitement, awe, respect. She loves learning from him, though there will never be time to gather more than a fraction of what he knows. But the very thought of things she must still glean from him spurs her love as keenly as his quiet ways and his stubborn resistance to romantic declaration.

After a while, too cold to remain standing against the night air – which Archie does not seem to feel – Myrtle shuts the window. She senses the kitchen is cleansed, but keeps this thought to herself. In their long marriage she has learnt which inconsequential thoughts to harbour, and which to pass on to Archie. One of the skills needed for a happy marriage, she has always believed, is to spare your spouse the general grain of thought that daily fills your head: choose, instead, only the particles that have some hope of interesting, enlightening or informing.

'You *are* cold, too,' Archie is saying. He is rubbing her arms, her shoulders, her cheeks – gently, with his thumbs. He is urging her to leave things till the morning. Myrtle sees the fan of cards on the table, where Annie left them: single reminder of an earlier part of the evening whose discomfort has been quelled by Archie. Relieved, but longing for further comfort, Myrtle follows her husband out of the room to bed.

'Is Ken happier, do you think, now everything's resolved?' Myrtle asks Annie. It is three weeks since the row, which has never been mentioned. Myrtle knows her enquiry is a risk.

Annie looks up from her cards.

'I'm not sure it's all been resolved in his mind.' She suddenly giggles. 'You know what? He never made that last job. Archie saw to that, getting him so drunk. He had a head on him next morning . . . didn't get out of bed till three in the afternoon. I said to him you've lost yourself a hundred pounds, Ken. There goes our last chance of a few savings. He didn't seem to care – his head was throbbing that badly. Savings! he said. You'd have spent it in an afternoon. I don't know what he thinks I am.'

Myrtle smiles kindly, as she always does at Annie's moments of most profound self-illusion.

'Anyway, I've persuaded him that all I really want is this big plaid coat I saw in a catalogue. A hundred and fifty-nine pounds. It would last me for ever, Ken, I said. He said that shouldn't be too far beyond our resources if I can hold out for a week or two . . .'

Now Myrtle sighs, and in her anxiety not to be trapped into a conversation about Annie's material desires, which could lead back into the dangerous territory, she finds herself taking an unwise path to deflection.

'Archie's been contemplating buying a bit of land,' she says. 'There's a small field going: Farmer Ricks is selling off his horses. It's nothing much, just over an acre, but protected.'

Annie eyes her with plain contempt.

'You're to be *landowners*? What would you want that old field for?'

Myrtle pauses, regretting her mistake. She should never have mentioned the matter at this time. Annie, in this mood, is bound to be unreceptive to the idea that she and Archie have so enjoyed for the past few weeks. It came to Archie the morning after the row: its planning has taken up the shore leaves ever since.

'Archie has it in mind to plant this coppice, this small wood.'

'What on earth for?' In her amazement, Annie puts down her cards.

'He's always liked trees. He thinks it would be a challenge, finding trees to withstand the weather up here . . .' Aware she is losing Annie's comprehension, and having plunged recklessly in so far, Myrtle decides to go one dangerous step further. 'Besides,' she says, quietly, 'Archie and I have nothing to leave behind. You've got Janice. We've nothing. No one. We just have this feeling we'd like to plant something.'

'Well.' Annie's astonishment is enfeebling. 'I don't know what to make of that. Seems to me to be a funny way to spend money.'

Myrtle, desperately wanting Annie to understand, tries further to convince.

'Just imagine: in twenty years or so there'd be this wood – for birds, wildlife, people to walk in, bluebells . . . Don't you see?'

'Not really.' In silence she wrestles for a long time with thoughts that Myrtle cannot guess at. 'It must be nice to be rich,' she says at last. 'Able just to go and buy a field if you want one.'

'We're not rich,' says Myrtle, quickly. This is another conversation she would prefer to avoid.

'Oh no? You got a fair price for your father-in-law's house, didn't you?'

'Most of that was sunk into the new boat, you know that.'

'You got this place for nothing from your ma. You don't know what it's like, paying rent.' Annie's mouth is twisted, resentful. She reflects in silence again. 'The funny thing about you and me,' she says at last, 'is that you're rich and you don't care about money. We're poor and I mind very much.'

'We're not rich, I tell you: we're far from rich. A few thousand in the bank. If we buy this field and trees there'll not be much left.'

'A few thousand in the bank! We're up to the limit of our overdraft, I'll have you know. You in your cushy position can't understand the worry of that.'

'Of course I can, Annie. And I know what it must be like, all the expense of a growing daughter –'

'You've no idea what it's like, the feeling of having nothing to fall back on. Don't try to pretend you can understand that.'

'Let's not talk about money –'

'Aye: it's always the thing that's come between us. In my book, the rich and the poor can never be true friends.'

'That's nonsense! Besides, you know we're not rich, Annie, though I'm not denying we've a bit more than you, and we don't spend much –'

'You're rich in my eyes.'

'What can I say? Except that money's not the most important –'

'It's bloody important if it's not there.'

'And, besides' – Myrtle feels herself flustered – 'you know that you can call upon Archie and me whenever –'

'Thanks. But never. You know we'd never do that.'

Both women are flushed. Myrtle feels provoked, defensive about her modest savings. Annie, consumed by the resentment of the Duns' wealth, is unreasonably angry. She would like Myrtle, for once, to shout at her, respond in equal anger. But that is never Myrtle's way. Myrtle's way is to hand out patient advice.

'Perhaps,' she says, 'if you could sometimes resist the extravagant things you always seem to crave . . . that might ease the strain.'

'I'll take no such criticism from you,' Annie explodes. 'Who are you to criticise my innocent longings for a microwave, a coat, whatever?' Her voice is breaking. 'You're always criticising, Myrtle. When you keep back the words I can see them in your eyes. I get fed up with your disapproval.'

Suddenly she is sobbing. She lowers her head on to her folded arms: hair tumbles, speckled with lights. Myrtle is unnerved, shocked.

'Whatever's the matter, Annie? You can't expect us to agree on everything. That would be very dull. We've never done that, have we? And ever since we were children we've spoken our minds to each other, haven't we? That's part of friendship, isn't it? Come on: sit up. Tell me what's really the matter.' She pushes back the auburn hair. Annie looks up, her stricken face streaked with mascara.

'Hell: it's nothing to do with you and me, with money, with criticism.' Annie sniffs, dabs at her eyes with her sleeve. 'Put it all down to a difficult time at home. Ever since that night here, the new agreement between him and Archie, Ken's been . . . well, not the man I know.' She sits up, swats her face with a piece of kitchen paper but makes no improvement on the dark state of her cheeks. 'He's become *obsessed* with earning more money. Obsessed with providing me with things he thinks I might want, things he thinks will make our marriage . . . better.'

'Oh Lord, Annie. I thought everything was well, now. Archie's not said a thing, except that all's back on track now.'

'Archie wouldn't know. Ken's keeping his word. No more deliveries. The van's up for sale, though God knows who'll take an old load of junk like that off our hands. But he just keeps on and on . . . how's he going to afford this and that for me? I suppose it was my own fault in the first place, asking for things. Pressing him too hard. But now he thinks he'll never keep me unless there's a constant stream of *things*. I keep saying he's got it all wrong. I've got everything I want – except just the one coat.' She manages a half-smile. 'And the kind of husband I once imagined. But he's so convinced by his own idea it's become a sort of madness. He starts up soon as he's through the door, goes on and on. I find myself longing for him to go back to sea. Few days' peace. Even Janice is pleased when he's gone. Home tomorrow, aren't they? It'll all start up again. I don't know what to do.'

'I'm so sorry. I'd no idea anything was – well, seeing Ken so little, there was no chance for me to guess.' Myrtle's sympathy and concern rise automatically: she also feels both helpless and tired. A picture of Ken, all those years ago on the bus, comes to mind: Ken eaten with a sudden obsession. She had listened. Perhaps her attention had helped. 'Tell him to come and see me,' she says. 'Perhaps I could –'

'He never would,' says Annie. 'He's not that sort, a confessor. He keeps things to himself – always has. You remember him at school? Still, I'll say something. Thanks.' She looks at her watch. 'I must be going, Janice needs more bloody shoes.' She stands, her smeary face calmer. 'Sorry I flared up, said stupid things.'

'That's all right.'

The two women briefly hug, a less exuberant version of their old childhood embrace, but a signal that misunderstandings, differences, have been wiped from the slate again for a while.

'You'll never know how much Janice loves her lessons with you,' she says suddenly, gaily. 'If she does well, it'll be all because of you.'

'Janice is a good girl,' says Myrtle. 'I'm proud of her.'

Sometimes, for all that she loves Annie, Myrtle wants to be rid of her. She wants not to have to think of her troubles, provide sympathy, listen, comfort, assure. She wants a month's rest from the card games: she wants to be relieved of Annie's presence for a long time. Such irrational feelings induce guilt, but nonetheless, on sudden, unsignalled occasions, they assault Myrtle with a strength that confuses and saddens. This is one of those times. She is glad when Annie is gone.

The few weeks since the row have been particularly happy for Myrtle and Archie. Each time he has been home they have been involved in the negotiations for their field. (What Myrtle kept from Annie was the fact that the contract is ready for signing. This will be done tomorrow, when Archie gets home.) Myrtle has been engaging herself in the study of trees. Catalogues arrive. She goes through them slowly, marking the possibilities she can point out to Archie. She selects reference books in the library, makes notes. For the first time since her mother died, what with Janice's lessons and the planning of the copse, her days are fully occupied. She revels in the feeling of busyness, and the joy of working towards something again with Archie. Not since the renovation of the house, after Dot died, have they shared anything so closely and with such anticipation.

On the day before Archie's return, Myrtle is kept busy going through papers with the solicitor. Her walk is much later than usual. The evenings are getting lighter, but by the time she arrives at the field twilight is pressing down, causing her to think of their wood at the end of the day – longer, denser shadows, branches smudged into an indistinct mass of purplish brown. She feels intense excitement, and equal impatience for the few hours till Archie's return to pass. He expects to be back at seven a.m. Soon as the catch is unloaded they will be off to sign the contract, and then home to study the latest suggestions for planting on Myrtle's list. As Myrtle walks among the trees in her mind, watching the real sky close down into the kind of lively darkness that is a familiar harbinger of spring, her mind is so entirely free of Annie and her problems that she feels no guilt. She thinks only how fortunate it is, in the kind of uneventful life that she and Archie lead, that the occasional excitements that flare in the quietness are all the more precious for their rarity. The evening passes in greater than usual anticipation of Archie's return. Restless, Myrtle paces the room, studies the stars, knows she will not sleep at her normal hour.

It's three a.m. when Myrtle last looks at her clock. She then dozes for a while, dreams of branches, many of them fallen and rotted on the paths. There is birdsong but, more loudly, the harsh crack of a pheasant's cry. The dream is faintly disturbing. But when she wakes it goes quickly from her, overridden by the thought of the day to come.

At 6.30 Myrtle is sitting at her table drinking a cup of tea. She does not put on the lamp, but watches light slowly unfurl across the small bit of sky framed by the window. In ten minutes she will put on her cloak, for it's a chilly morning, and go down to the harbour. She enjoys the moment when *Skyline II*, snub-nosed and a little battered now, pushes its way through the harbour's entrance. She likes to watch the way Archie skilfully manoeuvres the vessel into its place beside others tied to the wall. She knows that if she witnessed the homecomings regularly, they would become commonplace events of no great significance or wonder. As it is, Myrtle goes to greet Archie's arrival so rarely that her pride and pleasure never fade.

She picks up her mug, puts it by the sink. Her hand, she notices, is shaking. Her excitement is laced with nervousness – she can't think why, except that she's unaccustomed to important events: and the buying of their piece of land, and the planning of their coppice for posterity, is an event quite out of the ordinary. No wonder she is shaky. Archie will laugh, she thinks, when she tells him of her child-like sensations this morning. He may even confess he was in a particular hurry to get back. *The next time I'm standing by the stove* she thinks, *the contract will have been signed. We may be too excited to eat much breakfast.* All the same, so that Archie will not guess at the extent of her ungrounding, she takes two plates from the shelf and sets them on the table.

As Myrtle goes to swipe her cloak from the peg behind the door, the telephone rings. She curses it. On her way, now, she does not want to be held up for a moment.

The crackling, as she picks it up, tells her at once it's a ship-to-shore phone. The voice she can't immediately distinguish. Ross, perhaps. Shouting.

'Get an ambulance down to the harbour. At once! Quickly.'

'What?'

'There's been an accident.'

'Who?' The line is indistinct. Her immediate thought is Ken. One of his mistakes . . .

'Myrtle –?'

But she has slammed down the receiver, fled down the outside steps, left open the door. As she runs, she remembers an accident not long after they were married. Archie cut his thumb badly at sea. He arrived back with his hand a balloon of blood-soaked bandages. Went straight to hospital. No ambulance needed then. Whoever it is must have cut something more seriously this time.

Myrtle has run so fast that when she arrives at the harbour icy knives of pain are shooting up through her chest. Several boats are already in, unloading their catch. Not *Skyline II*. No sign of her. A group of fishermen some yards away are talking. One of them turns to Myrtle, shakes his head. What do they know? What have they heard? Should she ask? And Christ! She has forgotten to ring the ambulance! In her thoughtless panic she has failed to carry out the vital order. Myrtle turns to run to the telephone box outside the chandler's. At that moment she sees the ambulance tottering down the hill, an aged, cream-coloured vehicle with no sense of urgency. Ross, or whoever, must have rung someone else as well. Thank God. And the ambulance's blue light isn't flashing. Its siren isn't screaming. It parks unhurriedly on the harbour wall. It must know this mission is no great emergency.

Others have gathered. Some of the wives. Word has flown round. It always does, when something out of the ordinary happens. Weddings, funerals, accidents: there they suddenly are, the villagers, a mixture of loyal support and curiosity. Witnesses to an event that can be talked about, exaggerated, diminished, until it's superseded by the next happening.

A largish crowd has gathered by now. Myrtle moves along the harbour wall. She does not want to catch anyone's eye. She looks out to sea. There is a low, light mist. If Archie has to deal with an injured member of his crew, she realises, the signing of the contract may have to be postponed. Well, never mind. What is a few days? She sees that there's no horizon. It's one of those moments when the sky – a deep storm blue – is an arc that curves right into the water, no demarcation line, making one vast bowl of the elements. It's a miracle, she thinks, that on such occasions every fishing boat at sea isn't consumed by this void. Then she thinks how silly she is: for it's all an illusion to one standing on the land, a trick of the eye.

Jutting through the low mist, which lazes round its bows, comes *Skyline II* at last. Her meridian-blue paint is bright against the flat grey water. She moves very slowly, like something filmed in slow motion, moving and yet seemingly at a standstill. Myrtle runs back to the place where she will berth. Others are there before her, gathered round the ambulance. A stretcher, and its scarlet folded blanket, are waiting on the ground.

Myrtle clasps her hands. Their rough skin is very cold. Someone offers her a jacket. She wonders at this, but she shakes her head. Someone else shouts the *Skyline*'s nearly here . . . Head down, Myrtle swerves only her eyes to see the familiar shape of the boat nosing very close to the harbour wall.

Two ambulancemen, in livid orange coats, move to the edge of the wall. Myrtle moves to stand beside them. She looks down at the sullen brown water slapping at the slime-covered wall. She looks at the iron ladder cut into the wall – the ladder that Archie and his mates hurry up and down as if it is no more difficult to negotiate than a domestic staircase.

'Are you going down first, Jock, then? Or am I?'

'You go. You're nippier on your feet.' The two men laugh. Somewhere in the tightness of her own terror, Myrtle understands their lesser anxiety.

Skyline II is below them now, perfectly in place. A blast of smells rises up: fish, salt winds, iodine. The engine stutters quietly, then cuts out. The crowd is curiously quiet. Ross is running up the ladder, rope in hand, to tie up. His flesh is green-white under his stubble. As his face appears over the wall, Myrtle enquires with her eyes. But he doesn't see her. He doesn't see anyone.

'Hurry,' he whispers to the ambulancemen. One of them lowers himself, dithers a foot among the top rungs of the ladder. The other picks up the stretcher. Myrtle forces herself to look down.

Among the clutter of the deck a body lies covered in blood-soaked rugs. It looks too big to be Ken, and Annie is nowhere to be seen. Only a sprout of hair is visible, and a hand. The fingers are splayed: it could be a bleached starfish. Squiggles of blood pattern the small clearings of deck. Dozens of dead fish lie beside the body, tipped from a box that was meant for the hold. Their silver scales are streaked with blood. They lie among bloody footprints. Chains and nets are splattered with blood . . . The man must have erupted like a volcano of blood. It's everywhere.

Myrtle hears an echoing moan within her, like the call of dolphins in the sea's depths. She thinks she may faint, but clasps her own hands tighter and her vision clears. Someone has an arm round her and is saying things that make no sense. Both ambulancemen are on board now, making a space for the stretcher.

The crew all seem to be there, too: helpless, alert. As the body is lifted gently on to the stretcher, the blanket falls from one arm. Myrtle sees it is Archie's jersey, but for a moment the fact means nothing to her. Once the fisherman is in place, the two ambulancemen stand rigid with concern. How will the stretcher come up the wall? Myrtle can feel the whole crowd wonder, too.

In the end, she does not see how it is done. Once the mates have leapt forward to take charge of this particular part of the procedure, she turns away, unable to watch, for by now the connection between Archie's jersey and the wounded man has made insane sense. When she next looks – seconds, minutes, hours later, time is so contorted she has no idea – the bloody red parcel of her husband is rising above the ground of the harbour wall. It swings perilously for a moment, then is secured firmly at each end by Ross – sweat pouring down his face, and another member of the crew. The ambulancemen appear over the wall, hurry after the stretcher, their gratitude to the mates visible on their faces. Myrtle finds herself pushed towards the open doors of the ambulance. Ross takes her elbow, helps her up the steps.

She sits opposite the bunk where Archie is lying. His hand hangs down under the sodden rug: the great white starfish hand, the only thing not smirched with blood. She leans over and touches it. It's icy cold. She's pushed gently back into her place by the ambulanceman who is doing something to Archie she does not want to see.

The doors are slammed shut, cutting off the numerous faces of the now large crowd of fishermen and their wives who have come to see what has befallen Archie Duns. Myrtle is aware that Ross is by her side. She wonders vaguely, where is Ken? Surely Ken ought to be here with Archie? And where is Annie? Why isn't Annie here?

The ambulance moves forward, its siren shrieking. Myrtle looks through the clouded window. In the watery view beyond it – everything streaming, shredded, no shape or line unbroken – Myrtle sees Ken vomiting over the harbour wall. Annie stands beside him. Something in her stricken figure makes her seem on a different planet from her husband, for all her physical closeness to him. As the ambulance gathers speed Annie's shocked white face is a thin frame round the great black hole of her open mouth. The image dances in the blackened window all the way to the hospital: ugly, ugly.

Myrtle sits on a plastic chair in a small hospital waiting room that once might have been part of a corridor. There are shiny tiles halfway up the wall, the colour of beetroot. The detached part of her mind asks who on earth could have chosen such a colour for such a room, where people await bad news. She longs for the balm of blue or green on which to rest her eyes. She shuts them. The beetroot makes her feel sick. Cold sweat is guttering down her back. Ross, sitting beside her, keeps patting her knee. She has no energy to ask him to stop. Where is Annie? Still not here.

A long time has passed since the bloody mound of Archie was rushed past her through rubber doors which swung shut in her face. She managed to ask a doctor in a white coat, gashed with Archie's blood, what hope there was.

'Your husband's suffered a terrible injury, Mrs Duns,' was all he said, and ran from her.

A nurse had shown Ross and Myrtle into this beetroot cell. Tea was offered. Tea! Myrtle shook her head. Her throat was closed, so she was unable to ask Ross a single question, or utter a word. Her query to the doctor had used up her entire store of energy. So she and Ross sit in silence in the airless, stuffy place – the silence occasionally jabbed by the cry of a seagull beyond the shut window. Myrtle studies the pile of old magazines on the low table, their paper crumpled to a repellent softness. The cover of the top magazine is a photograph of a symbolically perfect wife. She has blonde hair that ripples like frogskin. She smiles a smile of china teeth. She wears an apron covered in orange roses. *Make your man an old-fashioned meal* is the headline that flies across her neat little hips. How can you make your man an old-fashioned meal if your man is no longer there? The question throbs through Myrtle sharp as frostbite.

Suddenly the door opens. The nurse – a tinge of anxiety just visible on her impassive face – ushers in Annie, and Ross's wife, Jean. Jean is very pale, her face glassed with sweat. Annie is red in the face, eyes bruised with tears. She is making a lot of noise, sobbing. She dashes over to Myrtle, flings her arms round her neck. Myrtle, rock hard in her upright position on the plastic chair, doesn't yield. She seems scarcely to notice Annie is there.

'Stop that noise, Annie,' says Ross. 'Doesn't help any of us.' His arm is round his wife's shoulder.

Annie, jarred by the note in his voice, stops crying at once. She disentangles herself from Myrtle and sits on the empty chair beside her.

'Is there any news?' she asks.

Myrtle turns to her. Despite Annie's distress, her smeared face and swollen eyes, Annie is pretty again. Myrtle shakes her head.

'We're waiting,' she says. 'Waiting, waiting.' Then she asks: 'Where's Ken?'

'Ken?' The question is flat, so empty, it is as if Annie has never heard of Ken. 'I don't know.'

There are footsteps. The door opens again, cautiously. A doctor Myrtle hasn't seen before comes in. Thick glasses make his eyes look as if they are set inches back into his head. There are two wings of sweat on his top lip, like a transparent moustache. He looks at Myrtle.

Ross and his wife stand up. 'Jean and I will wait for you outside,' he says, and they leave the room.

Annie puts a shaking hand over Myrtle's. The doctor swallows. He takes a biro from his top pocket and looks at his clipboard as if expecting to find good news there.

'I'm afraid I have to tell you, Mrs Duns, that your husband has passed away. We did everything we could.'

Passed away? For a moment the phrase is confused in Myrtle's mind with *passed by*. 'He's just passed by,' someone once said when she was looking for him. *Passed by* it couldn't be: though perhaps it was.

'You mean he's dead?' she asks at last.

'I'm afraid so. He stood no chance, really.'

Annie's fingers are cold spiders all over the clump of Myrtle's hands. She tries to shake them off. Annie is whimpering.

'I'm so sorry,' the doctor adds.

'Horrible for you, having to break this sort of news,' Myrtle hears herself saying in a voice that is bright, controlled.

'We never get used to it. There's no best way of doing it. Now, if there's any way we can help . . . When you feel ready, we can make arrangements.'

'Thank you. I can manage. Annie here will come home with me.' There is a feeling of alcohol in Myrtle's veins. She is so in control it is uncanny. The doctor coughs.

'I don't know if you'd like to see your husband –'

'No thank you –'

'– pay your last respects?'

'No.'

'Go on,' says Annie. 'You must say goodbye to Archie.'

'I want to remember him alive, not dead,' snaps Myrtle. She glares at Annie, then at the doctor. Her eyes are hard and dry as glass, not a tear in them. No tears behind them ready to soften.

'Very well,' says the doctor. 'Whatever you wish, of course. People feel differently. But if you change your mind, just let us know. Mr Duns will be tidied up within the hour.'

The doctor looks as if he's aware of his own clumsiness. He backs out of the room, inclining his head a little in Myrtle's direction, muttering further words of regret.

When he has gone Annie says:

'I'll go and see him if you like.'

'No.'

'Someone ought to see him.'

'Why?'

Annie shrugs.

'Last respects,' she says. 'Though I suppose that doesn't mean much.'

'No.'

'Oh Myrtle, how could this happen?'

'How did it? That's the question.' Myrtle stands up very fast. Her hands hang at her sides, heavy as buckets. Annie shakes her head.

'I don't believe any of this,' she says.

'It's happening,' says Myrtle, 'and I want to go home now.'

Annie goes to fetch Ross and Jean. Ross screws the balls of his thumbs fiercely into his eyes to scotch the tears. The three of them walk with Myrtle back to the house. The few people about lower their eyes as the small troop passes, and murmur words of sympathy. The news, it seems, has reached every corner of the village. Myrtle keeps herself very upright, silent. She remembers what Dot said when Jock died: you have to keep going till everyone's gone away.

At the house Myrtle runs up the steps. The front door is open. For a second she can't remember why. She goes in and the comfortable sight that has met her on a million ordinary entrances into the kitchen is there as always. The only difference is that the contract for the buying of the field lies on the table awaiting their signature – hers and Archie's.

Myrtle is surrounded by kindness, sympathy, friends, company, offers of help, offerings of flowers. She is brought soup and pies and shortbread biscuits, in the pathetic belief that at some point she will feel hungry. For the rest of the day people come and go – Archie's schoolfriends, his mates, their wives. They try to find words, try to hide their tears, marvel at Myrtle's apparent calm. 'When she takes it in,' she hears one of them whisper as soon as she is outside the door, 'she'll crack.'

But Myrtle has no intention of cracking. All she wants is to be left alone. Annie is a constant presence, making endless mugs of tea and finding her way among the biscuit boxes with an efficiency she has never before shown. She offers to stay the night, but Myrtle insists she wants to be alone. Annie accedes to this wish at last, cries again, and hugs her friend.

'You're so strong,' she says. 'No one can believe it.'

'Where's Ken?' Myrtle asks.

'I don't know. When he comes home shall I send him over?'

'Aye. Tell him I want to know, from him, how it was.'

'I will.'

'I don't want to know from anyone else.'

'I'll make sure of that. Promise me you'll ring if you want me in the night.'

'Promise.'

'And I'll be round in the morning first thing. Oh God, Myrtle. What did Archie ever do –?'

Myrtle cannot contain her impatience, though she tries to be gentle.

'There's no accounting for the Lord's decisions, I've always known that. Now, thank you for being here . . .'

When Annie has gone Myrtle moves brusquely about in the emptiness, drying mugs that the many visitors have left to drain by the sink. She watches her actions from some distant place outside herself. She watches herself move towards Archie's old jacket hanging on the door. She watches herself, for a moment she can't help despising, bury her head in its coarse wool stuff that is alive with the smell of him. She sniffs hungrily at his sweat mixed with the salt winds and sea spray that are embedded in its texture. Then she moves quickly to the table, picks up Archie's pen. On the back of the unsigned contract she begins to make a list of arrangements that must be made for the funeral. She stays up till midnight, but Ken does not appear.

Five days later, an hour before the hearse is due, Annie comes round. She wears a black velvet beret – plainly bought especially for the occasion – which balances precariously on her curls. A sprig of heather is pinned to her dark coat. She carries a bunch of bright flowers wrapped in a cone of cellophane.

'Didn't think he'd want anything too gloomy, knowing Archie,' she says, dumping them on the table.

Knowing Archie. Annie didn't know Archie at all. Her claim is annoying, but Myrtle manages a faint smile.

'Thanks,' she says. 'Lovely. Do you want to come in the hearse with me? There's room.'

Annie nods, pleased by the offer. To be involved in the local importance of a death is no less gratifying than being singled out in any other important event. She sits, undoes her coat.

'Ken came home last night,' she says.

'Did he say where he'd been?'

'No. But then I didn't really ask. It's not as if I cared.'

'It was worrying,' says Myrtle.

'Aye, on top of everything else. I'm sorry for the extra –'

'That's all right. I'm just glad he's back. It must have hit him badly, his old friend . . . for all their differences. I'm glad they'd made it up, the quarrels. Is he coming to the funeral?'

'He didn't say. But I imagine so. He wouldn't miss Archie's funeral.' She glances at the clock. 'Half an hour. Shall we have a game?'

Annie takes a pack of cards from the pocket of her old navy coat and begins to shuffle them. Myrtle pulls the bunch of flowers towards her so that she can read the message. Annie's writing is fat and unruly, just as it was when she was ten years old. *Dear dear Archie*, it says, *missing you already and always will. Much much love, Annie*.

Much much love? Annie had no such thing for Archie, nor he for her. As for missing him: Annie's could only be a thin, polite sort of missing. Again Myrtle has to quell a stab of annoyance. She knows this is no time to be ungrateful for the small hypocrisies of death.

'All right, is it? Took me ages to think what to put.'

'Fine, fine,' says Myrtle.

'Ken'll bring his own bunch, I daresay.'

They concentrate on their game of cards till the hearse arrives. Annie sits one side of the coffin, which is covered in spring flowers, Myrtle the other. Tears pour down Annie's cheeks, drip from her jaw on to her coat. Myrtle's own eyes remain hard and cold, solidified in their sockets, so that on the journey to the church she sees nothing

191

but the transparent salmon skin of the driver's ears that stand to attention under the brim of his official black hat.

Late that night, when it's all over – the ceremony, time, reality, all an incomprehensible flotsam in her mind – Myrtle goes automatically to the kitchen window to close it. Her exhaustion, a weariness unlike any she has ever known, seems to walk beside her: she longs only to lie down, now, beside it, and sleep it away. But she takes a moment to look up at the clear night sky, full of stars as it was that last time she and Archie contemplated it, Archie so full of his teasing.

In a single glance Myrtle sees the Bear. It shines out at her more clearly than any of the other gatherings of stars, impossible to miss, to confuse. The sadness of not being able to please Archie by her discovery is what causes her finally to weep, and she knows that widowhood has begun.

Part II

It's early morning, two years after Archie's death, at the fish market. In the large shed, where neon bulbs fizzle sourly against sunlight, the floor is covered with plastic crates of fish. Through the spiky coverings of crushed ice, their heads all face the same way. Myrtle, shawl over her head, wanders about the wet floor looking at them. She sees how in death every one is different. Some look resigned. Some are still open-mouthed in indignation. Some have a chinless, weary look as if the catastrophe of being caught in a net was of no consequence. All their eyes are open. They have in common huge black pupils almost filled with highlights. Their irises are uniformly the colour of moonstones. Within hours each one of these thousands of creatures will be reduced to separate flesh and bone by a few lethal flicks of a knife. Tomorrow they will be replaced by a shoal just as large, their fate just the same.

The place is crowded. Men in grubby white coats and yellow rubber boots stomp about among the crates making notes, shouting prices. There is a sense of customary speed, urgency. Many of the fishermen, having dumped their fish, want to go straight back to sea for a further twenty-four hours before taking a couple of days off. Political problems in the fishing industry are taking their toll. They must go much further, these days, to find their fish, come back with a much reduced catch. The good days of plenty, and rich takings, are over. The fight for survival, now, by those who have not abandoned it all and gone off to the rigs, is harder by the week. What would Archie have made of it all? He would have shared in his mates' dejection. He might even have turned in the *Skyline II* for a smaller boat, as many of the men along the coast had done, and gone fishing up in the northern waters.

Myrtle leaves the shed for the harbour's edge and looks down at the fat, grubby boats, each one scabby with rust. From one of them fish are still being unloaded. The boxes are hauled up on primitive cranes, dumped on the ground with a stinging crash of ice, loaded on to a trolley and wheeled into the shed to be sold. On the decks of the boats are large piles of green net, tidily rolled up, plastic floats bunched over them like giant necklaces. They are a favourite look out place for gulls. A few are perched on the floats now: enormous birds standing on stilt legs, birds of voracious eye and savage beak. As a load of boxes swings on the crane from the boat to the land, a single flat-fish falls to the ground. The gull whose anxious watch happened to be in the right direction is the one who swoops and catches it. The fish is bolted down, too big for the beak but tossed back with much jerking of the head: then the neck is swollen to a puff of goitre feathers. The gulls who missed their chance keep up their moaning. There is no sharing among birds who must fight for survival.

'They're starving,' says a voice behind Myrtle. She turns to see Alastair Brown, the harbour master. He, too, is watching the desperate little scene. 'The Lord knows what'll happen to them.'

Alastair Brown is a newcomer to the village since Archie died, a Cornishman by birth, who likes to give the impression that he has inherited Mediterranean blood. Perhaps it is to underline this fiction he wears dark glasses, no matter how overcast the sky, or dim the lights in the shed. These perch importantly on a nose shaped like a parrot's beak. No one has ever seen his eyes. His excessive black hair is disciplined by quantities of Brylcreem, a trick he has learnt from watching videos of forties films, the passion in his life only second to fish and the sea. Beneath his impeccable navy Guernsey, he always wears a clean white shirt and the kind of sunset-streaked tie that is laughed at, behind his back, for being poncy. In all, he is a singular character, standing out in a community of unflamboyant men, but agreeable and efficient at his job. His small vanities give rise to friendly amusement, but he is generally liked.

Alastair Brown is a bachelor. On his arrival in the village he was treated to the scrutiny of every unmarried woman of approximate age. Some fancied his harbour-side house, much in need of a woman's touch; some saw themselves as the first to rip off the dark glasses, stare deeply into the long-hidden eyes, and get on with things. Polite though he was to all these ladies eager to win his favours, no definite relationship seemed forthcoming. An occasional drink in the pub was all they secured, not a hint of anything more promising, for all their competitive declarations to each other of his serious intent. Sometimes he is seen leaving his house with a small tartan suitcase on a Friday night. There is a rumour that Dundee is his destination. Further rumour suggests there must be a Dundee woman who has something the locals lack. There would be no surprise if Alastair Brown came home one day with a bride on his arm. Should this ever happen, the wife would receive a restrained greeting.

Annie, unsurprisingly, was one of the many who cast both eyes and hopes on the suave harbour master. Bolder than many of the others, she wooed him first with free cups of coffee in the café, which he accepted with grace and pleasure. But he made no suggestions of returning her hospitality. Annie grew impatient. She had never met a man remotely like Alastair Brown before. Although she admitted to Myrtle her attraction to him was set more on his originality than his body, she saw him as a challenge that could not go untried. She laid her plans and was rewarded in part.

The reward was to be granted entry into Alastair's house. This was something none of his other pursuers had achieved. Annie's way was to knock on his door one night, and his politeness prevailed. Without asking why she had come, he invited her in to join him watching the end of *They Were Sisters*, one of his favourite forties films. He ushered her to an upright chair, gave her a glass of milk and whisky, and returned to his own armchair for the rest of the film. It was soon apparent to Annie he was so engrossed in Margaret Lockwood that she was able to look about, taking in his habitat, as she later told Myrtle, quite freely.

She saw a sparsely furnished, bachelor sort of room, though there were shelves of books and a glass case full of antique nautical instruments. Also, the curtains were plainly interlined, and might even have been a silk mixture. From such clues Annie was able to guess that Alastair Brown, harbour master extraordinary, was a man of some means. As the credits of the film came up at last, her enthusiasm to get to know him better increased.

She handed him a small paper bag that had been resting on her knee, explaining this was the reason for her unannounced visit. She hoped he would not think her . . . Annie could not immediately find the right word, but Alastair Brown did not notice as he pulled a multi-coloured tie from the bag. As he looked at it in some surprise – she could not tell for the life of her, she said to Myrtle, whether he liked it or not, as the black glasses concealed most of his expression – Annie explained she had come across it at a car boot sale and thought it just the thing for his collection. He responded to this piece of infor-mation with silence. Annie, by now unnerved, went on to explain that as it had only cost ten pence she felt it could not be considered as a gift with a message. To this Alastair Brown was bound to agree. A defi-nite smile indicated his approval was gathering. He thanked her, put it back in the bag, and said it would indeed be a valuable addition to his collection. Then there was more silence.

But Annie, encouraged by his signs of feeling honoured by her attention, felt she should go one step further in her mission – having got this far, having got *into* the house, unlike any of the others – before she left. She asked him if he ever took off his glasses: it was the question the whole village was asking, she added, lest he should think the impertinence was solely hers. Alastair Brown answered by re-arranging the angle of his spectacles across his beak nose. Finally, he said *no* was the answer to that question. Except, of course, in bed.

When it came to tactics, Annie told Myrtle in her recounting of this whole story, never had she been so stretched. She decided to pause for a moment, then take the plunge. Take the bait – she was convinced it was bait – he had offered her. She wondered if he would pay her the compliment, she said, sweeping her own lashes about in the way that could be relied on for effect, of allowing her to be the first one to see his eyes. Alastair Brown remained unmoving, in astounded silence. But there was something that did not suggest he was insulted, just amazed. To counteract any alarm she may have caused him, Annie gave a small laugh, and quickly explained that, of course, it had never entered her mind that bed was the only place in which he could be seen with naked eyes. No such cheeky thought, she tried to convince him, had entered her head. But how about a compromise? How about snatching off his glasses just for a moment, and in return she would give him a kiss? Annie laughed again, suddenly feeling the power of her own ingenuity. She felt things were going well. But she laughed alone.

Suddenly Alastair Brown stood up very fast. He put his hand to his mouth. In his smart navy jersey, he reminded Annie of a station master about to blow his whistle, keen for the train to leave his station. The dark glasses, in which she could see a miniature portrait of her own confused face, were turned hard on her. *That would be most improper*, he said. *That would not be the done thing at all: and now if you don't mind, Mrs Mcleoud, I'll show you to the door.* His dismissal bit deeply into Annie as he led her to the door, shook hands, and bid her a polite goodnight. Alastair Brown was her only failure since the day in the woods with Archie.

Myrtle, entertained by the story, had managed to make Annie promise not to repeat it to anyone else, both for her own sake and Alastair Brown's. Annie had kept her word. She remained the only one to have entered his house, but even that small triumph she managed to keep to herself. Alastair Brown continued to be approached in various ways by women from villages all up the coast – the news of an available bachelor of means, a harbour master to boot, had travelled fast. There was nothing to suggest any of them had been any more successful in their overtures than Annie, although speculation that something was afoot was renewed when there were fewer sightings of Alastair Brown and his tartan suitcase bound for weekends in Dundee.

While subtle competition for his favours continued, the story began to go around that the woman he was actually waiting for was the widow Myrtle Duns. She was one of the few women who, with no inclination ever to set up with a man again (though this fact was known only by Annie) had never shown the slightest interest in, or even warmth towards, Alastair Brown. They were mere acquaintances. Their communication extended to no more than a few polite words on the rare occasions they ran into each other. Annie was not slow to pass on the rumour to Myrtle. The absurdity of the whole idea made Myrtle smile. She could not imagine what fuelled it, but put it down to the foolishness of empty minds. She hopes Alastair Brown has not heard the gossip too. It would be embarrassing, make their brief encounters awkward.

The morning at the fish market, when the harbour master observes the seagull's plight, is only the fifth or sixth time he has offered a polite comment to Myrtle in the year that he has been in the job.

Myrtle, scornful of those who see her slightest exchanges with Alastair as evidence of anything other than common decency to a neighbour, is ready to go along with his friendliness.

'You're right,' she says. 'Archie was always concerned about the gulls.'

Alastair Brown is standing beside her now. He rests a bare hand on a stack of full fish boxes. One of his fingers is only an inch from an open mouth frilled with spike teeth. He picks up a handful of crushed ice, watches it melt and run down his thumb. The hand is not that of a fisherman. The skin is wind-burnt but unblemished. Myrtle looks at it with interest. 'Going to be another fine day,' he says at last.

'I think it is, aye.'

'And hot,' he says. 'Almost like Cornwall.'

As Myrtle does not respond to this, Alastair Brown turns and moves towards the ice house. She follows for a few paces, then stops. Ice is being pumped from the machine, through the baggy overhead tube and straight into the hold of one of the boats. The process makes a loud scrunching noise, like hundreds of feet on gravel. Ken must be at work, she thinks, and stops, not wanting to go any further. She does not want to run into Ken. After Archie's death he never went to sea again. Two months later the one-man job came up at the ice house and he took it. His knowledge of what's going on at sea is now vicarious, his life duller. But Annie likes the regularity of the wages. And Ken, Annie says, likes the fact he has more time for reading. He spends many of his free hours up at the library. He doesn't tell Annie what he reads, but she suspects it's 'poetry and stuff'. He has become very quiet in the last two years: reverted to the taciturnity of his boyhood. But none of this is any concern to Myrtle. Her wish is simply to see him, even in the distance, as little as possible.

Alastair Brown is at the door of the ice house. He turns and waves to her. She waves back. He goes in. She stands just where, as a small child, she used to stand holding Dot's hand, watching the men unload sacks of ice from a van that came from Edinburgh. She remembers the excitement when the ice machine was first installed. Most of the villagers came down to watch it work the first time, marvelling at the speed with which the stream of ice tumbled down into the hold of the first boat in the queue. Now, of course, the modern device no longer holds any awe. Like all improvements, it soon became the norm. Even the old men who used to hunch the heavy bags from vans to boats are no longer impressed. The marvel of progress is a short-lived thing, Myrtle thinks.

She turns her eyes to the harbour mouth, half expecting, as always, to see *Skyline II*. But the boat has been sold. She works from Aberdeen. She'll not be coming back here again. Ross and two of Archie's crew have a small boat now. They fish up on the west coast, near Inverness, away for several weeks at a time. Myrtle averts her eyes from the place where *Skyline II* used to berth. She does not want to see the strange red boat that has taken her place. She looks at her watch. Eight o'clock. A quarter of an hour before she must be at school. Time to fill in. She has managed to structure her life pretty well – part-time job at the school now, the planting of the coppice, one day a week at the Evergreen Home, Janice's lessons a few hours a week: yes, she is busy. But unexpected moments fall upon her, still, jagged as broken glass, cutting, empty. Just as she thinks both her mind and body are employed, the scorch of singleness assaults her, reminding her that whenever the small occupation that engages her comes to an end, she must return to an empty house, an empty bed, an emptiness that reaches far back beyond the horizon.

Myrtle becomes impatient at such moments. She turns quickly now to leave the harbour and walk up the hill to the shed where Martin does his filleting in the mornings.

Martin is hard at work on his first load of fish – several crates must be ready for collection by midday. He stands behind the slab, intent on the fish he is preparing. The thin blade of his knife makes the barest sound of splitting silk as it runs through the raw flesh. The only other noise in this bleak little work place is a dripping tap over the sink. Martin spends six hours a day here. Myrtle wonders at his constant cheerfulness. She chooses a place to stand on one of the few dry patches on the stone floor, looks down at his hands, so skilful, so fast – trained to chip stone, not to slice fish.

'Myrtle! Tea?'

'No thanks.' There is a single mug by the sink. On the ceiling, in the bulbs of the special lights, there are small coils of such intense blue that they hurt Myrtle's eyes. She cannot imagine how he can work in such alien conditions.

'So what are you doing? Here so early?'

'I don't seem to be able to stay in bed much after five-thirty. I wake up so alert. I went down to the harbour.'

'What's going on down there?'

'Nothing much. I ran into Alastair Brown.'

They smile at each other. Martin is aware of the rumour. He throws the carcass of a small haddock into a crate on the floor. It's already half full of slobbery skins and milky spines. Stripped of their flesh, they are bent like the fronds of delicate plants. He lays the fillets beside a row of others, iridescent little silvery strips of matching neatness.

'Any progress in his courting?'

'Don't be silly! We've scarcely exchanged a word since he's been here.'

'Maybe he's a slow mover. Though I have to say I don't see him as quite the ideal man for you, should you ever want to marry again.'

'I'll never want to do that.'

'No. Well. That's understandable.' Swish, swish goes his knife. Off comes a head. Its gold eyes, not long enough dead to have dulled, look at Myrtle. 'Have you thought any more about the headstone? It's been, what? Almost two years now. I'm keeping aside that fine bit of marble I showed you. You only have to give me the word.'

'I have thought, yes. Thought and thought. "Archie Duns, husband and fisherman", I thought. How about that? And the dates, of course.'

Martin's thumbs fumble swiftly through the fish while his eyes look up to meet hers.

'That sounds fine to me,' he says. 'That sounds good. I'm sure God prefers understatements. I mean, wandering around as many cemeteries as I do, you'd think the dead *en masse* were saints – such tributes. So you're not thinking about adding something from the Bible, too?'

'I'm still trying to find something. I'm being a little slow, I know. I want to get it absolutely right.' Martin nods. 'I must be on my way. Assembly's in three minutes.'

'You're liking it, the job at school?'

'Oh aye, it's grand. It's what I've always wanted, teaching. Nine- and ten-year-olds are my lot. Wonderful, that age.'

'Shall I bring you up a piece of haddock on my way home?'

'You're always bringing me fish.'

'And why not?'

'Well, that would be nice.'

'See you later, then.'

Myrtle pushes through the doors of thick transparent plastic, breathes fishless air, sees a ribbon of pale sun on the sea. She looks forward to the warmth of her classroom – a much more cheerful and painted place since she herself was there. She looks forward to the recitations, one by one, of *When fishes flew and forests walked* . . . They are good learners, her class. She is proud of them. The school bell echoes down the wynd: she hurries. She's been up so long almost a whole day seems to have passed. This evening there's Martin's piece of haddock to look forward to, and in the afternoon Annie is coming round for a game of cards. That is what she looks forward to most of all, for they have not had the chance to see each other for a while.

The evening after Archie died, Martin went round to see Myrtle. He found her alone at the table surrounded by a small chaos of paper, lists. There were signs of last night's weeping in her eyes, but she seemed calm, and glad to see him.

'I'll be the one to dig Archie's grave,' he said. 'It's all arranged.'

'Thank you. That would be best.'

'And . . . as for the headstone, when it comes to the time to think about it, you can rely on me to find the finest bit of marble.'

Myrtle, grateful for a visitor who did not offer well-meaning platitudes, made an attempt to smile. The softness of his Canadian drawl was comforting as wool on skin.

'You're a good man, Martin,' she said, and turned her eyes to the window. She gave a small, self-deprecating laugh. 'Why, I haven't even found the right epitaph for Mother, yet. Years late. And now there's Archie. I'll do my best, try to concentrate when things have –'

'There's plenty of time. You've enough to think about at the moment, arranging the funeral. Is there anything I can do?'

'I think it's all done. I've been making arrangements all day.'

'If there's anything, anything at all . . . you know you only have to call on me.'

'I know.' Myrtle nodded. 'Thanks.'

They fell into silence for a while. Several times Myrtle cocked her head as if she heard footsteps outside. Once she put up her hand, as if expecting to find Archie's reaching over her shoulder. But when all she grabbed was air she gave an impatient sigh, annoyed with herself for such foolishness. Eventually she said:

'I don't know how it happened. I don't know what sort of accident it was. Nobody has told me. I don't want to ask. I expect one of them will come and explain when they can find the words. Ken was meant to come. Annie asked him. I've been expecting him. But no sign of him yet.'

'I'm sure he will.' Martin moved uneasily in his chair. He had heard bloody rumours.

'Also, I don't know when he died. Was it in the boat, in the ambulance, in the hospital? I don't know. No one told me. I didn't ask. I couldn't ask. I held his hand, but did he know I held it? Did he know I was there? I'll never know. How will I live without knowing?'

'All these things . . . You must try not to let them torment you in the next few days. You must keep your strength for yourself and others.'

Myrtle looked at him with interest. She was suddenly more alert.

'That's an unusual thing to say to someone whose husband's just died . . . Others. But you're right, of course. My mother told me that when my father died she needed all her energy to comfort those around her. I've had to do a fair bit of calming down. Annie's wept herself to a standstill crying for Archie, crying for me, crying for herself. I don't feel much like tears, myself. One burst of weeping last night, when they'd all gone, and I saw the Bear, and there was no Archie to congratulate me. But now I feel quite dry – bone dry, parched, scraped, arid. The machinery that should be making my widow's tears is too feeble to start them. There's no power, there. There's nothing, nothing, nothing. No Archie. Nothing.'

'I can understand.' Martin had to turn his head away lest she should see the tears that had sprung to his own eyes.

'But how can it have happened, Martin? The accident, whatever it was? Archie was the most conscientious man you could ever find when it came to safety. If one of the crew was ever careless, endangering others, Archie'd come down on him like a ton of bricks. What could have happened? Dear God, what could have happened? My Uncle John knew a man who was decapitated when the winch broke – cables snapped. That can't have been . . .'

'There's no use asking yourself these questions when the answers aren't ready.' Martin stood up, aware of his clumsy sympathy, sharing her emptiness. 'I'm sure Ken will be the one to tell you. He was Archie's oldest friend, despite their differences of late. He was the one there, he saw the horror, he knows he has to be the one to tell you when you're ready, and he's ready. Imagine how he must feel. He'll need to give himself a little time to gather his strength to come to you. After the funeral, perhaps.'

'Aye: you're right again. I'll wait.' Myrtle shrugged, and stood too. 'It's not *how* I really want to know – I'm a coward, there. It's not *when*, really, either. All I want to know is *why*? Why did Archie die? Why?'

Martin shook his head, unable to speak. He wanted to stretch out a hand to her, touch her hair, her cheek, her bruised eyes – make some small physical gesture to show he understood the magnitude of her sorrow. But he felt that to do so would be inappropriate.

Restrained acts of friendship are often of more value than those whose show is innocently mistimed. Martin merely shook his head as he went to the door, sensing it was time for Myrtle to be alone again. He knew she was a woman to whom solitude is consolation, and he had no wish to intrude a mite too far into her aloneness. With promises of returning next day, he left with a swiftness that was much appreciated by Myrtle, who went back to her lists of things that must be done to ensure Archie's funeral was the sort of occasion due to such a man.

Myrtle and Annie sit at their usual places playing cards. It's a bright afternoon. The kitchen is filled with light. The aged wall clock ticks – relentless, hollow, nagging the concentration. One of Archie's old navy jerseys still hangs on the back of the door. The wool on a sleeve is snagged in a couple of places, making small holes that Myrtle means one day to darn.

Annie arrived a little late for the game, and flustered. Soon after Archie died she left the job in the museum café to be a receptionist in a hairdresser. Within a week she grew tired of making scant appointments, and left for a series of other equally unsatisfactory jobs. Eventually she returned to the café where she was welcomed back and offered a promotion. Now, she is in charge of three waitresses and the punctual delivery of the homemade cakes is her responsibility. She works longer hours than she needs, lingers over a cup of coffee with whoever else is on duty long after the last customer has gone. Anything, as Myrtle observes, to put off the moment of going home.

Myrtle is used to reading Annie's hands. Today she sees that they are a little shaky as they arrange the cards. Indication of some sort of confrontation: a thin blade of dread stabs at Myrtle's innards. There have been too many confrontations with Annie since Archie's death. Too many arguments, disagreements, promises not to be so stupid again, apologies . . . Peace, then, for a week or so – untroubled friendship almost like the old days, before Annie – always Annie – provokes some new unease between them.

Today Myrtle knows she is not going to get away with a peaceful, silent game of cards. Some accusation, that she cannot guess at, is boiling within Annie, whose eyes glitter dangerously. Annie slams down her cards.

'Myrt: I can't not say this any longer. I think you should see someone. Everybody thinks so.'

'Everybody?' The thought of people discussing what might be best for her makes Myrtle feel sick, cold. 'See someone?' she says lightly. 'What sort of person?'

'You know: one of those people who help. A counsellor.'

'Why should I want to see one of them? Why do you suppose I need help? What sort of help do you think a counsellor could be?' Despite herself, she knows there is scorn in her voice.

Annie sighs. There is suffering in her face. Afflicted by so much do-gooding earnestness, Myrtle thinks.

'The fact is, it's almost two years since Archie died, and as far as I know, you've never broken down, never given in to hysteria, never acted like any normal woman whose husband has been killed in a ghastly accident. You didn't even cry at the funeral. Just watched all the rest of us snivelling, a superior expression on your face.'

'Is that how you saw it?' Myrtle tries for patience. 'I appreciate your concern,' she says, aware of her own formality, 'but I've no intention of seeing anyone. I don't believe in that sort of help. I don't want it, I don't need it. The fact that I'm not a weeper shouldn't be any cause for you to worry that I'm not behaving "normally" as you call it. It's just how I am. We're all made differently, so naturally we all react differently. There's nothing very odd about that.'

'You're impossible sometimes,' says Annie. 'So stand-offish, even to me. So sure of your own strength, your own independence. So unwilling, since Archie's been gone, to let anyone get near you.' She begins to fiddle with a line of cards, not meeting Myrtle's eye. 'The fact is, you've been acting strangely. Shutting yourself away, almost hermit-like. I know you enjoy your teaching, and you love your pupils, and Janice. And I know a lot of your time is taken up planting your wood – none of us ever invited to see it, mind. And I'm not saying you're not just the same to me, in a way. Here I am: cards as usual. Chit-chat, cups of tea. But the thing is, you can't deny it, you've gone away from us. You've left me, your friends, for somewhere of your own where no human company seems to be needed.'

'I'm sorry,' says Myrtle, 'if it feels like that.'

'All I'm trying to say is, it's time for you to try to return to a less secret, solitary life. For God's sake, Archie wouldn't have wanted you to become a sort of nun just because he had died. He'd want you to carry on as normally as possible.'

'I do,' says Myrtle. 'At least, I'm trying.'

'And quite apart from that, you don't tell me much now, about how you're feeling – it's as if you don't trust me any more, don't need me as a friend any longer, don't want me to know what's going on in your – well, your soul.'

'I don't,' says Myrtle, firmly. 'I'm sorry if this distresses you, but I don't. In the first place I could never describe it. And if I could, I wouldn't want to. Not even to you.'

'I see.' Annie's wounded look now meets Myrtle's. 'It didn't used to be like that.'

'Perhaps you don't quite remember. You were the one who always confessed everything – well, not everything, but a good deal. I was the one who said less.'

Annie's head snaps back.

'What didn't I tell you? Far as I remember, I told you everything.'

Confronted by this untruth, Myrtle feels reckless. She answers before she can stop herself.

'You never said a thing about your love for Martin. That is, you admitted you fancied him. But you never said anything about the seriousness of your love for him.'

'For Martin?' The blood blows across Annie's face, reddening it from forehead to chin. Then quickly as it has come it drains away, leaving her a ghastly white. 'Who told you about Martin?'

'I'll never tell you that.'

'The bastard. It must have been him. No one else knew.'

'It was a long time ago. You can trust me.'

There's a long silence. Then Annie says:

'Well, since you know, I don't mind telling you it's true. I loved

Martin. I mean I really loved him. I would have married him in five minutes, had he asked. But he didn't love me. Funny, really. I've had so many men, never a shortage. I suppose I didn't want to admit to you of all people my *failure*. I'd always been so good at getting every man I wanted. Although all *they* ever wanted was the same thing, and it was never love – except Ken.' She gives a small, self-deprecating laugh. 'Whereas you, big, solid, plain Myrtle – you've only ever looked at one man, and that man turned and saw you and loved you completely. He may have died too soon, but you've been so lucky. You don't know how lucky.'

'Aye, I do,' says Myrtle. 'There's not a day I don't remember that. But you shouldn't underrate Ken's love for you. You've a devoted husband there . . .'

'Ah! Ken. The loving husband. We scarcely speak these days.'

'There you are! That's another thing you haven't told me.'

'Not something I want to talk about, think about.' Annie sounds weary now. 'I keep myself busy as I can so I don't have to think. I'll find it hard ever to forgive that man.'

'But you should,' says Myrtle. 'I mean, I have. And if it wasn't for Ken, Archie would be here today.'

'You're a bloody saint, then. A bloody *stupid* saint.' The harsh words are forlorn. 'How can I forgive a man who caused *your* husband to die, Myrt? And he hasn't laid a finger on me since Archie . . .'

'I'm sorry,' says Myrtle. 'Perhaps, time –'

'Time? What's time got to do with anything? You of all people must know that. Time makes no difference, does it?'

'Not to . . . no,' agrees Myrtle. Annie pulls on her coat.

'I don't know where we've got to. Nowhere, I think. I came here to try tactfully to suggest you need help, and you snap my head off. You take the chance to tell me you no longer want to tell me things, but can't resist letting on that you know about my pathetic love for Martin in the past. You also scoff at me for not forgiving Ken for killing your husband – something you, the saintly Myrtle, apparently have done. I don't know where that leads us. I feel totally . . . and then I go and tell you about Ken not wanting me any more – or maybe it's just impotence brought on by guilt. I don't know. I'm not sure I care.' Tears begin to run down her cheeks. 'Maybe I'm the one who needs the help, you're the strong one. Well, you've always been the strong one, really. I've always relied on you. Taken you for granted, perhaps. I hate your new distance.' She holds out her arms. 'Please come back.'

Myrtle holds out her arms, with some reluctance, and allows Annie to shift her sad head on her shoulder. She murmurs vaguely comforting words, assures Annie she hasn't gone, she'll always be there, but since Archie died there are great tracts of life she wants to deal with entirely on her own. Annie nods, wipes away her tears. Myrtle has no idea whether or not her friend understands, or has taken comfort. And in a strange, hard way that puzzles her, she doesn't care very much. A selfish longing to be alone consumes her. She disentangles Annie from her arms and goes to open the door. But Annie does not move. Myrtle can tell from her face that a sudden thought has come to her to lighten the sombre air between them.

'Shall I tell you something, Myrt?' she asks. Her red eyes are mischievous now. 'Seeing as you know about Martin, all past history . . . I have to confess I wrote him smashing letters. Know how? I went up to the library – yes, I did – studied a few books of love letters between famous people. Well, I took a bit from one, a bit from another, nothing too high-faluting, joined them up with a word or two of my own. I was proud of them, I can tell you. It was good fun.' She is laughing now; so is Myrtle. 'Martin must have been that surprised. Don't suppose he ever imagined I was a talented writer.' She stands. 'But I tell you something else – he's the only one I'd ever have gone to all that bother for. If he ever says anything about those letters, you won't let on, will you?'

'Of course not. Never.' The laughter, which has lifted them, dies. 'But please, Annie, never say again that Ken killed Archie. He didn't. It was an accident. You know that.'

'Ken's fault. You know *that*.'

'And please don't come round suggesting any more counsellors.' Myrtle manages to say this lightly. 'You should know I'm the last person in the world who'd welcome some stranger's prurient questions, some futile attempt at understanding. How on earth could that be a comfort? It'd be the greatest intrusion . . . If I've inherited anything from my mother, it's how to deal with things on my own.' She manages a smile as Annie goes down the steps.

'I'll remember that,' says Annie. But she can't return the smile.

When Annie has gone the picture of Ken's confession returns to Myrtle, as it has done many times since Archie's death. She fights it, but it will not go away because it is never absolutely clear. No matter how carefully she scours Ken's explanation, it is always misted. She is still unable to see, to understand, how exactly those terrible moments were. She accepts that full realisation may always elude her, but knows she will never be able to give up the search.

Ken came to the funeral, silent, pale, unweeping. He stood far away from Annie and made no attempt to speak to Myrtle. As she stood throwing a handful of earth into the grave, she was aware of his slipping away down the path. His mysterious exit merely added another puzzle to the dreadful mysteries of the day: why had Archie died? Who among the mourners knew? Was it only Ken who was party to the whole truth? Such questions, that day, merely dappled Myrtle's more profound reflections and were put aside. She would find the answers eventually, but while his coffin lay exposed in the jaws of newly cut black earth, they seemed irrelevant.

Two weeks later Ken paid his visit to Myrtle. He confessed he could find no adequate words to express his sympathy and sorrow – this news was greeted with an impatient, dismissive wave of Myrtle's hand. All he could do, he said, was to explain what happened.

'This is difficult for me to say, Myrtle,' he began, 'but if I don't tell you the truth I'll never be able to live with myself.'

'I daresay it will be just as difficult for me to hear the truth as it is for you to explain it. But I'd be obliged if you'd just get on with it.' Myrtle had never heard herself speak like that, so roughly.

Ken kneaded his hands, lowered his eyes, further unnerved.

'There was this argument. Archie and me.'

'Argument?'

'I'm afraid we'd got round to squabbling again. At sea.'

'I thought you'd sorted out all your differences.'

'We had. I was about to sell the van, as you know. No more deliveries. I kept my word. But I just couldn't get it out of my mind that we on *Skyline II* were being a bit foolish . . . the only honest ones. Christ . . . I wasn't doing *much*. Just selling a few fish that the bloody stupid law says should be thrown back. Not the *Skyline*'s, of course. I'd never have done that. I was just helping a friend, delivering a crate or two for him. All I said to Archie was that if others were doing it, why not us? By that I didn't mean I had any intention of carrying on – I'd given my word. I just wanted to know why we should be in a minority, these hard times . . .'

'You were stuffing crates between the furniture?' Ken nodded. 'You're a fool, Ken.' Myrtle's voice was a knife-slash. 'Besides, you knew nothing in the world would persuade Archie to contemplate anything dishonest.'

'Of course I knew that. But this wasn't exactly dishonesty on a large scale. Just the occasional crate or two, if I happened to be going in the right direction. Didn't think there was much harm in that.'

'What friend?'

'You can't expect me to tell you that. But once again there was a shortage of money. Annie always wanting more than we had. This was to have been my last try at persuading him. Then I would have given up – hell, I'm not a crook, just worn down by disappointing my wife. Anyhow, that day I made my suggestion – fully expecting him to say no, fully expecting to sell the van when we came ashore, the job on the boat being more important to me than anything . . . and Archie lost his temper. I've never seen a man so angry, bawling me out. Only thing concerns him is his rage with me. Just for that moment he lost his concentration. Then the chance in the million happens: winch snaps. Cable snaps back at the speed of light, gets him in the throat . . .' Here Ken's voice was so thickened by a rising sob that it was hard to distinguish his words. But Myrtle, hearing the facts at last, felt no mercy. Now she desired to know the full horror. Better to live with the reality than ghastly imaginings.

'And then?'

'One minute he was punching the air, screeching blue murder at me. The next – a cracking noise when the wire broke. Archie stopped shouting and was slewed over on the deck.' Ken's sobs were articulate by now. 'Blood gushed out. Never seen so much blood. Jugular sliced. He didn't make a sound. No cry, nothing. To be honest, Myrtle, it happened all so quickly, and it was all so terrible, the most terrible thing I've ever seen, that it's still confused in my mind.'

'Yes, yes.'

'In the daytime, that is. Asleep – nightmares – clear as anything. Then when I wake the confusion starts again . . .' He broke off to blow his nose, tried to stop the sobbing.

Myrtle's hands were folded in her lap. She sat very upright, eyes on something out of the window.

'One of the many things Archie always believed in was that a fisherman should keep his concentration. Let it lapse for a moment, he used to say, and disaster can strike.' She spoke in the high, thin voice of her younger self. Ken looked up, half expecting to see Myrtle the child. 'If you hadn't been having a row, and God knows how you must have put your crazy idea to provoke him to that sort of anger, Archie wouldn't be dead. He'd be here now.'

'Possibly,' said Ken. His sobs were ebbing. 'He could still have had his back to the winch, might not have got out of the way in time . . .'

Myrtle turned on him, rigid in her contempt.

'You know that's not true, Ken Mcleod, so don't go trying to soothe your conscience with any such delusions. Archie's reactions to danger were quicker than a wild animal's. He could sense disaster a mile off. There's no possible chance he would have been caught by that wire if he hadn't been concentrating on your loathsome suggestions instead of the job in hand –' Her normal voice had returned now, deep and scarred. Ken stood up, shoulders hunched as if against rain.

'Myrtle, please. I know how it is for you – it's bad for me, too. How am I going to live with myself?'

'I don't know.'

'I don't suppose there's anything I can say by way of –'

213

'No, nothing. Don't try.'

'You'll never forgive me – how can I cope with that?'

'Oh, that. No need to worry there.' Myrtle gave a small laugh. 'Forgiveness – if that's what you want. I forgive you. You didn't set out to murder Archie, just to goad him. Your foolishness, trying to persuade an honest man to agree to a dishonest arrangement – was beyond belief. But that's not the point. Forgiveness isn't going to bring him back. The thing you should worry about is keeping out of my way. As you can imagine, I don't want our paths to cross any more, Ken. I don't want any more to do with the man who . . . I'm warning you, keep out of the way. Not easy in a place this size, but possible. Nothing's changed between me and Annie, of course. She's my friend, whatever. Not her fault, your –'

'Annie's not all innocence in this. Her pushing me –'

'I'll not hear a word against Annie, and besides, I'd like you to go now.'

'Very well.' Ken shrugged, wiping his eyes with the weight of a man who has run out of words. He left the room in silence.

When he had gone Myrtle remained in her chair, in the quiet of her empty kitchen. Visions of the accident crowded her vision, worse than anything she had imagined. Archie's bloody head, almost severed from his body, rose before her, no matter how she shifted her eyes. She heard herself moaning, the quiet cooings of a strangled dove. Archie's voice was in her head, smatterings of things he had said over the years. His presence was so strong she was convinced his absence was some madness within *her*, and soon he would be back to comfort. In her stillness she realised she was waiting for him: she also knew the uselessness of that wait. It was the first time the absurdity of her position struck her with a feeling of utter helplessness. It was to strike again and again in the months to come.

Ken, for his part, kept to his word. He avoided Myrtle: there was no occasion for them to speak. Until the afternoon of Annie's outburst, the two friends never mentioned Ken's name. He became a ghost between them.

*

In the five minutes before Martin arrives, Myrtle wonders if she has been too hard on Annie. Annie meant well. Others, concerned for her, mean well too. But their presumptions annoy her. Their anxiety is an intrusion into her dearly held privacy. It provokes unreasonable anger. She wants to be left to deal in her own way with her aloneness. She wants to be the sole witness to her own foolishness, eccentricity, small spasms of irrational behaviour. These things will pass, she believes. The chasm that surrounds her will never be filled, but the footholds will become stronger. In time the rawness of skin and soul will lessen, and she will be less wary of the proximity of others. The figure of her own mother, widowed, is bright in her mind. Dot was dignified, strong, at ease with her husband's death: her way was to carry on abiding by his rules – their rules – and to regard his absence as a temporary matter of not much more significance than a long trip to foreign waters. Dot's belief in the reunion with her husband was buoyant – her cheerfulness, by day, made the loss easy for others. (There were a few occasions on which Myrtle had heard her weeping in the night – occasions when she knew any offer of comfort would be abhorred, and so left her mother to battle undisturbed.) Dot was more approachable in widowhood, Myrtle realises, than she is herself. She vows to try to be less distant, less defensive. She is aware her need to grieve privately causes some people concern, even offence. She wishes she could make them understand she is not lonely, just alone. And aloneness, if accommodated in the right spirit, has as many riches as a peopled world.

Myrtle gets up from the table and moves round the room. Under her long skirts her feet shuffle in shy dance steps. Her body sways. Her big hands sprawl on her hips, clutching at the material gathered round her waist. She moves cautiously as a ship coming into berth: from table, to stove, to chair. As she passes the door she slows down even further. The smell of Archie's jersey is still there. Like his voice in her head, it has not faded a jot. *Stop moving about, Myrtle wife. Sit down, won't you?*

Perhaps this is madness, she thinks. But she has found this crisscrossing the room, weaving in and out like the wool of a darn, is comforting. It furnishes a miniscule part of the emptiness, in the same way that nets interrupt the depths of the sea. And no one has caught her at her dancing: no one has proof of her occasionally eccentric behaviour. So why do they think she is in need of help? I'm as fine and strong as any woman can be whose husband has been dead for nearly two years, she tells herself – though perhaps I'm becoming stuck in too rigid a groove of self-discipline. Perhaps the time has come to shift a little . . .

When Martin arrives with his parcel of fish, he finds Myrtle still moving about, humming to herself, her eyes unfocused. He sees it takes her a moment or two to disentangle herself from her reflections. Then she looks at him gladly, unembarrassed that he has caught her in this private act, and suggests they should walk out and see how the trees are doing.

This is the first time Myrtle has invited anyone to the coppice. As they walk up the road she feels an irrational guilt. The wood was Archie's idea: he should be the first one to check its progress. But Martin is talking about other things – how he had cut his hand quite badly, yesterday, still not highly skilled at filleting. He is trying to describe how hands deal so differently with different materials. There could hardly be a greater contrast between the rubbery flesh of fish and the unyielding hardness of marble, he says: and yet his own hands felt it much easier to chip the stone than to knife through the flesh. Odd. It would be a luxury to cut through silk with sharp scissors, he adds. Or even fine tweed. Perhaps he should have been a tailor – a bespoke tailor. And what is a bespoke tailor, incidentally? He once looked it up in a dictionary but couldn't find it. Did Myrtle know what the word *bespoke* means? She shakes her head, eyes dazzled by the poppies flaring along the hedgerows. Martin's voice is soothing, no matter what he says. It's a fine warm evening. In the distance a tractor stutters up and down the seam of rich dark soil, The Golden Fringe, as it's known locally, near the sea. The tractor is very old, topples to one side, caught in a net of gulls. For a moment the daft idea comes to Myrtle that if it wasn't for the gulls it would keel over completely. The guilt she felt at the beginning of the walk has disappeared.

And when it comes to showing Martin round the wood, she begins to enjoy herself. The enjoyment runs up the veins of her arms, tingling, an active thing. They walk up and down the paths that Myrtle has spent months designing between the trees – young saplings, each one strapped into a protective covering, just a few thin branches and tiny leaves sprouting out at the top.

'Imagine all this in ten years' time,' says Myrtle. 'Ground ivy, moss, bluebells, primroses, birds nesting in the branches.'

Martin is impressed. He strokes his chin, nods his head.

'You organised all this yourself? Choosing the trees, planning the planting? It's quite something.'

'We'd decided on a good many things together, it wasn't all me. At one moment, soon after Archie died, I thought I should abandon the whole project. But then I thought, no: the whole idea had given him so much pleasure. He was so looking forward to getting it under way. I thought the least I can do is to go ahead, do the best I can alone. And I have to say it's taken up a lot of time, which has been a good thing.'

They reach the centre of the wood, the place where all the paths end.

'This,' says Myrtle, 'I'm going to keep as a clearing. I might put a bench here. Somewhere to ruminate in my old age.'

'I could make you a bench,' says Martin. 'I haven't worked with wood for years, but I enjoy a bit of carpentry.'

He's not sure Myrtle has heard his suggestion, for she does not answer, but moves to the place she judges to be the very centre of the clearing. She turns to him.

'Here,' she says, 'I want a rock. Do you think that would be possible? I want a rock to be a memorial stone to Archie.'

'I think that would be possible.'

'Could you find me one? Could you help me to arrange the transport? It'll be quite difficult, I know.'

'I'll see what I can do.'

'It would need some sort of . . .'

'. . . simple carving. Name and dates. On the rockface, or perhaps a separate piece of stone. I'd like to do that for Archie.'

'If you could, I'd be so pleased – though you've already done the headstone. You've done a lot for Archie. Do you like it here? Can you see how it will all be eventually?'

Martin nods again. He knows he is the first person to be invited to the wood, and is touched by her pleasure and excitement. She moves, smiling, towards him, pointing to the only path they have not tried. Then she trips over a hidden stone, and falls. It's not a bad fall, though she whimpers briefly and clutches an ankle. In a moment Martin is by her side. He kneels, briskly examines the ankle like a doctor.

'It's nothing but a slight twist,' says Myrtle. 'Give me a hand.'

Martin grips the hand she offers, puts the other one beneath her elbow, heaves her to her feet. For a moment they stand as close as is necessary for Martin to provide support while Myrtle tries putting weight on her foot. There is a stab of pain, but nothing unbearable.

'It's fine,' she says. 'Thanks.' She frees her hand and arm from Martin and moves awkwardly away from him, turning her head so that he shall not see the scarlet flush that has spread over her. This is the first time since Archie died she has had any physical contact with a man. She hates having let him touch her, albeit innocently, helpfully. The guilt rushes back. First she brings a man to see Archie's wood before any one else, and then in the memorial place itself she lets him hold her hand. Grip it quite hard. An enjoyable sensation. This is betrayal indeed.

'Let's go back this way,' she says, and hobbles down the new path.

'Sure you're all right?'

'Sure. It's only a very slight twist.'

Walking ahead of Martin gives her the chance to rethink her opinion of herself as her face cools down. With surprising speed she changes her mind. Archie, she tells herself, would have been delighted that their old mutual friend Martin was the first visitor to the wood. He would also have thought it the natural and right thing to do, to help Myrtle up when she stumbled. So why on earth had she been so put out? Why had such an innocent event caused her such anguish? Could it be because that moment of being in Martin's grasp was an unbidden comfort? Leaning on him, she had felt strong, hopeful – hopeful of what she could not say: something to do with the kindness of a good man still having the power to touch her.

She and Martin walk slowly back along the road to the village. The poppies' heads are bowed now, their petals closing. The tractor has gone, the net of gulls dispersed. One or two are left floating across the sky, aimless in the arc of fine silver webbing formed by evening clouds. When they reach the house Myrtle, her calm restored now, invites Martin in for a glass of beer. But he declines.

'I promised Annie I'd deliver a bit of fish for her supper. She's not too happy, I reckon. Having a difficult time, I guess.'

'She is, too,' says Myrtle quickly. Martin waves.

'Take care of that ankle,' he says. 'And thank you for taking me to your wood. It's a grand place. Archie would have been proud of what you've done.'

Myrtle begins to climb the steps to the front door.

'Would you mind . . .?' she says.

'. . . not saying anything to anyone? You can rely on me. I shan't say a word.'

As Myrtle fries the slivers of fresh haddock Martin has given her, she wonders whether Annie has invited him to join her and Janice for supper. The thought ruffles her very slightly. To deflect it she takes out her old copy of *Sorab and Rustum* to prepare herself for Janice's lesson tomorrow. As always, she looks forward to Janice's visit. The child loves the poems Myrtle has chosen to study – she has a particular liking for narrative poetry. Tomorrow will be the introduction to Matthew Arnold. Myrtle reads as she eats – a habit she has acquired of late, although often she becomes so engrossed in the book that the food grows cold. Tonight, most of Martin's haddock is left to become unappetising on the plate, and has to be thrown away.

Unlike many who are widowed, Myrtle does not suffer from night-mares. Deep and dreamless sleep returned to her not long after Archie was buried. Instead, it is the day-pictures that assault her – jagged little sections that sometimes lock together easily, but sometimes a piece is missing from her memory, and she panics. Recently she has been unable to recall, after the wedding, their arrival in Mull. She remembers the dour house, the friendly landlady, the Swiss sort of bedroom, the delicious breakfasts . . . But their actual arrival at this house has gone from her. Unnerved, Myrtle wonders how important this vanishing is. Does it mean rebellion by a mind overtaxed by remembering? Should she try to stop indulging in memory of things past, and fix her mind instead on the nebulous stretches of the future? This is difficult. She does try, sometimes. But there are no peaks in the mist. Nothing clear to aim for, no apparent path. No conscious desires.

And of late a new and strange phenomenon has come to trouble her: the sky. In her rational mind Myrtle knows this inconvenient phobia must have sprung from the trauma of Archie's death. But in the moments before she has time to reason with herself, scoff at her absurdity, fear clammies her skin and jolts her heart.

The menace of the sky began one evening when, on impulse, she walked down to the harbour. This was something she often made herself do, to try to overcome her loathing of the place from which *Skyline II* was gone, but where Archie's friends still berthed. Used to absence, they were, perhaps, by now. On this particular evening there was a fine sunset: ruddy cloud densely reflected in the harbour waters, staining their brown to rust. It was a sky much like the one on the morning that Archie, mortally wounded, came ashore for the last time. Then, Myrtle remembered, as she waited for the boat to appear, she looked up and thought someone had shot the sky. Blood oozed from the clouds, streaked across gashes of peacock blue. On the recent evening she had forced herself to visit the harbour – almost two years since Archie's death, for heaven's sake – a similarly murderous sky had returned with all its old menace: she was overcome by a cold and enfeebling fear. Hurrying home, she stumbled several times, like a woman much older than herself. Safely in the kitchen, a sense of her own absurdity came quickly to her rescue. She laughed out loud in the silence, made herself a cup of tea. There was nothing for it but to deal with the undesirable surprises of widowhood with as much patience and reason as she could muster.

But from that evening it seemed that it was not just the sunset that unnerved her. A dun sky, next morning, was just as alarming. On the way to school she felt it hunched over her, ready to pounce, flatten, destroy. Safe indoors, the clamour of her class put flight to such silly fears, but she dreaded the journey home when the bell rang at three, and found herself small needless tasks to postpone her departure. She took a hold on herself – *always take a hold on yourself when the going gets rough*, Dot used to say – and left by four. The afternoon sky was lighter, more cheerful, cloudless. But still it oppressed, weighed heavily, filled her with unease. Subsequently, every outing required a summoning of strength. She could not give in, she knew, to some peculiar form of agoraphobia; she could rely on herself to beat this irrational fear. Out of doors, she kept her eyes down, unable to look up, dreading the whiteness of cloud shapes in her vision. She could no longer remember how she had ever taken pleasure in the massive skyscapes that arched over this part of the Scottish coast. She could only pray that her strange new fear was nothing more than a passing inconvenience bred of widowhood. Determination to overcome the distortion of her widow's senses was the task she now set herself, convinced that in time it would surely evaporate as mysteriously as it had descended.

Janice arrives a little early for her lesson. Her clumpy shoes clatter on the stone floor as she spins about disturbing the peace. She is pink-cheeked and bright-eyed as she empties her satchel of books on to the scrubbed table. Myrtle senses a time-spin moment. She knows this restless mood so well: Janice is Annie at thirteen, inflamed with antici-pation, almost visible sparks flying off her. Janice is a more serious pupil than Annie ever was. But Myrtle doubts she will be wholly able to concentrate on the poem today.

They sit. Myrtle eyes Janice fiercely. She wants to make quite sure the girl is aware of her priorities. She is here to study Arnold. She must put aside whatever the event is that has caused this obviously excited state.

Myrtle picks up her open book. She begins to read.

For very young, he seemed, tenderly reared;
Like some young cypress, tall and dark and straight,
Which in a queen's secluded garden throws
Its slight dark shadow on the turf,
By midnight, to a bubbling fountain's sound –

'Oh, Myrtle, I'm sorry. I can't concentrate on the words today. It's a great poem and that, but I'm all of a dither.'

'So I can see.' Myrtle fixes Janice with a look in which interest is underlined with impatience. 'What's the matter? What's clogging your mind?'

'Clogging?' Janice laughs. Her hands fidget about, moving pencils, rubbers. Myrtle frowns at the iridescent green nail polish. She also notices the girl's eyelashes – long, but not half the length of her mother's – bunched clumsily together by mascara which looks as if it was put on a long time ago. Myrtle feels a swell of unease which spoils the morning. She allows a beat or two of silence. Janice breaks it with her announcement.

'I'm in love,' she says.

'In love?' Myrtle feels her face being scanned: Janice is eager for a reaction. Myrtle tries to remember the boys in Janice's class: indeterminate youths as disparate as were the boys of her own generation. There must be Rosses and Kens and similar others there. Not an Archie, of course. There could never be another Archie.

'Don't ask me who,' says Janice.

'Right, I won't. It's nothing to do with me. Would you like a cup of tea?'

'Couldn't touch a thing, thanks. Shit: it gets you in the guts, doesn't it?'

'That's horrible language,' says Myrtle.

'Sorry. Slipped out.' Janice giggles. 'Those kind of words are ordinary among my friends.'

'Pity. They're not necessary.'

'No: but everyone uses them. I'd be different if I didn't, wouldn't I?'

'You should be brave enough to do and say what you think is

right. Following the others just for the sake of it is pretty feeble, I'd say. Not admirable.' The unease is making Myrtle fiercer than she intended. She doesn't know why Janice's sudden crude language has hit her so hard. Annie has always sworn: it is hardly surprising Janice takes after her. But until this morning, at this table, Janice has always been careful with her language. Annie has probably warned her that Myrtle is a prude in that way. And perhaps I am, Myrtle finds herself thinking. Why else should the child's sudden lapse be so oddly shocking?

Janice's hands come to rest at last on the open book in which the poem awaits. She is taken aback by Myrtle's admonition – a rare thing. But still she is unable to drag herself back to the story of *Sorab and Rustum* which only a week ago she had found so compelling.

'As I was saying, it gets you – it messes everything up, this love business.' A pout mushes the words. She puts a hand on her stomach. 'Can't eat, can't sleep, can't think of nothing else.'

'Anything else.'

'Well, you know what I mean. Spend all my time looking out for him. Anything just to catch a glimpse.'

Myrtle's glance, despite herself, is sympathetic. She decides to risk a single question.

'Is this love requited?' she asks.

'Req – what?'

'Does he love you back?' Myrtle is anxious the lesson should not altogether disappear. She does not want the short hour to give way to discussions of teenage fancy, for all that she understands Janice's heightened need to explore.

'Love me back? Fancy me, you mean? Don't suppose he even knows I exist.'

'Then you shouldn't waste too much time on him.'

'How can I help it? How can I stop what I feel? I only have to see him and my legs turn to jelly and my knees wobble out of joint and my heart batters like I'm going to die – don't you remember ever feeling like that?'

Myrtle smiles.

'I think most people have gone through that sort of experience at some time or other.'

'Bloody awful.'

'Janice, please.'

'Sorry.'

'Does your mother know?'

'Course not. Couldn't talk to her about that sort of thing. Please don't tell her. Promise not to tell her.'

'Promise.'

'What shall I do?'

'Such feelings wear off. Such turbulence fades. It can't last at such fever pitch for long.'

'Hope not. And yet –'

'Besides, at your age there's nothing much you can hope for, is there? I mean, except for friendship. Teenage crushes rarely develop into anything more lasting, more mature.'

'I know all that.' Janice is petulant. 'But I still can't do anything about it. It's, like, *gripped* me. It's all over me. It's much more than just a teenage crush, as you call it.'

'Janice, you're not yet thirteen and a half. You are a teenager. This is just part of the growing-up process which seems to have hit you rather hard, rather early. If I were you I should try to concentrate on the other bits of your life that give you most enjoyment. Our lessons, for instance.'

'Sorry. I'm trying.'

'Like a biscuit?'

'Please. I'm starving, though I feel sick when I eat.' She looks very young.

Myrtle gets up and goes to the tin. When her back is to Janice she asks:

'Didn't you manage the nice piece of haddock last night?'

'What haddock?'

'I thought Martin brought round a bit –'

'Oh he did, aye.'

Myrtle has a quick struggle with herself, and loses.

'And did your mother ask him to stay and share it for his pains?' she asks, despising herself.

Janice drags her eyes back from some remote place, blushing, as if she knows Myrtle has a picture in mind of the boy she loves. But Myrtle has no such thing, nor is she trying to envisage him.

'She did, I think,' says Janice, 'but he said he had to be on his way.' There is a sadness about her now, thoughts far from Martin and his fish. 'I couldn't eat the stuff. I've always hated fish, except fish fingers. My dad says I'm a living shame.'

The smallest reference to Ken causes Myrtle to wince, but she is determined the child shall have no clue as to what she feels.

'Try this,' she says, and hands Janice a slice of recently made gingerbread. Amorphous relief at the news about Martin – a sensation she would not like to scrutinise for fear of what it might reveal – flows through her. In this deliquescent state she thinks she has been too hard on the child, and berates herself. She returns to her seat, watches Janice hungrily eat the food, her eyes with their pathetically clotted lashes never still, confused, grateful.

'Oh Myrtle, thanks,' she says.

'It's something most people go through,' says Myrtle. 'When it's over – and you might be surprised how soon that is – you'll look back at yourself and laugh.'

'No I won't,' says Janice, very serious, licking crumbs from her fingers. 'I'll never laugh about this.'

'Well, whatever. But you won't do anything foolish, will you?'

'What d'you take me for?' She giggles but looks scornful. 'Can you remember when it happened to you? Fancying a guy – *really* fancying a guy for the first time?'

The warmth Myrtle felt for Janice's father comes back to her: the uncomfortable knowledge that hers had been unrequited love, and then the blasting of her hopes, all the same, when Ken betrayed her.

'I do believe I can,' she says, 'but that's not a story for today. There's not much time left and we've hardly read a thing.' She picks up the book, and Janice sighs.

Later, when Janice leaves, Myrtle feels she has failed to divert the

child's thoughts. It was impossible to regain her interest, concentration, enthusiasm. She remembers Ken's keenness for poetry as a boy:
then how it fizzled out, once he fell in love with Annie, and he read no
more. She hates to think of Janice going the same way as her father,
and hopes this childish state is but a temporary phase.

It's a Saturday morning. The exercise books Myrtle was intending to
mark she finished late last night. They sit in a neat pile on the table.
She wishes she had left them for this morning, as she had planned.

There is nothing to do. With no one to cook for, no plans to meet
Annie, the hours stretch emptily ahead. It's one of the few times since
Archie has died, Myrtle realises, that she has been at a loss as to know
what to do. She is grateful for the rarity of such occasions. But, in the
meantime, how best to fill the hours? Saturday mornings used to be
such busy times, speeding along in their happiness . . .

What Myrtle would like to do is to walk to the coppice, see how the
trees have progressed over the last few days – their new growth never
fails to astound her. She would like to reflect further on the placing of
the rock and the bench. But her enemy the sky bars her from leaving
the safety of the house. Through the window she can see it's a hard,
unbroken blue: a bright glare she cannot face flooding directly down
upon her. Perhaps it will be less menacing this afternoon, she thinks:
perhaps she will try to confront it then.

She sits at the table, big hands slabbed on its familiar wooden surface, cogitating on the feebleness of one who is supposedly so strong.
A long silence is interrupted by a knock on the door. By now Myrtle
has acclimatised herself to the thought of a solitary day devoid of
tasks, and small anticipated pleasures are beginning to stir. Not ten
minutes ago she would have been delighted by a visitor. Now, she is
not so sure.

Alastair Brown, it is. The shaky smile on his face indicates he has
been practising its uneasy stretch for some time. His navy blazer looks
suspiciously new. He holds a bunch of yellow roses secured in a cone
of transparent, spotted paper. Its edge is painted to look like a lace frill.
Whatever will florists think up next? Myrtle finds herself pondering.

'Mr Brown?'

'Mrs Duns?'

'Might I step over your threshold for just a moment? Might I come in?'

'Of course. Please do.'

Myrtle shuts the door behind him. She can't see his eyes, hidden as always behind dark glasses. But his head is bowed. He seems to be concentrating very intently on the roses. Then with a small shrug of impeccably blazered shoulders, he puts them quickly down on the table – a gesture almost of distaste. The scrunched paper that he has been holding glints with tiny flecks of his sweat. Myrtle sees his hands are shaking. He slips them into his pockets, aware of her eyes. The rigidity of the blazer is now destroyed by bulges. Myrtle offers him coffee.

'That would be a kindness,' says Alastair Brown.

While the kettle boils he filters back and forth round the kitchen. His innocent movements cause Myrtle a feeling of betrayal. The presence of any man in this kitchen, Archie's place, seems like infidelity. She watches Alastair Brown's dark glasses come to rest on various objects, and they swoop across the view out of the window. What can he be thinking? Why has he come? Plainly he's ill at ease. The sophisticated man from sophisticated southern parts, so apparent in his strutting down at the harbour, has left him here. His whole being suggests he has misjudged the wisdom of calling on Myrtle. He should never have embarked on this visit, he is cowed by regret. He's made a mistake, but it's too late to escape without some explanation.

Myrtle hands him a mug of coffee. He thanks her too profusely. She sits in her usual place at the table, indicating he should sit opposite – she doesn't want him to take Archie's seat. Sitting, he stares at his strong coffee. Then he makes so bold – Myrtle can see his struggle – to ask if she could oblige him with a touch more milk. He's quite unusual in his fondness for milky coffee, these health-conscious days, he says, with a thin little laugh.

Milk is added. Silence hangs between them again. Myrtle, growing more curious about the reason for the visit, finds it welcome despite the unease. Whatever Alastair Brown's mission, it will break the morning, the pleasures she had begun to anticipate would probably not have been so interesting as this strange call. He stirs his coffee, so that the small chipping sound of spoon against china will temper his words, perhaps.

'Not having been here at the time of your husband's death,' he begins at last, 'I offered no condolences. But I imagine that when a spouse dies the time for sympathy does not run out.'

'No,' says Myrtle.

'I've taken my time in coming here to offer my . . . but, as you can imagine, I could not be sure it would be appropriate.'

'It's very kind of you to . . . thank you.'

Alastair Brown allows another silence while he forms his next words.

'I hear – I mean, in a small place like this one hears everything, doesn't one? – that you are a very brave and gallant widow, crying on nobody's shoulder, as happy as can be expected in yourself. I hope that is the case.' Myrtle senses that behind the dark glasses Alastair Brown's eyes shut with relief now the worst part of his little speech is over. His taut shoulders rise, and he continues. 'I can see that after many years of happy marriage to have one's companion snatched away *untimely*, as it were, would put quite a different light on the rewards of solitude. It must make it less desirable. Strange.'

Myrtle nods. She sees her visitor's confidence rising. She sees his careful balancing of words is giving him a certain pleasure, now he is under way. She smiles, not consciously to encourage him further. But Mr Brown takes the small movement of her lips as the green light.

'I also hear,' he says, 'as I daresay you do, that my rejection of all the kind offers of help and friendship from local ladies – and, indeed, it has to be said, from others further afield – is because there is a rumour that the woman I am in fact awaiting is the Duns widow, the elusive Myrtle. You, Mrs Duns.'

Myrtle raises her eyebrows. She senses she is blushing, can think of no reply.

'But worry not. This is not the case. This is merely a silly rumour that has got out of hand. My reason for coming here this morning is to assure you absolutely, Mrs Duns, that there's not a jot of truth in the foolish story. The thought had never crossed my mind. I mean, we've scarcely met. But I didn't want you to suffer any embarrassment. I thought it best to come here and, well, put my cards on the table.'

Myrtle allows herself a long moment in which to think how best to answer.

'That's very kind,' she says again. 'Thoughtful. I had of course heard something of the silly rumours, but I naturally dismissed them. Still, it's good to hear from you yourself that the whole idea seems as absurd to you as it does to me.'

The muscles round Alastair Brown's mouth relax. Myrtle warms towards this awkward man: she's concerned to vanquish his fears for her discomfort. She would like to put him completely at his ease, and wonders how to guide a conversation into a new direction, deflect him from his concern – which may have caused him weeks of worry – over this visit. But before she can come to any decision Alastair Brown braves his next difficult point.

'But there is something I should like to put to you, Mrs Duns, now we have cleared up the matter of the rumours, cleared the air. I hope you won't take this as speaking out of turn. But – I hope you will understand this – there is something I am after, something very precious, very innocent, but proving very elusive to a bachelor of middle years.' He turns his head towards the window. Miniature curtains flap in the black discs of his glasses. 'What I am after is companionship.'

Myrtle, intrigued and amused by his formal use of language couched oddly in his Cornish brogue, is scarcely taking in the thrust of the words themselves. Alastair Brown pauses only for a moment to register a blurred query in her eyes, then hurries to enlighten.

'As you must know yourself, Mrs Duns, to be a single figure in a society crowded with couples has its drawbacks. It's assumed one is looking for a partner, and to that end all sorts of kind people offer up enthusiastic suggestions – but not, unfortunately, for companionship alone. You must have experienced this. Even in your two years of widowhood you must have turned down numerous suitors anxious to enter your life.'

'You flatter me,' says Myrtle, feeling herself redden again, 'but that really isn't the case.'

'Whatever. For my own part – and forgive me if this sounds like vanity – a good many ladies have pressed their suits upon me' (the visual image forces Myrtle to control a smile) 'and I've had to discourage them because their own aims have not exactly coincided with mine. What they are after is fun, romance, a sexual relationship, but all pointing towards the big commitment on the horizon – marriage. Well, I don't want that, ever. I've no wish to be a married man, though I have every wish to be a companionable man. I can offer plain food by my fireside, a drop of double malt, old films on the telly – as you may have heard from your friend Mrs Mcleoud' – here he allows himself a wry smile. 'I can offer excursions up the coast in summer in my little boat – but nothing more, really. Nothing of significance. My old mother lives in a home in Dundee. I feel obliged to visit her regularly. She's pleased to be back in these parts – born and bred in Dundee. Never liked Cornwall.' He breaks off to sigh. 'What a dull life, you must be thinking. But it's all I have to offer. In return I would enjoy an occasional agreeable female presence, someone who's looking for nothing beyond my meagre –'

'I'm not thinking it's a dull life,' Myrtle interrupts.

'Then you're a woman in a million.'

'Just one of simple tastes, like you. I've little ambition beyond getting through each day to the best of my ability.'

'Funny, I'm of that school, too.' Alastair Brown now smiles more openly. Myrtle's few words encourage him to reveal further thoughts pertaining to himself.

'It's also funny, you know, that any woman should ever consider pursuing me. I mean, not only do I lead a very quiet life and have little money and no car or other attractions, but I'm scarred . . . Of course, they don't know that. Dark glasses signal mystery, don't they? Stupid idea.' He taps a lens with his finger. 'They're also considered an affectation. I've heard the scoffing, believe me. But dark glasses that never come off are a challenge, I suppose. Well, mine don't come off for a very good reason.'

With no warning, the harbour master suddenly snatches off his glasses. They fall on to the table. He turns to face Myrtle.

'This, Mrs Duns. Take a good look and you'll see the reason I can never hope to offer any woman –'

He stops. Myrtle is too surprised to contain a gasp. One eye has a permanently lowered lid. The rim of white that shows beneath it is a cloudy brown, the iris invisible. The unsteady iris of the other eye is of no recognisable colour; the eyeball is surrounded by a mess of scarred and puckered skin. The result of some botched operation, perhaps, Myrtle thinks, but nothing very shocking. She stares back at the eyes thrust defiantly towards her. Ashamed of her initial reaction, she now attempts an impassive face.

'Accident,' says Alastair Brown.

'I'm sorry,' says Myrtle.

'So you understand.'

'I don't think you should be quite so sure that a scarred face will put people off.'

'But I do think that. I'm sure of it. I've had experience. I've seen people backing away, aghast. That's why I never take off . . . I can see all right. Sight's luckily not impaired. But you have to admit, I look pretty monstrous.'

Myrtle shakes her head. She can understand his wounded eyes might inspire distaste in some people, but to her the scarred face remains curiously fine, with its strong parrot nose and engaging smile. Reflecting on all this, she fails to come up with quick words of comfort. Alastair Brown, again with the air of a man who has made a mistake but knows it is too late to retract, puts the dark glasses back on. The metamorphosis, Myrtle is forced to admit to herself, is instant. His strange attraction once more positively confronts her. In the backwater of her mind, unformed, the thought occurs that progressive friendship with this man could be beneficial to both parties. But for the moment she intends to be cautious. Show her reserve.

'You've seen enough,' he says. 'I'm sorry. I didn't mean to . . . I'd be grateful if you would keep this to yourself.'

'Of course.'

By now it is time for more coffee, the right amount of milk. Myrtle's composure has returned. She feels pity for the man. She's intrigued by his mixture of vanity and lack of confidence. Perhaps they often go together, she thinks.

The morning is slipping by curiously fast. When will Alastair Brown leave? Will he further expand on his wish for a companion? As if sensing her thoughts, he pushes the cone of roses across the table towards her.

'I'll be off in a minute,' he says. 'These are for you.'

'Thank you.'

'But just to return for a moment to my request for a companion. I came to you with the thought that perhaps, as a widow, you might be looking for something of that nature yourself. Nothing more.'

'I haven't consciously thought in those terms,' says Myrtle, anxious in her delicacy, 'but I like to see friends. I'm no hermit.'

'Then from time to time we could get together? Share a herring?'

'Why not?' Myrtle smiles. Alastair Brown smiles back.

'Do you like old films?'

'I've not seen many.' The thought of even an occasional evening with the harbour master in front of his television causes Myrtle a lack of enthusiasm she has to conceal. She does this by shifting herself into a very upright position, back straight, signifying formality, a hint of unapproachability.

'I could try to convert you. Stewart Grainger, Margaret Lockwood . . . another world.'

His eagerness touches Myrtle. She thinks her defensive position might look too severe, and the last thing she wants to do is to offend so gentle a man. She slumps a little in her chair, and allows him a glimpse of her natural sympathy.

'I do enjoy a game of cards,' she says.

232

'Why, so do I!' His eagerness is almost pathetic. 'Though I haven't played anything but patience for a good many years now.'

Myrtle notices his second cup of coffee is untouched. She plans a small lie merely to ensure the visit will have a definite cut-off time, for she feels that given the slightest measure of encouragement Alastair Brown could still be sitting at her table at noon.

'I have an engagement at twelve,' she says, 'but we could play a game now, if you like.'

The effect of this offer upon Alastair Brown is out of all proportion to the invitation: he beams at the prospect, though even in his keen anticipation of further time in Myrtle's company, he does not abandon his well-mannered hesitation.

'I would not want to prevail upon your kindness,' he says.

'You're not prevailing on anything.' Myrtle, a little impatient, slaps down the cards.

'Now you're making a mockery of my language.'

'Well, it is quite distinctive,' Myrtle answers in a teasing voice. 'You can tell you watch a lot of old films.'

'I don't assume such language down at the harbour, with the men, as you can imagine.'

'I can. They'd have no idea what you were on about. You're plainly not a man of your time.'

'Nor do I want to be,' says Alastair Brown, cutting the pack with an elegant flick of his wrist which indicates a suddenly frivolous and easy heart. Myrtle observes that he has decided that his visit is not a mistake after all, and he's beginning to enjoy himself.

Two hours pass. Myrtle and the harbour master are still silently at their cards. Myrtle seems to have forgotten her engagement: her visitor has not reminded her. A plate of buttered scones is on the table beside them, but both are concentrating too hard to bother with food. Alastair Brown is taxing Myrtle. He is a good card player, much better than Annie.

The door opens – no knock – and Annie hurries in. She regards the two bowed heads. Myrtle looks up, dragging her concentration from her fine hand of cards to her friend's incredulous face.

'Oh, Annie,' she says, 'Mr Brown, here, has just dropped by –'

'I'm so sorry.' Alastair Brown, rigid with confusion, leaps up at once. The legs of his chair make a horrible squawk on the floor. His cards fall from his hands to splatter over the table. 'I just dropped in for a moment –'

'So I see,' says Annie. 'And why not?' Her eyes are on the roses, still in their cone of paper but thrust into a jug. 'Well, don't mind me. I was just dropping in, too, to see if Myrtle was all right, to see if she fancied a game of cards. But I see I've been beaten to it.'

'Sit down,' says Myrtle, her fluster receding. This is ridiculous, she thinks: why should she and Alastair Brown be so put out by Annie's appearance? 'Have a scone.'

'Not on your life.' The words are quiet and furious.

'I for one am on my way,' offers Alastair Brown. He pulls at his parrot-beak nose, fingers working fast. 'Thank you for your hospitality, Mrs Duns. I enjoyed our game. Perhaps we can have a return match, one day.' This is said with a small defiant toss of his head in Annie's direction. 'Mrs Mcleoud, good to see you again, too –'

He is gone. Annie looks down on Myrtle, who is calmly gathering up the cards. Then she sits in her usual place.

'So? What was all that about?' she asks.

'Annie!' Myrtle gives a small laugh. Her friend's entrance may have made her uneasy for a moment (though why this was so she cannot imagine), but it has done nothing to affect her good humour. 'Mr Brown –' she begins.

'Alastair, to me –'

'– maybe, to you. Mr Brown, to me, dropped by unexpectedly. He had one cup of coffee, left the other untouched, refused a scone and played several games of two-handed rummy. He's a good man at cards.' She smiles. Annie sniffs.

'So they're true, then, the rumours? Harbour master pants after the widow Duns.'

'Don't be ridiculous. He strikes me as a lonely man. Short of friends up here.'

'Not for the lack of opportunity. There's several keen to befriend him.' Annie is mellowing. She drags her look to the roses – a slow, vacant trawling of the intensely blue eyes that Myrtle knows so well. It means a thought has occurred to her.

'Well, he's all yours. Not my type, anyway. Leaves others free.'

'What do you mean?'

'Och, never mind.' Annie smiles. 'How do you fancy the roses?'

'There's not much choice, locally, is there?'

'Did you ask him why he always keeps his glasses on?'

'No.'

'Pretentious.'

'He might have something the matter with his eyes.'

'Doubt it. But you always go for the kindest explanation, don't you?' Annie begins to shuffle the cards. 'Actually, I came over to tell you something funny. I came to tell you Janice is in love.'

Myrtle dislikes the triumphant way in which Annie produces the news that Myrtle already knows. She barely raises her eyebrows.

'Thirteen,' goes on Annie, 'imagine. Well, I suppose I was a good deal younger than that, wasn't I? Had every boy in the class lined up for his turn, didn't I?'

'You did,' says Myrtle. 'Who's the boy?'

Annie shrugs.

'She's a dark horse, Janice. Won't tell me. She'll only say I'd be surprised. A lot of boys walk her home after school. Some of them stop off for a bite of tea, or go off for a walk. God knows what they do. She comes back very pink in the cheeks, sometimes.'

'They start so young these days – the pity of it. Perhaps you should make it your business to find out what she's up to.'

'No younger than some of us, thank you very much.' Annie laughs. 'Find out what she's up to? She'd never tell us. I have my suspicions about a certain Gus Gowering – I'm keeping my ear to the ground.'

'What's been your advice to her?'

'Advice?' Again Annie laughs. 'What advice can a mother give a daughter that she's going to listen to these days? Course I said don't do anything silly, but go for it, I said. Have fun.'

'Hope the whole business won't detract from her work,' says Myrtle, shoulders rising prissily. 'She's doing so well.'

'Heavens above, Myrtle, you have to keep up with the times. You're too nervous, over cautious. Of course a crush on some spotty boy isn't going to put Janice off her work.'

'It put you off yours, if you remember,' says Myrtle, giving her a sharp look. But she's in no mood to quarrel with Annie today.

'Feel like a quick game?' Annie is dealing out the cards. '*If you remember, I didn't have half Janice's brains.*' Then, after she has reflected on this for a while in silence, she goes on: 'You'll find me pretty boring to play with after Mr Romantic Hero Harbour Master, I daresay. But at least you're familiar with my game.'

'Don't be silly, Annie.'

'You know you can nearly always beat me, unless by some fluke . . .' She cuts the cards.

Half an hour later a white envelope is slipped through the door. Myrtle, her back to the door, does not hear it drop on to the mat. Annie, vicariously expectant, puts down her cards and hurries to pick it up.

'From Martin,' she says.

'How do you know?'

'He left me a note once. Sort of writing you'd always recognise.' She looks at Myrtle with such powerful curiosity that Myrtle, despite herself, slits open the envelope and takes out a single sheet of paper. She reads quickly to herself.

Bench settled. All in place. Hope you won't take this as a liberty. I'll be up at the coppice at 5.30 for your approval if that is convenient. If it isn't ring me and I'll remove it at once and apologise for acting with such haste. I was spurred by what I thought was a good idea. Yours, Martin.

'Something urgent?' There's an edge in Annie's voice.

Myrtle feels herself blushing as deeply as she did some hours ago in front of the harbour master, and is annoyed with herself for such irrationality.

'Nothing at all urgent,' she says. 'Martin's arranging some sort of memorial thing for Archie. This is news that he's found the very thing.'

'Oh? And where's that going to be?'

Later, Myrtle realised she could have avoided the truth with another truth – explained about the headstone for the grave without an inscription. As it is, in her silly confusion, she blurts out the thing she has been keeping from Annie.

'Up in the wood,' she says.

'Up in the *wood*?' Annie's eyes flare indignantly. 'The wood where none of your friends are allowed? Only Martin taken up there? Martin the privileged?'

'What's the matter?' Myrtle is astonished by the resentment she seems to have caused. 'You know perfectly well the reason. I've told you a thousand times. I want you to see it when it's a *wood*, when the trees have grown. At the moment there's nothing much to see . . .'

'As your oldest friend, I wouldn't have minded being shown the nothing, the bare ground, before the bloody trees were even planted. I wouldn't have minded being in at the beginning of things. But oh no – only Martin –'

'I'm sorry.' Their eyes lock. Annie's are hostile, hurt. Her mouth droops, petulant. 'I wouldn't have thought it was the kind of thing to interest you much, a wood,' says Myrtle.

'Don't know me very well, then, do you?' Annie is huffy as a child. 'How come Martin's the lucky one?'

'I wanted him to find me a bench to put there. Something I can sit on and think about Archie.' She sighs patiently, aware that such a concept is beyond Annie's understanding.

'I'd say that's a morbid plan, isn't it?'

'Not to my mind.'

'Archie would have wanted you to get on with your life a bit, wouldn't he? Even get married again. Give the harbour master a chance.' Annie can't resist a smile. As always, her good humour returns as quickly as it has disappeared.

'Don't be silly,' says Myrtle, smiling too. It's too often it happens this way, between her and Annie. One moment they are at loggerheads, then one of them breaks away, teasing, giving in to sudden mirth which the other immediately employs too. 'You do go on.'

'He's a kind man, Martin,' says Annie. 'Everyone knows that. I mean, he showed no resentment over my silly behaviour. He never mentions it. Real gentleman!' She pauses. 'He's bringing me a dressed crab tonight. If I'm patient enough, who knows? One day he might have more to offer than fish.'

'He might, too,' agrees Myrtle, keeping her eyes firmly on the cards.

When she arrives at the coppice, 5.30 precisely, Martin is already there. He sits at one end of the bench, eyes on a wheeling swallow.

The bench is a firm and ancient thing of dark wood: not at all what Myrtle had in mind. But quickly she sees it is better than her imagining. She appreciates its air of permanency, as if beneath its thick legs roots descend far into the earth to join with the young roots of the trees. Already it looks as if it has been here for years. Martin jumps up. He seems nervous.

'You didn't object to my plan, then?'

'Of course not.' Myrtle's happy smile is partially due to the fact that in her haste to arrive on time she had given no thought to the sky, and it had not troubled her.

'What do you think?'

'I like it. It's good, solid.'

'Funny thing is, it's been outside my workshop for as long as I can remember. It was there when my parents bought the place, but I've never sat on it before. I suddenly thought, on my way home last night – why, it's just the thing. A seasoned bench. You wouldn't want something too new-looking in a place like this, would you? Here, try it.'

Myrtle sits at the other end. She puts an arm on its wide wooden arm. She shuffles herself, feeling the safety of the thick planks beneath her skirts.

'Oh Martin,' she says, enthusiasm rising, 'it's lovely. Thank you very much.'

'Needs a bit of sanding down. A coat of protective stuff.' He looks pleased, relieved. 'I'll come up at the weekend. It's a much better bench than anything I could make. I'm not much of a carpenter, really.'

'I must pay you for it.'

'You'll do no such thing. I'm just happy it's found a good resting place. Reckon it'll see us all out.'

Myrtle smiles up at him.

'Thank you,' she says again. And then: 'Would you mind if I sit here alone for a while?'

'You do that.' Martin turns away at once and walks down a path edged with waist-high saplings. Myrtle watches him till he is out of sight. She is grateful for his instant understanding. Annie would have chided her for planning to indulge in morbid thoughts.

But once she is alone Myrtle does not think of Archie. She looks up at the broad evening sky, lavender blue unbroken by cloud, and is aware that the fear has gone. Yes: her new, strange fear is no longer there. The vastness above her is no longer intimidating, nor does it threaten. The irrational alarm seems to be conquered, its disappearance as mysterious as its coming, just as she had believed it would be. That, surely, must be one small step in some new direction.

Myrtle's eyes follow the tiny arrow of the swallow. What strange rites people go through on their own, she thinks. What subtle junctions they make for themselves between one era of their lives and another . . . She stands, stretches, yawns, looks round at her wood of healthy young trees, then sets off for home knowing that there has been some change of the tides within her, and Archie would be glad.

On the road just outside the village Myrtle sees Janice running towards her. The child is wearing a light-coloured dress with a fidgety hem that rises and falls in small waves as she moves. She reaches Myrtle: pink cheeks, high spirits.

'What's up with you, Janice?'

'I'm just so *happy*.'

'That's good. Done your homework?'

'Oh, Myrtle . . . I'm going to. I was on my way.'

'This is hardly your way home.' Myrtle hears herself sounding severe. Janice shrugs, gives a small skip.

'You know what? I told my mum. I told her I was in love, there was someone I really fancied.'

'Did you, now?'

'She laughed. She said: have fun. She said: don't do anything I wouldn't do. That gives me a pretty free rein, doesn't it?'

'I don't think you should speak of your mother like that,' says Myrtle.

'But it's the truth. I know it's the truth – my mum was up to all sorts. I've heard things. Well, I'm proud of her. She's so pretty. When she was young she must have been . . . *ace*, wasn't she?' Janice scans Myrtle's face. Finding no response, she changes tack. 'I just ran into Martin,' she says. 'He said he'd just been doing some business in your wood.'

'He delivered a very good bench,' says Myrtle. 'We were trying it out.'

'You mean,' says Janice, incredulously, 'you and Martin were just sitting on a bench talking? Is that how you try out a bench? God, grown-ups do the most boring things in the world. Just *sitting on a bench* – fun? I don't believe it.'

At last Myrtle is laughing and they reach the village.

'Run along, no more skiving,' says Myrtle, ruffling the child's hair. 'I want the whole of the second stanza off by heart, remember?'

'No hassle,' says Janice, turning away. As she runs off, Janice is Annie, one evening in early summer. She was twelve years old and wearing a similar dress with a flippety hem. She and Myrtle were walking back towards the village when Annie suddenly burst into tears. She confessed to Myrtle she could not live unless some boy paid attention to her. Myrtle cannot remember which of the many it was – Hamish, perhaps. But she remembers Annie's despair, her claim never to have fancied any boy so much in her life. She then admitted she'd gone round to his house the evening before, knowing his father was at sea and his mother was on late shift at the pub. She'd just boldly walked up to the front door, knocked, heart battering fast. Hamish had let her in, none too pleased to be interrupted from some puzzle he was doing. She followed him into the front room where he carried on with the puzzle – a picture of an old steam train, Annie said. When he asked her what she wanted Annie could think of nothing to say. So she took up a pose by the fireplace and began to undo the buttons of her shirt, just as she had seen some actress do on television. When Hamish glanced at her, she lifted her skirt above her knee. He went white, she said. A ghastly white. Then he started shouting at her. Annie couldn't remember the words precisely, but they were all insults: she was a slag, a slut, she'd end up as the village tart, get into rare trouble if she didn't mind out. Just as Annie was about to run from the room, tears streaming down her face, the hostile Hamish came over and rammed his face down on to hers. He kissed her, bit her, so rough. He squeezed her breast till she cried out in pain, and pinched the top of her bare arm. Then he dragged her to the front door and pushed her out into the night, shouting that perhaps now she had learnt her lesson. Annie's mouth was bleeding: she had to wipe the blood with the hem of her skirt, and creep upstairs at home without her mother hearing – well, that wasn't difficult, her mother was deep in some romantic novel as usual. She had cried herself to sleep and at school next day explained away her swollen lip convincingly: a neighbour's dog had bitten her, she said.

Myrtle remembers Annie shaking in her arms as she told her this story. She remembers when cars went by the passengers gave them funny looks. So they went into a field, sat out of sight behind a hedge. There Annie showed Myrtle the bruises on her arms and breast, and Myrtle, in her horror, could find no words. They clung to each other for immeasurable time. Eventually Myrtle begged Annie never to do anything so silly again. She promised she wouldn't: she had learnt her lesson, she said. But within a few weeks she was fluttering her beautiful lashes at some other boy, and impatiently brushed aside Myrtle's warnings. Now, as Myrtle watches Annie's daughter skipping into the dusk, bent on some foolish action, she feels a profound sense of misgiving – a feeling horribly familiar from her childhood, when she had helplessly watched Annie's compulsive behaviour.

'Janice,' she calls. She wants to say something – warn her, stop her, though exactly how she can put it she has no idea. But Janice is out of sight. She does not hear. Myrtle sighs. She knows she must do something before it is too late. But what? Perhaps Martin will have an idea, she thinks. Martin, so full of good sense, will know what to do, and he can be trusted to keep the matter to himself. Comforted by this thought, Myrtle makes her way home, tipping back her head fearlessly to confront the sky which by now is mottled with darkening cloud. For the first time since Archie died she feels hunger, and looks forward to the vegetable soup that has been simmering on the stove.

Life, Myrtle senses, is beginning to speed up. She is aware of a feeling of pace, activity, which is hard to analyse. But her door seems to open more often. People seem to come and go more frequently, as they used to when Archie was alive. Annie comes again to play cards several afternoons a week, other fishermen's wives invite her to drop by, Martin arrives regularly with a piece of fish, and the harbour master, in his quest for companionship, makes formal applications to come round once a week for a game and something to eat. He has invited her several times to an evening of herrings cooked in oatmeal, and old films, but Myrtle has always managed to switch the invitation. By now she feels a certain affection for Alastair Brown, but the desire to enter his territory still eludes her. She promises she will come, one day, but not just yet. The harbour master waits patiently, fearful that if he presses too hard he may risk impairing their delicate friendship.

One Tuesday evening there is a particular feeling of bustle. Myrtle is marking books at the kitchen table when Martin comes in – these days, although he knocks, he also takes the liberty of pushing open the door at the same time. The confidence of this action indicates a deepening of their friendship, thinks Myrtle, though she realises that Martin himself has probably not given the matter any conscious thought. Now, Myrtle is surprised. She was not expecting Martin this evening. He never comes on a Tuesday, the day he collects marble from a yard near Edinburgh. She sees that, for once, he does not carry a newspaper parcel of fish.

'Bench finished,' he says. 'Sanded, sealed, looks terrific. I've been up there most of the afternoon.'

'That's wonderful. I'll go and see it tomorrow. I don't know how to thank you.'

'For heaven's sake. I don't want any thanks from you. I loved doing it. Now all we have to settle is the inscription for the headstone on Archie's grave.'

'I know.' They both smile. Ever since Archie died Myrtle has been searching the Bible for a suitable sentence, and has failed to come up with the perfect thing. 'I'm making my final choice,' she says

Martin is pacing about, uncalm. He has the air of one who has just achieved something and can't quite contain the delight that has given him.

'Look here,' he says, 'I have to go north next week, collect a consignment of marble. Somewhere up near Perth. I was just wondering . . . if you might like to come with me. I mean, it would only be a very minor outing, but I was thinking it's about time you went somewhere. Got out a little. You've scarcely left the village since Archie died, have you?'

Myrtle puts her hand on to the thick black handle of the kettle, its enamel worn into the shape of her palm. She leans against the stove, needing support. The implications of this innocent invitation have ungrounded her. Martin watches her carefully. He sees the force of her hesitation.

'It wouldn't be *much* of an invitation,' he says. 'Not exactly a historic day out. But the van's quite comfortable, and it's fine country up there in the hills. I have to pick up the stuff by five. Then we could find ourselves somewhere for an early supper – be back here soon after nine.' Myrtle has turned very pale. The internal argument with herself, the weighing-up of her various feelings, is almost visible. 'Earlier, if you like,' says Martin, gently. 'Or we could skip supper altogether.'

The ancient growl of the kettle is the only sound in the room for a while.

'That's a very kind thought, Martin,' Myrtle says at last. 'A lovely invitation, and I'm tempted.' She pauses. 'But I think I'm not quite ready for it yet . . .'

'Ready for what?'

'Ready for . . . sitting beside a man, being driven by someone who isn't Archie . . .' She gives a small laugh. 'It sounds silly, I know.'

'I'm sorry,' says Martin. He suppresses a sigh. 'I was trying to find the right moment. I misjudged.'

'I find it hard to judge, myself. At the moment, anything beyond these walls, within the village, the wood – and you're the only one who comes there – it would seem like infidelity.'

Martin smiles. Wry, disappointed.

'It's been two years, Myrtle.'

'I know. And things are beginning to change. I'm beginning to feel a little . . . speeded up. Less unsafe. But there's still a way to go.'

Martin moves closer to her. She can see he considers putting an arm round her shoulder, but resists, and she is grateful for that.

'I understand,' he says. 'I'll try to be patient. Then one fine day I'll suggest we go off for a drink to some far-off place – at least two miles away – and you'll say yes. You might even enjoy yourself and think it was just what Archie would have wanted. So I hope I'll persuade you in the end.'

They are both smiling at this light rendering of his hopes. And shortly after that, having refused a cup of tea, he leaves.

For all his cheerful countenance, Myrtle knows he is a disappointed man. She reruns the short scene between them in her mind, wondering whether she has hurt him as well as disappointed him. Her refusal of his agreeable invitation, she knows, was irrational, foolish. It would have been an enjoyable day and – Martin was right – she needed to get out of the village, see a broader landscape. She trusted him absolutely: he had become the best male friend she had. He had never given any indication of what Janice would call 'fancying' her: indeed, the only time they had had any physical contact was when she had fallen in the coppice. She had no fears that his attitude would suddenly change, and he would take the liberty of making some untoward physical gesture. So why had she been overwhelmed by reluctance to accept his offer? Myrtle could not answer her own query. She could only be sure of an amorphous apprehension that had stopped her. And now she was faced with the worrying question: had her decision endangered the depth of their friendship? Would Martin, once rejected, keep to his word and wait patiently for a more opportune time? Or might he feel it was not worth bothering again . . .? The thought was a painful one. Myrtle had it in mind to run after him, say how silly she had been, she'd love to come to Perthshire with him after all. But so quick a change of mind and action was not in Myrtle's nature. It would be undignified, the act of a torn young girl rather than an almost middle-aged woman who should know her own mind, stick to the firmness of her purpose. Having taken down her jacket from the hook, Myrtle puts it back.

There is another knock at the door. Webbed by her quandary, Myrtle moves with restless heart to open it. She hopes it might be Martin returning: this time she would not be so foolish. Yes, she would say. Yes, I would love to come. And there would be the outing to Perth to look forward to, a bright star in her mind.

It is Ken. They stand looking at each other. Myrtle makes no attempt to hurry her thoughts from the new possibility of Perth to the disagreeable reality of Ken's presence. He wrings his hands.

'What are you doing here?' Myrtle asks at last. 'You know I've no wish to see you. I told you not to come here any more. It's not as if we have anything further to say to one another . . .'

'Please: let me in for a moment. It's important.'

Myrtle stands aside to let him enter. She doesn't know why she has done this. Still preoccupied by Martin's visit, perhaps. Or touched by Ken's look of desperation. Ken hurries over to the window.

'Thanks,' he says. 'I won't keep you long – I've done my best to keep out of your way.'

'That's true,' agrees Myrtle. Since his visit soon after Archie's funeral they have scarcely exchanged a word. 'Is all well at the ice house?'

'Hardly stimulating, but fine,' says Ken. 'But that's not what I've come to talk to you about. I need your help. Annie! Your friend Annie's off her rocker. She says she's going. Leaving.'

Myrtle, to hide her surprise, takes mugs down from the dresser. She has been aware of Annie's discontent for the last few years – a feeling which doubled in strength after the tragedy of Archie. But there has been no recent mention of the marriage being in serious trouble.

'Has she said anything to you?'

'Not a thing.'

'That's curious. I mean, with your being such friends.'

'Even the best of friends cordon off certain areas,' says Myrtle. 'What's the problem?'

Ken irritates Myrtle by a long, noisy sigh.

'Hard to say. I've done my best. Earn the money, try to keep out of her way. She's on about Archie all the time. Won't listen to a word I say. There seems to be no such thing in her nature as forgiveness. She doesn't know the meaning of redemption. I don't know how to persuade her there's nothing further I can do about something in the past – no way on earth I can bring Archie back, God that there were. Regret doesn't get you bloody anywhere, nor does the confessing of sins, far as I can see . . . And now even Janice seems to have turned against me. Suddenly she's very cold. God knows what Annie's been saying to her.'

'I'm sorry,' says Myrtle. Despite herself, she has pity for the man. 'I know nothing of all this. And why does Annie suddenly want to go?'

'Just says she can't stand being under the same roof as me any longer. If you ask me, there's probably someone else. Leopards don't change their spots, do they? And I still haven't been allowed to lay hands on her since the day Archie died. She must be getting it from somewhere –'

'Ken –'

'Well, you know Annie. If there is someone, though, beats me who it is. Martin's the only one who comes round, bringing his do-gooding pieces of fish – I hear he hands it round half the village, wants to be in everyone's good books. It couldn't be St Martin she fancies, boring man. No: I think there's someone visits her up at the café, someone from St Andrews. I've seen her talking in the street to some fellow in a kilt, some smarmhead with a big car. I may be wrong, but all I do know is Annie wouldn't go off to be on her own. No chance of that. She wouldn't last a minute without a man. As for me, I wouldn't last long without her, I can tell you that. She may be a right bitch, Annie, but I love her. Do you mind if I sit down?'

Before Myrtle can answer, Ken sits, rubs his eyes so fiercely Myrtle finds it a wonder he doesn't look up at her with crushed eyeballs.

'What do you want me to do?' she asks.

'I don't know. Find out what's going on. Suggest it'd be best for her to stay – that is, if you believe that yourself.'

'Of course I do, provided you can work things out somehow.'

'You'd best not tell her I've been round, said anything. She's forbidden me ever to come here. She'd go mad.'

'We'll have to risk that,' says Myrtle. 'I'm not prepared to enter into some devious arrangement. I'll do what I can, but she'll have to know you've been here. Otherwise what reason would I have for suddenly enquiring about her private life? We don't go in for those sort of conversations, so much, these days. Annie fights shy of my disapproval, and she knows there's a lot in her life I can't agree with.'

'Very well. You know what's best. I leave it to you.' Ken stands, a trace of relief on his face. Myrtle sees the blades of his shoulders stick sharply through the thin, worn wool of his jersey. He is a bad colour: dry skin flakes through a dense stubble on his chin. 'Thanks, Myrtle. You can imagine how grateful . . . letting me in like this. It's taken me weeks, making up my mind whether or not to come. It was only her outburst last night decided me. You're a good – well, I suppose not a friend any more.' He scratches his head. The dry hair stands up in silly points.

'It'd be difficult ever to forget the part you played, that's for sure. But you know in my heart I can't bear you any hatred. Anger runs its course. I just needed a bit of time. But all the avoiding – I'd say there's no point, any more. It might help with Annie, if she sees my forgiveness as well as knowing it exists. Come round whenever you want.'

Ken rubs his eyes again, incredulous. He goes to the door.

'You're a woman in a million, Myrtle,' he says. 'No wonder Archie . . . And if you don't mind my asking, how are you doing after all this time?'

'I'm doing fine.'

'I miss the man every day of my life. I miss life on the boat, the sea, I could do with a week's wind on my face. But that's nothing as to how . . . well, we were friends, till the end, all those years. Matter of fact, despite our quarrels, we were still friends.' Ken speaks with the soft urgency of one who hasn't been listened to for a long time. Myrtle gives him a sympathetic nod. 'This room brings it all back, Christ it does.' Ken opens the door. 'I never knew you could miss a man so much.'

'Oh, you can, too,' says Myrtle. 'Aye, you can.'

When Ken has gone, Archie – whose presence has occasionally been less vivid of late – comes roaring back, so close to flesh and blood it is only the rational part of Myrtle's mind that stops her from putting out a hand to touch him. This is natural, she supposes. There are so many memories of Archie and Ken together – playing as children, working on the *Skyline II* as grown-ups – it's no wonder that seeing Ken again brings the pictures back with such terrible clarity.

Archie's jersey, she notices, still hangs on the back of the door. Its blue wool is muted with dust. It wasn't his favourite jersey. That had been the green, the one that Dot had knitted for him years ago, which he had been wearing when he died. Myrtle takes the jersey down, slaps at it with one hand. Sprays of dust fly out, their minute particles fired by a shaft of sun through the window. For a split second the dust is thus turned to sparks, as if blown from some fire of life that still exists within the jersey: Myrtle smiles to herself for entertaining such fanciful thoughts. All the same, unnerved, she rolls it up – its old smell of salt and sea and sweat faintly haunt the air – and stuffs it into the bin. Should have done this long ago, she thinks, pleased with herself. But her eyes are filled with unusual tears. Archie's voice is so loud in her head – nothing profound, just a jumble of ordinary greetings and farewells. *Good to be back, Myrtle wife* . . . It was always good to be back, sad to go. Myrtle realises that all his homecomings and departures through the years are now rolled into just two acts so familiar that they cause a burning sensation along her skin: Archie, clean-shaven, clean-clothed, bag in hand, brief kiss, fading footsteps, the empty week ahead whose thud never dimmed. Then, the returning Archie: tired, unshaven, dirty, wet, fish-smelling, salt lips – Archie *back*, his presence causing a magic change in the room that makes it tip and sway so that Myrtle herself, until she has grown accustomed to it, knows the feeling of what it is like to be on a boat tossed by the sea.

'But Archie, you're gone for ever, now,' she says out loud, brusquely. (Of late she has caught herself talking out loud sometimes, and puts it down to the tricks of the solitary life.) 'And I must . . .' What she must do is to employ her old standby, deflection. This evening she is lucky enough to have some positive action to hand. Annie must be confronted as soon as possible. Och, quite a day, she thinks, pulling on her coat, and averting her eyes from the bareness of the door now that Archie's jersey no longer hangs there.

Myrtle has not been to Annie's house for some time. As she hurries up the path she sees through the window that Annie is lying on the sofa watching television. From Janice's open window upstairs comes the persistent thump of rock music. Myrtle lets herself in. There is dread in her heart. She loathes confrontations, but her blood is up.

Annie furrily turns on the cushions, a lazy-cat movement that makes a backwash of dark streaks in the dralon fabric, as Myrtle comes in. Her bare feet nuzzle each other, twirling in a sensuous way that Myrtle finds repellent. The minute toenails are skilfully painted dots of scarlet. The sight of them further – unreasonably – enrages her. Annie smiles up at her friend's censorious face, enjoying the disapproval.

'Here's a surprise,' she says. 'I was just watching a quiz show. If I'm actually watching something Ken doesn't dare switch to his blasted football.' She flicks the remote control, drags herself into a sitting position, pulling her legs under her skirt. 'So what brings you here –?'

'Ken's just been round,' says Myrtle. She sits, back to the window.

'He's obviously said something to put you in a rare old mood. I told him not to come round to your place, ever.'

'I'm glad he did.'

Annie sniffs, indelicately. Strokes her throat, languorous.

'What was he on about, then?'

'He's says you're threatening to leave. If that's so, I felt we ought to talk about it.'

Annie begins to laugh. It's her usual beguiling laugh, but behind the cooing Myrtle detects a note of scorn.

'Could this be called interfering, Myrtle, by any chance? Poking you nose into matters between Ken and me that have nothing to do with you?' She is doubled up with laughter, now. Hands are running through her hair. When she raises her head her pretty teeth glint whitely as they did when she was a girl. Myrtle stares at her, unsure what move to make next.

'You could call it that, I suppose,' she says, when at last Annie stops laughing. 'But when it's something this important, surely –'

'You know me,' butts in Annie, 'always threatening to leave Ken. He should be used to it now. We had a particularly noisy row the other night. I shouted a few home truths, suppose that alarmed him.'

'You mean you're not about to go?'

'Course not. It might come to that one day. But not yet. Where would I go? What would I do? What about Janice? There's her to think of.'

Myrtle feels herself falling more deeply into the chair. Relief makes her heavy, calm.

'I'm glad to hear it,' she says.

'He shouldn't have come running to you. Our troubles aren't your business.'

'Don't be stupid, Annie. Ken's in a bad way. He needed my help – not that there's much I can do. One can't hope to sort out other people's marriages. All I said was I'd try to talk to you, make you see sense.'

'No need for your good advice, thanks very much. We've always had different ideas about right and wrong, haven't we? All our life your good advice has started off by condemning me for something or other. Well I'm sick of your disapproval, if you want to know. I'm quite able to make my own judgements, thank you. If it'll give you any satisfaction I don't mind telling you I'll stick around with Ken till

I can't bear it a moment longer, and that'll probably be some time yet. But you might as well know it's a high price to pay for a roof over my head. I can barely stand the sight of him, those soulful eyes begging for forgiveness that I'll never hand out – never in my life will I grant him that satisfaction, so don't waste your breath trying to persuade me.'

There is a long silence.

'I told him I'd be glad if he comes round when he wants to,' says Myrtle at last. 'No point in carrying on with all this silly avoidance. You know I forgave him right from the start. It's time to show I mean it. Two years of never meeting is enough. It's unnatural. He was Archie's friend. I'd like to see him from time to time: Archie would have wanted that.'

'That's up to you then.' Their eyes meet.

'For God's sake, Annie, remember it was an accident. Ken's had punishment enough.'

'There speaks St Myrtle. Well at least he's got *your* forgiveness.'

'That's not enough.'

'That's all he's getting.'

'I wish you weren't so adamant.'

'You've always wished me to be things or do things that wild horses wouldn't make me . . .' She swings one leg on to the floor. Curls the toes through the pile of the swirling carpet. 'And I suppose Ken took it upon himself to mention a certain gentleman with a large car?'

'He did say something.'

Annie laughs, merrily this time.

'Silly bugger! Jealousy's his problem, always has been. Can't bear anyone to look at me, yet can hardly meet my eye himself. The chap he's referring to gave me a lift home one night from the café – raining cats and dogs. Ken happened to be coming down the path just as we arrived. Went berserk. Banged on the windscreen, shouted bloody murder, hauled me up the path by the scruff of my neck. What's all this about, Ken? I said, when we got indoors. He's a boring old businessman from St Andrews, owns a chain of stationery shops, drops in when he's passing this way and gives me a nice big tip, I said, but he's never stepped an inch out of line, never laid a finger on me, and can you imagine me lowering myself so far as *him*? I said . . . But of course Ken didn't believe me. Then I showed him the marks *he'd* made on my arm. He takes one look and breaks down sobbing. He's a jealous *wimp* if you want the truth. Trouble is, I never loved him in the right way to begin with, did I? I should never have married him.'

'Be that as it may, I'm pleased to hear there isn't anyone else,' says Myrtle.

'No: the Jaguar man hasn't been back since, as you can imagine. He was my best customer, too. I miss the tips.' She smiles, casts a wan look out of the window. 'There's no one I've met recently I fancy in the slightest, so you needn't worry. I'm beginning to think there may never be anyone else again. The sterile life from here to the grave.'

It's Myrtle's turn for a small smile. When Annie subsides into self-pity it's time to change tack.

'Do you remember,' she asks, 'how when we were first married we so hated it when the men went off? Leaving us to empty days? All the worry on our own?'

'You took all that harder than me,' says Annie. 'I'd do anything, now, for Ken to be off to sea for a week . . . have an evening to myself. The husband back every night wanting his meal on the table, complaining about his day in the ice house – fishermen's wives don't know how lucky they are having time to themselves . . .' She happens to glance back at Myrtle, sees the tight mouth and big clenched fists on the arms of the chair. Remorse comes too late. 'Oh God, Myrtle,' she cries, 'what am I saying? I don't mean that! Really I don't. How could I be saying that to you of all people, you with no choice but being alone for the rest . . .' She leaps up, rushes to put an arm round Myrtle. 'Please believe – what was I doing?'

'Just carrying on in your usual blundering way,' says Myrtle. She stands up, pushing Annie from her. 'Blurting things out with no thought for others.'

'I'm sorry.'

'Easy enough to say you're sorry.'

'But I really am. No excuses. And I should have told you about things here. I often thought about it, then I thought no, it's too complicated. I didn't want to involve you. Besides, you don't tell me much these days. It's not like it used to be. Your disapproval makes it difficult to decide where to begin . . . No, don't go. Stay a bit. Have a cup of tea.'

But Myrtle is sweeping out of the door.

'I'm away,' she says. 'Another time.'

In her brisk walk home Myrtle allows herself to wonder what it would be like were she and Annie no longer friends. Such a situation is unimaginable. But in the safety of her own kitchen her friend's voice rings out. *You with no choice but being alone* . . . It's odd that Annie, in her cruel moments of truth, can be so accurate. It occurs to Myrtle she should have reacted to this statement with indignation, although she secretly acknowledged its accuracy. But the fact was she could not be bothered. Let Annie think what she likes. She had wished for no further argument at the end of a long day. All the same, Myrtle wishes she could prove her wrong. But that is a possibility not worth a moment's thought. Drained by her day, Myrtle sits at the table and listens for Archie's voice. But at moments when she most needs it, it fails her. The dead can be as elusive as the living. They go from you, they return in their own unheeded time. Myrtle stretches out her hands on the table, trying to make sense of all this. It is an occasion for the interminable passing of widowed hours. Then a full moon slides into the window, interrupting.

Five days have passed since Myrtle turned down Martin's invitation to Perth. She has not seen him since then. But they have been busy days – the new feeling of bustle continues – and she has not thought much about his absence. It has lain gently as hoar frost on her mind, untroubling. But now, on the sixth day of no sign of him, anxiety begins to glitter. She fears she may have caused him offence, though doubts this can be so – a man of his sensitivity and understanding. She wonders what she should do, hesitates to be the one to get in touch.

On the afternoon of the sixth day a strong wind from the sea attacks the coast. Myrtle walks home from school clutching at collar, scarf, flapping books in her basket. It occurs to her she has very good reason to get in touch with Martin: she has found at last an epitaph for Archie's headstone. Martin has been awaiting her decision for ages. He will be pleased.

The wind scrapes across her eyeballs causing streamers of tears. She has no free hand to wipe them away, so feels them tickling and irritating across her cheeks until they dry. Her vision is blurred. But in the distance, on the other side of the street, she sees Martin. At least, she cannot be quite sure . . . She blinks rapidly. In the few seconds that her eyes are clear she sees it *is* him. A woman walks beside him. They are arm in arm.

Too fast for any logical thought, Myrtle moves into the porch of a newsagent – thus she can watch their progress but can't be seen by them. For a second she contemplates going into the shop, hiding. But curiosity overcomes her. She decides to stay where she is for a few moments, to recover her composure, then be on her way. They will be sure to see her. What happens then will be up to Martin.

Myrtle watches Martin and his companion walk slowly up the street. Like everyone else abroad today, they concentrate on fending off the wind. Neither of them speaks, though Martin is smiling. The woman's hair, a reddish colour, stands straight up from her head making her look like an aggressive character in a children's book. She is much shorter than Martin, obviously thin beneath the ballooning stuff of her windcheater. She carries a plastic bag from a tourist shop, indicating she is not a local. She and Martin are now but ten yards away. Myrtle judges it time to move from her hiding place.

She is aware of the battering of her heart, and is puzzled. Why should she be so shocked, amazed, at the sight of Martin with a woman? It had never occurred to her that he might have a girlfriend, but it had also never occurred to her there was no one in his life – simply, she did not think of Martin in those terms. He was her dearest friend and for the most part they skirted one another's private feelings by mutual, though unspoken, consent. He had once told her that there was someone he loved: but that was long ago. Myrtle assumed that he had resigned himself to a bachelor life, and was quite happy. Sometimes it occurs to her her lack of curiosity about the part of his life hidden from her is due to a fear of discovering some unwanted truth. At other times she tells herself the depths of Martin are not her business, and do not bother her. She appreciates the ease of their friendship and is satisfied with its present form.

As she moves back on to the pavement the wind renews its attack, once more pulling strings of tears from her eyes. So it is as if through watered silk she sees Martin wave, smile, begin to cross the street. At once she summons a generous smile in return, and tastes the salt tears gathering in the corners of her mouth. She is determined to welcome whoever this woman may be: how good, how very good that Martin has found someone, perhaps, with whom to share his life.

They face each other, a yard apart. Martin greets Myrtle, shouting through the wind. He puts his arm round the woman's shoulders. She is dabbing at her upright bunch of hair but to no avail: it remains erect, silly. But she's smiling. She has a friendly face, no denying. Freckles running into each other.

'My sister, Myrtle,' Martin is shouting. 'Gwen. Suddenly over from Canada – no warning. Sorry I haven't been in touch. We took a small trip up to Perth . . . Wanted to show her the scenery.' Gwen is nodding and bobbing and slamming her hand at her hair. She and Myrtle are smiling at each other, trying to concentrate against the annoyance of the elements. Myrtle's heart is thumping still, but benignly, now.

'Why don't you both come and have a cup of tea?' she shouts. Martin moves nearer to her. 'We're on the way up to the cemetery. Want to show the sister some of my work. Could we drop by later?'

'Supper?' shouts Myrtle. Then she remembers something that would undoubtedly change the tone of the evening. 'Alastair Brown is coming round, but . . .'

'We'd like that. We'll be there.' More nodding and smiling, clutching and waving. Then they go their separate ways.

Myrtle turns into the wind. She sails home as if carried by a buoyant sea, dipping and tossing like a small boat, the familiar streets running like smudged watercolours through the tears in her wind-blown eyes.

Home, the practical part of her nature takes over. Her mind whips through the almost empty fridge. She will have to add vegetables to the venison stew which was meant to last her for several days. She will have to make a quick treacle tart (the harbour master's favourite), iron rough cotton napkins unused since Archie died, and unlock the special cupboard where his whisky is kept along with a couple of bottles of wine.

It has been so long since Myrtle has entertained more than one guest that she finds herself in an unusual dither. Her hands shake as she rolls the pastry. She has to run to the shop for a pot of cream, then go back again for forgotten candles. The wind clamours through the cracks in the frame of the small window, making the curtains restless. Time goes so fast there is no moment for Myrtle to change her old skirt or brush the salt-stiff chunks of her hair. She knows, as she opens the door, she is unattractively flushed, all awry, far from the picture of a calm hostess.

But the evening – she feels from the start – works. Alastair Brown, new yellow satin tie poised like a tulip beneath his chin, is plainly surprised but gratified to find himself one of a *party*, as he calls the evening. He and Martin know each other slightly and seem keen to refurbish the acquaintance. There is an enjoyable moment when each takes it upon himself to open the bottle of wine – a slight race, indeed, to be first with the corkscrew. (This Martin wins, knowing its place in the drawer. The harbour master wastes precious seconds looking for it on a shelf near the stove.) But having had his small triumph, Martin is adamant the harbour master should be the one to open the bottle. Alastair Brown does not take much persuading. He even admits that once in his youth he worked as a wine waiter in Paris, so he's not unacquainted with dealing with even the most obstinate of bottles. All this is explained with a lightness of touch, amid laughter. But Myrtle is conscious that an almost invisible sense of competition has been established – perhaps the men are not even aware of it themselves – as to whose proprietorial rights are strongest in this kitchen. Myrtle knows it's not her favours they are sparring for – they merely want to make quite sure the other one is familiar with the home of china and glass, the right hooks for the coats, and the whereabouts of the box of matches. (There is another slight race to light the candles.) All this Myrtle secretly enjoys.

As the men fall into conversation about fishing matters, she is able to study Martin's sister. Gwen, she judges, must be a few years her junior: a good-looking woman now that her hair has fallen back into place – sharp-jawed, like Martin, and they share the same cautious, beguiling smile. She answers Myrtle's questions about her life in Canada: divorced, no children, she teaches physical education in the village school, and in her spare time writes plays which are from time to time put on by the local drama club. She misses Martin and her parents. But the school and her pupils have become her life, and she could not envisage changing it again now. Myrtle listens eagerly as Gwen describes the Canadian system of education, and the venison simmers on the stove till almost nine o'clock.

Myrtle's cooking is much appreciated. There is more general conversation over supper, and Myrtle reflects she has never seen the harbour master in better spirits (he is often very silent, melancholy, during their card games) and she is pleased to see him enjoying himself with abandon. He tells an almost disproportionate amount of anecdotes, encouraging laughter in stories against himself. Myrtle can see that Martin, initially prejudiced by blazer and important tie, is warming to this strange man – and here Myrtle feels a sense of small achievement. Two lonely men: if they could become friends that would be to their mutual advantage. For the third or fourth time during the evening she feels a warm rush of both surprise at her own ability to have organised this spontaneous evening, and pleasure at seeing it work so well.

It's past midnight when Gwen and Martin leave. Gwen is to return to Canada at the weekend. Martin says he will come round when she has gone. It is plain, in the out-of-character profusion of his thanks, he has much enjoyed the evening.

The harbour master, still sitting at the table, does not have the look of a man much inclined to make his immediate departure. He has poured himself yet another of his strange drinks – whisky with a touch of milk. Myrtle has lost count of how many of these he has consumed since he arrived. He looks up at her. It's disconcerting, on such an occasion, not to be able to see the expression in his eyes: all Myrtle can see is her own head reflected down to a couple of pinpoints. Alastair Brown stands up, begins to unbutton his blazer.

'Let me help with the washing-up,' he says.

'No, please. I can do it in a moment in the morning.' There is urgency in her voice. Myrtle is suddenly very anxious that the blazer should remain in its buttoned-up state: she has no desire to see the harbour master in shirt sleeves, let alone taking Archie's place beside the sink, dishcloth in hand.

'Very well. Whatever you wish.' His quick agreement with her suggestion fills Myrtle with relief. 'But the night is young. Should we have just one game of cards while I finish my nightcap?'

'It's not that young,' says Myrtle, lightly. 'Getting on for one o' clock.' She has no wish to offend, merely to speed him on his way. At the back of her mind she is beginning to feel the pressure of what might be in her visitor's mind, and must be avoided. 'So I think it's too late for me. I'm past concentrating.'

Alastair Brown leaps to his feet as if a bomb has gone off beneath him – one hand rebuttoning the blazer, the other clinging to the dazzling yellow knot of his tie. He is a man mortified by his own impropriety, ashamed by his untoward act. He should have seen how late it was, how tired Myrtle must be. These musings are clearly visible to Myrtle who, shocked by his incredible leap from the chair, tries to contain a smile. She realises that although the glasses of whisky were small, the number consumed has fired the harbour master's sense of companionship beyond its normal calm. He stands looking down at her, a little unsteady, bending gently from side to side like a young tree in its first breeze.

'Oh, what came over me, for heaven's sake? Forgive such an inconsiderate thought. Of course it's too late for anything but bed –' Here he

gives a hare-leap towards the door, realising that once more he has
said the wrong thing. 'I'm on my way, you see, on my way, on my . . .'

Myrtle swiftly follows him to the door. He is having trouble with
the handle.

'Calm down, Alastair.' She does not often use his Christian name.
It has effect. It also gives the harbour master courage to make a final
gesture. He takes both Myrtle's hands in his – backing away from her
as he does so to indicate this is the total extent of his intention – and
rubs them gently, as a woman judges the texture of cloth between her
fingers.

'This was a wonderful evening,' he says. Her hands are still in his.
'I've not enjoyed myself so much for a long time.'

'Good.'

'I think that went for all of us, Gwen and your friend Martin.'

Alastair bows his head and squeezes Myrtle's hands more seriously.

'You're a fine-looking woman, Myrtle,' he says, dark glasses pointed
towards her skirts.

To humour him, Myrtle thinks quickly, is the best way. If she tries
to release her hands there will be a tussle. She does not want that.
Perhaps the mention of Archie will caution him.

'Archie used to say he loved my smile,' she says, 'and my height and
my weight. But in all his love for me he never tried to pretend he saw
me as any kind of beauty. That would have been foolish. Luckily for
me, looks weren't a priority in Archie's mind.' She laughs lightly. Her
plan has worked. Alastair releases her hands. But his train of thought
is not deflected.

'God knows, Myrtle,' he says, 'you underrate yourself. You do
something to a man. I know I asked only for companionship, but I
find myself wanting more: your calm, your strength.' He pauses. 'Your
love, even.'

Myrtle is unnerved by the seriousness of his declaration but also,
despite herself, intrigued.

'You're like a distant mountain in my life,' Alastair goes on, 'which
more than anything in the world I want to –'

'Climb?' suggests Myrtle. She is still trying to make a joke of it all.

Alastair smiles reluctantly. Then his mouth is on hers, the glasses cold against her cheeks. He is kissing her. There is no taste of salt on his nibbling lips. No suggestion of sea, fish. Nothing like Archie. Instead, intimations of tea, whisky, milk. As the harbour master's tongue worms gently round her teeth she is both scandalised by her own behaviour, and excited. She shifts her position. Alastair moves back at once, though again he holds her hands.

'Have I offended you?'

'No.' No: he hadn't offended, exactly. Though elements of shame were shooting through the odd desire.

'I had no intention . . . Not for the world would I do anything to frighten you, to lose our friendship. I just wanted so much to touch you.' He lets go of her hands, wipes his mouth with a folded hand-kerchief. Smooths his hair. Replaces himself as if at the end of some violent lovemaking, rather than a mere kiss.

'That's all right.' By now, curiously, it is all right. Myrtle's heart is still skittering.

'You won't hold it against me?'

'Of course not.'

'Then farewell, dear Myrtle. I'm on my way.'

He goes. Myrtle quickly shuts the door behind him. She does not want to watch his descent down the steps. She wants to return to the table, regard the detritus of the evening, rerun it in her mind. The success of it all, and the unexpected ending, have filled her with spinning energy. As for Alastair Brown . . . her admiration for the dignified and gentle way in which he comported himself, when his feelings over-came him, has added to the warmth of Myrtle's own affection. He is a good man, to be trusted. She is glad he has come to the village: Archie would have wanted her to make new friends. One day, perhaps . . . she can imagine the sympathy she feels for Alastair could change into a kind of love. There could even be some kind of permanent arrange-ment – though she cannot conceive of either leaving this house, or sharing it with anyone but Archie. Still, they are well matched, she and the harbour master. As if from a distance, Myrtle can see that: a middle-aged widow of determined character, quiet and plain, unlikely to attract the rare outsiders who pass through the village. And a kind, scarred, shy, in some ways pitiful man. Yes, they could be suited. There is a final truth to be faced: the kiss, now, does not seem like a betrayal. Rather, it was a relief – relief to know physical pleasure could still flare. The sensitive Alastair Brown has stirred in Myrtle something she had thought might never exist again. This realisation adds to the sense that her life is in some curious way speeding up, and she is glad.

By two a.m. Myrtle has finished the washing-up. Everything is back to normal. She goes to the window, looks up at the Bear. The wind has died down, but is still just strong enough to carry the smell of the sea into the room. She closes the window: wonders, wonders.

The next afternoon Alastair Brown is waiting for her at the bottom of the steps when she arrives home from school. He offers to take her bags and basket, but she refuses. He had occupied a part of her mind this morning, while she was baking, but had been banished from it this afternoon in class. His unexpected presence was not altogether welcome. She is in a hurry. There is a load of books to mark, then she wants to write down the epitaph for Archie – she felt she could judge it more properly once she has written it – and send it with a note to Martin. Myrtle can see that the harbour master is clearly in some kind of an agitated state. Her previous feelings of warmth are suddenly overcast with annoyance. But she invites him to follow her in, knowing quite well her sense of hospitality will overcome any inconvenience, and once more they will share a pot of tea.

Alastair Brown's cheeks are pale beneath the dark glasses. His inflamed behaviour of the night before has obviously caused him deep remorse and probably a sleepless night. He paces the room, wringing his hands, in an elaborate warm-up to his apology. He does not take off his waterproof jacket, indicating his stay will not be a long one. Myrtle thinks it suits him better than his blazer. He looks stronger in it, hardier. More appealing, endearing . . . attractive – not a word Myrtle is accustomed to using without care, but it comes to her now. By the time they are sitting at the table with their mugs of tea, her previous irritation has fled. It's replaced by sympathy.

'I do hope my inappropriate behaviour last night has not caused you the anguish it has caused me, dear Myrtle,' the harbour master begins. 'I know the boundaries of companionship, and I know they must not be overstepped. My only excuse is that I got quite carried away by the enjoyment of the evening. I do apologise.'

'There's no need,' says Myrtle, smiling. 'So stop tormenting yourself.' She pauses for a moment to calculate, then goes on: 'If you ask me, I'd say the number of drams of whisky you drank may have exaggerated in your mind the exact nature of your behaviour. As far as I was concerned, you were the perfect gentleman.'

'Oh, Mrs Duns, Myrtle . . .' Alastair Brown interrupts the flight of his mug to his mouth, returns it to the table and wraps his hands round its hot china. He bows his head. Once again, in his relief, he is tempted to overstep the boundaries he has just mentioned, and once again he exerts all his strength to resist the temptation he feels. 'You've no idea how good it is to hear you say that,' he murmurs. 'Your understanding means more to me than I can –'

'Yes, well, let's put the whole incident aside now, shall we?' Myrtle is brusque in order to deflect his course. 'And for heaven's sake don't brood any more on something of so little importance. I wouldn't want you to do that.'

When he looks up Alastair Brown struggles with his mouth and produces a tepid smile. It's this grappling with himself, and winning, that inspires Myrtle's admiration.

'Of so little importance?' he says, sadly. Then quickly continues: 'I know that there's no use asking you round to my house one evening – I know you're not ready for that, though I should like to think I will entertain you there one day. But now the weather's improving . . . I couldn't help wondering if I could persuade you for a little jaunt up the coast in my boat? We could take a picnic – just go for an afternoon.' His glasses are on her face. '*The Swift* is nothing very grand, of course, but a friendly little boat. My mother, who hates the sea, used to trust me. I think she rather enjoyed our little excursions.'

Myrtle remembers her recent foolishness in turning down Martin's equally innocent invitation to Perth.

'Of course: I'd love to come one afternoon,' she says. 'When it's warmer. In a few weeks . . .'

The harbour master, like a man who has snatched what he wants and feels he must escape before it's taken back from him, makes one of his sudden leaps towards the door – his physical agility in leaping about is becoming familiar. He has not even finished his tea.

'Then *there's* a plan to look forward to,' he says, and runs excitedly from the room, leaving the door open behind him.

Myrtle goes to shut it a moment later, to find Annie on the doorstep.

'Just collided with your fancy man again,' she says.

'Och, Annie, I was just about to get down to my marking.'

'So you've time for him, but not for me.'

'Don't be so daft. Come on in. I'll make a fresh pot.'

Since the confrontation concerning Ken, Annie has been round more frequently than usual. Their mutual avoiding of the subject of Ken (Myrtle's belief that the best of friendships can only be maintained by the avoidance of matters likely to cause conflict) has caused only the faintest shadow between them: Annie has been in high spirits, full of stories about weird customers at the café – her mimicry can always make Myrtle laugh – and the cantankerous old witch who is her new boss.

Today she is in no less good humour, though her face is serious.

'Come on, what's going on?' she says, taking her usual place. 'You and the harbour master. There must be something. He's always here.'

In the moment that Myrtle has to form her answer, a dozen alternatives spin through her mind. She rejects the thought of lying: decides that while there are so many things she wants to keep from Annie, she deserves to be let into some secrets. And so far the subject of the harbour master, while decidedly intriguing, is not yet of great importance.

'Nothing,' she says. 'Honestly. He's just a friend. He knows that's all I want. I don't think he'd overstep the mark.'

Annie laughs.

'Seems pretty keen to me,' she says. 'All these visits. Are you sure you're not being naive? Anyhow, I've been trying to imagine it: my friend married to the harbour master. Must say I find it difficult. Has the thought never crossed your mind?'

'Never.'

'Suppose I must believe you.'

'Archie's only been dead two years.'

'How long must a widow wait?'

'Depends what she wants.'

'I mean, how long must it be to feel something for a new man when the man she's always loved has died?'

'God knows. It's not something I think about.' Here, Myrtle questions herself silently. Is this quite true?

Annie sighs.

'You know what? I've been trying to imagine what it's like being you.'

Myrtle laughs. She decides to confront Annie with the thought that immediately springs to her.

'You've been overtaxing your imagination then, lately, haven't you? You're not usually by way of thinking how things are for other people.'

'Right as usual,' concedes Annie with a pretty smile. 'But I suddenly find myself curious. I mean, I imagine widowhood must be so empty: you must feel so empty.'

Myrtle dislikes the way this conversation is going, for the impossibility of conveying to anyone precise feelings of loss will make it worthless. How would Annie ever understand, for instance, the continuing strangeness of this very room since Archie no longer lives here? The physical changes in inanimate things only visible to her? But Annie is in a rare mood of sympathy and concern. Myrtle tries to be patient.

'I don't feel empty,' she says. 'I've never felt that. To feel empty is the easiest assumption to make about someone left on their own through death. It may be true for others: not for me.' She pauses, taking in Annie's incredulous eyes – she feels renewed love for her at this moment, the sort of love she felt as a child when Annie listened to Myrtle's stories with wonder and awe.

'That sounds to me like boasting,' says Annie.

Myrtle places her big hand somewhere near her heart. 'Then I've put it badly,' she says. 'It's not meant to sound self-satisfied. What I'm trying to explain – and I don't like even attempting these sort of hopeless explanations – is that I feel over-full of new things. The wreckage within has to be sorted out – a long process, I daresay. But I think that there's a lot that can be rescued. So I wait, quite patiently.' She is heavy with the inadequacy of her explanation.

'Not at all as I imagined, then,' says Annie after a silent reflection. 'You make me feel there's hope for you, no reason for pity. I'm glad about that: I'm not much good at pity.' She shifts, sips her tea. Myrtle has never seen her look so grown-up. 'You know what? I've been thinking about what you said . . . how we hated the men going off to sea and all that, and how lucky I am for all that way of life to be over now, have my man all the time while you've . . .'

'You've been doing a lot of thinking!' Myrtle smiles. She's relieved that Annie's interest in her widowed state is spent.

'Yes, well: twenty years too late I'm beginning to grow up, perhaps. Anyway . . .' She looks directly at her friend. 'I let Ken have it last night. First time for so long.'

Myrtle's answer is the merest lift of an eyebrow. Although she scorns herself for her inability, she has never been able to respond to Annie in Annie's naturally crude language.

'It was nice,' Annie goes on, entertained by Myrtle's prudish blush. 'I don't suppose it'll mean anything amazing like me suddenly falling in love with him, but perhaps it'll make things easier. This morning, on her way out of the door to school, Janice says to me: "Mum, do you realise it's the first morning for months you haven't shouted at Dad at breakfast? What's got into you?" So maybe . . .'

Both are smiling. But Myrtle is drained by the unusual exchange with Annie, the harbour master's apology, the short night. She wants to put everything aside, now: get down to her marking. She sees Annie is still restless, excited.

'Trouble is,' she goes on, 'if you can't stop thinking about another man, then it's difficult to concentrate on a husband you've never really loved.'

Myrtle can bear no more. She takes a pack of cards from the drawer.

'How about a quick game? Just one, before I get down to work.'

Annie nods. She has the unfocused look of one torn by conflicting thoughts: the bittersweetness of a secret though unrequited love, the equal bittersweetness of physical release provided by an unloved husband. Myrtle regards her severely, defying further confidences. She has no wish to know any more about the two men in Annie's ill-ordered life. Annie responds silently to the look of familiar severity that locks her friend's features. With distracted fingers she picks up the pack of cards, begins to shuffle.

The peace when she has gone is not to last. Myrtle tries out the epitaph several times, finds it satisfactory. She writes a brief note to Martin, which she will post – no energy to walk up to his cottage this evening. Then she begins to go through the exercise books, marvelling as always at the singularity of each of her pupils. Some have treated the set essay, *The Storm* – please concentrate, she had said, on the sounds and smells and colours and noises – with great enjoyment, while others have scarcely been able to scrape together a sentence. But her concentration on her pupils' work is interrupted by the telephone. It is the matron of the Evergreen Home, desperate for help: two members of staff are sick. Myrtle has not been to the home of late: she agrees to go as soon as she has finished her books.

It is almost dark by the time she arrives at the Evergreen. As soon as she is through the door the smells of floor polish and reheated stew, urine only half suppressed by disinfectant, and the sickly odour of drying clothes come giddyingly back to her. She is greeted by the grateful, harassed matron, and hurried to the parlour, as it is still called. There, every chair in the semicircle round the television is occupied. Heads are slumped so low on chests it's as if some invisible slayer has just been in and broken every neck. Hands droop from the arms of floral chairs lifeless as old gloves. Sharp planes of kneecap and shin bone give edges to sloppy rugs. Bandaged feet, plump in gaping slippers, are absolutely still on the swirling carpet. Myrtle swings her eyes carefully from one to another of them: her old ability at assessing comes back to her. She concentrates very hard, determined not to look out of the window where the horizon will still be just visible – the horizon worn to nothing by Dot's constant gaze as she searched so long for *The Skyline*, convinced of its return.

'All this lot – bed,' says the matron. 'It's way past time. If you could start moving them, I'll get the Horlicks. Careful of Mrs Jackson, there. She's falling to pieces.'

For the next few hours Myrtle does her best. She spoons drinks, that take an age to cool, into dithering mouths bereft of teeth. She tries to understand confused murmurings – mostly grumbles: helps find words that won't come to etiolated minds. She peels off warm wrinkled stockings: sees her hands are splattered with particles of dry skin that blow off flesh-starved legs beneath. She tucks in narrow beds in narrow rooms, a single photograph or ornament the only reminder of a previous life. She pats the gristle of shoulder bones beneath crocheted shawls, and wishes each old thing a good night, wondering for which one it will be the last. Then, refusing to accept payment, she hurries away.

On the walk home, Myrtle decides never to go to the home again. She admits to herself that due to pressure of conscience this decision could one day be reversed. But for the moment she is angry and depressed: not so much by the sadness of the home's function, as by the thought of being the widow who can always be counted on to help out. She wants passionately to rebel against that role, has absolutely no intention of helping out any more. While her own lack of charity adds to her rage, nothing, for the moment, will change her mind.

She is by now very tired, and longs for bed. But she has forgotten her torch and the darkness of the night means she cannot hurry. She looks up. There is no moon, but a mass of small, hard, dense jet clouds, as if the contents of a coal scuttle had been scattered in the sky. Myrtle is glad when she reaches the houses at the end of the lane that runs down from the home. She scoffs at herself for having felt afraid, but is relieved by the lights.

She turns a corner and sees the figure of a man just ahead of her – he has obviously just come out of the pub. It's Ken. She calls him. He turns, and is at once by her side. She can smell whisky, smoke.

'Why, Myrtle! I'll walk you home.' He takes her arm, so much more firmly than he did all those years ago. It's plain he's in very good humour.

'You been out enjoying yourself?' he asks.

'I've been up at the home, helping out.'

'You're a good woman, Myrtle. A good woman. A woman to be relied on.' His own high spirits preclude interest in further information about her evening.

'I'm not, you know. I've all sorts of uncharitable thoughts.'

'Well,' says Ken, not up to finding a pertinent response to this surprising fact, 'I'll tell you something: I'm a happier man, Myrtle. I'm definitely a happier man.'

'Good. I'm glad.' They have reached Myrtle's house. She takes her arm from his. 'Thank you for walking with me.'

'I'm not swearing on this, mind,' says Ken, 'but I think maybe change is in the air. God knows why, but I think maybe Annie's coming round . . .'

'I hope so,' says Myrtle. She is halfway up the steps. 'Goodnight.'

Ken turns back the way he has come. He hurries off with a bounding step, a lightness of heart, knowing what awaits him at home. Myrtle, visualising their night, is caught unawares by a thrust of something very painful to which she would be ashamed to put a name. Physically, the pain stabs so lividly she doubles up, clings to the iron handrail for support. This *jealousy* (for that is what, undeniably, it is) clashes with the previous anger that has been furthered by Ken's praise of her worthiness. Alone on this alien night outside her own front door, Myrtle wonders how just twenty-four hours can bring such change of feeling. The joy of last night is now far away as the hidden stars. She is cold, and loathes herself for her base feelings. How, just two years since Archie's death, can she possibly be jealous . . . of such a thing as Ken and Annie's renewed physical joy?

The picture of the harbour master presses into her mind. It would be so easy.

Then: the picture of Martin, laughing with his sister last night. That would be less easy . . . It takes Myrtle a long time to pull herself into an upright position, find her keys and let herself into the dark emptiness of the house.

Once Martin's sister has returned to Canada he resumes his old habit, dropping round to see Myrtle every few days. Sometimes they go up to the copse, express surprise at the growth of the trees, and 'test out', as Martin calls it, each one of the paths, now bushy with new rough grass. The day he gets Myrtle's note about her final decision for Archie's epitaph, he hurries round after his morning's filleting, knowing this is the day she does not go to school until two.

'This is a cause for celebration,' he says. 'I'll get working as soon as I can.'

Behind his smile Myrtle sees a look of unusual weariness. A muscle flickers under one eye. The smile faded, his mouth is grim in repose. He sits in his usual place at the table. In the warm air a smell of fish comes powerfully off him. Myrtle fetches a bottle of beer from the fridge, and sits too. She decides to ignore the signs of trouble. Her belief is that if someone wants to talk about what is on their mind, they will do so. There is no need to enquire. Instead, she asks if his sister enjoyed her stay.

'I think she did. She'd never been out of Canada before. She needed a break – running a smallholding on her own, it's a lot for a single woman.' Martin pauses. 'The real reason for her visit was to tell me she'd set up with some man. He wants her to move in with him in Vancouver. She's thinking about it.' He swigs at his beer, tosses back his head, closes his eyes for a moment. 'I've decided to give up the filleting job, end of the month,' he says. 'It's not a way to spend the mornings. Besides, the pay . . .' He opens his eyes. 'I went round to Annie last night. Ken there for once. Quite a surprise.' He flicks another smile, conveying nothing. 'The girl Janice was there, in a foul mood. God knows what had got into her. When I arrived she dashed straight up to her room and stayed there.'

'Teenagers,' says Myrtle. 'She tells me she's in love with some boy. Perhaps that's the trouble.'

'Annie said that was the explanation, too.'

'Aye, I believe it is.' Myrtle is conscious of her disloyalty.

'But you teach Janice, don't you? Private tutoring: lucky her.'

'I enjoy it. She's a clever girl, loves poetry. Ken was just the same at her age. He would have liked to have tried to get into Edinburgh. But his father scoffed at him. He came from a long line of fishermen, could not imagine his son not wanting to follow the family tradition. Ken argued a bit, but his father was a strong man and in the end he gave up, went to sea. He was on my father's boat, then joined Archie. I don't think he ever really enjoyed fishing. He's happier in the ice house. As for the learning, his ambition seemed to slip away. He said there was no time to read any more, though I believe that lately, since Archie . . . I've seen him coming out of the library sometimes. Still, he's proud Janice is so bright. I think he'd like to see her achieve what he himself never managed.'

'He's an awkward man, distant. But I like him. Daresay they're not the ideal parents.'

'They're not indeed,' says Myrtle. 'Janice is spoiled rotten one minute, ignored the next. And Annie's showing signs of wanting to relive her own youth through Janice – urging her to go for it, whatever that means. If Janice manages to escape some terrible trouble, it'll be no thanks to her mother. Though of course she'll never be quite so desirable. There was no one prettier than Annie along this coast when she was younger. Janice isn't blessed in quite the same way – lucky, perhaps. She's pretty enough, though more like her father.'

'She's pretty enough to cause trouble,' says Martin. 'I've seen the look in her eye. She should be warned.'

'I try,' says Myrtle, 'but I doubt I make much impression.'

Martin stands, makes to leave. In the ten minutes with Myrtle his expression has mellowed. She assumes he has been worrying over the decision about the filleting. On his next visit she is determined they will further discuss his work: she will encourage him to seek jobs further afield, advertise his skills as a stonemason.

'You're a wonder, Myrtle,' he says, as he goes. 'So many of us wouldn't know what to do without you.'

When she is alone Myrtle does not think about this remark, but puts it away to reflect on later. She crosses the room with her dipping gait, half dancing, enjoying her imitation of a small boat on a buoyant sea, her silly secret. Outside there is blue sky. It's very warm. She looks forward to walking back to school, sun on her bare arms. Then she remembers: now this good weather has settled in there's no excuse to delay for much longer the excursion on the harbour master's boat. This she has been looking forward to and dreading in equal measure. She cannot work out why both feelings accost her so strongly: and now her strongest desire is to get the whole thing over and done with. She is convinced the picnic will be some sort of turning point, will straighten things in her mind – though, again, the precise nature of her thoughts is not easy to define. I'm floating, she thinks, on a sea of unknown depths: no idea which way I'll drift, what I'll do. But at least I'm not drowning any more: I'm stronger, though the missing is unchanged, will never change. Myrtle picks up her school bags and hurries out. The new shift of pace in her life is tentative but still exciting, which is curious, because until quite recently she thought nothing would ever be exciting, or joyful, again.

With the delicacy and tact that he considers his speciality, Alastair Brown proposes a date for their excursion, and makes arrangements. Myrtle insists only that the whole thing should be secret. She is puzzled by her own insistence on this point, but instinct tells her it should be so. She does not relish the idea of gossip at her expense – and such inaccurate gossip it would be, too.

On the morning of the appointed day she prepares herself – a head-scarf, by way of slight disguise, and a jacket in case the weather should change. While tying the scarf in a knot that makes no attempt at elegance, she thinks with amusement how very differently Annie

271

would prepare – does prepare – to go out on a date. Hours of elaborate making-up, half a dozen dresses slipped on and off till the right one is found, sparkling combs flitting in and out of the much-tossed hair. Myrtle wears her oldest summer skirt, nothing on her face, and ties back her hair.

With a certain nefarious enjoyment she slips out of the house and makes her way to the bus stop. She enjoys the journey five miles along the coast to a neighbouring fishing village – though lobster boats are the only ones left there now – where she is to meet Alastair Brown at the harbour. There is hot sun, the sea a tightly stretched blue a shade deeper than the cloudless sky. The gleaming tooth of Bass Rock is unusually clear in the distance. On each side of the road tall daisies glint among the ripened wheat, while further inland a field of violent yellow rapeseed burns between proper green fields. Myrtle remembers she has not been out of the village, except to the copse, for a very long time. The short journey feels like an adventure.

At the harbour – the very place Annie was awarded her Fisher Lass's sash – Alastair Brown sits at a wooden table provided for customers at the stall where lobsters and crabs are sold. Annie, walking down the hill, sees him before he sees her. She is puzzled. Surely he is not breakfasting on shellfish at this time of the morning? No: nearer, now, she sees he is holding a mug of tea, a commodity not usually provided by the owners of the very small business. Myrtle taps him on the shoulder.

'The VIP treatment, I see?' she says, knowing the flippant remark is quite out of character. But what with the breeze coming off the water, and the sun, she feels lighthearted, careless. Alastair Brown jumps to his feet like a man surprised: perhaps this is to disguise the fact that he has been waiting, anticipating, for a long time.

'Case of one HM treating another,' he explains. 'My friend Captain Travers lives up in that cottage, saw me sitting here, brought me some elevenses. Don't worry: he'll keep my unexplained visit to himself. If we hurry on down to the boat he won't even see you.' He pulls his shoulders back, stands very upright, a glimmer of self-importance visible in his stance. Myrtle reads his mind. He is not averse to the fact that he has been treated with propriety by a retired naval captain. Myrtle smiles, to convey her appreciation of this fact. But despite the captain's boosting gesture, Alastair Brown is nervous. He pulls the peak of his waterproof cap further down over the glasses: the sun is small diamonds in the black lenses. His hands jump in and out of the deep pockets several times before one of them dares to land on Myrtle's arm, and they move towards the steps in the harbour wall that lead down to the water.

The Swift, unsurprisingly, is an immaculate little boat. Myrtle can't help wondering just how recently she has been repainted: her scarlet sides are dazzling. It occurs to her the new paint might have been planned to coincide with this outing – but then she hastily puts the vain thought aside. There is no doubt the harbour master has taken great trouble. Everything is swept and polished, nothing is out of place. There is a cushion on one of the wooden seats. A wicker picnic basket is lodged under another. Myrtle finds herself touched, and pleased that someone should go to all this trouble for her . . .

She takes her place on the cushion. Alastair Brown wedges himself into the tiny cabin that houses nothing more than a seat and steering wheel. Slowly *The Swift* putters out of the harbour and gathers a little speed on the open sea. The water's tautness, seen from the bus, Myrtle realises, was an illusion. Here, it dips and sways in a lively way. Sometimes a small wave is driven to break, its peak flurrying for a moment like a white bird before its feathers are dashed back into the darker water.

Myrtle's old fear of the sea has not quite left her. A trace of apprehension still lingers, though less troubling than on the day of the Fisher Lass outing. But she cannot be completely at ease, bouncing about in so small a boat, and is glad Alastair Brown seems content to keep close to the coast rather than heading out for the Lammemuirs. To her surprise she soon realises that he himself shares her unease. She had always supposed him to be a man knowledgeable about all kinds of boats. Perhaps he felt more at home on a larger craft. As captain of *The Swift*, he is far less in command than when safely pacing the harbour. And he does not seem well acquainted with the workings of his boat. Sometimes there is a surprising leap forwards followed by a slackening of speed. To judge from his hands racing on the wheel, and his jerking head, both activities surprise him. He does not have the air of one who actually likes the sea. He might much have preferred a picnic somewhere on a hillside, Myrtle thinks, but has calculated that to go to sea is a more appropriate invitation from a harbour master.

The sun is hot by now, despite a breeze. Three or four gulls fly in convoy behind the boat, mewling softly. Myrtle is lulled by the rocking, and the heat. She is back on her much longer sea voyage, the day Annie was *The Skyline*'s Fisher Lass – a much rougher day: that moment she was tipped against Ken, that moment he took her arm and dragged her to her feet. Then he was gone. There was no chance to cling to him. Disappointment snagged at her, but only mildly, for in truth her feelings for Ken were only faintly stirred – or did she remember that wrongly? Looking back now, it seems obvious she was merely searching for someone to love, to fancy, and Ken, not much sought-after or seeking, seemed the best bet. She also remembers the seasick way her stomach lurched when Archie smiled at her that day – nothing more than a friendly smile, confirming he was not the sort of boy she could even contemplate befriending . . . but all the same, the thought of Annie determined to seduce him, and succeeding, increased the sickness. Never in her maddest dreams, that day, could she have foreseen how things were to turn out, what havoc and surprises the whirligig of time can bring forth.

And now, more or less middle-aged, wiser, she sits looking at the waves, trying to read the signals in her stomach, and finding this almost as difficult as when she was young. She recognises a blunt-edged excitement, a feeling of pale anticipation, akin to what she felt about Ken – nothing very specific, nothing either certain or troubling. Just the comfortable sensation that is the nature of good companions. No sooner has she made these calculations then Archie appears – Archie! How he would laugh, the very idea of her off on a sea picnic with the harbour master! His voice is so loud she jerks her head round, expecting to find him beside her. But boat and sea, empty

274

of him, tighten the void within her. She closes her eyes, feels the balm of sun on her lids, knows without doubt that the rest of her life, whatever it may be, will be a double life: on the one hand there will be reality to deal with – on the other, always haunting that real life, will be the spirit of Archie.

Myrtle is jolted from her cogitations by a definite slowing-down of the boat. The harbour master shouts that he thinks it's time to eat. Myrtle agrees. Sun and wind have made her hungry.

They go to within a few yards of the shore. There is no one on the small grey beach, just rocks scarved with blowing seaweed.

'Shall we wade ashore? We'd be sheltered. Make ourselves comfortable.'

Myrtle pictures herself hitching up her long skirts, fighting off possible suggestions from Alastair Brown of carrying her ashore. She sees a picnic in a rocky corner as perhaps he sees it: an opportunity . . . She sees a second kiss. She sees further. Her pity and affection for the harbour master, her new desire for arms around her, could wing beyond set boundaries here under the sun, lulled by the plash of the sea. Is this what she wants? There's no time to calculate.

'I'd rather stay here,' she says.

'Very well. Whatever you wish.' If the harbour master is disappointed, he conceals it nobly. He drops the anchor, moves to sit opposite Myrtle – thus the boat is nicely balanced. He pulls the wicker basket between them, and with hands that visibly tremble, begins to sort out plates and carefully wrapped packages. There are crab and watercress sandwiches, homemade lemon biscuits from the bakery, peaches and grapes. Myrtle is touched by the trouble he has taken. It's a strange feeling to be handed things, waited upon, looked after again. Agreeable. She accepts a glass of dry cider, chilled in a special box. For himself, the harbour master has brought a carton of milk. What a strange man he is. They sit in easy silence for a while, gently rocking.

As Myrtle's guest, playing cards, Alastair Brown is not a keen talker. He produces short sentences from time to time, conveying disparate bits of information which Myrtle has strung together, but still has no coherent picture of his life. But now, on this sea picnic – a time he has perhaps been waiting for with impatience and some trepidation – he takes his opportunity to tell Myrtle the story of his life.

'I've been to most parts of the world,' he says, with the sudden rush of a man who usually has no one to talk to, 'but find there's still nowhere to beat this part of Scotland, or Cornwall.'

He tells her that he was born in the small village of St Germans, near Plymouth, though the family moved to Truro when he was six and lived in a cottage by the sea. At eighteen he found a job with a firm that transported animals to foreign parts, hence his experience of the world. 'Though it was mostly in the company of a mule or an elephant on a leading rein,' he said. 'Up and down ramps in terrible heat, in and out of aeroplanes – not how I'd imagined my life, really.'

The sun and cider have made Myrtle sleepy. She shuts her eyes but keeps up a small smile to show she is listening. In truth his story becomes a little hazy – the many jobs, the death of his parents within a week, his inability to find in any of the kind women who come his way the necessities of a wife; his love of milk stemming from some week on a farm of Jersey cows . . . How was it he decided to leave Cornwall and move up here? Myrtle cannot be sure. Through the mists of her sleepiness it is all very endearing but confusing. Soporific. Almost asleep, she suddenly feels a hand on one of hers. She snaps open her eyes.

'I've been looking forward to today,' the harbour master says.

Myrtle broadens her smile, shifts on her cushion. She hopes that this will show she has felt the same. She leaves her hand beneath his, lest moving it away in under a minute would seem impolite. She notices the skin on her forearm is a ruddy pink. Burnt a little. Annie would have come on such an expedition armed with lotions and creams against the sun.

'Hope I haven't bored you, babbling on.'

'Not at all. What a life you've had. I've hardly been anywhere. The Shetland Isles, Newcastle – my furthest north, my furthest south. Haven't even quite made it to Perth, and I've always wanted to go there. Archie and I had plans for a holiday in Italy one day. But now . . . I can't see myself moving. I love it here.'

'Ah! *La bella Italia!*' The harbour master is suddenly vivacious. 'I once had to fly a crate of mallard out to Rome. Some very rich Florentine prince had this sudden desire for English ducks on his pond – lake. He agreed to pay the company I was working for a fortune to send someone out at once – very impatient, Italian princes. So four hours of driving through the Italian countryside in a hired car, ducks quacking beside me, is my only rather reduced experience of Italy, I'm afraid . . . I have to say I've always had it in mind to return in different circumstances.' Myrtle laughs. Her response triggers a squeeze of her hand, which she now gently removes. The harbour master begins to gather up the picnic things. 'You could take off your scarf, here,' he says, subdued again.

Myrtle has forgotten her scarf. She unties it. Her hair blows about. The wind on her neck is wonderfully cooling. A gust snatches the scarf, drops it in the sea. At once Alastair Brown leaps to Myrtle's side of the boat, leans perilously over, hands outstretched, calling to the floating scrap of cotton as if it was a duck. The boat tips alarmingly. Myrtle, convinced they are about to capsize, pulls at the harbour master's jacket. He falls back into her arms. The boat rights itself. He quickly moves back to his old seat, put out by his failure.

'Sorry, sorry, sorry, so very sorry,' he says. The incident has unnerved him. 'I'll get an oar. I'll easily reach it with an oar.'

'Please: don't bother.' Myrtle cannot bear the thought of another attempt at rescue. 'It's not at all important. I've plenty more scarves.'

'Oh my dear Myrtle: I'm not very competent. As you can see, I'm not a man nimble in my ways.' His melancholy sense of failure, like his crab sandwiches, touches Myrtle. She is now the one to make a gesture. She puts a hand on his arm.

'It's a lovely day,' she says. 'I'm enjoying myself so much. How lucky we were with the weather.' Behind the black glasses, she is convinced, his eyes are incredulous. His mouth falls open, wavers in his search for words.

'Dear, dear Myrtle,' he says, 'I was so worried it might all have gone wrong – well, we might have capsized.' He gives a small laugh. 'I was so anxious to make it a happy day for you.' Here, Myrtle retrieves her hand once more. He pauses, searching for pre-planned words. 'I'm bound to admit – and forgive me in advance if this is untoward – but I'm bound to admit that a not inconsiderable amount of hours a day are spent wondering . . . how best to please you.' He pauses again, glasses two black scanners turned on Myrtle's face. They listen to the tap-tapping of small waves against the bows. 'I find that my desire merely to be a companion, since the other night, has changed immeasurably. I know that any possible alternative to your husband, to Archie, is beyond contemplation, at least for several years. But if ever you so had it in mind to require anything beyond our happy companionship – our card games, further days at sea, perhaps – then you must know that I would be far from averse . . . to changing the solitary nature of my life.'

It sometimes happens that serious moments in one person's life give rise to irrelevant humour in another's. Even as the harbour master labours with his convoluted declaration, Myrtle finds herself editing it down to the kind of simple English she does her best to encourage in her pupils. Disentangling her thoughts from this private précis, she takes some time to answer.

'What you say is a great comfort,' she begins at last. 'Och: I'm lucky to have you as a friend and can only hope that any . . . visions you may have of a change in the future won't disturb our present friendship.' Even as she speaks the inadequacy of her reply – also something which would not earn high marks for her pupils – sears through her. She can see it brings disappointment, dashed hopes. But she has not expected such serious sentiments. There has been no time to prepare a more delicate response. She can only try to reassure her companion-turned-suitor she will take his words seriously, be grateful for them. 'I'll think about what you said. I won't forget it.'

'I'd be grateful for that. Well, now: I've had my say, and I'll not bother you with the matter again. We'll go on just as before.' The harbour master stands, looking at his watch. 'I rather think it's time we were getting back.'

The boat tips rapidly from side to side as he returns, with great dignity, to start up the engine. Myrtle thinks that never has she felt such admiration for this awkward man. The admiration veers into heightened affection, an affection so lively that, cocooned here in the blues of sky and sea, under a high sun, she wonders once again if it might be possible to turn it into something deeper . . . indeed if one day the harbour master's visions of a future together could be a possibility.

The unexpected thoughts cluster in her mind: she stretches her bare arms out along the sides of the boat. They move off, heading back the way they've come, but keeping even nearer to the shore. Myrtle studies Alastair Brown's parrot profile. He lifts the carton of milk to his mouth, drinks. And swiftly as the new thoughts of a possible future have come, they evaporate. There is no reasoning, here, Myrtle tells herself: but the heart can be a wayward thing. She suddenly now knows, beyond any doubt, that the idea of life with the milk-drinking harbour master is not, and never will be, something she would want. The sun and sea air must have pressed her to take leave of her senses, causing momentary imaginings to flutter wildly. But now they are quite dead – dead for ever, as realised absurdities so quickly become. The fact that she contemplated even for a moment . . . is folly beyond her dottiest imaginings. But that is how it is, she tells herself, when you allow yourself to be misguided by a vague longing to love again. When you are confused by the sensations of a single kiss, having had no physical contact with a man for two years. She is grateful to have come to her senses.

Myrtle reflects on these things so hard that perhaps her thoughts are transferred to the harbour master on his seat, shoulders grimly hunched. For back in the harbour – the homeward journey is so much faster than the outward one – his spirit seems withdrawn. There is the pretence of a smile, a helping hand as Myrtle climbs out of the boat, courteous thanks for having given up her day. Myrtle's own thanks, and her evident delight in the day, seem not to touch him. He says he will come round for a game of cards one day soon, and Myrtle leaves to make her way home. On the bus she is convinced he was aware of the swift turn her thoughts took on the homeward journey. She hopes that the time would never come when she would have to be more specific, be forced to spell out to him the reason she must turn him down . . . Then, tired from so much serious cogitation, her mind darts to an unlikely idea: after all these years without one, she thinks, perhaps the time has come to consider buying a television . . .

Archie had always been a radio man, keen never to miss a shipping forecast. He liked news bulletins three times a day, and the gardening programmes. The thought of owning a television would never have occurred to him. His time at home he had wanted to spend talking to his wife, or doing small jobs around the house. He regarded the idea of people slumped round a screen, night after night, as a waste of life. Better study the stars. Myrtle agreed with him, though sometimes felt a yearning to watch a good play or documentary. On a few occasions, when Archie was at sea, she had joined Annie to watch a particular programme, and had later confessed to Archie. He had laughed, but not minded. But of course he had not suggested that they should get a set, too. Excited by her new idea, Myrtle convinces herself that he would understand that in her life alone a television – sparingly used – might be a companion on the few evenings when neither Martin, Annie nor the harbour master did not come round.

She is so preoccupied with these thoughts – the sea picnic and its implications have gone from her mind – that it takes a moment when she reaches home to register a child sitting at the bottom of the stone steps. Janice. A furious and sulky Janice, by the look on her face. She stands as Myrtle approaches.

'Where've you been? I've been waiting half an hour,' she says.

'I've been out.' Myrtle is confused, put out by the child's hostility.

'What about my Saturday lesson?'

'But I thought . . .? I mean, you haven't been for the past three weeks. You said you didn't want any more Saturday lessons this term, just the Tuesdays.'

'Changed my mind.'

'Well I'm sorry, but you didn't let me know.'

'I told Mum to tell you when she came round yesterday.'

'She must have forgotten.'

'She never remembers *anything* except the time of her hair appointments.'

'I'm sorry you had to wait: come on in.'

The kitchen is cool – the thick stone walls keep it cool on the hottest day – and rubbled with shadows of late afternoon. Myrtle can feel the skin of her face and arms burning. She opens the window, makes tea. She's glad to be home.

Janice slams her books down on the table, sits in her usual gawky position, knees together, calves widely spread, clumpy shoes of hideous green turned to glare at each other. Her grumpiness fills the room. The day on the boat with the harbour master hangs thin as gossamer somewhere in the back of Myrtle's conscience. More strongly burns the idea of the television: she looks forward to thinking more about that when Janice has gone.

'I've written something I thought about *Michael*,' Janice says, 'though I have to tell you, I think Wordsworth's bloody gloomy.' She pushes an open exercise book towards Myrtle.

'Janice, your language,' says Myrtle, despite herself. She scans the offered paragraph, a crude attack on the poet quite unlike anything Janice has ever written before. Janice watches her face.

'You know what? The other day at school I mentioned Wordsworth by mistake, and course none of the others had ever heard of him. Turned out they'd never heard of any of the stuff I do with you – Arnold, Coleridge, Keats, Shelley, anyone like that. Well, why would they? We're not taught that crap at school. Only poetry we get is John Hegley. I like him, mind. They thought I was bananas, wanting to know *more* poetry: I pretended I'd seen some programme about Keats and the others. If they thought I was having extra lessons they'd think like I was a bloody swot, do me over. You'll never, ever tell anyone, will you?' Her eyes are hard, but hold a suggestion of tears.

'Janice, what's happened? Of course I won't tell anyone.'

'What's happened is, I'm not interested any more. I don't want any more lessons, thanks very much. I've gone off of poetry. I've got other things on my mind. That's what I've come round to tell you.'

Myrtle sighs, thinks quickly. Janice is in no mood to be persuaded.

'Well, I'm sorry to hear all that. I've enjoyed our lessons. I thought you had, too.'

'Oh, I have.' Janice shrugs. 'It's just I don't want any more.'

'I would be very sorry,' says Myrtle slowly, 'to see you go the same way as your father. He was a clever boy, very keen on literature. He wanted to go to university. But he went to sea and his interest seemed to dry up. Such a pity.'

'First I've heard of it. Anyways, I don't want to go to university. I want to be an air hostess. Travel. Get out of this dump.'

'I see. But remember, there's a chance you may change your mind. All sorts of things that seem very firm, quite positive, at fourteen, get shifted by events, growing up. That may seem unbelievable now . . .'

'I tell you, I'm right off those old poets.' A single tear glitters down Janice's cheek. She wipes it away with the back of her hand, suddenly childlike. 'I tell you, they'd never leave off if they ever found out at school.'

'I know it's hard,' falters Myrtle, 'to be brave enough to do something different from the crowd. But it's always worth trying to stick to what *you* really want, what *you* really believe in, no matter how much ridicule that may earn you –'

Further tears are running from Janice's eyes now. She pummels at them with scornful fists, gives a choking laugh.

'Have you ever been mocked by a whole class? Jeered? They nearly died laughing when I mentioned bloody Wordsworth –'

Myrtle passes Janice a clean, folded handkerchief from her pocket. She remembers similar occasions. Her classmates were always laughing, scoffing. Until the last two years at school she always had to try to conceal her love of learning.

'Sometimes,' she says, 'if you stick out for your own thing, don't follow the crowd, you get recognised in the end . . . one other person thinks it worth following you, and then they all do the same, sheeplike . . . and you find yourself a leader.' She remembers she had thought this might happen to her, but it never did.

Myrtle knows she is not doing well. Janice laughs more loudly, nastily. She stands.

'Very funny.' she says. 'I can just see my class – a lot of mega-thugs, in case you didn't know – all suddenly thinking Janice Mcleoud and her swotty love of old poets is the hip thing . . . And anyways, I don't want to be lectured by you,' she says. 'One thing I liked here was you never lectured me.'

Myrtle stands too. She forces a smile, attempts lightness.

'I can see I'm getting nowhere. I'll not try further. How's the boyfriend?'

For a second Janice's face crashes, then she sticks up her chin, controlling herself.

'I don't know if you've ever fancied someone so rotten it gets you everywhere like all the time, so you can't stop thinking for a moment of anything else, but it's a bloody nightmare.'

She gives a leap towards Myrtle – childlike, again – flings her arms round her shoulders, leans her head on Myrtle's breast. Myrtle feels the sharp thinness of her. She takes the handkerchief, wipes away the tears, strokes the frenzied head. But she does not clutch the child tightly to her, indicate she wants her to stay, for fear of alienating her further.

'Anyways, thanks, Myrtle,' Janice says, pulling herself away.

'Come round whenever you want. I'm always pleased to see you.'

Janice runs out of the door, dragging her satchel, bangs the door purposefully behind her. She has left her open exercise book on the table. Myrtle picks it up, drags her eyes down to the last sentence.

Wordsworth is a load of crap, she reads, and feels the pleasures of the day seeping from her.

A few days later Alastair Brown returns at his usual time. They settle down to a game of cards.

It's very warm in the kitchen, despite a thread of air that hangs between open window and open door. After many days of sun the thick stone walls have relinquished their cooling influence. A wasp travels from point to point on the ceiling, its voice the faint sizzle of frying fat. The harbour master asks permission to take off his jacket. Beneath it he wears a shirt no other man in the village would contemplate – a fancy garment of blue, yellow and green stripes, expensive cotton, sharp collar. He also wears turquoise cuff links set in gold.

Myrtle smiles.

'Those are very smart,' she says. 'Did you get them abroad?'

'Hong Kong airport. Over there to deliver a panda.' His answer is deadpan. Myrtle sees that his spirits are still withdrawn. He is behaving in his usual companionable way, makes no reference to the day out. But something has gone from him. Myrtle pours glasses of home-made lemonade. They play in silence for a while. Then a small frown dislodges the harbour master's glasses. He has to move them back into place.

'I suppose,' he says, eyes on his fan of cards, 'that for the wife of a fisherman, widowhood is in some respects easier. I mean, you must be so used to absence, to being on your own.' The difficulty he has saying this indicates to Myrtle it's something that has been occupying his mind, a thought he wants confirmed, perhaps to ameliorate a problem concerning his feelings for Myrtle.

She is silenced by his observation. She cannot believe that a man of such keen sensitivity, in some ways, is so lacking in imagination. But she is careful not to seem to snub him in her reply.

'It may appear like that,' she says, nicely. 'I can quite understand that's how it could. But it's not so. This is an absence that will never end, that you carry round with you for the rest of your life, never get used to. You can't avoid its normal presence – it's always there, whatever else happens. And the hardest thing is that you know that sometimes it won't just remain passive: it'll leap out, take you in a stranglehold, causing havoc again with all the things you believed you'd managed to get into some form of order . . .' She is speaking quietly, as if to herself. 'But there! What am I saying? I don't like to try to explain such things: I was just trying to answer your question. Fishermen's wives – I believe we all must feel the same – never quite get used to the constant absences, the anxiety that's always there. But at least there's hope, a very good chance, the men will be back. The occasional disaster puts paid to any feelings of complacency – but the men know their sea, they're not fools, they don't take risks. So anxiety when they're gone is only caused by instinctive lack of trust of the water, the fear of a sudden storm. But in reality, each time they go out there's very high hope they'll come back. Archie's death is the end of that hope for me, but I must go on hoping for the others.'

Alastair Brown lays down his hand of cards, bows his head.

'I'm sorry, Myrtle,' he says, 'I seem to have presumed something very foolish, very thoughtless, and yet I found myself thinking about it so much. I've said the wrong thing again.'

'Oh no. No you haven't.' Myrtle is quick to reassure. She hates his distress. 'Lots of people wonder how it is to be widowed, just as they wonder about all sorts of states of life. They ask. You can't tell them. You can't ever explain the sensations, any more than you can explain the precise feeling of a physical pain to a doctor. Other people can only guess.'

The harbour master now shuffles sadly.

'It was clumsy of me to suggest,' he says. 'But I'm honoured – believe me I'm honoured – that you should have explained so well things which you have no reason to explain to another living soul . . .'

'You're a good friend to me,' Myrtle says. 'You asked. It would have been cowardly not to have tried to answer.' Once again she finds herself drawn to this awkward man, and yet detached. Nothing could induce her to make any physical gesture of reassurance, today, as she had on the boat, lest he misunderstand it and find his hopes revived. Yet the pathos of the man moves her deeply, and she hates her inability to help him. She can only hope he understands.

As they return to their game, in silence again, Myrtle sees in the harbour master a melancholy that is familiar: it was what she herself lived with for years before she met Archie – the aridity of resignation. Alastair Brown looks like a man who has dared to hope, been rebuffed, and now must return to the emptiness that had been his life before the hope beguiled him. Myrtle feels guilt. She knows that with a few words she could change his life. But she cannot say them. The harbour master knows she cannot say them. They are joined in their sadness.

The air of mutual anguish is scattered when Annie comes running in, laughing, restless. She wears a muslin summer dress that mists her limbs, clings to the points of her knee bones, breasts. She fiddles with a long pink silky scarf flung round her neck, tosses her hair. In the low shadows of the kitchen she could be eighteen again, running in to urge Myrtle out: how pleased Myrtle was when Annie seemed genuinely determined to include her in some plan, how she loved her. She loves her again now: it suddenly comes upon her, a vibrant, smothering warmth, a gladness at her presence, her existence. She has felt angry with Annie on many occasions of late, so it's a relief to find the intrinsic feeling, the one that bound them as children, is still there. Also, she is grateful for this visit. Annie's entrance is perfect timing. Now Myrtle will be spared any further explanations when Alastair Brown decides to leave.

Which he does at once. The presence of Annie always causes him unease: he is never able to put from his mind past scenes with women who have been keen to get closer to him than he has to them. Annie, he imagines, has probably put wicked stories round the village concerning his lack of enthusiasm, his inability to take his chance.

'Here, take over my hand,' he suggests, getting up.

'Willingly, Alastair. Myrtle and I've not played in an age. I think it's my turn.' She looks up at him with an enchanting smile that makes him hurry on with his jacket – so fast does he try to slide his arms into the sleeves that he finds himself in a muddle, further exacerbating his general state of confusion. Annie slumps dramatically down in his chair, as if exhausted but elated by some secret event. She pulls the rumpled skirts above her brown knees, turns in her toes – a childhood habit never outgrown. One glance at the scarlet nails twinkling through the peep-toes of pink stiletto slingbacks, and the harbour master gives one of his customary hare-leaps to the door. Myrtle follows him out.

'Thank you for coming,' she says. 'Come again soon.' Then, with no forethought, no intention, she bends forward and kisses him on the cheek. The gesture causes them equal astonishment – Alastair Brown cannot know this, but Myrtle has never kissed a man on the cheek in her life: meaningless social habits are not her way. She is stunned by her own boldness, at this unpremeditated act which is more surprising, in a way, than her yielding to Alastair Brown's kiss the other night. She watches the harbour master skim down the steps, adjusting his glasses, tugging at his tie. At the bottom he turns to give a small, etiolated wave – the wave of a man grateful for kindness shown, but fully aware of the limitations between them that will always exist.

Myrtle turns back into the kitchen. Annie is still shifting on the seat in the fretted shadows. The odd sliver of sunlight spears a part of her arm, makes miniature forks of lighting through the blue of her eyes. Annie is always happiest in summer. The sun is her spur. Her skin, warmed, rubs against hard surfaces, nestles into cushions or rugs. Myrtle sees all the signs: Annie today resembles the Annie of so many youthful summers, when she declared herself inflamed with love for some boy. Myrtle can't help laughing.

'So!' Annie is laughing too. 'Caught you and the harbour master at it again. I think it's bloody marvellous. When's the happy day?'

'Don't be so daft, Annie. He's a good man, a good friend, but that's all.'

'I've heard that one before. You might as well tell me the truth, you know. All these years.'

'I'm telling you the truth.'

'In that case, it's a pity.'

'You're in high spirits.' Myrtle fetches clean glasses, ice. Pours more lemonade. Annie gives her a triumphant grin.

'Ken took the afternoon off. Have to take our chance when Janice is at school.'

'You're happier, then? Things still going better?'

'I'd say they're far from perfect, but a few per cent better. We don't row so much, but we have our time cut out dealing with Janice and her moods. She's all over the place at the moment. Don't know what's got into her. Bloody nightmare to live with, I can tell you.'

'She'll come round. She tells me she doesn't want any more tutoring, but I daresay she'll change her mind.'

'She told me. I'm sorry. She was enjoying your lessons so much. You were an inspiration in her life – everyone needs one of those. Hope she'll come to her senses. All due to hormones, of course, I suppose. But I wasn't ever like this, was I, Myrt? Down in the dumps for weeks because some crass boy wouldn't respond?'

'I don't ever remember a boy who wouldn't respond to you,' says Myrtle, and Annie laughs again, delighted at the truth of this. Then her thoughts return to Janice.

'Still, in some way she's brought us closer. That and . . .' Annie looks away from Myrtle. 'I don't know. I suppose my anger's petered out. You can't go on blaming someone for ever. I've come to see Archie's dying was enough punishment for Ken. Daresay I've been too hard on him, on your behalf, even though I know you forgave him long ago. Then, he's been so patient, I'll say that. I respect patience. And he's tried not to inflict his despair on us – Janice and me. I respect that too. It's made me feel much fonder of him. Not the kind of love I felt, still feel, for Martin – but a nice comfortable sort of old fondness. We're used to each other. And now the sex is back – that's terrific. That's grand.'

'Oh Annie, I can't tell you how relieved I am. How pleased,' says Myrtle quickly. 'It's what I kept hoping for.' She makes no mention of the single piece of information that troubles her: Annie's admission of her continuing love for Martin. But perhaps by now that is just an old habit, remembered more than felt. Whatever the truth, a warning registers in Myrtle's mind: she must never confess to Annie that her own friendship with Martin provides a growing warmth in her life. Annie interrupts her reflections.

'I think you should seriously consider Alastair Brown,' she says. 'Imagine it: of course you couldn't love him like you loved Archie, but he could widen your life. He could urge you into the modern world – I was saying to Ken only the other night, Myrtle must be the only person on the coast who still doesn't have a television, doesn't even want one.'

'All that may be going to change, it so happens.'

'The things you keep from me! That's good news. Wonderful. But also, you've never been anywhere, you don't show any signs of wanting to explore other places, holiday abroad. I said to Ken let's go to Spain next year, Benidorm or somewhere, see the world. He liked the idea. But you! Wild horses wouldn't drag you further south than Edinburgh. Think about it: you've forty years of good life ahead and if you never set foot outside this place you'll never meet anyone. Seems to me the harbour master is a golden opportunity. Could be your last chance.'

Myrtle smiles. She is not in the least offended by Annie's light-hearted criticisms, or worried by her concerns.

'I've no particular wish to meet anyone else,' she says. 'I like it here. I can't imagine moving.'

'You know what? You're really, really old-fashioned – like people in the olden days who never went anywhere. But you've got the opportunities, enough money, and what do you do? You stick around here, quite happy. I bet you Archie would have wanted you to see a bit of the world . . . Are you mad at me, saying all this?'

'Not in the slightest. You must understand, I'm rooted here, happy. I feel safe being where I've been with Archie. Of course, one day, I might venture further afield, see a little. But I'm in no hurry. I'm one of those who finds more than enough in a small world.'

'Wish I could feel the same way. I keep wanting to be off, though God knows where to. What'd I do? You're stumped, really, without some rich bloke behind you. Ken's doing his best, I'll say that. He gets a regular wage, but we'll never be rich. He says one day we might go to Australia. Don't know how I'd feel about that or even if we'll stick together long enough to make any real plans. One thing'd stop me: missing you.'

'You'd get used to that. I'd come and visit you one day.'

'Bet you wouldn't.'

'Well, no, to be honest, probably not.'

'Don't suppose we'll go. It's only an idea.' Annie's previous exuberance has mellowed. She picks up the cards. Myrtle glances out of the window. Annie laughs. 'You still checking on the weather and there's no need now. I like that. Fine calm day. No worry.'

'Habit,' says Myrtle. 'I always glance at the sky first thing in the morning. Sometimes I can't help thinking thank God Archie's not out in that . . . Then I think of the others.'

'You're a rum one, Myrt. Pretty out of place in this modern world. I don't know what goes on in your head sometimes. Here: cut.'

Myrtle takes up half the pack. They play until late. Dusk curtains the room. The glass jug, refilled with lemonade, glows like a low-watt lamp between them. The silken wood of the table supports their fore-arms, elbows – the feeling of the wood so familiar it's as if this particular evening is a concentration of a thousand games played here through the years. Annie says Ken is getting takeaway for Janice this evening, so she can have a night off. Myrtle says there's cold meat and tomatoes in the fridge. They smile at each other, enjoy the thought of a late supper when the game comes to an end. Fluctuations in the moods of friends, Myrtle thinks, are their life blood. This evening all the love and awe and admiration she has ever felt for Annie are reassembled in the darkening room. In the void left by Archie, this peace with Annie, sometimes so elusive, she knows must not be allowed to escape. Their importance to each other must continue for the rest of their lives.

Their evening is a merry one. They talk about the old days, laugh at old jokes, tread safe ground. There is no mention of the forgiveness of Ken by Annie, but Myrtle is certain that – possibly not con-sciously – that has been achieved. She knows there will never be a time she does not worry about Annie's firecracker ways, her thought-lessness, her dubious morality. But since Archie's death, and Janice's troublesome behaviour, a kind of maturity seems to be reaching Annie at last. Also, now that the two frozen years between her and Ken seem to be thawing, her natural high spirits and her energy are return-ing. But even as she reflects upon these things Myrtle knows she could be wrong. So often in the past Annie has wiped out Myrtle's feel-ings of love and trust by a single, foolish – often unkind – act. So often she has had to start all over again, rebuilding her affection for her friend. It has been a wearying and depressing business, but never so bad as to think of giving up. Now her parents and Archie are dead, Annie is the most important person in the world to Myrtle, and on an evening like this it is impossible to imagine ever falling out with her again.

When at last Annie leaves it is almost midnight. Myrtle goes out of the door with her, pauses at the top of the steps, just as she had with the harbour master. The women hug each other for longer than usual. The warm boulders of the night press against them. When they draw away each sees the other cloudily – there is an unclear moon: the few stars play *pianissimo* in a sky that is hardly dark.

'Bugger Australia,' says Annie, as she runs down the steps.

A week later, another warm summer's evening, Myrtle prepares to walk to the graveyard. Martin has sent word that he has finished work on the headstone and would like her opinion on a few last details in the carving.

Myrtle walks with lightness of step towards the cemetery. Agreeable evenings seem to have been gathering: this is to be another of them. The matter of the headstone sorted out, Martin is to come back with her for the red fish he brought her that morning, which she will grill with a little butter. They will sit talking in their easy way. Myrtle may ask his opinion about the idea of a television for the autumn. She sees the quiet pattern of her life stretching for years ahead – the unaccountable restlessness, and worse, which struck her recently, seems to have faded. Now it will be cards with Annie, suppers sometimes with Martin, visits – though no more secret excursions – with the harbour master: the pleasure of teaching at the school and the time to read all the books she has always wanted to read. What else could a widow, bound for ever to her husband's spirit, ask?

Myrtle lets herself through the gate, shuts it behind her. She decides to spend a moment in the church before going to meet Martin at Archie's grave. She moves fast along the path of crushed stone whose heat, through her open sandals, she can feel. Inside the church it's almost winter-cold, dank. Plaster on the walls is crumbling, flaking – a small snow-pile has fallen to the floor near the pew into which Myrtle slips to take a seat. She looks round at the bareness. There's a single vase of flowers on the altar, gladioli and daisies, both wilting. The two candles, their ivory wax slumped but rigid, remind Myrtle of rigor mortis. They are coming to the end of their life. She remembers the dozens of candles that the church liberally blazes for weddings, but more particularly for the funerals of fishermen. Myrtle cannot count the number of services round coffins she has been to here: every seat full, every voice imploring God to hear us when we cry to thee for those in peril on the sea. Her father, Archie . . . they sang the hymn for Dot, too. It was her favourite.

Myrtle likes it here, the few moments of 'peace and holy quiet'. She covers her face with her big hands and tries to imagine the unfurnished golden vastness that is her idea of heaven. She tries to pray that her dead family are reunited, but she cannot imagine how, or visualise them. Are there chairs in heaven? She finds it impossible to picture, so instead her prayer turns to thanks for all she has been left with. Then she returns to the porch.

The heat of the evening drenches her again. She puts up a hand, touches the warm stone. She turns towards the sea: the family grave is close to the wall that divides graveyard from shore. She can just see the kneeling figure of Martin – bright blue shirt – working with his chisel, back to her. His figure is backlit by the sun: the illusion is of a halo surrounding him. The halo also frames a second figure, a slight young girl, it seems to be, leaning against the headstone.

Myrtle moves on to the short, neat grass between the graves, approaches warily. She wants to see more before she herself is seen. Ten yards from Archie's grave she stops, conceals herself behind a mausoleum of rotting mossy stone, an edifice about the size of a beach hut. Although both figures are still blazed with sunlight, she can now see them quite clearly. The girl is Janice.

Janice leans against the headstone, one skinny arm drifts along its top. She wears a very short dress of the same muslin stuff that Annie was wearing last week. It clings to hips and small breasts, only knickers underneath it. Her free hand swoops to the buttons at the neck: languorously, like some caricature film star, she undoes two. The gesture, like her stance, is a mature design of provocation. She flutters her eyelashes, as she must have seen her mother do a thousand times: she bunches her mouth into a ridiculous pout.

'*Look*, Martin,' she suddenly screams. 'For shite's sake look at me. Please!'

From the speed with which Martin rises to his feet Myrtle can measure his anger. For a second she registers the two figures – the man with a hand on the girl's shoulder, shaking her, shouting at her, and the girl's open, screaming mouth, both on fire among the sun's rays, burning. She runs towards them. Janice screams louder. Martin turns.

'Janice! Whatever can you be thinking –? You little trollop, you –'

Myrtle is too horrified, too angry to fashion useful words. She pushes past Martin, drags Janice away from the headstone – the idea of the child touching it causes a sour nausea in her chest – and slaps the defiant, upturned face.

The screaming stops. Silence: then a gull protests overhead. Myrtle is aware of Martin's arm on hers, pulling her away.

'How dare you?' Janice's face is still upturned, still defiant, sneering. 'You'll be sacked for this.'

Myrtle is conscious of little beyond her thundering heartbeat. Martin is pulling her further away.

'Leave her alone,' he says.

'You lay another finger on me and you'll be locked up for assault,' says Janice. There are red slashes on her cheek, imprint of Myrtle's hand.

'*Do up your buttons*,' says Myrtle. Her voice is a long way off, nothing to do with her, unable to say the hundred things she wants to say. 'What do you think you were doing?'

Janice smiles, the nastiest smile Myrtle has ever seen on a child: a smile that has never come from Annie or Ken.

'What would you know about anything? What would you know about desperateness that eats into you so you can't do anything night or day? What would you know about passion, desire, months and months seeing Martin being nice to my mum, kind to you, and not even *noticing* me?'

'I think you should run home now, Janice,' says Martin.

'You're *fourteen*, Janice . . .' Myrtle, shaking, ashamed at her violence, tries to imitate Martin's gentleness.

'So? What's that got to do with anything? I wasn't doing anything wrong. Only trying to make Martin *notice* me. Say something to me. Realise I exist.'

'Go on,' says Martin again. 'Home. I think we should forget all this as quickly as possible.'

'Forget?' Janice laughs. She fiddles with the buttons of her dress, doesn't do them up. She picks up a jersey from the ground, slings it round her shoulders. 'Right. I'm off. Leave you two to it. Perhaps – hey! Perhaps that's what got you, Myrtle. Perhaps you fancy Martin yourself! That would be a good laugh! Well, I shouldn't bank on your chances there. You're old and plain and no man in his right mind would give you a second –'

'Get away!' Martin now shouts, all gentleness gone. 'Now. Go on.'

Janice, barefoot, runs through the tombstones towards the gate.

Myrtle sits down on Archie's grave. Martin lowers himself to sit beside her. He hides his head in his hands. Myrtle longs to weep, but she cannot.

'Whatever did I do?' she asks at last. 'Hitting someone else's child . . . Hitting Janice, who I've loved since she was a baby. Janice: three years of lessons we both loved. What happened to me? What's happened to her?'

Martin raises his head. He puts an arm around Myrtle.

'She deserved it. She's out of control, that child. Disturbed. I suppose I should have told you what's been happening. In fact I had made up my mind to tell you . . .' He sighs. 'For months now, she's been tracking me down – nothing physical, like today. But making suggestive remarks, doing all she can to provoke me. As for the letters . . . page after page of how she loves, thinks, dreams, will wait for ever – pathetic, childish stuff. I stopped opening them. I told her I would read no more. Then she started ringing . . . pornographic stuff this time. What she'd like to do – before I slammed down the telephone. I was going to go to Annie and Ken: I didn't want to get the child into trouble. But she needs help. She's in a bad way . . . And now this.'

'Oh, God,' says Myrtle.

'I found her waiting here. I tried to humour her, begged her to stop being silly, go away. But no good. I daren't get angry – she'd have accused me of child abuse in a flash. I could only pray you wouldn't be late.'

'And there was I in the church . . . What do we do now? I've hit a child. I've hit Janice. She may have deserved it – that's no excuse. That's goodbye to my job, she's right. And that's the least of it.'

'No,' says Martin. 'It won't come to that. We'll work it out, rationally, with Annie and Ken. They know how peculiar Janice has been of late. They'll understand.'

'I can only hope so,' says Myrtle, 'or things will be very bad. Just when I thought . . . Annie and I were on an even keel again . . .' Her voice breaks, but still she does not cry.

They remain sitting on the grave for a long time, listening to the occasional gull, and the striking of the church clock. The sun is hovering on the horizon, about to disappear: the sea is grazed with gold light. Poppies in a vase that Myrtle arranged on the grave yesterday are a clutch of smaller suns, their petals flakes of sunlight clinging together against the onset of night. Myrtle can smell fish from Martin's hand. She stares at the fine-grained marble of Archie's headstone where Martin has done his careful work. But she has no heart to discuss that now.

'Would you mind, another evening?' she says, and struggles to rise. 'I can't concentrate on the headstone just now. But it's beautiful.'

'Of course.' Martin helps her up.

'And would you mind if . . . I cooked the fish tomorrow? This evening I'd rather . . . Well, I've no doubt Annie will be round. I'd rather face her on my own.'

'Fine. Shall I walk with you to the house?'

'I'll be all right, thanks.'

'You look as if you're in a state of shock . . .'

'You look pretty shocked yourself.' It's only now Martin is standing that Myrtle is aware of the strained lines under his eyes, and the grave sadness of the eyes themselves. They hold each other's hands for a moment, then Myrtle turns to go.

'The poor wee girl,' she says. 'Whatever's happened to her? Whatever's happened to me? What did I do?'

She makes her way through the gravestones and their long shadows. In just an hour, she realises, she has travelled from the highest of spirits (the smuggest of spirits, perhaps) to dejection that is equally low. And there is no voice from Archie to tell her what to do.

Home, Myrtle has scarcely settled to a few moments reflection when Annie comes bursting in, cheeks scarlet, furious-eyed.

'You hit my child,' she says, quietly. And then shouts: 'You hit Janice. How dare you?'

'She deserved it,' says Myrtle.

'It's not up to you to decide what anyone else's child deserves. You know nothing of Janice beyond your superior books. You know nothing, what's been going on. The last thing in the world the child needs is to be attacked by you. I could have you up for assault. Martin the witness. But don't worry. I'm not going to. I'm going to give you a piece of my mind in a way that'll give me far more satisfaction –'

She rushes at Myrtle, swings at her cheek with a hard open hand. She slaps with every ounce of strength in her furious body. The blow, surprising in its force, sends Myrtle tottering backwards to the stove. Her cheek stings, flames. One of Annie's fingers must have caught the corner of an eye, for Myrtle's sight in this eye is unfocused through a tear. Her heart is beating wildly, but she feels no desire to shout back. A heavy, almost slumberous calm seems to have drugged her. She regards Annie, and herself, as if from some far-off place – as if she is watching a fight between two unknown people.

As soon as Annie has struck her blow, she steps back, shocked. She grasps the hand that struck the blow in her other one as if to withhold it from further damage. But her fury is not spent. She is still defiant, chin still tipped high in the air, eyes lashing.

'That's what you deserve, Myrtle Duns, and I'm bloody glad I was the one to do it. Maybe it'll make a chink in your bloody superiority, your high-mindedness, your arrogant ways, your general . . . *smugness*.' She peters out, backing away. 'Often, St Myrtle, you know what I think? Often I think you're nothing less than a cow. A *cow*,' she repeats, and backs to her usual chair at the table, sits. 'And don't you go thinking that in a few days' time we'll make up as usual. Because we won't. You've gone too far this time. There'll be no more of this . . .' She snatches up the pack of cards from the table, raises her hand above her head and throws them with an uncontrolled gesture. Myrtle's eyes follow some of the cards as they drop like heavy leaves in various places all round the room. She listens to the quiet taps, separate sad notes, as they land on floor, wood, iron of stove. When they have all landed, there is a moment of absolute quiet again. Then Annie thrusts her head into her hands and begins to sob. Myrtle fingers her cheek. After a while she says:

'Of course I shouldn't have struck Janice. I'm sorry.'

'You bloody shouldn't.' Annie's shoulders are heaving. She smears her mascara as she wipes her eyes with the clenched backs of her hands.

'Spontaneous fury. I couldn't believe what I was seeing. It was mad, I know. I've no explanation, beyond the shock. For what it's worth, you can imagine how I feel, letting fly like that. You know I love Janice as if she –'

'I don't give a toss how you feel. Serve you right if you're up to your neck in remorse for ever and ever.' Annie's voice is high, childlike. Suddenly she looks up, locks eyes with Myrtle. 'Are you quite sure,' she asks, 'your fury wasn't something to do with the fact that the man Janice was being stupid with was *Martin*?'

Myrtle's mouth opens. Her big hand leaves her cheek, drops heavily to her side.

'Of course not,' she says. 'I don't know what you mean.'

'Then you're not as clever as you claim. Don't tell me Martin doesn't mean something to you – you're always asking Janice if he's been bringing us a piece of fish for supper. Martin the only one allowed up to your stupid wood. I've got eyes.'

Myrtle sighs.

'Martin's a good friend, he's been wonderful since Archie died. So has Alastair Brown, in a way.' Here Annie gives a sneering little laugh. 'I don't know what I'd have done without them,' Myrtle falters on, 'without you.'

'You'd have managed. You're so bloody good at managing, remember?'

'Martin and Alastair Brown are only friends, no matter what you think. This isn't the time for any alternatives in my life.' She lifts the kettle, automatically calculates how much water it holds. Puts it on the stove.

'I don't want any of your tea.' Annie stands, tears over. 'I'm going.'

'Before you go, shouldn't we talk about Janice? I've been worried about her for some time.'

'Janice is none of your business. Spare yourself the worry.'

'For Lord's sake, I've known her all her life: taught her, looked after her, I love the child. I don't know what's got into her lately, but something very disturbing.'

'You don't know the half of it,' says Annie. Her hostility is waning. Myrtle pours two mugs of tea. Annie shakes her head, but takes one. Myrtle sees there is no time to work out moral complications. She knows only where her loyalties lie. For the first time in her life she is going to lie to Annie.

'She's been mentioning this boy she's fallen for, but she wouldn't tell me his name,' says Myrtle.

'Boy!' Annie gives a small laugh. 'It's a wonder you didn't guess: it's Martin. Some boy.'

Myrtle spins round from the stove to face Annie. One eye is still blurred with tears.

'Martin! I didn't guess. He told me just now. Did you know?'

Annie shrugs. There's a long pause.

'Not till an hour ago when Janice comes screaming in,' she says. 'I must admit. And that's not the all of it.' She goes to the window. 'As I told you, I once really loved Martin. None of the others came anywhere near him, in my book. I didn't get anywhere. But I've never stopped loving him.'

Myrtle feels a great desire to say she is sorry about that, but she keeps her silence.

'So you can see what it was like when Janice comes running home in tears to tell me you hit her because she was having a bit of fun with the . . . man she's been doing her nut for these last months, and that man is the man I love most in the world.'

In this icy revelation Myrtle senses a core of toughness. Annie, she has no doubt, will sort out Janice in her own way. The chances are

Annie will win Martin in the end, though God knows what that will do to Janice.

'The pity of it,' are the only words she can find.

Annie drags her eyes from the sea, sighs deeply. She is not completely stricken by the drama, somehow. Now her score is paid – her eyes smile across Myrtle's scarlet cheek – she seems in no hurry to go.

'Janice has certainly been acting crazy, lately,' she says. 'I haven't known what to do. Ken's been sympathetic but useless, says he's not going to interfere. When he heard Janice just now, hysterical, he said the best place for him was down his mum's. Left me to sort it out.'

'Why haven't you said anything of all this?'

Annie shrugs.

'Playing your game,' she says. 'Keeping things that most matter from a best friend. That's always been your way, your superior show of strength. Thought I'd try it.'

'Annie,' says Myrtle.

'Anyhow, she wasn't doing anything wrong. Only having a bit of fun – something you don't know much about. Flirting – just trying to make him look at her, say something nice.'

'That may be what she intended. It didn't look like that. She was acting provocatively. Reminded me of a child prostitute –'

'You prissy old woman!' Annie flares up again. 'That's always been your trouble! How dare you call Janice a –'

'Let's not shout at one another any more,' says Myrtle. 'The point is, whatever the truth of what she was up to this evening, something's got to be done about her.'

'Yes, well, thanks for pointing that out. But I'd be grateful if you'd not interfere. I'll deal with it. She'll get over her silly obsession, I daresay. Martin when he comes up with the fish never gives her a glance. She'll soon learn how hopeless it is, what a waste of time. I'm buggered if I'm going to stop him coming round. She'll soon find some boy of her own age, forget all about this silly crush on Martin.'

Myrtle can see how it will all be: the confusion, the anger, the hurt that will ensue. She looks round the safe harbour of her kitchen, and the ordinary things of everyday life have scattered. Anguished feeling between Annie and herself is subversive as always – it's shifted the walls, scattered the comfort, blasted all that is familiar. She is amazed and disturbed by the effects that both heights and depths of feeling can have on inanimate things.

Annie has finished her tea, bangs down the mug on the table. Her face is a mess of mascara, her hair a stormy tangle of curls. Myrtle tries to replace the sight of her with the picture of their last, happy meeting. Annie laughing, smiling, loving. But she can't. Annie in all her wrath and confusion – and perhaps regret – is too strong to be supplanted by the alternative creature that Myrtle loves.

'I hope we can get over all this,' she hears herself saying.

'We can't. I'm not as good as you at forgiveness, remember? Far as I'm concerned, the end of a friendship can be every bit as savage as the end of a love affair. Pity, but there it is. There's too much against us now to carry on. So best not to have anything more to do with each other, isn't it? Safer. And I don't want you anywhere near Janice any more, that's for sure. I'll deal with her, deal with Ken, deal with the whole crowd . . . Don't look at me like that. I'm not in need of your pitying looks, thanks very much. If you don't like what's happening – well, too bad. Blame yourself. Janice is an innocent child, head over heels about some man, acts stupidly one day, but he hasn't a clue what she's on about, she's never given him so much as a sign before about how she feels . . .' Annie is near Myrtle now, looking closely at her still reddened face. 'That's what she told me: that's what I believe. If she'd been causing Martin any aggravation he'd have told me, wouldn't he?'

'I daresay.' Myrtle turns her head from her friend's glare, glances at the horizon. Even that is unsteady. She is in no doubt that she must keep her knowledge to herself. To reveal what she knows would not help, now.

'So I'm going,' says Annie. 'I'm off. You won't miss the cards. The harbour master's a much better player.'

She hurries to the door. Everything within Myrtle cries out to her to delay Annie – say stop, this is ridiculous, let's not leave it like this. But no voice emerges from the chaos within her. She does not watch Annie go, but stays leaning against the stove, arms folded. After a long silence the telephone rings: Martin. He wants to know how she is, if he would like her to come round. Myrtle explains that Annie has gone, and she would prefer to be on her own. Martin asks no other questions, and Myrtle is grateful for that but assures him she will see him tomorrow.

After a while Myrtle lights the lamps, and the moths, which have been waiting on the window ledge, begin their fluttering, daring themselves to go ever nearer the lights. Myrtle takes no notice of them, but stoops down and begins to pick up the cards.

It has been the bleakest week since Archie died. Myrtle has spent many hours in reflection, cursing her own untoward behaviour in the churchyard that has brought about this crisis – condemning herself for not having enquired further into Janice's obsession, which had been plain to see, and tried to help her. She also blames Annie: a self-obsessed, irresponsible mother, always wanting to win her child's approbation by giving in to her wishes, however unsuitable. But she has learnt that it has never been any good, criticising Annie's abilities at motherhood. Annie has always been deaf to all constructive suggestion concerning Janice. In the past they had many a useless quarrel: Annie's case was always that Myrtle could not know what it was like, being a mother, so was not one to give advice. In her greater rages she would claim Myrtle's criticism was fired by jealousy, the bitterness of the barren state. So, long ago, Myrtle had given up, kept her silence as she watched Janice yearning for the barriers of discipline that are every child's right, and being alarmed by the empty spaces granted by her parents.

Myrtle also goes over the last quarrel, the lacerating words. Despite the wounds they have left, she misses Annie. She misses Janice. She fears for them both. She plays patience, waiting for one of them to come round. But Martin tells her Ken has hired a caravan and the whole family has gone off somewhere. This is so unusual – Myrtle has never known the three of them go away together – that she is further alarmed. The days are very long, listless. She has noticed that when she goes out to shop she causes a disagreeable stir. People who are her friends, acquaintances, give her looks that she cannot quite read, but she feels the tension, the disapproval. She holds her head high and ignores them, with as much dignity as she can manage, until she reaches the safety of her kitchen. There, she slumps at her empty table, fiddles drearily with a pack of cards, wonders at the length and grimness of the hot summer days. Never has she missed Archie so much. The ache, which she had thought so recently was beginning to dull, has now returned more piercingly than before. And the exciting feeling of the new bustle in her life has disappeared as fast as it had come. Perhaps it had all been an illusion, wishful thinking. But now there is no bustle, nothing but the maturing of the trees to look forward to.

The harbour master remains loyal. The day after Annie ran out he appeared with a bunch of poppies and daisies and long grasses. Myrtle was touched by the thought of him pottering along the hedgerows in his blazer, choosing the flowers. He told her he had heard the silly rumours (they had spread so fast?) but she could rest assured he would always stand by her, always be there if needed. Once again Myrtle found herself on the brink of unbending, giving herself up to him to ensure companionship for life. Once again she withheld. Alastair Brown was not the right man for her. Remembering her own moment of weakness, she gives a small scoffing smile and shuffles the cards. She is grateful to this sad, kind man, but knows gratitude is no reason for commitment. She believes he understands the situation but has not given up hope.

Indeed, in the stifling week since Annie's departure the harbour master has been round three times: gentle, his sympathy alive in his quietness. He asks no questions and Myrtle makes no effort to explain. They merely play their card games and drink iced lemonade, glad of each other's company. By now, there is that ease between them which comes to people who recognise their friendship will never converge, but never fade. The small element of tension is fired by their different desires, but it does nothing to trouble their pleasure in each other's company.

Martin, too, comes round most days – brief visits, bringing small slivers of fish, for Myrtle says she has no appetite. He tells her he saw

Annie only for a moment before she went away. She shouted at him, slammed the door in his face. He could hear Janice crying upstairs, and Ken shouting from somewhere. The whole household was in an unhappy state, he said. He left quickly, had no intention of returning.

'They'll have to sort it out for themselves,' he said.

But he and Myrtle did not speak of Annie after that. Instead, Martin – a little wanting in spirits, Myrtle thought – reported progress on the finishing of Archie's epitaph, interrupted that memorable evening. It was coming along well, he said. He hoped it would be completed in a matter of days.

In the long hours between visits from her two loyal friends, Myrtle sits thinking that, if you look around, everywhere you see people frightened of beginnings, frightened of endings. She is not unusual in that, and this present time is both some kind of ending, and some kind of beginning that she cannot envisage. She is a little afraid, but Archie's voice comes to her, strong, firm, wise – encouraging her in some way she cannot exactly comprehend, but comforting.

It's a week to the day that Annie left with her terrible threats, and Martin comes round to say he has finished the engraving. He would like her to come and see it.

They walk together through the plushy warm air of a late summer evening. They stand by the headstone: the epitaph is finely carved. Martin has done a wonderful job. But Myrtle does not want to stay long. The ghost of Janice, leaning against this very stone, in her outrageous pose, is still too new, too raw. So after a few moments, when Myrtle has given her thanks, they decide to walk on up to the copse. They have not been there for some time.

The saplings are strong, and bright with young leaves – noticeably taller since the last visit. The sight of them provides Myrtle with the first dart of real pleasure since Annie left. She cries out loud in delight, tripping fast up and down the paths, ruffled with new grass now, so that Martin has to hurry to keep up with her. They reach the clearing at the heart of the wood. They sit on the fine old bench which is Myrtle's memorial to Archie – to which, Myrtle knows, she will return for many years ahead until she is too old or infirm to walk. In silence she and Martin look about them: at the trees, the brightness of the grass. And they look up to the arc of unclouded blue sky, where swallows swoop in lazy whiplash circles. On the back of a languid breeze the smell of the sea reaches them.

'The rock?' says Myrtle. 'I'd still like to put a rock here. Did you manage to find one?'

'I've been looking,' says Martin. 'And I'm glad to say I think I've found the perfect thing – I was going to tell you. I found it on a small beach, a cove, a couple of miles up the coast. I was looking for drift-wood for an artist friend. I suddenly saw this handsome rock, all by itself, looking out to sea. I thought: that's the one for Myrtle. Only trouble will be transporting it. There's no access to the beach for a van. But I'll work that out somehow. I'll have it here soon. It'll have to be soon.'

'That's wonderful news,' says Myrtle. 'It'll go so well, here. I look forward to it.' She pauses. 'It's the thing I most look forward to, now.'

In the silence that follows she hears Martin sigh. He allows a few more moments to pass before speaking.

'I've news for you, Myrtle,' he says at last. 'I fear it's not a good moment, but time is running out. I would have told you last week, but then there was all the . . . disruption. Anyhow, I'm going back to Canada.'

Myrtle turns her head and looks at him.

'I'm off at the end of the month if everything's tied up by then. It was my sister who made up my mind. She came over to tell me she couldn't really cope with the smallholding any more – the house and bit of land where we lived with our parents as children. It had become all too much for her. Besides, she's met this man. He wants her to move in with him, somewhere near Vancouver. It will be good for her. I'm pleased. Her only worry was selling the old place. She didn't like the idea, wondered if I might consider . . .'

As he speaks, Myrtle sees the days, weeks, months, years ahead. No Martin with his fish and his devoted friendship. Perhaps no Annie for a very long time – though surely, in the end, things would be all right between them. She sees the stacks of books to be marked, the possibility of a television set. She sees the harbour master, his black hair turning to grey, beating her at cards for years and years to come. She sees her own funeral: the widow Duns laid to rest beside the good fisherman Archie, who died many years before her.

'So I've been considering,' Martin goes on, his voice striking her again, 'I've been thinking very hard. The decision was very difficult. But I think the right one. After all, there's not a great deal of satisfying life for me here. I scrape around for work, earn very little, feel I'm not doing enough. I'm haunted by a sense of unfulfilment. Besides that, though I've been here a long time, I still feel I don't really fit in – never have, never will. I'm a friend of a lot of the fishermen, but I'm not one of them. I don't have their understanding of the sea, I don't even like it. I hate cutting up their fish to try to earn a bit more. I don't like the doleful atmosphere in the village for days on end when the men are away. I shall miss my parents, though they've said they might join me in the homeland in a few years' time. I shall miss this place, the people, friends . . . But I'm tired of the sense of my own uselessness, here. In Canada, I could be working to some real purpose.'

Myrtle sees herself in the kitchen, through the seasons, listening for Archie's voice, living with the spirit of him but denied the flesh, and wonders if that is how it should be, if that is the proper plan of things. She thinks of Annie's return: surely they will forgive each other. But also she sees years of watching the friendship become more threadbare as ever more wearying quarrels outweigh the love. Perhaps friendships, like love affairs, have their appointed time, and when too much has blasted them it is better they should end . . . Unimaginable though that is.

'Besides,' says Martin, 'there's one other thing.' He pauses. Then speaks so quietly Myrtle has to strain to hear his words. 'I once confessed to you there was just one woman I loved – had loved for years. I never told my love because of the impossibility of a life together. She married another. She was widowed. She became my greatest friend, and I never stopped loving her. I waited for a very long time, wondering how long it takes for widowhood to heal – for the desire for fresh life to become acceptable. I tested the water very gently. I asked her to come for a small trip to Perth with me.' Here, he allowed himself a small, grim smile. 'But no, she said: she wasn't ready to come even as far as Perth. I took that as a final no, for she must have seen where I was leading, and wanted to stop me in my tracks before I did anything that might upset our friendship.'

'Oh, Martin,' says Myrtle, turning to face him, cheeks blazing. 'Believe me. I never for one moment supposed . . .' She sees his eyes are dull with resignation.

'And so I gave up, I suppose,' he says. 'But I never left off loving her, I never will. But when my sister made her suggestion . . . well, I thought, there's nothing to keep me here. Hope runs out. The sensible thing to do is to return home, work hard to make it the thriving farm it once was. It's a remote, lonely place, but I've never minded solitude. Rather like it. And who knows, I may meet someone who'd like to join me there, even become my wife.'

Myrtle thinks of some Canadian wife, without a face, greeting Martin as he comes through an open door into his childhood house. Outside there are mountains, fir trees, sky of a blue unknown in Scotland. No sight of the sea.

'And so, I'm off to Canada. It breaks my heart, but it would be foolish not to go.'

Myrtle remembers the times she's been jealous – yes, jealous – of Martin taking fish to Annie. How puzzled she was by that. Her keen regret over refusing his invitation to Perth – puzzling, too. She remembers the flash of lightning between them the day Martin helped her to her feet just yards from here – a moment recognised but ignored by them both. She remembers how constantly she has relied on him since Archie died. But because of her concern about fidelity to a dead man, she has not allowed herself to accept what her feelings have become for one who is alive.

Myrtle looks away from him, slides her eyes back up to the evening sky. We could write, she thinks. I'd write more than Annie, of course, but still. Maybe she'd come for a visit one day – always wanted to see the world. Myrtle sees a single swallow, spinning so fast it's hard to imagine how the bird will right itself as it tumbles towards the ground. But it does: and the next moment it's soaring very high again in unpremeditated pleasure. She keeps her eyes on its flight.

'I could always come with you,' she says.

Then for a long time she and Martin remain sitting on the memorial bench, looking at each other in astonishment and wonder.

<u>LAND GIRLS</u>

Angela Huth

Now a major film

The West Country in wartime, and the land girls are gathering on
the farm of John and Faith Lawrence.

Prue, a man-eating hairdresser from Manchester; Ag, a cerebral
Cambridge undergraduate; and Stella, a dreamy Surrey girl stunted
by love: three very different women, from very different back-
grounds, who find themselves thrown together, sharing an attic
bedroom and laying the foundations for a friendship that will last a
lifetime.

'Angela Huth's riveting novel . . . is evocative and entertaining'
Mail on Sunday

'It had me in its grip and I couldn't rest until the final page . . . It is
satisfying and rare to read a book whose characters are dealt the
fates we feel they deserve . . . A beautifully spun tale that absorbs
without the need to address "issues"'
Literary Review

'A good story, told with wit and a keen observation of detail'
Times Literary Supplement

Abacus
0 349 10601 0

Now you can order superb titles directly from Abacus

☐ Another Kind of Cinderella	Angela Huth	£6.99
☐ Invitation to the Married Life	Angela Huth	£6.99
☐ Land Girls	Angela Huth	£6.99
☐ Nowhere Girl	Angela Huth	£6.99
☐ South of the Lights	Angela Huth	£6.99
☐ Virginia Fly is Drowning	Angela Huth	£6.99

───────── ⬭ ABACUS ⬭ ─────────

Please allow for postage and packing: **Free UK delivery.**
Europe: add 25% of retail price; Rest of World: 45% of retail price.

To order any of the above or any other Abacus titles, please call our credit card orderline or fill in this coupon and send/fax it to:

Abacus, 250 Western Avenue, London, W3 6XZ, UK.
Fax 0181 324 5678   Telephone 0181 324 5517

☐ I enclose a UK bank cheque made payable to Abacus for £ . . . .
☐ Please charge £ . . . . . . to my Access, Visa, Delta, Switch Card No.

Expiry Date ☐☐☐☐   Switch Issue No. ☐☐

NAME (Block letters please) . . . .

ADDRESS . . . .

Postcode . . . . Telephone . . . .

Signature . . . .

Please allow 28 days for delivery within the UK. Offer subject to price and availability.

Please do not send any further mailings from companies carefully selected by Abacus ☐